'Dynamic storytelling and a fully imagined magical world . . . Dennard's rich descriptions, insightful characterizations and breathtaking action sequences will keep readers on their toes'
Publishers Weekly

'Two devoted friends dreaming of independence contend with unfathomable magic and the schemes of empires in this action-packed series opener . . . Epic adventure and steamy smooches make for a crowd-pleasing formula'
Kirkus

'It's great to read a fantasy book where sisterhood and no-nonsense women take the lead . . . Triumphantly fun, *Truthwitch* casts off the current trend for gritty fantasy with a joyous laugh and a cheeky wink'
SFX

'A rollicking, swashbuckling adventure . . . Just the thing if you'd like to be swept away from real life for a while'
The Bookbag

Windwitch

Before she settled down as a full-time novelist and writing instructor, Susan Dennard travelled the world as a marine biologist. She is the author of the Something Strange and Deadly series as well as the Witchlands novels. When not writing, she can be found hiking with her dogs, exploring tidal pools, or earning bruises at the dojo.

To find out more about the Witchlands novels, please visit **thewitchlands.com**.

BY SUSAN DENNARD

The Witchlands Series
Truthwitch
Windwitch

A Witchlands Novella
Sightwitch

Windwitch

The Witchlands Series: Book Two

Susan Dennard

TOR

First published 2017 by Tom Doherty Associates, LLC

First published in the UK 2017 by Tor

This paperback edition published 2018 by Tor
an imprint of Pan Macmillan
The Smithson, 6 Briset Street, London SE1 5NR
Associated companies throughout the world
www.panmacmillan.com

ISBN 978-1-4472-8232-7

3 5 7 9 8 6 4 2

A CIP catalogue record for this book is available from the British Library.

Typeset by Palimpsest Book Production Ltd, Falkirk, Stirlingshire
Printed and bound by CPI Group (UK) Ltd, Croydon, CR0 4YY

Visit www.panmacmillan.com to read more about all our books
and to buy them. You will also find features, author interviews and
news of any author events, and you can sign up for e-newsletters
so that you're always first to hear about our new releases.

FOR JENNIFER AND DAVID

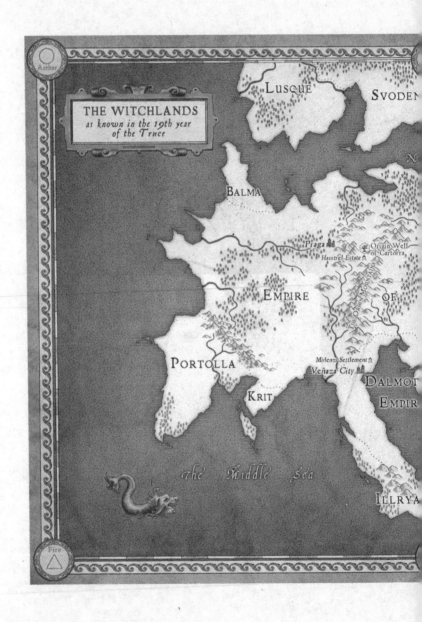

THE WITCHLANDS
as known in the 19th year
of the Truce

LUSQUE

SVODEN

BALMA

Praga

Origin Well
of Cartorra

Hasstrel Estate

EMPIRE

OF

PORTOLLA

Midenzi Settlement

Veñaza City

DALMOT

EMPIR

KRIT

ILLRYA

The Middle Sea

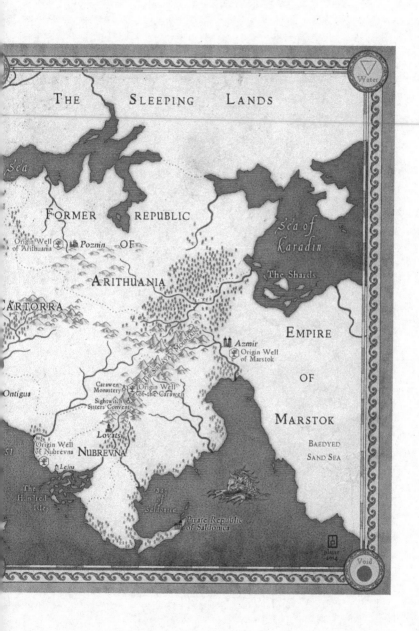

Windwitch

BEFORE

*B*lood on the floor.

It weeps sideways, pooling in a moonbeam before the gentle roll of the ship sends it trickling back the other way.

The prince releases the sword's hilt and rocks back two steps, heart banging against his ribs. He's never taken another man's life before. He wonders if this will change him.

The blade stays upright, lodged in the wood, even as the young man skewered beneath it tries to stand. Each time the assassin moves, the hole through his abdomen stretches wider. His innards glitter like silver coins in this half-light.

"Who are you?" the prince's voice rasps out. The first sound he has made since awakening to a shadow in his cabin.

Thank Noden his father's swords hang above the bed, ready for the grabbing when assassins strike.

"She's . . . waiting for you," the would-be assassin answers. He attempts once more to rise, this time reaching for the hilt with his bloodied left hand.

No pinkie, the prince notes absently, for his mind is turning over the word *she*. There is only one *she* who would do this. Only one she *who wants the prince dead*—and she has told him so herself many times.

The prince turns, lips parting to shout the alarm, but then he hears the man laughing behind him. A hacking sound with too many dimensions. Too much weight.

He turns back. The man's grip is falling from the sword. He topples back to the wood, with more blood, more laughter. His right hand pulls something from a pocket in his coat. A clay pot tumbles free. It rolls across the planks. Through the blood. Out the other side, painting a long, glistening line across the cabin floor.

Then the young assassin gives a final, bloody chuckle before whispering, "Ignite."

The prince sways upon the barren cliff and watches his warship burn.

Heat roars against him, the black flames of the seafire almost invisible atop the waves. Only their white, alchemical hearts shine through.

The noise consumes everything. The violent crack and pop of tarred wood that has braved more storms and battles than the prince has years.

He should be dead. His skin is charred to black, his hair singed off entirely, and his lungs burned to embers.

He doesn't know how he survived. How he held the seafire back long enough for every man and woman on board to abandon ship. Perhaps he won't survive. He's barely standing now.

His crew watches from the beach. Some sob. Some scream. A few even search the shore, the waves. But most simply stare as the prince does.

They don't know that an assassin has come. They don't know that she is waiting for news of his death.

The princess of Nubrevna. Vivia Nihar.

She will try to kill the prince again, if she learns this attempt has failed. Then his people, his crew will be at risk once more. Which is why, as he sinks to the ground, he decides these sailors must never learn he still lives. They must think him dead, and Vivia must think him dead too.

One for the sake of many.

Darkness creeps along the edge of his vision now. His eyes finally shut, and he recalls something his aunt once said: "The holiest always have the farthest to fall."

They do, he thinks, and I am perfect proof of it.

Then Merik Nihar, prince of Nubrevna, slips into a black and dreamless sleep.

ONE

There were advantages to being a dead man.

Merik Nihar, prince of Nubrevna and former admiral to the Nubrevnan navy, wished he'd considered dying a long time ago. He got so much more done as a corpse.

Such as right now. He'd come to Judgment Square at the heart of Lovats for a reason, and that reason was tucked inside a low hut, an extension of the prison behind it, where records were kept. There was one prisoner in particular Merik needed information on. A prisoner with no left pinkie, who now resided beyond the final shelf, deep in Noden's watery Hell.

Merik sank into the hood of his tan cloak. True, his face was scarcely recognizable thanks to the burns, and his hair was only just beginning to grow back, but the covering offered safety in the madness of Judgment Square.

Or Goshorn Square, as it was sometimes called, thanks to the enormous goshorn oak at the center.

The pale trunk, as wide as a lighthouse and easily as tall, was dented to high hell-waters, and its branches hadn't seen green in decades. *That tree*, Merik thought, as he eyed the longest branch, *looks like it might soon join me in death.*

All day long, tides of traffic poured through the square, driven by curiosity. Who would be forced into public shame? Shackled to the stones without food or reprieve? Who would feel the burning snap of a rope—followed by the cold kiss of Noden's Hagfishes?

Desperation brought people in droves. Families came to beg the Nubrevnan soldiers for mercy on their loved ones, and the homeless came to beg for food, for shelter, for pity of any kind.

But no one had pity or mercy to spare these days. Not even Merik Nihar.

He'd already done all he could—given up all he could for a trade agreement with the Hasstrel estate in Cartorra. He'd almost negotiated one with the Marstoks as well, but ultimately death had come too soon.

A family blocked Merik's way now. A woman and her two boys, each of them shouting at anyone who passed by.

"No crime in being hungry!" they hollered in unison. "Free us and feed us! Free us and feed us!" The older boy, wildly tall and skinny as a brittlestar, rounded on Merik.

"No crime in being hungry!" He heaved in close. "Free us and feed—"

Merik sidestepped the boy before twirling left around his brother and finally shooting past the mother. She was the loudest of the three, with her sun-bleached hair and a face lined with fury.

Merik knew that feeling well, for it was fury that fueled

6

him ever onward. Even as pain cut through his body and blisterings on his chest were scraped open by homespun.

Others in the area picked up the chant. *Free us and feed us! No crime in being hungry!* Merik found his steps settling into a quick clip to match the rhythm of that cry. So few people in the Witchlands had magic, much less magic of any real use. They survived by the whim of nature—or the whim of witches—and their own unrelenting grit.

Merik reached the gallows at the oak's fat trunk. Six ropes dangled from a middle branch, limp coils in the midmorning heat. Yet as Merik tried to skirt the empty stage, he caught sight of a tall figure, pale-headed and hulkingly framed.

Kullen. The name grazed across Merik's heart, sucking the air from his lungs before his brain could catch up and say, *No, not Kullen. Never Kullen.*

For Kullen had cleaved in Lejna two weeks ago. He had died in Lejna two weeks ago. He would never be coming back.

Without thinking, Merik's fists shot out. He punched the gallows stage, pain bursting in his knuckles—at once grounding. At once real.

Again he punched. Harder this time, wondering why his insides spun. He had paid his dues to Kullen's ghost. He had bought that shrine on the hillside, using the one remaining gold button from his admiral's coat, and he'd prayed for the Hagfishes to give Kullen quick passage beyond the final shelf.

After that, it was supposed to stop hurting. *This* was supposed to stop hurting.

Eventually, the tall figure was gone and Merik's bleeding knuckles stung more brightly than the past. Merik forced himself onward, elbows out and hood low. For if Safiya fon

7

Hasstrel could reach that pier in Lejna despite Marstoks and Cleaved in her way—if she could do all that for a nation that wasn't even her own, for a trade agreement with her family—then Merik could certainly finish what he'd come here to do.

Curse his mind for going to her, though. Merik had done so well at avoiding memories of Safi since the explosion. Since his old world had ended and this new one had begun. Not because he didn't *want* to think about her. Noden save him, but that last moment he'd shared with her . . .

No, no—Merik would not dwell. There was no point in remembering the taste of Safi's skin against his lips, not when his lips were now broken. Not when his entire body was ruined and wretched to behold.

Besides, dead men weren't supposed to care.

On he charged through filth and body odor. A tide that fought back. A storm with no eye. Each smack of limbs against Merik's shoulders or hands sent pain scuttling through him.

He reached the irons. Fifty prisoners waited here, shackled to the stones and crispy from the sun. A fence surrounded them, indifferent to the people pressing in from the outside.

They begged the guards to give their sons water. Their wives shade. Their fathers release. Yet the two soldiers who waited at the fence's gate—inside, to keep from being trampled—showed no more interest in the hungry of Lovats than they did the prisoners they were meant to guard.

In fact, so bored were these two soldiers that they played taro to while away the time. One wore an iris-blue strip of cloth at his biceps, a mourning band to show respect for his dead prince. The other kept the band draped across a knee.

At the sight of that cloth—just lying there, unused—a fresh, furious wind ignited in Merik's chest. He had given so much for Nubrevna, and this was all it had earned him: a hollow, false grief. Outward shows, like the wreaths and streamers draped across the city, that couldn't truly mask how little anyone cared their prince was dead.

Vivia had seen to that.

Thank Noden, Merik soon arrived at the hut, for he could keep his winds and temper contained for only so long—and the fuse was almost burned up.

The crowds spat him out before orange walls streaked in bird shit, and Merik cut toward a door on the south side. Always locked, but not impenetrable.

"Open up!" Merik bellowed. He knocked once at the door—a mistake. The newly splintered skin on his knuckles sloughed off. "I know you're in there!"

No response. At least none that Merik could hear, but that was all right. He let the heat in his body grow. Strengthen. *Gust.*

Then he knocked again, feeling the wind curl around him as he did so. "Hurry! It's madness out here!"

The latch jiggled. The door creaked back . . . And Merik shoved in. With fists, with force, with wind.

The soldier on the other side stood no chance. He toppled back, the whole hut shuddering from the force of his fall. Before he could rise, Merik had the door closed behind him. He advanced on the man, his winds chasing. Tearing up papers in a cyclone that felt so blighted good.

It had been too long since Merik had let his winds unfurl and his magic stretch wide. Fire built in his belly, a rage that

9

blustered and blew. That had kept his stomach full when food had not. Air billowed around him, sweeping in and out in time to his breaths.

The soldier—middle-aged, sallow-skinned—stayed on the ground with his hands to protect his face. Clearly, he'd decided surrender was his safest option.

Too bad. Merik would've loved a fight. Instead, he forced his eyes to scour the room. He used his winds too, coaxing them outward. Letting the vibrations on the air tell him where other bodies might wait. Where other breaths might curl. Yet no one hid in the dark corners, and the door into the main prison remained firmly shut.

So at last, with careful control, Merik returned his attention to the soldier. His magic softened, dropping papers to the floor before he eased off his hood, fighting the pain that skittered down his scalp.

Then Merik waited, to see if the soldier would recognize him.

Nothing. In fact, the instant the man lowered his hands, he shrank back. "What are you?"

"Angry." Merik advanced a single step. "I seek someone recently released from a second time in the irons."

The man shot a scattered glance around the room. "I'll need more information. Sir. An age or crime or release date—"

"I don't have that." Merik claimed another step forward, and this time the soldier frantically scrambled upright. Away from Merik and grabbing for the nearest papers.

"I met this prisoner"—*I killed this prisoner*—"eleven days ago." Merik paused, thinking back to the moonbeam. "He was

10

brown-skinned with long black hair, and he had two stripes tattooed beneath his left eye."

Two stripes. Two times in the Judgment Square irons.

"And . . ." Merik lifted his left hand. The skin bore shades of healing red and brown, except where new blood cracked along his knuckles. "The prisoner had no pinkie."

"Garren Leeri!" the soldier cried, nodding. "I remember him, all right. He was part of the Nines, back before we cracked down on the Skulks' gangs. Though the second time we arrested him, it was for petty theft."

"Indeed. And what exactly happened to Garren after his time was served?"

"He was sold, sir."

Merik's nostrils flared. *Sold* was not something he'd known could happen to prisoners, and with that thought, disgusted heat awoke in his lungs. Merik didn't fight it—he simply let it kick out to rattle the papers near his feet.

One such paper flipped up, slapping against the soldier's shin. In an instant, the man was trembling again. "It doesn't happen often. Sir. Selling people, I mean. Just when we've no room in the prison—and we only sell people convicted for petty crimes. They work off their time instead."

"And to whom"—Merik dipped his head sideways—"did you sell this man named Garren?"

"To Pin's Keep, sir. They regularly buy prisoners to work the clinic. Give them second chances."

"Ah." Merik could barely bite back a smile. Pin's Keep was a shelter for the poorest of Lovats. It had been a project of Merik's mother, and upon the queen's death, it had passed directly to Vivia.

11

How easy. Just like that, Merik had the found the sinew binding Garren to Vivia. All he lacked was tangible proof—something physical that he could hand to the High Council showing, beyond any doubt, that his sister was a murderer. That she was not fit to rule.

Now he had a lead. A good one.

Before Merik could loose a smile, the sound of metal scraping on wood filled the room.

Merik turned as the outside door swung in and met the eyes of a startled young guard.

Well, this was unfortunate.

For the guard.

Out snapped Merik's winds, grabbing the guard like a doll. Then in they whipped, and he was flung straight for Merik.

Whose fist was ready.

Merik's torn knuckles connected with the guard's jaw. Full speed. A hurricane against a mountain. The guard was out in an instant, and as his limp form crumpled, Merik threw a glance at the first soldier.

But the older man was at the door to the prison now, fumbling with a lock to escape and muttering, "Too old for this. Too old for this."

Hell-waters. A flash of guilt hit Merik's chest. He had what he'd come for, and hanging around was simply asking for more trouble. So he left the soldier to his escape and slung toward the hut's open door.

Only to stop halfway as a screeching woman tumbled inside. "There's no crime in being hungry! Free us and feed us!"

It was *that* woman, and her two sons straggled in behind.

Noden hang him, but hadn't Merik had enough interruptions for one day?

The answer was no, apparently he had not.

Upon spotting the unconscious guard and then Merik's unhooded face, the woman fell completely silent. Totally still. There was something in her bloodshot eyes, something hopeful.

"You," she breathed. Then she stumbled forward, arms outstretched. "Please, Fury, we've done nothing wrong."

Merik yanked up his hood, the pain briefly louder than any sounds. Brighter too, even as the woman and her sons closed in.

Her hands grabbed Merik's hand. "Please, Fury!" she repeated, and inwardly Merik winced at that title. Was he truly so grotesque? "Please, sir! We've been good and given our respects to your shrine! We don't deserve your wrath— we just want to feed our families!"

Merik tore himself free. Skin split beneath her fingernails. Any moment now, soldiers would be pouring in from the records office, and though Merik could fight these boys and their mother, that would only draw attention.

"Free us and feed us, you said?" Merik scooped a ring of keys from the unconscious guard's belt. "Take these."

The cursed woman cowered back from Merik's outstretched hand.

And now he was out of time. The familiar sound of a wind-drum was booming outside. *Soldiers needed*, said the beat, *in Judgment Square*.

So Merik flung the keys at the nearest son, who caught them clumsily. "Free the prisoners if you want, but be quick about it. Because *now* would be a good time for all of us to run."

Then Merik thrust into the crowds, bobbing low and moving fast. For though the woman and her sons lacked the good sense to flee, Merik Nihar did not.

After all, even dead men could have lives they didn't want to lose.

TWO

This was not Azmir.

Safiya fon Hasstrel might have been a poor geography student, but even *she* knew this crescent-moon bay was not the capital of Marstok. Though weasels piss on her, she wished it were.

Anything would be more interesting than staring at the same turquoise waves she'd been staring at for the past week, so at odds with the dark, dense jungle beyond. For here, on the easternmost edge of the Contested Lands—a long peninsula of no-man's-land that didn't quite belong to the pirate factions in Saldonica and didn't quite belong to the empires either—there was absolutely nothing of interest to do.

Paper whispered behind Safi, almost in time to the sea's swell, and overtop it sang the infinitely calm voice of the Empress of Marstok. All day long, she worked through missives and messages on a low table at the center of her cabin, stopping only to update Safi on some complicated political alliance or recent shift in her empire's southern borders.

It was excruciatingly dull, and the simple truth was, at least in Safi's opinion, that pretty people should *not* be allowed to lecture. Nothing negated beauty faster than boredom.

"Are you listening, Domna?"

"Of course I am, Your Majesty!" Safi twirled around, her white gown billowing. She batted her eyelashes for an extra dose of innocence.

Vaness wasn't buying it. Her heart-shaped face had hardened, and Safi didn't *think* she was imagining how the empress's iron belt rippled and grooved like two snakes sliding past each other.

Vaness was, according to scholars, the youngest, most powerful empress in all of the Witchlands history. She was also, according to legend, the strongest, most vicious Ironwitch who had ever lived, having felled an entire mountain when she was only seven years old. And, of course, according to Safi, Vaness was the most beautiful, most elegant woman who had ever graced the world with her presence.

Yet none of that mattered because gods *below*, Vaness was tedious.

No card games, no jokes, no exciting stories by Firewitch flame—nothing at all to make this wait more bearable. They'd dropped anchor here a week before, hiding first from a Cartorran cutter. Then from a Cartorran armada. Everyone had been braced for a naval battle . . .

That had never come. And while Safi knew this to be a good thing—war *was* senseless, as Habim always said—she'd also learned that *waiting all day long* was her own form of private hell.

Especially since her entire life had been upended two and a half weeks ago. A surprise betrothal to the Emperor of

16

Cartorra had pulled her into a cyclone of conspiracy and escape. She'd learned her uncle, a man she'd spent her whole life loathing, was behind some massive, wide-scale plan to bring peace to the Witchlands.

Then, because Safi's life wasn't complicated enough already, she'd discovered that she and her Threadsister Iseult might be the mythical Cahr Awen, whose duty it was to heal magic across the Witchlands.

The empress cleared her throat emphatically, snapping Safi's mind back to the present.

"My treaty with the Baedyed Pirates is incredibly important for Marstok." Vaness lifted her eyebrows sternly. "It took years to come to an agreement with them, and thousands of lives will be saved because of it—you are not even listening now, Domna!"

This was not *entirely* untrue, yet Safi took offense at the empress's tone. After all, she'd been wearing her best I-am-a-perfect-student face, and Vaness really ought to appreciate that. It wasn't as if Safi ever bothered to school her features with her mentors, Mathew and Habim. Nor even with Iseult.

Safi's throat tightened. Instinctively, she grabbed for the Threadstone resting against her collarbone. Every few minutes, she'd haul out the uncut ruby and stare into its flickering depths.

It was supposed to light up if Iseult was in danger. Yet not a flash so far. Not a peep. This had soothed Safi at first—it was all she'd had to cling to, really. Her *only* connection to her Threadsister. Her better half. Her logical get-Safi-out-of-trouble half. The person who never would have let Safi agree to join the empress.

In hindsight, Safi could see what a fool's bargain she'd made, offering up her Truthwitchery so the empress could root out corruption in her Marstoki court. Safi had thought herself *oh* so noble and *oh* so self-sacrificing, for by joining Vaness, Safi was helping the dying nation of Nubrevna win trade.

The truth was, though, that she was stuck. On a ship. In the middle of nowhere. With only the Empress of Insipid for company.

"Sit with me," Vaness ordered, cutting through Safi's self-inflicted misery. "Since you clearly do not care for Baedyed politics, perhaps this message will interest you."

Safi's interest perked up. A *message*. Already this afternoon had turned more enticing than yesterday's.

Resting her hands on her own iron belt, she crossed the lolling cabin to an empty bench opposite the empress. Vaness rifled through a stack of mismatched papers, the slightest scowl knitting her brow.

It brought to mind a different face often pinched with a frown. A different leader who, like the Empress of Marstok, put his people's lives forever above his own.

Merik.

Safi's lungs expanded. Her traitorous cheeks warmed. It was only *one* kiss they'd shared, so really, this blush could stop now.

As if answering her thoughts, Safi glimpsed a single name atop the page Vaness now withdrew: *Prince of Nubrevna.* Her pulse quickened. Maybe this was it—maybe, finally, she would have news of the world and the people she'd left behind.

Before she could learn anything or catch any words, though, the door to the empress's cabin burst wide. A man rushed in, dressed as a sailor in Marstoki green. He spotted Safi and Vaness, and for two heartbeats, he simply stared.

False. The word fretted down Safi's spine, her Truthwitchery tingling. A warning that what she saw was a lie. That duplicity now gaped at her while he lifted a single hand.

"Look out!" Safi tried to grab for the empress, tried to yank them both down for cover. But she was too slow. The sailor had pulled the trigger on his pistol.

It fired with a *crack!*

The shot never connected. It halted midair, a spinning ball of iron mere inches from the empress's face.

Then a blade cut through the attacker's back and a bloodied steel tip erupted from his belly. A singing slice that severed spine and organ and skin.

The sword ripped back. The body fell. The leader of Vaness's personal guards appeared, dressed in black from head to toe, his blade dripping with blood.

The Adder High. "Assassin." He offered the word so calmly. "You know what to do, Your Majesty."

Without another word, he was gone.

The iron shot finally dropped from the air. It clattered to the floor and rolled, the sound lost to a sudden roaring of voices outside.

"Come," was all Vaness said. Then, as if she feared Safi might not listen, she tightened the iron belt at Safi's waist and *yanked* her toward the door with her magic.

Safi had no choice but to hurry after, despite the swelling

horror in her throat. Despite the questions flinging across her mind.

They reached the assassin. Vaness slowed long enough to glance down. She sniffed dismissively, lifting her black skirts, and stepped across his corpse. Her feet tracked blood on the other side.

Safi, meanwhile, made sure to step around.

She also made sure not to look at the man's dead eyes. Blue and staring straight at the caulked ceiling.

Outside, chaos had taken hold, yet Vaness faced it all without emotion. A flick of her hands and the iron shackles at her wrists melted outward into four thin walls that encased her and Safi. *A shield.* The empress then cut left across the deck. Voices hollered in Marstoki, all of them muffled and tinny.

Yet fully understandable. A second assassin was thought to be on board, and the Adders and the crew had to find him.

"Faster," Vaness commanded Safi, and the belt towed harder.

"Where are we going?" Safi shouted back. She saw nothing inside this shield save the perfect, clear sky above.

Soon enough Safi had an answer. They reached the warship's launch gig, stored astern and suspended for easy release into the waves. Vaness melted her front shield into a set of steps, which she immediately ascended.

Then they were in the swinging boat, iron spreading around the gig's edges. Walls to keep them safe. But no roof, no protection against the voice now roaring, "*He's belowdecks!*"

Vaness met Safi's eyes. "Hold on," she warned. Then her hands rose, chains clanked, and the gig lurched.

They dropped to the waves. Safi almost toppled off her seat, and spindrift sprayed in—followed by a sticky, salty breeze as Safi righted herself. It was all so calm, so quiet down here. Her knees bounced—how could it be so serene when violence ruled nearby?

The calm was a lie, for a single breath later, a burst of brilliant light stormed above the shields, glittery with glass and power. The boat flew back, tipping dangerously.

Last of all came the thunder. Violent. Scalding. *Alive.*

The ship had blown up.

Flames charged against the shield, yet the empress held the onslaught at bay. Paper-thin, the shields spread, coating the entire gig. Protecting Vaness and Safi against raging heat and cuffing the hell-fires to a muted roar.

Blood dripped from the empress's nose, and her muscles quaked. A sign she could not hold her shield against the madness forever.

So Safi snatched up the oars from the gig's belly. Not once did she consider if this was what she should do—just as she would not *consider* swimming when trapped beneath a tide. There were oars and a shore to aim for, so she acted.

Seeing what Safi intended, Vaness formed two holes in the shield for the oars. Smoke and heat gushed in.

Safi ignored it, even as her fingers burned and as her lungs filled with salty smoke.

Stroke after stroke, she carried Vaness and herself away from death, until at last the gig *thunked* against dark gravel. Until at last, the empress allowed her iron shield to fall. It coiled back into decorative shackles at her wrists, giving Safi a full view of the black flames burning before them.

Seafire.

Its dark thirst could not be slaked. Wind could not snuff it out. Water only fanned its resinous flames all the higher.

Safi scooped her arms around the flagging empress and dragged them both into the soft waves. She felt no relief at having survived this attack. No heady satisfaction surged through her because she'd made it to shore. She felt only a growing emptiness. A gathering dark. For *this* was her life now. Not boredom and lectures, but hell-flames and assassins. Massacres and endless flight.

And no one could save her from it but herself.

I could run right now, she thought, eyeing the long shoreline—the mangroves and palm trees beyond. *The empress wouldn't even notice. Probably wouldn't care either.*

If Safi aimed southwest, she would eventually reach the Pirate Republic of Saldonica. The only civilization—if it could be called that—and the only place to find a ship out of here. Yet she was almost certain that she could *not* survive in that cesspool of humanity alone.

Her fingers moved to her Threadstone, for now that Safi's life hung on a knife's edge, the ruby had finally flared to life.

If Iseult were here, then Safi could charge off into that jungle without a second thought. With Iseult, Safi was brave. She was strong. She was fearless. But Safi had no idea where her Threadsister was, nor any clue when she'd see her again—or *if* she'd see her again.

Which meant, for now, Safi's chances were better with the Empress of Marstok.

Once the warship had burned to a flaming skeleton and the heat of the attack had drawn back, Safi turned to Vaness.

22

The empress stood rooted to the ground, stiff as the iron she controlled.

Ash streaked her skin. Two lines of blood dried beneath her nose.

"We need to hide," Safi croaked. Gods below, she needed water. Cold, soothing salt-free water. "The fire will draw the Cartorran armada to us."

Ever so slowly, the empress cracked her gaze from the horizon and fixed it on Safi. "There might," she growled, "be survivors."

Safi's lips pressed thin, but she didn't argue. And perhaps it was that lack of argument that set Vaness's shoulders to sinking ever so slightly.

"We aim for Saldonica," was all the Empress of Marstok said next. Then she set off with Safi stalking behind, across the rocky beach and toward the gathering dark.

THREE

Stasis, Iseult det Midenzi told herself for the thousandth time since dawn. *Stasis in your fingers and in your toes.*

Not that she could feel her fingers or her toes. She'd been sprinting downhill in this freezing mountain stream for what seemed an eternity. Twice she'd fallen, and twice she'd dunked herself head to foot.

But she couldn't stop. She just had to keep running. Although to *where* had been a recurring question. If she'd read her map correctly all those hours ago, before the Cleaved had picked up her scent and started chasing, then she must be somewhere near the northernmost tip of the Contested Lands.

Which meant no settlements to take refuge in. No people to save her from what hunted behind.

For a week, Iseult had been traveling toward Marstok. The dead, lowlands around Lejna had eventually turned steep. Hilly. Iseult had never been anywhere that wasn't flat enough to see the sky. Oh, she'd seen snowcapped peaks and craggy foothills in illustrations and she'd heard Safi describe them, but she never could have guessed how *small* they would make

24

her feel. How cut off and trapped, when hills blocked her vision of the sky.

It was made all the worse by the complete absence of Threads. As a Threadwitch, Iseult could see the Threads that build, the Threads that bind, the Threads that break. A thousand colors to shimmer over her at every moment of every day. Except that without people, there were no Threads—and without Threads, there was no added color to fill her eyes, her mind.

Iseult was and had been alone for days. She'd trekked over pine needle carpets, and only the hundreds of trees creaking in the wind had kept her company. Yet no matter the terrain, Iseult had moved carefully. Never leaving a mark, never leaving a trail, and always, always moving east.

Until this morning.

Four Cleaved had picked up Iseult's trail. She had no idea where they'd come from or how they had followed. This salamander-fiber cloak that the Bloodwitch Aeduan had given her two weeks ago was meant to block her scent from the Cleaved, yet it had, thus far, failed her. Iseult could feel the black corruption of Cleaved Threads still hunting.

And they gained ground with each passing minute.

I should wrap the Threadstone, Iseult thought vaguely, a distant thrum of inner dialogue to weave between her stamping, splashing footsteps. *Wrap it in a bit of cloth so it doesn't keep bruising me when I run.*

She'd thought this particular refrain at least a hundred times now, for this wasn't the first time she had found herself sprinting over rough forest terrain. Yet every time she'd finally been able to pause and duck beneath a log, she'd been so focused on catching her breath or straining her witchery for some sign of pursuing Threads that she'd forgotten to wrap the Threadstone. At least until it started bruising her again.

Other times, Iseult would tumble so deeply into day-dreams that she'd forget her surroundings entirely for a bit. She'd imagine what it might be like to actually be the Cahr Awen.

Iseult and Safi had gone in the Origin Well of Nubrevna. They had touched its spring, and an earthquake had rolled through the land. *I have found the Cahr Awen*, Monk Evrane had then told Iseult and Safi, *and you have awoken the Water Well.*

For Safi, that title made perfect sense. She was sunshine and simplicity. Of course she would be the *Light-Bringer* half of the Cahr Awen. But Iseult was not the opposite of Safi. She wasn't starshine or complexity. She wasn't anything at all.

Unless I am. Unless I can be.

Iseult would drift asleep with those thoughts to warm her.

Today, though, was the first time Threadstone had ever flashed—a sign Iseult was truly in danger. She just hoped that, wherever Safi might be right now, she wasn't panicking at the sight of her own blinking stone.

Iseult also hoped that the stone flared only for her, for if it glowed because Safi was also threatened . . .

No, Iseult couldn't worry like that. All she could do right now was run.

To think, it had been only two weeks since all hell-fire had broken loose in Lejna. Since Iseult had lost Safi to the Mar-stoks, had rescued Merik from a collapsed building, and had decided she would go after her Threadsister no matter what.

26

Iseult had scoured the ghost city of Lejna after that, until she had found Mathew's abandoned coffee shop. There'd been food in the kitchen, and clean water too. She'd even found a sack of silver coins in the cellar.

When no one had come for her after eight days, though, Iseult had been forced to assume no one ever would. Dom Eron had likely heard of Safi's kidnapping by the Empress of Marstok; Habim, Mathew, and Eron were likely headed after her now.

Leaving Iseult with no choice but to set off at a steady pace northeast, sleeping by day, traveling by night. For there were only two types of people in the forests of the Witchlands: those who *tried* to kill you and those who *got* you killed. Both camps were best avoided.

Yet in the darkness that Iseult traveled by, there were other things waiting. Shadows and breezes and memories she couldn't lock away. She thought about Safi. She thought about her mother. She thought about Corlant and his cursed arrow that had almost taken her life. She thought of the Cleaved from Lejna and the teardrop-shaped scar they'd left behind.

And she thought of the Puppeteer, who tried endlessly to invade Iseult's dreams. A Weaverwitch, she called herself, all while insisting Iseult was just like her. But the Puppeteer cleaved people and controlled their Threads. Iseult could— *would*—never do that.

Mostly, Iseult thought about death. Her own. After all, she had only a single cutlass and she traveled toward a future that might not exist.

A future that could end very soon, if the Cleaved behind

27

finally caught up. *When* they caught up, for Iseult was no good at this. It was why she relied so deeply on Safi—the one who could intuit with her bounding feet, escape with only instinct to drive her. Iseult was her own worst enemy in these breakneck situations, and she was letting fear drown out her Threadwitch reason.

Until she caught sight of the morning glories. A carpet of them alongside the stream. Seemingly wild. Seemingly harmless.

But not wild. Not harmless.

Iseult was out of the stream in a heartbeat. Her numb feet tripped her as she scrambled up the stream's side. She fell; her hands caught her, wrists snapping back.

She didn't notice, didn't care, for there were morning glories everywhere she looked. Almost invisible in the mottled shadows, but unmissable if you knew how to look. Unmissable if you were a Nomatsi.

Though it looked like an innocent deer path cut into the pines, Iseult knew a Nomatsi road when she saw one. Meant to protect the tribes from outsiders, these trap-lined trails were certain death for anyone the caravan had not invited in.

Iseult had certainly not been invited, yet surely, as a fellow Nomatsi, *she* would not be deemed "outsider."

She kicked into a stiff march away from the stream. No more running, for a single false step would trigger the Poison-witched mist these morning glories were meant to hide.

There. She spotted the branch in the ground, wishbone shaped, with one kinked prong aiming north and one aiming south.

28

The way out of the Nomatsi road. Or the way deeper into it.

Iseult slowed her pace even more, easing around pine tree after pine tree. She crouched over a mossy stone. She tiptoed, she stalked, she scarcely breathed.

The Cleaved were so close now. Black Threads curdled and strained into her awareness, hungry and foul. In minutes, they would be upon her.

But that was all right, for up ahead was the next branch hammered into the earth, seamlessly woven into the forest. *Clawed bear traps ahead*, the branch alerted.

To the Cleaved, though, it would alert nothing at all. Not until their legs were trapped in iron teeth too strong for any man to pry apart.

The urge to sprint shook through Iseult's legs. To bolt past these bear traps tucked in the fern-frilled clearing before her. She grabbed her Threadstone, squeezed tight, and kept her pace steady. *Stasis, stasis, stasis.* She counted six traps before she reached the other side.

Then she was past, and now she could run. Just in time too, for behind her, the Nomatsi road awoke. Poisonwitch mists erupted, a heated charge rising in the distance. It juddered through the air, scratched down Iseult's spine.

The Cleaved had triggered it, yet the mist had no effect. The hunters were still coming.

Iseult pumped her legs faster. Her breath came in punctuated gasps. If she could get just a bit farther, then maybe she could escape entirely.

The bear traps snapped to life, clanging like midnight chimes. A howling burst out, torn from depraved throats.

Four sets of Threads snapped and fought against the steel holding their legs.

Iseult did not slow. She had to get ahead while she could, for this lead might be short-lived. Ferns and pine needles crashed beneath her feet. She had no idea where her heels would plant next. All she could see were the masts of pine trees. Saplings, trunks, roots—she sprinted around them. Twisted her ankles and jammed her knees.

Speed was a mistake. Nomatsi roads weren't meant to be crossed quickly. They demanded time. They demanded respect.

So it should have come as no surprise when Iseult reached a clearing and the solid ground abruptly gave way. It should have come as no surprise when a net snapped up to yank her high into the trees.

She yelped. Then flew straight upward, only to stop, dangling and swaying.

Iseult's breath sawed in. Razored out. *At least*, she thought vaguely, *I still have my cutlass.* Though little good it would do her when she was hanging twenty feet in the air.

Or when a Cleaved strode to the center of the clearing, black blood trailing behind. His posture was bent. He was missing half his foot, and his skin roiled with whatever magic had erupted within to cleave him. Yet he moved with unusual focus. None of the mindless, frenetic violence typical of a Cleaved.

Then Iseult realized *why*. Severed Threads drifted lazily above him, stretching into the sky. Almost invisible.

The Puppeteer. Just as she'd done in Lejna to the Marstoki

Adders and sailors, the Puppeteer must have cleaved these men from afar. And she must now be controlling them too.

At that realization, Threads began winking out. One by one, the Cleaved still locked in iron traps were dying. As if the Puppeteer had decided their time was up and snipped apart their Severed Threads.

Yet the man below still lived. He continued to prowl, leaving Iseult with only one option: she would have to cut herself down and try to kill the Cleaved before he killed her.

Iseult never got to make that move, before the hunter scuffled over a second trap. A net ripped from the soil, slinging him upward. Ropes squeaked. He struggled and fought and howled, mere feet from Iseult until he too was abruptly silenced, his Threads vanishing in a hiss of shriveling black.

The Puppeteer had killed him, leaving Iseult all alone on a Nomatsi road.

Iseult couldn't help it: she laughed. She had finally claimed the pause she so desperately needed. She had finally evaded her hunters, and this was where it landed her.

Iseult's laughter quickly dissolved. Trickled away on a swoop of cold.

For if Esme had sent these Cleaved to hunt her, Iseult could only assume she would do so again.

Worry about that later, she told herself. For now, she had no opponents, and her biggest worry was cutting herself down without breaking any bones in the process.

"Oh, goat tits," she murmured, invoking one of Safi's favorite oaths and grabbing at her Threadstone—no longer flashing—for the burst of strength she liked to pretend it gave her.

Then without another word or thought, and with only Threadwitch focus to guide her, Iseult set to sawing herself free.

FOUR

As Merik dipped and wove down Hawk's Way, a crowded street that bisected Lovats from one end to the other and hugged the River Timetz, he prayed the storm rolling in would hold off just a few more hours. Long enough for him to get to proper shelter. Maybe long enough for him to find a proper meal too.

He needed his strength back before he ventured to Pin's Keep.

Each breath Merik swallowed was spiced with rain about to break. Thunder rumbled beneath the wind-drums' song across Lovats. *Soldiers needed in Judgment Square.*

Lucky for Merik, he was a full mile from Judgment Square now, lost in the mayhem of Hawk's Way, with its crisscrossing bridges and zigzagging side streets. The buildings leaned like sailors after a night drinking, and at each intersection, wreaths of last autumn's oak leaves hung from corner to corner.

The amber and yellow shades never failed to catch Merik's eyes when he passed. So much of the Nihar lands had never seen an autumn harvest—or a spring rebirth—in the years that Merik had lived there. So much of the soil still festered with Dalmotti poison.

But the poison had never reached Lovats far to the northeast, so braiding oak leaves with strands of sage and mint, with sunbursts of fire and green, was still quite possible here. These wreaths were for the royal funeral in three days. For *Merik's* funeral.

What a twisted sense of humor Noden had.

On Merik hurried, the call for soldiers still hammering strong, even as he hopped the worn granite steps into an ancient temple off Hawk's Way. This temple was as old as Lovats itself, and time had smoothed away the six columns waiting at the shadowy entrance.

The Hagfishes. Noden's messengers, tasked with carrying the dead beyond the farthest shelf, deep down to the god's court at the bottom of the sea. Now all that remained of the sculptures were iron rings at waist level and the faintest outlines of faces above.

Merik followed a line of light inside, aiming for the farthest wall of the temple. The air cooled with each step; the wind-drums' call softened. Gradually, all sunlight faded, replaced by two halfhearted lamps hanging above a stone Noden on his throne at the temple's heart.

The space was mostly empty at this time of day. Only two old ladies waited within, and they were currently headed out.

"I hope there's bread at the funeral," said one of the women. Her reedy voice bounced off the granite god. "The Lindays handed out bread at the queen's funeral—do you remember that?"

"Don't get too excited," her companion muttered back. "I heard there might not be a funeral."

This hooked Merik's attention. He slunk behind the throne and listened. "My nephew Rayet is a page at the palace," the second woman continued, "and he told me that the princess didn't react at all when she heard the news of the prince's murder."

Of course she didn't. Merik's arms folded over his chest, fingers digging into his tender biceps.

"Did your nephew know who killed the prince? That butcher at the end of Hawk's Way told me it was the Marstoks, but then my neighbor said it was the Cartorrans..." Her voice faded into muffled nothing, and Merik didn't try to follow.

He'd heard enough. More than enough. Of course Vivia would cancel the funeral. He could practically hear her drawling voice: *Why waste food on the people when the troops could use it instead?*

She cared only for power. For claiming the crown that the High Council had, thank Noden, still not given her. But if the king's illness worsened—if he passed on as everyone believed Merik had—then there would be no keeping Vivia from the throne.

Abandoning the statue of the god, Merik moved to the two frescoes on the back wall.

On the right stood Lady Baile, patron saint of change, seasons, and crossroads. Noden's Right Hand, they called her, and the lamp's fire shimmered across golden wheat in her left hand, a silver trout in her right. Her skin was painted like a night sky, black with pinpricks of white, while the fox-shaped mask across her face shone blue. She stood upon a field of green, all colors on the fresco recently refreshed, as were the golden words beneath her:

> *Though we cannot always see*
> *the blessing in the loss.*
> *Strength is the gift of our Lady Baile*
> *and she will never abandon us.*

Merik's gaze flicked to a copper urn resting before her, overflowing with wood and silver coins. Offerings for her kindness. A petition for her to whisper in Noden's ear, *Help them.*

In vibrant heaps at the urn's base lay wreaths of last year's leaves, of sage and mint and rosemary—gifts to honor the dead. Merik wondered if any had been placed for Kullen.

Then his chest clenched. He twisted away, fixing his gaze on the second fresco. On Noden's Left Hand. The patron saint of justice, of vengeance, of rage.

The Fury.

That was what the woman in Judgment Square had called Merik. She'd meant it as a title. She'd meant it as a prayer.

Bald, scarred, and hulking, the saint of all things broken bore only the name of his true nature. His one calling. He brought justice to the wronged and punishment to the wicked, and while Lady Baile was as beautiful as life itself, the Fury was more grotesque than even the Hagfishes.

The crimson and black pigments of his body had faded, never to be refreshed, as had the gray cavernous backdrop behind him—and the words below the Fury's clawed feet:

Why do you hold a razor in one hand?
So men remember that I am sharp as any edge.
And why do you hold broken glass in the other?
So men remember that I am always watching.

"And this," Merik murmured to himself, "is who that woman mistook me for." *This* was the monster she had seen when she'd looked upon him.

He turned to the Fury's empty urn. Always empty, for no one wished to accidentally attract his eye, lest they too be judged.

Outside the temple, the storm finally broke. Rain clattered down, loud enough for Merik to hear. Yet when he glanced back toward the columns, expecting to find people rushing in for shelter, he found only a single figure loping inside. She dripped water to the flagstones with each of her long steps.

Cam. Merik's only ally.

"Dried lamb?" she called once she was close enough. Her voice echoed off the granite flagstones. Like Merik, she wore a hooded tan coat atop her beige shirt and black trousers—all of it homespun, all of it filthy. "The meat's not too wet."

Merik forced himself to summon a glare. To scold: "What have I said about stealing?"

"Does that mean," she began, her black eyes glittering with lamp-lit mischief, "that you don't want it? I can always save it for myself, you know."

Merik wrested it from her grip. Hunger, he had learned, beat morality every time.

"S'what I thought." A gloating grin split her face, stretching

37

the white patches on her brown cheek. "Even dead men gotta eat."

Cam's whole body was speckled with those swaths of white skin. Down the right side of her neck they spanned, stretching onto her left forearm, her right hand. Obvious, if one was looking; invisible if one wasn't.

Merik had certainly never looked before. He'd never been able to recall her name—she'd simply been the *new recruit.* Then again, he hadn't known she was a girl either. She'd looked the part of a ship's boy on the *Jana,* and she'd played it well enough too.

Not once had Merik commented on Cam's sex though. And since she seemed determined to keep her secret, he had continued to address her as "boy." After all, what did it really matter in the end? *She* was the one who had stayed behind while the rest of the crew went to the village of Noden's Gift.

My gut told me you weren't dead, she'd explained to Merik, *so I searched and searched and searched until I found you.*

"Are the streets safe, boy?" he asked through a mouthful of tough meat. The lamb had been smoked too long.

"Hye," Cam mumbled through her own full jowls. "Though no thanks to you, sir. The Royal Forces are all riled up. Which"—she tore off another bite with vicious emphasis—"is why you should've let me come along."

Merik huffed a sigh. He and Cam had exchanged this same argument at least once a day since the explosion. Each time Merik had slunk into a small village to find supplies or gone hunting along the riverbanks for supper, Cam had begged to join. Each time, Merik had refused.

"If you'd been there," Merik countered, "then the Royal Forces would be hunting you now too."

"Not a chance, sir." Cam swatted the air with her lamb strip. "If I'd been with you, I'd have kept watch, see? Then that pickpocket wouldn't have nabbed this . . ." She fished a flimsy coin purse from her coat and dangled it before Merik's nose. "Did you even notice someone had picked your pocket, sir?"

Merik swore under his breath. Then he snatched it from her. "I had *not* noticed, and how did you get it back?"

"Same way I get everything." She wiggled her fingers at him. The glistening, jagged scar on the edge of her left hand shone.

As Cam relayed how she'd enjoyed Merik's adventure from a nearby rooftop, he settled in to the familiar rhythm of her storytelling. Unfiltered, uncultured, unabashed—that was how Cam spoke. Dragging out words for effect or lowering her voice to a tense, terrifying whisper.

For the past two weeks, the girl had talked endlessly. And for the past two weeks, Merik had listened. In fact, more often than not, Merik had found himself clinging to those moments when he could lose himself in Cam's voice. When he could ride the crests and waves of her story and forget, for just a few breaths, that his life had been swept away by hell-waters.

"The streets are crawling with soldiers now, sir. But," Cam finished, flashing one of her easy smiles, "with the rain going like this, I can get us into Old Town unseen. You gotta finish eating first, though."

"Hye, hye," he muttered, and though he would have preferred to savor the feel of food down his gullet—Noden's

39

breath, it had been so long—Merik choked down the final smoky mouthful of lamb. Then he pushed to his feet and offered a gruff, "Lead the way, boy. Lead the way."

Vivia Nihar stood before the Battle Room's massive doors, the grain in the pale, unpainted oak blurring like the clouds that gathered outside. Voices hummed through, serious and low.

No regrets, she thought, tugging at her navy frock coat's sleeves. *Just keep moving.* She smoothed her blouse underneath. It was the same set of phrases she thought each morning upon waking. The same phrases she had to recite to get through the day, through the difficult decisions. Through the hole that lived forever just behind her breastbone.

No regrets, keep moving . . . Where is the footman? The princess of Nubrevna was not meant to open her own blighted door. Especially not when all thirteen vizers of the High Council waited on the other side, judging her every move.

All day long, she was hounded by palace staff or city officials or sycophantic nobility. Yet now, when she actually needed someone to help her, no one was near.

With a frown twitching on her lips, Vivia squinted at a patch of light at the end of the long, dark hall. Two silhouettes fought to close the enormous doors—a sign that the clouds outside would soon thicken to a storm.

Oh, hang it. Vivia had too much to do to wait for footmen and thunderheads. As the king always said, *Sitting still is a quick path to madness.*

The oak creaked; the hinges groaned; the vizers in the long

40

hall silenced. Then Vivia was inside, and thirteen pairs of eyes were shifting from the single long table at the room's center ...

To her. Just staring like fools, every one of them.

"What?" She let the doors groan shut behind her. "Did Noden answer my prayers? Have the Hagfishes finally claimed your tongues?"

One of the vizers choked. Eleven snapped their gazes away. And one—the one who always opposed Vivia the most—simply picked at a hangnail.

Vizer Serrit Linday. Ever unimpressed. Ever unamused. *Ever* an urchin spine in Vivia's heel.

Her fingers curled, heat rising up her arms. She sometimes wondered if this might be the famed Nihar temper that her father so desperately wanted her to have.

But no. No, it wasn't. The flame was already dying, her mask already teetering at the edges. *Just keep moving.*

She set off for the head of the table, clicking her boot heels extra loud, extra hard on the flagstones. Let them think she was reining in her temper.

Clouded sunlight sifted into the Battle Room through a single glass window. It beamed onto the limp banners from generations past and highlighted just how much dust coated everything.

One of the window's dozen panes was broken and boarded up, leaving Vivia with a crude shadow to march through before reaching the table's head.

Six of the vizers saluted at her as she stalked by; seven did not.

Resistance. That was all Vivia ever met these days, and her

41

brother had been the worst of them. He had argued her every command and questioned her every move.

Well, at least he was no longer a problem. Now, if only the High Council would join him.

Will she become her mother, the vizers all wondered, *the queen by blood but with madness in her head? Or will she become her father, the Nihar vizer who now rules as regent and for whom command comes as easily as breath?*

Vivia already knew the answer. She knew it because she'd decided long ago to be a Nihar through and through. She would *never* become her mother. She would *never* let madness and darkness claim her. She would be the ruler the High Council expected.

She just had to keep acting. Keep moving. A little bit longer, and with no looking back. No regrets. For even if the High Council finally handed over the title she was born to, they could always snatch it back—just as they had done to her mother in those final days thirteen years ago.

Vivia reached the end of the table, with its worn finish and chipped corners. Thick vellum maps covered the time-pocked surface. Nubrevna, the Sirmayans, the Hundred Isles—all of the Witchlands could be examined at the stretch of an arm.

Right now, maps of the city lay open with fat rocks weighing down the curling edges. *Curse* them. The bastards had started the meeting without her.

From war to waste removal, nothing happened without the High Council's input. Yet all final decisions fell to the King Regent.

Or now, since Serafin rarely left his bed, the final decisions fell to Vivia.

"Princess," Serrit Linday crooned, leaning onto the table. Even though he was only a few months older than Vivia's twenty-three years, he wore old-fashioned robes. The kind Marstoki scholars and ancient spinsters favored, and like all Lindays, he wore the Witchmark of a Plantwitch on the back of his hand—a hand he was currently flexing as he rapped impatiently at the table.

"We were just discussing your plans to repair the dam, and we feel it best to wait. At least until after the funeral. The dam has lasted several years—what will a few more matter?"

Pretentious prick. Now Vivia's temper was actually sparking, although she kept her face bored.

To think that she and this vizer had *ever* been friends growing up. The Serrit she'd played with as a child was now Vizer Linday, and in less than a year, since replacing his deceased father on the council, Linday had become the worst of the thirteen noblemen standing before Vivia.

Noble*men*. Every single one of them male. It shouldn't have been that way, of course. The Lindays, Quintays, Sotars, and Eltars all had female heirs . . . who conveniently never wanted to leave their lands. *Oh, but can't our brothers/husbands/sons go instead?*

No. That was what Vivia would say once she was queen. *Whoever bears the vizerial bloodline stands at this table.* But until then, Vivia had to live with the *yes* passed down by her great-grandfather.

"Now, Your Highness," Linday went on, offering a smooth smile around the table, "I ran the calculations as requested, and the numbers are very clear. Lovats simple cannot support any more people."

43

"I don't recall asking for calculations."

"Because you didn't." Linday's smile widened into something crocodilian. "It was the Council that requested it."

"Highness," came another voice. Squeaky in a way that only Vizer Eltar could produce. Vivia swung her gaze to the rotund man. "The more people who enter the city, the more we vizers must shrink our portions—which is impossible! We all have our families and staff arriving for the prince's funeral, and at our current rations, I cannot keep my own beloved family fed."

Vivia sighed. "More food is coming, Eltar."

"You said that last week!" he squealed. "And now the funeral is in six days! How will we provide food for the city?"

"Additionally," piped up Vizer Quihar, "the more people we allow in, the more likely we are to let enemies into our midst. Until we know who killed the prince, we must close the Sentries and keep newcomers out."

This earned a chorus of agreements from around the table. Only one man stayed silent: the barrel-chested, black-skinned Vizer Sotar. He was also the only man with a fully operational brain in this entire room.

He flung Vivia a sympathetic wince now, and she found it . . . well, more welcome than she cared to admit. He was so much like his daughter Stacia, who served as Vivia's first mate. And were Stix here right now—were this Vivia's ship and Vivia's crew—Stix would lash out at these weak-willed vizers instantly. Mercilessly. *She* had the temper that Nubrevnan men respected most.

But Stix was inspecting the city's watchtowers today, like

44

a good first mate, while Vivia was trapped inside, watching slimy Serrit Linday quieting the vizers with a wave.

"I have a proposition for the High Council. And for you, Your Highness."

Vivia rolled her eyes. "Of course you do."

"The Purists have offered us food and the use of their compounds. Across Nubrevna and beyond." He motioned to a map that Vizer Eltar was so *conveniently* unrolling at the perfect moment. "Our people could be safe, even beyond our borders, if the need arose."

Sotar cleared his throat, and in a sound like stone on stone, he declared, "Placing our people outside Nubrevna is called invasion, Linday."

"Not to mention"—Vivia planted her hands on the table—"there must be some cost to this. No one—not even 'noble' Purists—act for free." Even as she voiced this argument, though, Vivia found herself staring at the unfurled map.

It was a simple outline of the Witchlands, but paint had been dripped wherever enemy forces were closest to Nubrevna. Yellow for Marstok, speckling the east and south. Black for Cartorra, scattered in the west. Blue for Dalmotti, gathering in southern waters.

And finally red, thick as blood, for the Baedyed and Red Sails pirates circling Saldonica and the Raider King's armies, still far to the north . . . for now. Heavy rains kept the Sirmayan Mountains water choked and uncrossable.

Come winter, that might change.

Vivia dragged her eyes from the map. From all those colors and all the senseless death that they might one day

45

become. "What do the Purists want, Vizer Linday? What is the price for their food and their walls?"

"Soldiers."

"*No.*" The word boomed from Vivia's throat. Explosive as a firepot. Yet as she straightened, sweeping her gaze across the table, there was no missing the interest that had settled over the Council. A collective relaxing of vizerial faces.

They had known what Linday planned to propose; they'd agreed to it long ago.

Serrit Linday ought to be castrated for this.

Vivia tossed a look at her only ally and found Sotar's dark face withdrawn. Disgusted. He, at least, was as surprised as Vivia by this turn of political sidestepping.

"The Purists," Vivia said, "will turn our people against the use of magic." She launched right to march around the table. "They consider magic a sin, yet magic—witches!—are the one thing that have kept Nubrevna safe and independent. You, Linday, are a Plantwitch! Yet you see no problem in giving our citizens and our soldiers to the Purists?"

Linday smirked as Vivia strode past, but other than a slight tipping back of his head, he offered no response.

"What about your family's Stonewitchery, Quihar? Or your son's Glamourwitchery, Eltar? Or your wife's Voice-witchery?" On and on she went, until she'd reminded every single vizer of the witches that mattered most to them.

Each imbecile Vivia passed, though, was suddenly quite interested in the state of his cuffs. Or his fingernails. Or some stain on the wall that only he could see.

Until Vivia was back at the head of the table. Then, it would seem, tiny Vizer Eltar suddenly found his testicles, for he piped up with, "At least if our people are with the Purists, it is fewer mouths to feed at the prince's funeral."

For a moment, those words knocked around in Vivia's skull. *Prince. Funeral.* They were a meaningless descant to the beat that thumped in her ribcage.

Then the words settled like sand in a tidal pool, and Vivia gripped the nearest map. Crushed it in a white-knuckled grip. *This* feeling she did not have to fake, for only a week ago she'd argued against that funeral with every breath inside her. *A waste of expenses*, she'd shouted. *A waste of precious materials, people, and time! The dam needs fixing and the people need feeding!*

The Council hadn't listened, though. Nor had her father. Of course not. Merik had been everyone's favorite. *He'd* had the Nihar rage, and *he'd* had the good sense to be born a man. Easy, easy—that was how Merik's life had always been. No resistance. Whatever he'd wanted, he'd gotten.

Even his death had been easy.

Before Vivia could offer more choice words on the funeral, Linday chimed in, "You make an excellent point, Eltar. We must properly honor the dead, and we cannot do so with this many people in the city."

Hagfishes claim him. Now that Vivia considered it—*really* considered it—castration was much too good for Linday. He deserved to be drawn, quartered, eviscerated, and then burned until none of his rotten core remained.

"Besides," he went on, more animated now that he held the room's attention, "all of our families will soon arrive for the funeral. We should not have to skim our own portions to feed a city overrun—"

47

Instantly. Mercilessly.

Water erupted from the pitcher at the center of the table. Thirteen perfect coils of it, one for each vizer—even Vizer Sotar.

"*Enough.*" Vivia's voice was low, and the water locked in place mere inches from each man's throat. Half had their eyes squeezed shut, and the other half were twisting away. "No Purists. Ever. Food *is* on the way, and we will continue to allow Nubrevnans into the city.

"And," she added, sliding her water whip a *smidgen* closer to the vizers, "you all could stand to lose a bit of fat from your bellies, so as of tomorrow, your rations will be reduced by another quarter. If your families are hungry, then tell them to stay home." She stepped away from the table, pivoting as if she were about to leave ...

But she hesitated. What was it her father always did so well? *Ah, yes.* The terrifying Nihar smile. She mimicked it now, looking back at the table. At the fools who inhabited it. Then she let the water flow, with perfect control, back into the pitcher.

It was a reminder that she was not merely a princess, nor merely a ship's captain. Nor *merely* the rightful queen of Nubrevna—if the Council would just agree to hand over the crown.

Vivia Nihar was a Tidewitch, and a blighted powerful one at that. She could drown them all with a thought, so let Serrit Linday and the rest of the High Council try to cross her again.

No more stalemates because they thought her unqualified and unhinged.

No more tiptoeing around a room because women oughtn't to run. To shout. To rule.

And above all: no more *blighted* regrets.

FIVE

The Bloodwitch named Aeduan hated Purists.

Not as much as he hated the Marstoks, nor as much as he hated the Cartorrans, but almost as much.

It was their certainty that angered him. Their condescending, unwavering certainty that anyone with magic should burn in hell-fire.

At least, he thought as he approached their grimy compound on the easternmost edge of the Nubrevnan border, *they treat all men with equal venom.* Usually shouts of *Repent, demon! Pay for your sins!* were reserved for Aeduan exclusively. It was nice to have the hate spread around.

Aeduan was late coming to the compound. He should have met his father's contact two days before, but instead he'd run all across Nubrevna, hunting a ghost for two weeks.

Now here he was, hundreds of miles away and facing crooked pine walls perched atop a hill's limestone edge. The compound looked as sick and barren as the land on which it rested, and Aeduan passed splintered trunks and ashy soil before he reached the two men guarding the tall entry gate.

Though both men wore matching brown Purist robes,

neither had the look of an anti-magic cultist—nor the scent of one on his blood. *Battlefields and tar.* These were men of violence, and they proved it when they lifted crossbows at Aeduan's approach.

"I seek one of your priests," Aeduan called to them. He lifted his hands.

"Which priest?" asked the skinnier of the two, his skin Marstoki brown.

"A man named Corlant." Aeduan slowed so the guards could see that his hands were empty—for of course, his knives were hidden within his buttoned-up coat. "He should have recently arrived."

"Your name?" asked the second man, his skin black as pitch and his accent Southlander—though which nation, Aeduan couldn't guess.

Upon giving his name, both men lowered their crossbows. The Southlander led the way through a side door near the main gate.

The interior of the compound was even grimier than the outside, all churned mud and clucking chickens and crude huts that would topple beneath a determined breeze. A string of men and women leaned against the main wall, each with baskets or empty sacks, waiting to enter the nearest hut. None spoke.

"They listen to one of our priests," the Southlander explained. "Then they get food for their families."

"They aren't Purists?"

"Not yet. But they will be." As the man uttered this, a boy stumbled from the hut, blinking as if coming up from a dream. In his arms was a basket.

51

Unbidden, a memory stirred in the back of Aeduan's mind. Another child, another basket, another lifetime, and a monk named Evrane, who had saved him from it all.

Evrane's mistake. She should have left Aeduan behind.

"*You are late.*" The words cut across the courtyard. Like mud from a riverbank, they slid into Aeduan's ears and oozed down his spine.

Instantly Aeduan's magic stirred. *Wet caves and white-knuckled grips. Rusted locks and endless hunger.*

Then from the faded wood of a hut, a shadowy shape peeled off. One moment, there were only the shaded planks. The next moment, a towering rope-thin man with Nomatsi features was standing beside it.

The mere presence of the priest grated against Aeduan's power with a primal sense of *wrongness.* Like watching an earwig scuttle across the room. The urge to smash Corlant would forever coil in Aeduan's muscles when they met.

Corlant flicked a lazy wrist at Aeduan's guide. "Return to your post," he commanded.

The Southlander bowed. "Blessed are the pure."

Corlant waited until the man was back outside the compound before slithering his attention to Aeduan. A long stare passed between them, with Corlant's eyebrows rising ever higher. Three deep trenches carved across his pale forehead.

"Has anyone ever told you," Corlant said eventually, "that you look more and more like your mother each day?"

Aeduan knew when he was being baited, yet Corlant was a friend of Aeduan's father. They'd grown up in the same tribe; they now thirsted for vengeance against the three empires. So as much as Aeduan might wish to crush Corlant—and might even imagine doing so from time to time—it was not a dream he could ever actually satisfy.

Once it was clear that Aeduan had no intention of answering, Corlant moved on to business. "Where is the money, boy?"

"I'm getting it."

"Oh? It is not here, then?" Corlant's nostrils fluttered, yet it wasn't with anger so much as hunger. As if he sensed something was amiss like a leech smells blood upon the water. "I was promised silver talers."

"And you will have them. Not today, though."

Corlant fidgeted with his chain, a smile curving up. "You've lost the money, haven't you, boy? Was it stolen?"

Aeduan didn't answer. The truth was, when he had returned to the tree trunk where he'd hidden the money he had earned from Prince Leopold fon Cartorra, he had found only an empty iron box and a handful of coins.

Lingering near the box had been a familiar blood-scent. Of clear lakes and frozen winters. It was the same person who'd conspired with Prince Leopold to betray Aeduan, so immediately Aeduan had set out to track it.

But after trailing west for a week, that smell had winked out entirely, leaving Aeduan with no choice but to give up and come here empty-handed. Money or no, he was still meant to meet Corlant for his next orders.

"Does your father know about this?" Corlant pressed. "For I will gladly tell him when next we speak."

Aeduan gazed pointedly into the middle distance before answering, "The king doesn't know."

A bark of laughter from the priest. He dropped the chain

with a hollow *thunk* against his chest. "Now this is unexpected, is it not?" He spun away, aiming for a cluster of huts in the back of the compound, and leaving Aeduan with no choice but to prowl after.

Chickens careened from Corlant's path, as did more men in brown robes. Men, Aeduan noted—the Purists were always men. Aeduan followed, careful to stay a footstep behind. Not because he felt Corlant deserved the lead, but because it pleased him to watch the man constantly crane his neck backward to speak.

"We are at an interesting crossroads," Corlant said over his shoulder. "You see, I need something done, and you need something hidden."

"I don't know what you mean."

Corlant's eyes flashed. "You seem to think you have more power than you actually do, boy." He paused before an open door. Beyond, a set of stairs sank into filmy darkness below the earth. "You may be Ragnor's son, but I have known Ragnor for far longer than you. When it comes to where his loyalties lie—"

"Neither of us," Aeduan interrupted. "The king would sacrifice us both if it meant winning this war."

Corlant sighed, a frustrated sound, before ultimately conceding, "You are right in that regard, boy. Which is all the more reason for us to cooperate. I need someone found. My men have had no success, but perhaps your . . . *skills* will prove more capable."

Aeduan's interest was piqued, for anyone this filthy priest wanted found was likely someone of interest—and likely a weakness for Corlant as well.

54

However, Aeduan forced himself to first ask, "What are my father's orders?"

"To do whatever I need." Corlant smiled.

Leaving Aeduan to imagine, once more, smashing the man like an earwig.

"What I need, boy, is for you to find a Nomatsi Thread-witch. Last I heard, she was in a town called Lejna on the Nubrevnan coast."

Something dark and vile tickled over Aeduan's skull. "Her name?"

"Iseult det Midenzi."

The shadows spread down Aeduan's neck. "Why do you want this girl?"

"That is none of your concern."

Aeduan moved his hands behind his back, fingers curling into hidden fists. No expression on his face. "What can I know, then? Information helps me track people, and I assume, *Priest* Corlant, that you want this girl found quickly."

Corlant's eyebrows lifted, the three lines returning. "Does this mean we have a deal, boy?"

Aeduan pretended to consider the proposition. Four breaths passed. Then: "Is it not against your oath to work with someone of my . . . talents?" He didn't want to declare his power aloud, not among people who opposed magic of any kind.

Corlant understood the implication, though, and anger flashed in his eyes. "You are unholy, yes, but you are also the king's son—and just as you need something, *I* need something. I will tell the king your money arrived as planned, and in return, you will hunt down this young woman."

Aeduan's fingers flexed taut. The urge to freeze Corlant's blood—to wrest the answers directly from his throat—pumped through Aeduan's veins. Questions, however, would only raise more questions.

He nodded. "I understand."

Corlant's forehead smoothed out. "Excellent." He smiled his foul smile and slid a hand beneath the collar of his robe, fumbling with some inner pocket, until at last he withdrew a sharp strip of iron.

A needle arrowhead. Nomatsi in style, and bloodied.

"This is her blood." Corlant offered the iron to Aeduan, who accepted it, his face carefully impassive. "When you reach her, boy, you will not kill her. She has something that belongs to me, and I want it back. Now tell me, how long until you find her?"

"As long as it takes."

The smile fell. "Then pray that it happens quickly, before my patience drains. Pray to the Moon Mother or the Cahr Awen or whomever it is you worship."

"I pray to no one."

"Your mistake."

Aeduan pretended not to hear. He was already spinning away.

After all, he had no time for prayer. Particularly since he knew no one ever listened.

SIX

Merik's steps were long and brisk as he followed Cam's wet, fuzzy head into Old Town.

He still wasn't used to her shorn hair—she'd chopped off the braids that all Nubrevnan ship boys wore only that morning. *What's the use in lookin' like a sailor when I'm not one anymore?* she'd asked on their ferry ride into the capital. *Besides, this way, no one will recognize me.*

Merik wasn't so sure about that. Though he'd seen others with dappled skin, it was rare—and Cam's lighter patches were especially pronounced against her dark skin. Plus, with that mangled scar on her left hand, she wasn't a person one was likely to forget.

She kept her hood low like Merik did, as they trekked onward through storm-soaked streets. Here in Old Town, in the northwest corner of the city and miles west of Judgment Square, the buildings sagged in on each other. Four families were often crammed into a single narrow house, and the streets seethed with humanity. Here, Merik could find shelter and ready himself for the trip to Pin's Keep.

Cam moved purposefully through traffic, her skinny legs

nimble as a sandpiper's. Having grown up on the streets of Lovats, she knew the best routes through town—and she had keen sense for when soldiers might appear.

Good thing, for soldiers strode everywhere, attempting to round up anyone with the Judgment Square tattoos beneath their left eyes. Every few blocks, Cam would twirl back, ready to guide Merik down a damp side street.

Even when there weren't soldiers, she would twist into alleys or shadowy thoroughfares, until Merik finally caught sight of a familiar building.

"Stop," he ordered. "We're going in there." He pointed to a narrow row house. Its sign declared a toy shop within, but its closed shutters suggested something else. "It's tenements now," Merik told Cam, as if this explained why they had come here.

It explained nothing, but Cam didn't ask for more. She *never* asked for more. She trusted her former admiral, former prince, even when Merik so clearly lacked any real plan. Any real clue.

Merik was the fish from the fable, lured into the cave after Queen Crab's gold, and Cam was the blind brother who followed happily. Foolishly. Right into the clacking maw.

Inside the decrepit shop, Merik sidestepped playing children and stretched his legs over huddled, hungry grandmas. It was far more crowded than the last time he'd come here, the hallway having become a living space of its own. An extension of each makeshift home.

Food is coming, Merik wanted to tell them, for no matter what Vivia had declared to him weeks before, he didn't believe that Nubrevnans would refuse food simply because it hailed from one of the empires.

Merik's thighs burned as he and Cam ascended three floors. He savored that pain, for it distracted him from what waited ahead.

And it reminded him that he could be truly dead. That he owed every of inch of his still living skin to Noden's beneficence and Cam's prophetic gut.

My gut, she'd told Merik after she'd first found him. *It always warns me when danger's coming, and it ain't steered me wrong yet.* It was exactly the sort of nonsense Merik was inclined to dismiss . . . Except that Cam's gut was the sole reason Merik still lived, and that mysterious organ had saved their skins at least six times on the journey to Lovats.

"Seventeen, eighteen, nineteen," Cam counted behind him. Each step got a number, and each number was breathier than the last. The girl's shoulders had started poking through her shirt these past few days, and Merik hadn't missed how Cam divvied out the bulk of their rations to Merik. Although he always argued that they should each get half, he suspected she didn't always obey.

Cam hit twenty-seven, and she and Merik shuffled onto the top floor's landing.

Twelve more steps down the crowded hall brought them to a low pine door. After a cautious glance up the hall and down the hall, Merik set to tapping a lock-spell rhythm on the frame.

His heart thumped faster. The wood melted into a distant, fuzzy grain.

Then the spell clicked. An iron bolt within slid free, and Merik found himself immobile, staring at the latch. At the familiar dent in the wood below it.

He couldn't do this. He'd thought he could face it, but now that he was here, it was a mistake.

"Sir," Cam murmured, "are we going in?"

Merik's blood was thudding like a hurricane in his ears. "This was . . . Kullen's."

"The first mate's." Cam dipped her head. "I guessed as much, sir."

In a burst of speed, Merik pushed open the door and charged inside. His eyes met the familiar space, and he listed sharply forward, only to freeze, tilted. Hanging in midair like a corpse forgotten at the noose.

A single beam of light crawled into the room from a narrow window. Almost cheerfully. Certainly mocking, it whispered over wide-plank floors, red-washed walls, and exposed low beams.

Too low for Kullen to ever move comfortably about. He'd knocked his head on them every time he'd passed through, just as he had on the *Jana*. Just as he had in the cabin he'd grown up in on the Nihar estate far to the south.

"Come, sir." Cam's calloused hand settled on Merik's arm. "People are watching. We oughta shut the door."

When Merik didn't move, Cam just heaved him forward two paces. A loud thump shook through the room, and power frizzed behind Merik as the lock-spell resumed.

"Ignite?" There was a question in Cam's tone, as if she hoped the lamps looping over the low beams were Fire-witched. They were, and at the voiced command, they brightened to life, revealing a dining area to the left.

Books were strewn across every surface. Each cover a different color or a different animal hide, and each spine with a

60

different title stamped into it. Books in the cupboard, books on the table, books stacked on three mismatched chairs.

One chair for Kullen. One chair for Merik. And one chair, the newest of the three, for Kullen's Heart-Thread.

Ryber. Merik's chest tightened at that name—at the beautiful black face it conjured. She had vanished after Kullen's death, leaving Merik with nothing but a note. While it was true that Merik had never grown close to her, never quite understood what she and Kullen shared, he would've welcomed having Ryber with him now. At least then one other person might understand what he was feeling.

Merik's gaze tilted right, to where Cam waited warily several steps behind.

"I can leave you alone, sir. If you want. Maybe go find us a real meal." She clutched at her stomach, which showed just how inverted her belly had become. "Don't know about you, but that lamb didn't fill me."

"Hye," Merik breathed. "There should be . . . martens . . ." His words faded off. He stumbled to the bed. Unmade and with more books tossed everywhere.

Tucked beneath the pillow was a coin purse from which Merik withdrew a single silver marten. But Cam's head wagged; her cheeks turned starfish red. "I can't use that, sir. People'll think I stole it." She waved at her dirty clothes, as if this explained everything.

Merik supposed it did. "Right." He dug deeper into the purse until he found a wooden marten. Then two more. "Here."

"Thank you, sir. I'll be back soon." She banged a fist to her heart, then waited for a dismissal. A reaction. Something.

Merik had nothing to give. He was a well run dry. No fury. No magic. Just …

Nothing.

He turned away, and Cam took the hint. Moments later, magic hissed behind Merik as the door opened, closed. He was alone.

He aimed for the dining area. Toward the books atop the table and chairs. Ryber had turned Kullen into a reader, beginning with a book gifted to him early in their courtship. The Airwitch had gone from reading nothing in his life to never stopping, buying every novel or history book he could get his hands on.

And it was the only subject he and Ryber ever discussed. Constantly, they hunched over a shared book or debated the finer points of some philosopher Merik had never heard of.

Merik's attention snagged on one spine now, a familiar title he'd seen Kullen reading on the *Jana* only hours before his death.

The True Tale of the Twelve Paladins.

Merik's breath caught. He yanked it off the table in a rasp of leather, a puff of dust. He peeled back the cover …

Different copy. He exhaled—hard. This edition had a torn first page; the one on the *Jana* had been smooth. And this one had white dust on the pages, paragraphs underlined and sentences circled, where the copy on the *Jana* had been clean.

Of course it was a different copy. The one on the ship was now ash—and even if it *had* somehow been the same edition, it would have made no difference. A book could not replace a Threadbrother.

Merik let the pages fall open naturally, to where a gold-backed card winked up at him. He peeled it over. *The King of Hounds*. It was from the taro deck Ryber always carried—that much he could recognize—and beneath it was a circled paragraph: *The paladins we locked away will one day walk among us. Vengeance will be theirs, in a fury unchecked, for their power was never ours to claim. Yet only in death, could they understand life. And only in life, will they change the world.*

Well, Merik was neither truly alive nor truly dead, so where did that leave him? No ship. No crew. No crown.

But with a clue to follow. A link between the assassin named Garren and Vivia, and a first step toward proving the princess was behind the explosion, the attack. Surely with such evidence, the High Council would never allow Vivia to rule.

Merely thinking of Vivia sent a fresh wave of heat down Merik's spine. It radiated into his arms and fingers. Burning, violent, delicious. All these years, Merik had tried to tame the Nihar rage. Tried to fight the temper that had made his family famous and uncrossable. After all, it was his temper that had propelled him into the Witchery Examination too young—that had convinced King Serafin Merik was more powerful than he truly was.

And all these years, Merik had tamped down the anger in an attempt to be as unlike Vivia as he could be, yet where had it gotten him?

It hadn't saved Kullen from his own storm.

It hadn't saved Safiya fon Hasstrel from the Marstoks.

And it sure as Noden's watery Hell hadn't saved Nubrevna from starvation and war.

So Merik embraced the rage. He let it course through each

of his breaths. Each of his thoughts. He could use the anger to help his hungry city. To protect his dying people.

For although the holiest might fall—and Merik had fallen far, indeed—they could also claw their way back up again.

The fourteenth chimes were ringing on stormy winds by the time Vivia found a moment to herself to trek beneath the city, deep into the core of the plateau.

Vivia had come here every day, without fail, for the past nine weeks. Her routine for each visit was always the same: check the lake, then search the tunnels for the missing, mythical under-city.

Vivia had left the Battle Room to find chaos. Wind-drums pounded the alarm for help in Judgment Square, and a full riot was under way by the time she arrived.

After an hour of ineffectually trying to wrangle escaped prisoners back into the irons, the sky turning darker and darker each minute, Vivia had ordered the soldiers to stop.

There was no point, not once the rain began to fall. Most people in the irons had committed crimes solely for the purpose of getting arrested, led by some misguided belief that if they could somehow get into prison, they could enjoy two meals a day. But the Lovats prison was already full, and so these fake, desperate criminals were left to time in the irons instead—where, of course, there was no food.

Still, a few dangerous convicts remained on the loose. Not to mention this new beast of a man who had freed the prisoners in the first place.

"The Fury," Vivia whispered to herself as she hiked deeper

underground. It was such a stupid thing to call oneself, and just begging for the Hagfishes' wrath. While those people in Judgment Square might have been gullible enough to believe Noden's vengeful saint had come to rescue them, Vivia knew whoever he had been, he was just a man.

And men could be found. Arrested. *Hanged.*

She stalked faster. This far beneath the surface, the air never warmed and few creatures lived. Vivia's lantern light crawled over rough limestone tunnels. One after the next. Nothing like the symmetric brick-lined Cisterns above, where sewage and Waterwitched plumbing moved. Whenever Vivia hauled herself back to the surface, dust would streak her skin, her hair, her uniform.

Which was why she always kept a spare uniform waiting in her mother's garden, tucked in a dry box. She also always worked alone, for these honeycombing caves were forever empty, forever secret. As far as Vivia was aware, she was the only person alive who even knew this world of magic and river existed.

Or so her mother had told her before bringing Vivia down here fifteen years ago. Jana had still been queen then, ruling and in power. The madness—and the High Council—had not yet taken her crown. *This is the source of our power, Little Fox,* she had told Vivia. *The reason our family rules Nubrevna and others do not. This water knows us. This water chose us.*

Vivia hadn't understood what Jana had meant back then, but she understood now. Now, she felt the magic that bound her blood to these underground waterways.

She marched into the final tunnel, where an ancient

Firewitched lamp warmed her vision. Brighter than her lantern, it made her eyeballs pound.

Keep moving. At least here, she *wanted* to keep moving. Here, she could stare into the darkness beyond, and it didn't matter if her mother stared back.

Inky water spanned before Vivia for as far as her squinting eyes could see. A vast lake where miles of underground river fed and flowed, a heart inside the Lovats plateau. This was where Nubrevna's true power lay. This was where the city's pulse lived.

On the lake's shore rested the skeletal ribs of an ancient rowboat, where Vivia always set her lantern and draped her clothes—and where she did so now, starting with the linen strip of iris-blue wrapped around her biceps.

Protocol demanded all men and women in the Royal Forces wear these mourning bands until the funeral, but they were a nuisance. A lie. Most of the troops had never known their prince, and they'd certainly never cared for him. Merik had grown up in the south, and unlike Vivia, who had risen through the ranks by her own sweat, her own strength, Merik had been handed a ship, a crew, and shiny captain's buttons.

Then, a few years after that, in the ultimate insult to Vivia, Merik had been handed the admiralty. Though Vivia had appreciated the indignation of her fellow sailors and soldiers at the time—the men and women she'd trained with—it hadn't made the pointed oversight by Serafin any less stinging.

Easy, easy. Everything in Merik's life had been *easy*.

In a rough burst of speed, Vivia finished her partial undressing, yanking off her boots and peeling off her coat.

Then she began her routine as she always did: she hissed, "Extinguish."

Darkness snuffed across the cavern, and she held her breath, waiting for her eyes to adjust . . . There. Starlight began to twinkle.

Not true starlight, but streaks and sprinkles and sprays of luminescent fungi that offered more than enough light to see by once Vivia's vision adapted. Four main spokes crawled across the rock, meeting at the ceiling's center. *Foxfire*, her mother had called it.

There should have been six spokes, though, and there *had* been six spokes until nine weeks ago, when the farthest stripe—at the opposite end of the lake—had winked out. Leaving five lines for another three weeks . . . Until another rivulet had vanished too.

Never had the light died in Vivia's life, nor during Queen Jana's. In fact, it had been at least two centuries since any of the six spokes had winked out.

It was a sign that our people were too weak to keep fighting, Jana had explained. *And it was a sign that the royal family was too weak to keep protecting.*

So the city's people had hidden underground, in a vast city carved into the rock. Where more foxfire grew in such huge magical masses that it was enough light for plants to grow— or enough light so long as Plantwitches were there to supplement and support.

The under-city is as big as Lovats above, my Little Fox. Powerful witches, the likes of which we no longer have today, built it centuries ago as a hiding place to keep our people alive.

Vivia had wanted to know more. *How was the city built,*

Mother? Why aren't there powerful witches like that now? How does the foxfire know we're too weak? And where is the city?

These were all excellent questions, but ones for which Jana had had no answer. After their ancestors' final use of the city, it had been sealed off. No records left behind, no clues to follow.

There was one question, though, that Vivia had never dared to ask: *Will you ever show this to Merik?* She hadn't wanted to know the answer, hadn't wanted to risk putting the idea in her mother's head. This had been their space, mother and daughter.

And now this was her space. Vivia's. Alone.

She stepped lightly to the lake's edge. Green light splayed across the surface, dancing in time to the water's flow. Flickering with the occasional fish or shell creature. The strength of the water poured into Vivia before her toes even hit the edge. Her connection to the ripples and tides, the power and the timelessness.

The lake embraced Vivia instantly. A friend to keep her safe. The waters cooled her toes, and as she dipped her hands into the vastness of it all, her eyes drifted shut. Then she felt her way through every drop of water that flowed through the plateau. This was her power. This was her home.

Vivia's magic snaked through the lake, bouncing over creatures that lived for all eternity in this dark world. Over rocks and boulders and treasure long lost and long forgotten. Upstream, her magic climbed. Downstream, her magic swept. Time melted into a lost thing—a human construct that the water neither cared for nor needed.

All was well with the lake. So Vivia shrank back into

herself, loss brushing along the edges of her being. It always did when her connection to the lake ended. If she could, she would never leave. She would plant roots in this lake and fall into it forever—

Vivia shook herself. No. *No.* She had to keep moving. Like the river, like the tides.

With her arms hugged tight to her chest, she stalked from the water. In moments, her boots were on—wet toes curling in dry leather—and she was scooping up her lantern once more. Yesterday, she had explored a series of caverns that spiraled above the lake. They'd ended at a cave-in, and on the other side, Vivia had sensed water. *Moving* water, like the vast floods that cleaned the Cisterns.

She wanted to try to clear a path through the cave-in's rubble, for though churning rapids might wait on the other side, churning rapids were no barrier for a Tidewitch.

Vivia was almost to a key split in the tunnels, when something landed on her head.

She flinched, hands flinging to her scalp. Legs, legs, legs spindled over her hair. She swatted. Hard. A black spot flew to the cavern floor.

A wolf spider, monstrous and fuzzy. Its legs stretched long as it scampered away, leaving Vivia to catch her breath. To slow her booming heart.

An almost hysterical laugh bubbled in her throat. She could face down entire navies. She could ride a waterfall from mountain peak to valley's end. She could battle almost any man or woman and be named victor.

But a spider ... She shivered, shoulders rolling high.

Before she could resume her forward, upward march, she spotted movement near her feet. Up the cavern walls too.

The wolf spider wasn't the only creature scratching its way to the surface, nor the only creature shaking with terror. A centipede—no, tens of them—curled out of crevices near Vivia's feet. Salamanders slithered up the walls.

Blessed Noden, where were all these creatures coming from?

And more important, what were all these creatures running from?

SEVEN

Half a day of walking.

Half a day of thirst.

The walking had been easy enough. Somehow Safi had lost her shoes in the surf, yet even barefoot, Safi had trained for this. And even with her foot smashed by an iron flail two weeks before, she could march for miles.

But the thirst ... That was a new experience, and it was made all the worse by the endless brackish water slithering through the mangroves, none of it drinkable.

Neither Safi nor the empress ever spoke. Not that it mattered. The jungles of the Contested Lands made enough noise for them both.

For hours, they trekked southwest, away from the shore. Away from any Cartorran armada that might be hunting or any assassins still on the prowl. They crossed mud that sucked them to their knees. Mangrove roots and cypress knobs. Vines that snagged, thorns that cut, and insects that clicked and feasted.

Until at last, they needed a rest.

Vaness was the first to sit. It took Safi several dragging

71

steps to even notice the sudden silence behind her. She snapped back her gaze. Empty jungle, and green, green shadows. Her heart lurched into her throat. Vaness had been right behind her.

There. Safi's eyes caught on a hunched figure atop a fallen mangrove. The black of Vaness's gown blended into the leaves and shadows.

Safi's heart settled. "Are you hurt?"

"Hmmm," was all the empress said before her dark head drooped forward, sweat-soaked hair cascading across her face.

Safi turned back. Water, water—that word pounded in her mind as she approached the empress. Vaness needed it, Safi needed it. They could go only so far without it.

Yet it wasn't dehydration she found shuddering through Vaness's small body. It was tears. The empress's grief was so pure, it sang off her. Hot, charged waves that kissed *true-true-true* against Safi's skin. She could almost see it—a funeral dirge to spread through the forest, rippling outward and growing perfect black roots.

She reached Vaness's side, but no useful words rose in her throat. This . . . this was too big for her.

Iron was not meant to weep.

Vaness seemed to understand. Shackles clanking, she cupped her face. Rubbed and swiped and erased the tears before saying, "They were my family." Her voice was thick. Almost lost in the jungle's endless cry. "The Adders. The sailors. I have known them my entire life. They were my friends . . . my family." A crack in her throat. A pause. "I did not think war would return so soon. The Truce only ended two weeks ago . . ." Her voice drifted off, leaving an unspoken truth to settle through the trees.

I ended the Truce by claiming you in Nubrevna. I brought this upon myself.

Then Vaness straightened, and like the iron she controlled, her posture steeled. When she met Safi's eyes, there was no sign tears had ever come—and there was certainly no sign of regret. "I will kill the Cartorrans who did this, Domna."

"How do you know it was Cartorra?" Yet even as Safi asked this, she knew the empire of her childhood—the empire that had sent an armada after her—was the only logical source of the attack.

Except . . . something was missing from that explanation. Like a key foisted into the wrong lock, the idea refused to click. After all, why would the emperor *kill* Safi? It seemed far more likely he would want his valuable Truthwitch kept alive.

Then again, perhaps he'd rather lose her forever than have her stand at his enemy's side. And, the assassin *had* had blue eyes.

"Henrick." Vaness spat the name, as if reading Safi's mind. "His entire navy—I will find them. I will kill them."

"I know." Safi did know. The truth of that statement burned off Vaness. It heated Safi's skin, boiled in Safi's gut—and she would revel in Emperor Henrick's downfall when it came. That toad-like leader of the Cartorran Empire, that sweaty-palmed man who'd tried to force Safi to marry him, tried to *force* her Truthwitchery into his clutches.

Safi offered her hand to the empress, and to her surprise, Vaness accepted. Her hands were surprisingly soft against

Safi's. Fingers that had rarely held weapons, skin that had never been worked.

Yet not once had Vaness complained today.

Iron might weep, but it did not break.

Scrapes and scratches Safi hadn't noticed before now fought for attention. Now that she'd stopped, her aching feet had decided they would no longer be ignored. Especially her healing right foot. Yet she forced herself to say, "We need to keep going, Your Majesty. We're still too close to shore."

"I know . . . Domna." Vaness uttered that title with a frown. "I cannot keep calling you that. Not once we are in Saldonica."

"Safi, then. Call me Safi."

Vaness nodded, mouthing *Safi* to herself as if she'd never used a first name before.

"But what shall I call you?" Safi asked, a spark of energy rushing through her at the prospect of a nickname. "Nessie? Van? V? Ssen . . . av?"

Vaness looked ill. She was clearly regretting this idea.

Safi, however, was only just getting started. Creating aliases had always been her favorite part of a heist, much to the annoyance of her mentor Mathew.

A bolt of fear hit Safi's chest at the thought of him. At the thought of all the men and women working for Uncle Eron. They wouldn't know where to find Safi now. Worse, they might think her dead and *never* come for her.

She swallowed, loosening her parched throat. Then she screwed her worries down deep, deep and out of reach. There was nothing to be done but hike onward.

And, of course, craft a new name for the empress. "Iron,"

74

she suggested as they resumed their trek west, following the sun toward Saldonica. "Steel? Oh, Iron-y." That made her chuckle.

Not Vaness, though, who now glared.

"Oh, I *know!*" Safi clapped her hands, delighted by her own genius. "I shall call you Un-*empressed.*"

"Please," Vaness said coldly, "stop this immediately."

Safi absolutely did not.

For hours, Safi and Vaness hiked. Mangroves gnarled into a jungle. Mahogany and oak, bamboo and ferns, interrupted only by swaths of yellow grassland.

Safi avoided the open meadows when she could. They were too exposed in case anyone followed, and the thick, waist-high grass was almost impenetrable. In the forest, the canopy grew so thick no sunlight pierced through, no plants could grow to block the earthen floor, which meant longer lines of sight. There was water in the jungle too. Twice the women came across a low streambed. Both times only a muddy trickle wavered by, but it was something. Even chalky, thick, and tasting of dirt, it was something.

They had just skirted another wide meadow when Safi noticed clouds pilling in. A storm would soon break, so they stopped at a fallen log. Stopping, however, made the pain return tenfold. Safi's soles screamed. Her ankles moaned. And the thirst . . .

Dizziness swept over her the instant she knelt beside the log. She almost fell to her hands. Limp muscles bound to weary bones, and the empress fared no better. It seemed to take all Vaness's remaining energy to crawl beneath the overgrown climbing vines.

At least, Safi thought distantly, the empress wasn't demanding. She endured her plight—and Safi's humor—as stoically as Iseult would.

Before Safi could join Vaness under the log, a water droplet slammed onto her scalp. More droplets followed, streaking down her forearm, leaving glowing white trails through dust and sweat and ash.

She had to catch this rain, no matter how much she'd rather use this moment to rest.

"Can you make a bottle?" Safi asked Vaness. "We need something to hold the water."

Vaness conjured a slow nod. She was past exhaustion, once more drowning in grief. Several bursts of rain later, though, two round canisters rested in her smooth palms. One from each shackle. Safi took them cautiously, as if any quick movements might frighten away the empress.

Her eyes were so empty in this darkness.

"I'm going to walk back to the last clearing we crossed. It'll be easier to catch rain in the open."

"Yes," Vaness said thickly. "Do that, Safi." She scooted back beneath the log, trusting Safi to return. Or perhaps no longer caring if she was forever alone.

Safi found a spot near the clearing's edge where ancient columns lay strewn across the earth. Half a crumbling wall too, and though Safi recognized marble beneath the ferns and vines, she didn't recognize the ruins. Some forgotten race, no doubt swallowed by an empire long ago.

Whoever they'd been, they didn't matter. Now all that

mattered was the rain. It stormed hard and clean against Safi's skin, and she let it pour down her body and into her mouth. She let it sink into her stained dress, her gnarled hair.

It felt good. It tasted good. Which was why the drumming of it covered the approaching footsteps. The tall grass covered the approaching bodies.

Safi's hands were up, scrubbing against her scalp, her eyes foolishly closed. Her focus was briefly—oh, so briefly—absorbed in the feel of fresh water on her lips, when a steel point dug into her back.

Safi didn't move. Didn't close her mouth or give any reaction that she felt the blade there.

"Stay still, Heretic, and we won't hurt you."

Four things about this command collided in Safi's mind at once. The person with the sword was male; he spoke in Cartorran with a mountain accent; he said "we" as if there was someone else in the clearing; and he'd called her "heretic."

Hell-Bard.

Safi's eyes snapped wide. Rain slid through her lashes, forcing her to blink as she lowered her gaze and found exactly what she expected to see.

A Hell-Bard towered five paces before her. Though a steel helm covered his face, there was no missing the enormity of his neck. He was the largest man Safi had ever seen, and the two axes he hefted in each hand were almost as long as Safi's legs. Rain glittered on the metal plates across his scarlet brigandine, on his chain mail sleeves and leather gauntlets—full armor that should have made noise. How had she not heard the brute coming, or seen him?

She swiveled her head just enough to glimpse the speaker

behind. What she saw didn't bode well. Though not as large as the giant, this Hell-Bard still cut a hulking silhouette. His armor was complete, his longsword expertly grasped in both hands, and the scarlet stripes across his gauntlets indicated he was an officer.

A Hell-Bard commander.

If a man is better armed or better trained, Habim had taught, *then do as he orders. It is better to live and look for opportunity than to die outmatched.*

"What do you want from me?" she asked the commander.

"For now, we want you to stay where you are." His voice echoed in his helm, and nothing in Safi's magic reacted. It was as if he spoke no truth yet also spoke no lie.

"It's wet," she tried again.

"Don't pretend it bothers you."

It did bother her. Safi's toes were numb. Her knees had turned to needles. But she also knew better than to press the point—especially since her witchery was so clearly failing her in the face of a Hell-Bard. Everything had narrowed down to the way the rain glanced off the man's armor. To the way the second Hell-Bard stood as still as the marble pillars mere feet away.

It was the moment Safi had run from her entire childhood, and Safi's training was taking over. All those drills and lessons and practice rounds with Habim, all those lectures and dark stories from Uncle Eron—they had become a part of her. Long before she'd ever met Iseult, Safi's teachers had hammered into her that she was strong, that she could fight and defend, and that no one should ever be able to back her into a corner.

78

Safi was a wolf in a world of rabbits.

Except when it came to the elite fighting force known as the Hell-Bard Brigade. With the sole purpose of rooting out unregistered witches in the Cartorran Empire, Safi had spent her life hiding from them—for of course her own magic was too valuable to ever reveal.

Since her first trip to the Cartorran capital when she was five years old, her uncle and tutors had told Safi there was no fighting the Hell-Bards. No defending against them. Uncle Eron, a dishonorably discharged Hell-Bard himself, knew better than anyone else what the Brigade could do. *When you see their scarlet armor,* he always told her, *you run the other way, for if you get too close, they will sense your magic. They will see you for what you really are.*

Safi might be a wolf, but Hell-Bards were lions.

Vaness is still out there, Safi thought. She who could block explosions with her witchery or crush entire mountains—a lion would be nothing against the Iron Empress.

And Vaness would notice Safi's absence. Sooner or later, she would come looking and see those overflowing canteens.

"Zander," the commander called, and the sword dug deeper into Safi's back. "Help Lev."

The giant nodded and twirled about to vanish in the grass, silent. Unnaturally so.

Safi twisted back toward the commander, ignoring how his blade cut through her gown, how he glared down at her, a shimmering pair of eyes beneath a dark helm.

"Let me go," she said, hollowing out her Cartorran vowels, lilting her voice into her most regal accent. His was the accent of Safi's childhood, the accent of the ignorant, mountain

79

estates. She would crush him with the voice of royalty. "You do not want me as an enemy, Hell-Bard."

The sword pressed farther. Pain, distant and cold, bit into her flesh.

Then a soft sound split the rain. He was laughing. A strange, foreign sound—like a sudden gust of wind. A new rise in the storm.

When he spoke next, his words were laced with amusement. "No, Safiya fon Hasstrel, you're right that I don't want you as an enemy."

Hearing her name made her gut drop low. The sense of falling, falling too fast rushed over her.

"But the reality is," he continued, oblivious of the bile rising in her throat, "I want your betrothed as an enemy even less. After all, Emperor Henrick holds my noose, so where he points is where I go. And whom he desires is whom I capture."

He has won, Safi thought, dumbfounded. Emperor Henrick had destroyed her ship, and now he'd captured her too.

The Sun card taken by the Emperor in a single poorly placed hand. *The Empress card is still in the deck.*

But it wasn't. The Empress had been drawn too, and that truth pummeled into Safi mere minutes later. The rain had eased into a gentle sprinkle when a new figure entered the clearing. With a crossbow in hand, the third Hell-Bard was by far the smallest of the three.

"Commander Fitz Grieg," the Hell-Bard said, her voice female. "We retrieved the empress."

Then came the giant. Zander. Across his arms hung a limp Vaness, a thick wooden collar locked around her neck.

Safi knew that collar. She'd seen it enough times growing

80

up, and terror of it was as much a part of her childhood as the Hell-Bards were. *The heretic's collar is what Hell-Bards put on their prisoners*, Uncle Eron always said. *The collar cancels out dangerous magic. Even wolves can be transformed into rabbits.*

For half a humid breath, panic set in. There was no escape now. No fighting, no running. Safi had gotten herself in a mess, and there was no one to come to her rescue.

What would Iseult do?

She had her answer immediately. It was Habim's favorite lesson of all: Iseult would learn her opponents. She would learn her terrain, and then she would choose her battlefields where she could.

"How long will the empress be unconscious, Lev?" The commander addressed the smallest Hell-Bard while he bound Safi's wrists behind her back with a wet, chafing rope. She didn't resist, she didn't fight.

But for all her seeming pliancy, Safi kept her fists curled inward, her wrists as wide as they could be.

"It was a large dose," said the Hell-Bard named Lev. Her voice was husky and slurred. An accent of the Pragan slums. "And her majesty's a small woman. I'd say she'll be out for at least a few hours."

"Can you carry her that long?" the commander asked, now pitching his question toward the giant as he gave a final testing tug on Safi's ropes.

Pain lanced up Safi's arms. Her fists were already aching. But she wouldn't release. Not until the commander had moved away.

"Yes, Commander," Zander replied. His voice resounded

so low, it was almost lost to the subsiding rain. "But we did pass a settlement an hour back. We might find a horse there."

"Or at the very least," Lev chimed in, "shoes for the ladies."

"Good enough," the commander agreed, and he finally—*finally*—moved away.

Safi relaxed her hands. Relief, small but there all the same, sang up her arms. Blood began to pump once more into her fingers.

A settlement meant a stop, and a stop meant an opportunity. Especially if Safi could learn something about her opponents before then. She hadn't initiated this, but she sure as hell-fires could complete it.

So when the commander barked, "Stand, Heretic," Safi stood.

And when he barked, "Walk, Heretic," Safi walked.

EIGHT

After leaving the Purist compound, Aeduan retraced his steps through Nubrevna's pine forests. He had no destination in mind, but since Corlant had two men tracking him, Aeduan needed to *look* as if he had a purpose.

He let them follow for a time before pushing his witchery to its full power. Faster, faster he ran until the men vanished from his senses entirely. Until at last he was far enough away to know he could pause undisturbed in a clearing where underbrush grew thick but shafts of cloudy light streamed in. Here, Aeduan examined the arrowhead.

Nothing. No blood-scent, just as the Threadwitch had no blood-scent.

There were different smells, though. Faint and mingling, as if others had handled the arrowhead. Corlant's scent hovered deep beneath the bloodstains. And then, lacing over the top, was a smell like hearth fires and teardrops.

Yet nothing for the Threadwitch Iseult.

Aeduan wanted to know why. Did she lack a blood-scent entirely, or was he simply unable to smell it?

He ran his thumb over the arrowhead, and a memory

unfolded. Hazy at first. *A face made of moonlight and shadows. An ancient lighthouse and a sandy beach. A night sky, with the Threadwitch's face at its heart.*

She had outwitted Aeduan that night, distracted him long enough to ensure her friend got to safety. Then she'd leaped off the lighthouse in a jump that would have killed her if Aeduan hadn't followed. Yet she'd known he would, and he had ultimately broken her fall.

After, when she'd spared Aeduan's life on the beach, her face had been cinched with pain and blood had bloomed on a bandage at her biceps.

An arrow wound, Aeduan knew now, and one that somehow connected her to Corlant. To a foul Purist priest in his father's employ.

Aeduan's breath loosed. His fingers curled over the arrowhead.

He was left with two choices, two ghosts he could try to hunt: the girl with no blood-scent or the talers with no trail.

Then the decision was made for him. He smelled his silver talers.

Before Aeduan had abandoned his iron lockbox in the hollowed-out tree, he had spilled his own blood across the coins. For his own blood he knew; his own blood he could always follow. Yet until this moment, he'd been unable to even *sense* those stained coins—much less track them down and reclaim them. It was as if they had been hidden beneath salamander fibers, and only now could Aeduan smell them.

There it was again, a slight tickling against his witchery, a lure bobbing atop a stream.

Aeduan was sprinting in an instant, a magic-fueled speed

that was twice as fast as before and not maintainable for long. But close. The scent of the talers was too close for him to risk losing it.

Distantly, Aeduan noticed other blood-scents. Foul ones. Tarnished ones. Men were so rarely a threat to him, so he ignored them and charged on. Over a stream, through a thicket of shriveling morning glories, then straight across a fern-covered clearing.

It wasn't until a bear trap clamped shut just below Aeduan's right knee, until iron teeth scratched against bone and the scent of his own blood gushed through the forest, that Aeduan realized he had charged directly onto a Nomatsi road.

Idiot. Thrice-damned idiot. He might not be able to navigate Nomatsi roads, but he could certainly avoid them. Now, whether or not he wanted his body to heal, it would. He could not pick and choose when that part of his witchery awoke. If he was hurt, his magic healed him.

Blood gushed, staining the pine needles and ferns to red and crawling outward in a lopsided sunburst to where, mere paces away, his coins waited. A satchel full. No more than forty if he had to guess.

Forty out of fifteen hundred.

Aeduan considered the three coins glinting in the weak sun. They had tumbled from the sack, silver stained with brown. Taunting. Laughing at him.

Two weeks of tracking the royal talers, and *this* was where the hunt had led him. To a clearing of bear traps, a ruined right leg, and too few talers to even buy a horse.

Aeduan's teeth ground, squeaking in his ears as he dragged

his gaze down to the bear trap. His leg was a mess. Nothing was recognizable below the knee. His entire calf was torn to the bone, strips of muscle and flesh hanging free.

Flies would come soon.

There was pain too, though Aeduan could ignore that. After all, pain was nothing new.

He sucked in a long breath, letting it expand in his belly. Roll up his spine. It was the first thing a new monk learned: how to breathe, how to separate. *A man is not his mind. A man is not his body. They are merely tools so that a man may fight onward.*

Aeduan exhaled, counting methodically and watching his blood trickle out. With each new number and each hiss of exhaled air, the world slid away. From the breeze on Aeduan's shinbone to the flies landing on hanks of muscle to the blood oozing outward—it all drifted into the background.

Until Aeduan stopped feeling anything at all. He was nothing more than a collection of thoughts. Of actions. He was not his mind. He was not his body.

As the last of Aeduan's breath slipped from his lungs, he bent forward and gripped the trap's jaws. A grunt, a burst of power, and the iron groaned wide.

Slowly—and fighting the nausea that washed upward in vast booms of heat—Aeduan pulled his leg from the trap.

Clang! It wrenched shut, flinging bits of flesh across the clearing. Aeduan scanned quickly around, but there was nothing else to avoid. He smelled corpses nearby, but corpses posed no threat. So he sat, witchery already healing him, one drop of blood at a time.

It took so much energy, though. Too much. And darkness was creeping in.

Yet right before unconsciousness could take hold, a smell like damp smoke tickled into his nose. Like campfires doused by rain. Against Aeduan's greatest wish and will, his mother's face drifted across his memory—along with the last words she'd ever said to him.

Run, my child, run.

After stretching her Threadwitchery senses as far as they could reach, and upon realizing no other Cleaved or hunters or life of any kind lurked nearby, Iseult sawed herself free from the net.

She hit the ground with a thump that she *barely* managed to roll into, then explored the area inch by inch. All signs pointed to a Nomatsi tribe having recently passed through. They'd made a sprawling camp in the woods, and judging by the traps and the tracks and the supplies scattered throughout, they had left in a hurry.

Too much of a hurry to disable their Nomatsi road, yet whatever had sent them fleeing, it was gone now. So Iseult grabbed anything useful she could find, grateful she wouldn't have to meet anyone. Wouldn't have to prove she was as Nomatsi as they were.

As she searched, she made a mental list of what she needed. *Oil for my cutlass. A whetstone. More portable eating utensils. A larger rucksack to hold it all.*

She moved deeper into the camp, pausing every few steps.

Stretching out her awareness and feeling for any Threads, for any living.

It was the first lesson Habim had ever drilled into Iseult: to constantly—*constantly*—make note of who was around her. Sometimes he would follow her, just to see how long it took her to notice him trailing behind. Slinking in closer. Slipping a blade from his belt.

The first time he'd done it, she hadn't noticed until he was almost upon her. It was his Threads that had given him away in the end. Yet he hadn't expected her to sense him at all, and Iseult had realized in that moment that she had an advantage.

She could see the weave of the world. At any moment, she could retreat inside herself and simply *feel* who was around her. What Threads twirled where, which people felt what, and how it might or might not connect to her.

She practiced that awareness. She became obsessed with it, really, and retreating into the weave every few minutes eventually became a natural instinct. Her range grew wider too. The more she reached, the farther and farther she found her Threadwitchery senses could go.

By the tenth time that Habim had tracked Iseult through the Veñaza City streets, she was able to notice him a full block away—and then sneak into an alley before he could catch her.

Today, in this abandoned campsite, Iseult moved no differently. Every few heartbeats, she sensed the texture of the forest. The placement of any Threads.

No one was near.

So piece by piece, Iseult found what she needed. Kicked under stones or hidden beneath grass—any forgotten item she deemed useful was stuffed into her satchel. Firewitched matches, a cooking spit, a ceramic bowl, and a tiny whetstone.

But the best discovery of all was an abandoned reed trap in a nearby creek. Iseult dizzily dragged it free to find three graylings and a trout flapping inside. She scaled them. She cleaned them. Then she set out to find shelter against the coming rain.

A lip of limestone was the first spot she discovered, and with the remains of a fire left behind, she deemed it as good enough as any for a campsite. Just in time too, for rain was slicing under the overhang, feeding the moss and vines that had crept inside the tiny shelter. Every few minutes, lightning cracked. Flashed over the washed-out campfire that Iseult now coaxed to life.

Iseult cooked a grayling, her eyes unfocused as she watched the skin blacken. It wasn't until she eased the fish off the fragile flame that she realized she'd lost her coins. For three cracks of lightning, she debated what to do.

She could leave them wherever they might be. Except Mathew's words whispered, *There's no predicting what might come, and money is a language all men speak.*

Fine. Back she would have to go. First, though, she would eat her grayling. Moist, delicious, fresh, she devoured it in seconds. Then she cooked and ate the second fish with a bit more care, a bit more attention to pleasure.

Eventually, the rain eased to a drizzle, so after cooking the remaining two fish—for later consumption—she doused the fire and retraced her steps. All the way back to the bear traps.

All the way back to the Bloodwitch.

For several long minutes, Iseult examined him. He was

89

clearly unconscious, stretched flat across the mud. His clothes were sodden and bloodied. His leg was a shredded mess.

A thousand questions scurried through Iseult's mind. Yet none were so bright as the command: *Run.*

She didn't move, though. Didn't even breathe, and without Safi there to guide her, without Safi's Threads to show her what she should feel, Iseult could only wonder why her lungs bulged against her ribs. Why her heart hammered so fast.

The sack of coins waited at the clearing's heart. Even with the rain having washed away parts of the scene, Iseult could make out what steps the Bloodwitch had taken. She saw tracks where he'd stumbled into the clearing from the west. Then came longer, deeper steps, where he had darted straight for the coins.

He is tracking the silver, Iseult guessed, and though the *why* and the *how* of it eluded her, she couldn't stop the certainty prickling down her spine. The silver talers were important; the Bloodwitch wanted them.

As Habim always said, *Use every resource available.*

Cautiously, Iseult entered the clearing. When the Bloodwitch didn't stir, even with the soft squelch of earth beneath her feet, she walked more boldly. Upon reaching her sack of coins, she peered inside. They glinted up at her, just as she remembered, their double-headed eagles dusted with brown. Coated in blood.

He must have tracked the blood.

Next, Iseult turned to the Bloodwitch. A stained bear trap sat within arm's reach, buzzing with flies. Hanks of skin and sinew clung to its closed claws. The Bloodwitch had stepped right into it, and now he was healing.

Dirt and dead flesh flowed from the furrows of his ruined muscle. It made an audible crunching and sucking sound atop the rain.

It was incredible to watch. Inhuman, really, this gift to heal one's body. The power of the Void. The power of a demon.

Yet when Iseult glanced at the Bloodwitch's sleeping, dirt-streaked face, she didn't see a demon lying limp before her.

She swallowed.

Despite having faced Aeduan thrice now, this was the first time she was able to look at him. To *see* him.

It was not what she expected.

Perhaps because in sleep, there was no tension of muscles about to attack. No disdainful nose in the air. No predatory awareness to cloak his eyes.

His face seemed peaceful, with his head tipped sideways and the lines of his neck stretched long. With his pale lips slightly open and his long, thick eyelashes fluttering on each breath.

He was younger than Iseult had imagined. No older than twenty, if she had to guess. Yet he *felt* old, with his voice so gruff. His language so formal.

It was in the way he carried himself too, as if he'd walked for a thousand years and planned to walk a thousand more.

This young man had stalked Iseult through Veñaza City. Had smiled cruelly at her, his crystal eyes swirling red. Then he had saved her too, in Lejna. With a salamander cloak and a single phrase: *Mhe varujta.* Trust me as if my soul were yours.

At the time, Iseult had wondered how he had known those words. How he had spoken Nomatsi like a native.

91

But now...now she could see. With his rain-sodden clothes plastered to a chest that rose and fell, there was no missing the lean shape of him. He was muscled, yes, but not bulky. This was a frame built for speed.

It was also a Nomatsi frame, just as the skin revealed through the tears in his breeches was Nomatsi skin. Pale as the moon.

Mhe varujta.

He wasn't a full tribesman, though. His eyes were not folded as deeply as Iseult's, his hair was not black as the night sky.

With more care and quiet than Iseult had known herself capable of, she knelt beside the Bloodwitch. His baldric glistened in the rain, the knife hilts rising and dropping in time to his breath. Iseult's fingers moved to the fat iron buckle resting in the groove between his chest and his shoulder. To unfasten it, she would have to touch bare skin, for the buckle had snagged in his shirt and torn the cotton wide.

Bare skin. Pale, Nomatsi skin.

A man's skin.

"Fanciful fool," she spat at last, and in a burst of speed she unhooked the buckle. Aeduan's skin was warm. Surprisingly so, given the rain's cold beat. Her fingers were certainly ice against him—

His breath hitched. She froze.

But he didn't awaken, and after a moment of staring at his sleeping face, she resumed her work. Faster now, towing the leather strap out from beneath him.

Goddess, he was heavy.

One heave. A second. The leather snaked free in a

92

twinkling melody of knife hilts and buckles. Iseult's lips curved in triumph, and she rocked back onto her knees.

With the baldric removed, there was no missing the blood on Aeduan's shirt. Not from a single wound, but from six small ones, each evenly spaced and an inch wide. Two below his collarbone, two on his chest, two on his abdomen.

Iseult slung the baldric over her shoulder and stole carefully away. She left the sack of coins where it was before walking all the way back to her campsite.

There she hid the Bloodwitch's knives and waited for him to wake up.

NINE

The sixteenth chimes came and went with no Cam or food to show for it. Unable to sit still—for it was a quick path to madness, as Aunt Evrane always said—Merik forced himself to move, to clear away books from the kitchen table, the cupboard's counter, the bed.

A knock. Merik spun around, dropping a book. His magic flared in ...

It was just the window. The shutter outside was open, and it had cracked against the warped glass. Merik's heart returned—albeit slowly—to his chest. His winds, though, didn't settle until he had reached the glass.

Outside, rain drizzled. A gray mist atop a shadowy city. With the weak lamplight behind Merik, there was no missing his reflection.

The Fury stared back.

Though bulbous and misshapen from the flaws in the glass, the hairlessness and red splotches were entirely Merik's own. Remnants from the explosion. Hurriedly, he screwed open the window, pinching his fingers on unfamiliar fastenings before latching tight the shutter.

But with the wooden shutters behind the window, the reflection—the similarities—grew more pronounced. Over the entire right side of Merik's face, and over his right ear too, was a large patch of shiny red skin with the faintest line of black to circle around. Dirt, he assumed, since it had been days since he'd had a real bath.

The explosion had hit Merik on that side, so his right shoulder, his right arm, his right leg—they had taken all the flames, all the force.

Merik bent a cautious glance to the front door, but it remained locked. Cam couldn't barge in when she returned, not without Merik to tap out the lock-spell. So with methodical care, he eased off his shirt. For eleven days, he'd examined these wounds, yet he'd witnessed only a fraction of the full picture. A sliver of the true monster that now stood before the window.

Eyes hooded, Merik scrutinized his body in the glassy glare. Dirt, if that was indeed what marked him, laced across the new pink flesh coating his right side. Down the black moved, gathering most densely at his chest. At his heart.

A bath was in order, he decided, once he had the time. Once the streets weren't crawling with Royal Forces. Once he'd gotten what he needed from Pin's Keep.

He stepped left, twisting to inspect his back. The dirt continued down his shoulder blades. The burns too, though far fewer.

"Destined for greatness?" he murmured as he slipped on his shirt. "I know you always said that, Kull, but look at me now. I should be dead, and you should still be alive."

As the words fell from Merik's mouth, a memory

percolated to the surface. *You should be dead, and Mother should still be alive.*

Merik snorted humorlessly. Aunt Evrane always used to say that Vivia hadn't meant what she'd muttered at the funeral. That the sight of their mother's body, smashed from the force of her jump off the water-bridge, had simply driven Vivia to thoughtless cruelties.

But Merik had known the truth then—and he knew it now too. Vivia had always blamed Merik for their mother's melancholy. With each new instance of Jana hiding in bed for days on end, of Jana bringing a knife to her own wrists, of Jana locking out her children for weeks at a time, Vivia had turned colder. And colder. For in her mind, their mother had descended into darkness only after Merik had been born.

Perhaps it was true, even if Aunt Evrane always insisted otherwise. *Jana's darkness awoke when she married my brother*, Evrane always said. *Not after she had you*. Yet Merik wasn't inclined to believe that claim. Particularly since Evrane's relationship with her brother was no better than Merik's was with Vivia.

Of course, Vivia had taken her hatred a step further than Serafin ever had: she had tried to eliminate Merik entirely. Not only would it clear the way for her to rule as she saw fit, but it also was revenge for the suicide Merik hadn't caused.

Vivia had failed to kill him, though.

So now it was Merik's turn.

*

When Cam returned, she was soaked through. Merik opened the door at her pounding, and she pushed inside, dripping water and leaving wet prints behind.

Merik waited until the door was shut to inspect the armful of food clutched at her chest. Hard bread, limp vegetables, and shriveled fruit—all wrapped in a jagged piece of wide-weave canvas.

Merik gathered it from her cold, rain-slick hands, his stomach rumbling, and after a gruff mumble of gratitude, he headed for the dry sink. Though some structures in Lovats had Waterwitched plumbing, Kullen's place was not one of them.

When Cam made no move to follow, he glanced back. "What is it?"

A gulp. Then Cam slunk forward, rubbing at her damp arms and avoiding Merik's gaze. "They're calling you the Fury on the streets, sir."

Ah. So that had stuck, then.

"Ain't too many soldiers out now," she went on, "but the ones who are . . . Well, they're all lookin' for you. For the . . . Fury."

With a sharp exhale, Merik dropped the vegetables and fruit into the sink—a limp head of fennel, four fat turnips thick with dirt, and six blue plums only slightly tinged with brown rot. The round loaf of barley bread was stale enough to break a tooth on, so Merik rewrapped it in the wet canvas and set it on the table to soak and soften.

His attention lingered there, brow knitting. "Will it be possible to reach Pin's Keep? With so many soldiers still searching?" He swung his eyes back to the girl, whose lips puckered sideways. An expression Merik was beginning to recognize as her thoughtful face.

"Are you sure, sir . . . That is to say . . ." She cleared her throat, moving abruptly to the sink, where, with surprising urgency, she set to scrubbing at the turnips with her knuckles. The scar on her left hand rippled and stretched.

"What?" Merik pressed, moving a single step closer.

Cam's cleaning turned all the more enthusiastic. "You sure you want to go to Pin's Keep, sir? What if . . . what if it wasn't your sister who tried to kill you?"

Heat fanned up Merik's neck. "It was her." No emotion, no emphasis. "I knew it was her before Judgment Square, and I have no doubt now."

"Just 'cos she runs Pin's Keep," Cam challenged, "don't mean she sent that assassin."

The heat spread, rising up Merik's spine. "I know it was her, Cam. I've been a hindrance to her plans ever since I moved back to the capital. And now—now," he went on, the heat spreading into his lungs, "I have a direct connection between Vivia and the assassin. I lack one final piece of proof, boy. Something tangible to give the High Council. I'm certain I'll find that at Pin's Keep."

"And what if you don't?" Cam's voice was a mere squeak now, yet something in her pitch gave Merik pause.

He fisted his fingers. The joints cracked. "Where," he asked, "is this coming from?"

She scrubbed harder, a loud *scratch-scratch* beneath her words. "It's just that, sir, I heard something on the street. Something bad. Something that makes me think . . . Well, it makes me think your sister ain't behind all this."

"And what did you hear?"

"That there was a second explosion." And with those words, her story tumbled out. "Just like the one on the *Jana*, sir, and people are sayin' it was the Cartorrans who did it. Or maybe the Dalmottis. But they're saying that whoever it was that blew us up, it's the same people who blew up that other ship too."

"What," Merik asked, even as his heart sank in a great downward rush, "other ship?"

"Oh, sir." Cam stopped mid-scrape of her turnip, posture wilting. "It was the Empress of Marstok's ship, and everyone on board was killed. Including . . . including that domna we carried on the *Jana*. Safiya fon Hasstrel."

Vivia found nothing new underground. Just more spiders and centipedes and amphibians on the run, and despite what had seemed like hours of moving stones from the cave-in, the rubble seemed as thick as ever.

Her frustration was good, though. She savored how it made her jaw work side to side as she strode down Hawk's Way, through a halfhearted rainstorm. She *used* the frustration to sharpen her mask into an uncrossable sneer, and by the time she reached the largest of the city's watchtowers, she was a Nihar once more.

She ascended the tower, nodding curtly as soldiers saluted one by one, fists against their hearts. It was so different from the Battle Room. No mocking stares. No waiting for her to trip and fall and fail. Vivia trusted these men with her life, and she knew they trusted her in turn.

99

"Bormin, Ferric," she said, naming each man beside the door at the tower's highest level before she strode outside into the rain. She crossed to the officer on deck: the tall, broad-shouldered Stacia Sotar—or Stix to those who knew her well enough to earn that privilege.

Stix's black skin was slick with rain, her white, tied-back hair plastered against her skull. She waved to Vivia, and her Witchmark—an upside-down triangle that signified her as a full Waterwitch—stretched long.

While Vivia could control water in liquid form, Stix controlled *all* aspects of the element. From ice to steam to this storm dribbling down. And while Vivia needed water nearby to draw from, Stix could summon vapor from the very air.

As always, Stix squinted with nearsighted eyes as Vivia approached. Once she realized who was on deck, she saluted. "Sir." She always called Vivia that—not *Your Highness*, not *Princess*. To Stix, Vivia was a ship's captain.

To Vivia, Stix was . . . *Too good for me.*

Vivia adjusted her face to match Stix's stern frown before she slipped her spyglass from her coat. Atop this tower, the highest point in the city, she could see clear across the mismatched rooftops and then straight across the valley and steppe farms in the distance. Even with the rain falling, the colorful farmhouses stood out amid all that brilliant green.

Vivia loved the sea. The never-ending swell of teal waves. The simplicity in knowing that all that stood between life and death was some tarred wood and faith in Noden's benevolence.

But she loved this view so much more. The weight of Lovats beneath her. The verdant life rippling ahead.

This was home.

The sea allowed men and women to pass for a time, but it was an uneasy alliance. Her fickle temper might turn on a thunderhead's whim. Like the Nihars. The land, though, welcomed men and women so long as they gave as much as they claimed. Partners. Friends. Thread-family.

Vivia wet her lips, swinging the spyglass left. Right. But no concerning thunderheads crossed her sight. Just gray, hazy gray all the way across the valley. Even the Sentries of Noden, at the end of the southern water-bridge, were crisp black silhouettes against the midday sky. The dam above the northern water-bridge looked as it always did: a featureless, sunlit wall with a shoddily mended fracture slicing down its heart.

One more thing the High Council refused to properly deal with.

Sighing, she raked her spyglass's view across the Water-Bridges of Stefin-Ekart that spanned from the mountains around the valley to the Lovats Plateau, each as wide as the river that fed into them. They hovered so high above the valley that clouds wisped below or alongside the ships packed hull to hull.

So many ships, so many Nubrevnans, and nowhere left to put them. *At least until I find the under-city.*

Stix cleared her throat. "Are you all right, sir? You seem . . . off."

Startled, Vivia almost dropped the glass. Her frown must have smoothed away. *No regrets. Keep moving.* With far too much force, she clacked shut the spyglass. "What news from the Foxes, First Mate?"

Stix ran her tongue over her teeth, as if contemplating

why Vivia had ignored her question. But then her face relaxed, and she said, "Good news, sir. It just came in, actually. Our little pirate fleet captured two more trade ships today. One with Dalmotti grain and the other with Cartorran seeds."

Oh thank Noden. Seeds were a victory. They would keep Nubrevna fed for years, so long as the land and the weather cooperated. Vivia couldn't *wait* to tell her father.

Of course, she showed none of this to Stix.

"Excellent," she said primly.

"I thought so too." Stix flashed a sly grin, baring her perfect teeth with the tiny gap in front.

Vivia's throat tightened. *Too good for me*. She turned away. "And . . . the missing ship?"

"Still no word, sir."

Vivia swore, relieved when Stix winced. *That* was the reaction she needed. The reaction her father would have earned.

The smallest ship in the Fox fleet had gone quiet two days before. Vivia could only assume the worst. There was nothing to be done for it, though. The Foxes were a secret. A backup plan that she and Serafin had formulated to keep Nubrevna fed. The crews had been hand-selected and sworn to secrecy—they all knew what was at stake. Every one of them had lost someone to famine or to war, so they wanted the Foxes to succeed as badly as Vivia and Serafin did.

Until the scheme was successful, though, no one—especially not the High Council—could know. Piracy was not precisely legal.

"We've also had no word from our spies," Stix said, words

even and businesslike. "Whoever was behind the prince's assassination, it does not appear to be one of the—"

The ground jolted. No warning, just a great lurch of the earth. So hard and so fast that Vivia's knees cracked. She toppled toward Stix, who toppled backward, arms windmilling. Vivia grabbed her, yanking her upright before she could fall over the parapet. The two soldiers weren't so lucky. They crashed to the stones.

Then everyone waited, bodies shaking in time to the fading quake. Stix gaped at Vivia, and Vivia gaped at the dam. At the crack that had been growing for decades up its middle.

But the stones held, and eventually Stix spoke: "Earthquake." The word hummed through Vivia's body. An impossible word. One that hadn't plagued Lovats in generations.

One that could, if it happened again, succeed in killing off the city before starvation or overcrowding even got the chance.

"Hye," Vivia agreed roughly. Her thoughts had scattered once she'd seen the dam was intact, and for a long stretch of time, the world was silent.

She let her eyes drift to Stix. Close enough now that the first mate didn't have to squint. It was too close—the sort of close that Vivia avoided, for though Stix would never ponder this moment again, Vivia would endlessly ruminate, evaluate, and yearn unrequited.

Then as suddenly as the tremor had hit, as suddenly as Vivia and Stix had pulled each other close, noise and movement resumed. Shouts from the soldiers. Shouts from the streets. Vivia hastily released Stix, lurching back a step. Both girls smoothed their shirts, fixed their collars.

"Check the city," Vivia ordered, "and I'll check the dam. I want a damage report in two hours. I'll find you at Pin's Keep."

Stix saluted, shaky yet strong. "Hye, sir!" She marched off, the soldiers dutifully following.

For several moments, Vivia eyed the water-bridges. Unlike the dam, they were bewitched by the same powerful witches who had built the under-city all those ages ago. Only magic could keep those massive structures aloft over a valley thousands of feet below.

Vivia couldn't help worrying, though, as she turned for the door, that if the magic of the underground was dying, then what of the magic above? For after all, whatever happened over . . .

Happened under too.

Merik felt like he was falling. As if he'd jumped off a water-bridge in the dead of night, just as his mother had, and now the shadowy valley zoomed in fast. Black skies and cold clouds.

And the Hagfishes waiting, mouths wide to catch him.

Safiya fon Hasstrel is dead.

Cam was still talking. A distant buzz of words, of which only snippets actually slid into Merik's ears. "Do you think your sister could have destroyed that ship too?" or "Why would she want to?" or "It makes no sense, sir." Yet Merik scarcely heard.

Safiya fon Hasstrel is dead. The words sifted through him. Numbing and cold. Shrinking the world down to a single, booming chorus in his ears. *Safiya fon Hasstrel is dead.*

It made no sense. Safi wasn't the sort of person who *died.* She was the sort who bent the world to her will. Who kissed the way she lived, with passion, impulse, life. Who smiled in the face of death, a challenge in her eyes, and then laughingly sidestepped it before the Hagfishes could yank her down.

This wasn't possible. Not again. Not someone else. Noden had already claimed too much.

Merik stumbled for the door. Cam's cold hands grabbed him. "Sir, sir, sir." But Merik shook her off and staggered on.

Magic skated over him from the lock-spells, briefly shattering the ringing in his ears. Then he was out of Kullen's home and hurrying downstairs. A blur of people and hunger and noise, before he finally joined the packed streets outside. Rain misted down—would it ever stop?—and each of Merik's steps fell harder than the last.

This is your fault, he told himself. After all, Merik had been the one to insist Safi reach Lejna, where the Marstoks had been waiting to claim her. If only he'd abandoned his contract with Dom Eron fon Hasstrel . . . If only he'd stayed by Safi's side atop that cliff instead of flying off to meet Kullen.

He'd lost Kullen in the end anyway. *But I could have saved Safi. I should have saved Safi.*

And Noden curse Merik, but how prophetic her last words to him had been: "I have a feeling I'll never see you again."

She'd been right, and it was Merik's fault.

He shambled onto a side street, no idea which one. As

soon as the rain droplets hit they steamed off the street, curling into a fog. Transforming the world into one indistinguishable uniformity. Every figure looked the same, every building blended into the next.

Another leftward veer, and this time Merik reached a familiar set of columns. Up Merik tramped, into the temple's darkness. The air turned instantly cooler; shadows sucked him in.

Twenty more paces, his feet dragging over the flagstones, and he was once more before the frescoes of Noden's saints.

It was then that the earth shook, dropping him to his knees. One heartbeat, two—the stones rattled. The city rumbled. Then as quickly as it had struck, the quake was past, leaving Merik with a booming heart and muscles braced for more.

But when more never came, Merik gulped in a calming breath and lifted his head to the fresco of the god's Left Hand.

To the beast that he had become.

"What should I do, Kull?" Merik gazed at the fresco's gruesome face, half expecting it to answer. But nothing came. It never would. Kullen—and these stones—would remain silent forever.

Except that in the silence came a thought. Something Aunt Evrane had always said whenever she scolded Merik: *The Fury never forgets, Merik. Whatever you have done will come back to you tenfold, and it will haunt you until you make amends.*

Merik slowly swiveled his wrists, reveling in how the new skin protested. How the blistered, dirt-lined strips tore apart.

He was haunted by his mistakes, but maybe . . . If he tilted his head at just the right angle, he could view this not as a curse but as a gift.

The assassin in the night. The fire on the *Jana*. The woman in Judgment Square. Each event had led Merik here, to Noden's temple. To a fresco of the god's Left Hand.

And only a fool ignored Noden's gifts.

Why do you hold a razor in one hand?

"So men remember," Merik whispered to the stones, "that I am sharp as any edge."

And why do you hold broken glass in the other?

"So men remember that I am always watching."

Take the god's gift. Become the Fury.

It was time to become the monster Merik had been all along. No more numbed distance. No more fighting the Nihar temper. Only vicious, hungry heat.

One for the sake of many; vengeance for those he'd lost.

It was time to make amends. Time to bring justice to the wronged. Time to bring punishment to the wicked.

Merik knew exactly where to begin.

TEN

Safi wished she were dead. At least then she could return as a ghost to terrorize these Hell-Bards.

They hadn't taken Safi or Vaness into the settlement. They hadn't even stopped nearby. Only the woman, Lev, had cut off from the group to vanish into the jungle. Which direction she'd taken, Safi couldn't guess.

One moment, Lev was there, walking silent as a deer behind the commander, who trod behind Safi. Then suddenly Lev was gone, and when Safi glanced back to scan the dense foliage, she earned a blade against her topmost vertebra.

"Keep moving, Heretic."

Heretic. It was the word for an unregistered witch in the Empire of Cartorra. It was the word for fugitives of the law.

And it was what the Hell-Bards were sworn to recognize and to eliminate. They could sense hidden witcheries. They could hunt hidden witches.

"My feet hurt, Hell-Bard."

"Good for you."

"My wrists hurt too."

"Fascinating."

Safi offered a sweet smile over her shoulder. "You're a bastard."

No reaction from within his helm. Just a metallic, "That's what they tell me."

Well, Safi was only just warming up. "Where are we going?"

The commander didn't answer that one. So onward she pressed: "When will we get there?"

Still nothing.

"What poison did you give the empress? Do you plan to feed us, or will starvation run its course? And do all Hell-Bards waddle like a duck, or is it just you?"

When he still refused to offer a reaction: "I *will* scream, you know."

A sigh bounced from his helmet. "And I *will* gag you, Heretic. That little trick you attempted by folding your wrists? It won't work with a gag."

That shut up Safi. Though not because of the threat in his words but rather the lack of anything else. No truth, no lies. None of the Hell-Bards registered with her witchery. How, she wanted to know, was such a thing possible?

It was the only thing Safi had learned about her opponents since capture, and it was of no use for an escape. Nonetheless, when an opportunity finally came, she was ready for it.

Vaness woke up.

It wasn't a gradual, groggy glide into awareness, but rather a panicked, predatory explosion. One moment, the empress lay limp in the giant's arms while Zander crossed a low gully. He had to lean forward to climb, his body awkwardly angled.

109

Meanwhile, Safi had paused ten paces behind, the commander's sword keeping her still. She watched Zander, impressed by how easily he carted Vaness up a rise almost as tall as he.

Halfway up the hill, though, Vaness became a hurricane.

She kicked. She screamed. She fell to the ground while Zander fought to stay upright.

The empress was on her feet before Safi's mind had even processed the awakening. And Vaness was running away before the giant or the commander—or Safi too—could chase after.

Vaness didn't get far, though. Zander's legs were twice as long, and he grabbed her from behind in mere seconds. She screeched like a Cleaved.

It was enough time for Safi to make a move. More than enough time. She dropped to her knees, spinning backward. With her torso, she tackled into the commander's knees, then lifted her left shoulder into his groin. Even with a long brigandine on, it had to hurt.

He certainly dropped fast enough, his back slamming into the streambed's wall.

Then Safi kicked—a hard side thrust of her heel into his exposed throat.

Except she missed and got a leather-clad shoulder instead.

The commander roared. A bellow of pain. Far more pain than the move should have earned, and he released his longsword—as if the muscles in his arm and hand had ceased to work.

He's hurt, Safi realized. She charged her heel once more into his left shoulder.

He doubled over.

She kicked again.

His knees buckled.

She kicked again and again until he fell back, hands clutched against his shoulder. Head lolling back. His helmet slipped off to reveal his face.

Safi froze.

It took her half a shallow breath to sort out what she saw. He looked so familiar . . . and yet so foreign.

Maybe it was the stubble that had grown across his jaw, or maybe it was the blood crusted down the left side of his face, as if his ear had been punched and the blood left to ooze for several days.

Or maybe it was simply the fact that the odds of the Chiseled Cheater being here—of him being a Hell-Bard commander . . .

It was unfathomable. Impossible.

Hell-Bard commander . . . what had Lev said? Fitz Grieg. Caden Fitz Grieg.

Never, *never* could Safi have guessed he'd be the Chiseled Cheater. *He* was the reason she was here. *He* had stolen her money after a taro game, and it was that trickery that had lit the fuse on all events to come.

If Caden hadn't stolen her money, Safi wouldn't have tried to steal it back the next day. If she hadn't tried to steal it back, she wouldn't have held up the wrong carriage. If she hadn't held up the wrong carriage, the Bloodwitch monk would never have gotten her scent. And if the Bloodwitch had never gotten her scent, she'd probably be free right now.

Free and with Iseult at her side.

Never could Safi have predicted that Caden would be the man behind that helmet. She had spit every time she'd said his name, and she'd vowed if she ever saw him again, she'd shred his face right off his high cheekbones.

Behind Safi, the sounds of struggle continued. Vaness's cries and kicks. Zander's grunts and clanking armor. Safi scarcely noticed. All she could do was absorb the Chiseled Cheater's face and try to assemble the pieces of a story she didn't understand.

Perhaps if she'd had a chance at actual escape, she would have tried. Perhaps if she'd seen a way to wrestle Vaness from Zander's grasp and that cursed collar, Safi would have tried that too.

But that wasn't the terrain before her, and she had too many questions churning to life like a stirred-up wasps' nest.

Which was why Safi didn't notice when Lev returned from her excursion to the settlement. It was why Safi didn't try to fight when Lev emerged directly behind her and kicked out her knee. Then, when the Chiseled Cheater, wincing, hefted up his helmet and became the Hell-Bard commander once more, Safi simply observed mutely. Even when they wound a rope around her ankles so she couldn't run or kick or fight, she let them.

Yet when the commander wrenched Safi around and growled, "Nice try, Heretic," Safi finally reacted. She grinned.

It *had* been a nice try, and worth the swelling right knee. Because she had learned more about her opponents than she'd ever expected. She knew the giant was strong but slow. The commander favored his right side in a fight because he was hurt—and his old wounds could clearly be reopened.

Best of all, Safi knew the Hell-Bards wouldn't hurt her. The commander could have as soon as the fight had begun. He could have sliced her open—just enough to slow her, and Lev could have taken Safi down with a lot more force than she'd actually used.

Yet neither Hell-Bard had hurt Safi or Vaness. Which meant they wanted both women alive. Unharmed. *Or rather, the Emperor of Cartorra wants us alive and unharmed.*

It gave Safi power, even with her legs bound and the empress collared.

The next time Lady Fate offered up an opportunity, Safi would be ready.

The sun was hidden by rain clouds when Aeduan awoke. He couldn't gauge how long he'd been out, but he was certain it was longer than he ever allowed himself. His magic had demanded energy from somewhere, and when food wasn't an option, unconsciousness it had to be.

It had been a shallow sleep. The kind where dreams fused with reality. Where he thought he was awake, but upon actual waking, he could see how strange the world had been. Bear traps as big as a man. Pine needles sticky with a blood that would never dry. Rain to flay off fresh skin.

And the scent of silver talers, ever present in Aeduan's nose.

His eyes snapped wide. With his new muscles protesting and the skin stretching too tightly, Aeduan hauled himself into a sitting position. His clothes were soaked through.

A quick glance around the area showed nothing save a

gray sky rippling overhead and fresh mud all around, while a quick inhale revealed nothing dangerous near. He turned his attention to his healed leg. The breeches were shredded, and the new pink wet skin gleamed in the cloudy light. It itched, but he ignored that, instead crawling stiffly on all fours toward the talers.

The bag hadn't moved since Aeduan's blind stumble into the bear trap. With his hands trembling ever so slightly from exhaustion, he lifted the sack and peered inside.

A branch cracked.

Aeduan lurched to his feet. His vision spun, yet he smelled no one.

"Don't move," said a voice in Nomatsi. Directly behind him.

The Threadwitch. Of course it would be her, yet Aeduan couldn't decide if Lady Fate was favoring him or cursing him.

He chose the latter when the Threadwitch said, "I removed your knives. They're hidden."

In his mindless drive for the coins, he'd entirely forgotten the blades. *Fool.*

He twisted toward her, calling in Dalmotti, "I do not need my knives to kill you, Threadwitch." Rain began to pelt his neck, his scalp.

The girl expelled a harsh breath before circling into the clearing. She wore Aeduan's cloak, turned inside out. Smart, even if it was against Monastery rules. One step became ten, until she paused at what would have been a safe distance against anyone but a Bloodwitch. Aeduan could tackle her before she blinked.

Instead, he let his arms hang limp at his sides. He *could*

114

attack, but information was better earned through conversation. At least so Monk Evrane always said.

Then again, Monk Evrane had also said this girl was half the Cahr Awen, that mythical pair their Monastery was sworn to protect. Aeduan found it unlikely, though—not merely that this girl could be half of that pair, but that the Cahr Awen even existed.

"Where are the rest of my coins, Threadwitch?"

No answer, and for three heartbeats they simply eyed each other through the rain. Droplets streaked down her face, leaving trails of white amid the dirt. She looked thinner than two weeks before. Her cheekbones poked through transparent skin, her eyes sagged.

"Where are the rest of my coins?" Aeduan repeated. "And how did you get them?"

Her nose wiggled. A sign, Aeduan guessed, that she was thinking.

The rain fell heavier now, pooling atop the mud. Rolling down the Monastery cloak that Aeduan wanted back. His own filthy wool coat was sodden through.

As if following his thoughts, the girl said in Nomatsi, "I've found us shelter."

"Us?" Aeduan asked, still in Dalmotti. "What do you think this is, Threadwitch?"

"An . . . alliance."

He laughed. A raw sound that rumbled from his stomach and clashed with the distant thunder overhead. He and the Threadwitch were, if anything, enemies. After all, he had been hired to deliver her to Corlant.

Aeduan was intrigued, though. It wasn't often people

surprised him, and it was even less often that people challenged him. The Threadwitch did more than that.

She perplexed him. He had no idea what she might say next. What she might do next.

Aeduan sniffed the air once. No blood-scents hit his witchery, yet something did prickle his nose . . .

The damp smoke. *Run, my child, run.*

"Dinner," the Threadwitch explained, stalking past Aeduan. She moved as if nothing had happened between them. As if the rain wasn't falling and she hadn't stolen his Carawen blades.

And as if turning her back on a Bloodwitch wasn't a fool's move.

Aeduan took his time walking. A few test steps with his newly healed leg. A stiff scooping motion to retrieve the abandoned coins. Then, when no traps sprang up to hold him and no pain burst forth, Aeduan shifted into a jog, following the Threadwitch wherever she might lead.

Safi's boots were far too large. They rubbed sores onto her heels—yet that was *nothing* compared to the raw skin at her wrists, where the Hell-Bard rope scraped and dug. Meanwhile, the rope at her ankles had sunk into the loose tops of her new boots and sloughed off the skin.

Each step burned.

Safi reveled in the pain. A distraction from the fire that gathered in her gut.

Hell-Bard Commander Fitz Grieg.

Caden.

116

The Chiseled Cheater.

There was that scar on his chin—it peeked out from his helmet. She remembered it from Veñaza City. Just as she remembered the confidence in his smile, and the manner he had of regarding a person dead on, no blinking. No looking away.

All those lifetimes ago in Veñaza City, Safi had thought that smile and the intensity of his stare were ... interesting. Appealing, even.

Now, she wanted nothing more than to rip them off his face.

Safi's boot snagged on a root. She tumbled forward. Rope fibers sliced into already bloodied flesh, and against her pride's greatest desire, she sucked in sharply.

"Stop, Heretic." The commander released her ropes before moving in front of her and helping her to rise. Then, from a satchel on his belt, he withdrew two strips of beige linen like the sort used for binding wounds.

"Give me your hands."

Safi complied, and to her shock, he wound the cloths around her wrists, blocking the harsh ropes from her open flesh. "I should have done this at the start," he said. His tone was neither apologetic nor accusatory. Merely observational.

It was then, while staring at the top of his dirty helmet, that a realization hit Safi. One that made her lungs hitch a second time.

What if *Caden* had told the Cartorran Emperor about Safi's magic? What if the reason Emperor Henrick knew Safi was a Truthwitch—the reason he'd wanted her as his betrothed—was *because of this Hell-Bard before her?*

117

The Chiseled Cheater had tricked her. Then the Hell-Bard commander had trapped her.

Safi was beyond anger. Beyond temper. This was her life now—forever running, forever changing hands from one enemy to the next until eventually the enemy severed her neck. It had been inevitable, really. Her magic had cursed her from the day she was born.

But Iseult . . .

Iseult was out there somewhere, forced on the run as well. Forced to give up the life she'd built in Veñaza City all because of Safi. All because of the Chiseled Cheater.

Cold hate spread through Safi's body. Throbbed against the ropes, pulsed in the tips of her blistered fingers and toes.

The hatred grew when they resumed marching. Hours of agony until at last the Hell-Bards halted for a break. Zander tied Safi to a lichen-veiled beech, and she let him. Even when the knobs of old branches poked into her back, she didn't fight him. Nor when he pulled up her arms, straining them behind her and forcing her back to arch. Then he tied off the rope high—so uncomfortably high—and her feet low. She was trussed up like the duck Mathew always roasted on her birthday.

Though Safi couldn't see the empress being tied to a tree behind her, she heard the same twanging stretch of ropes. The same crackling pop of shoulders stretched too far. There would be no running, no fighting any time soon.

She also heard the empress asking, with such sweet politeness, "May I have some water, please?"

The giant grunted Lev's way, and as Lev marched toward Safi, water bag in hand, Safi realized the Hell-Bard commander was nowhere in sight. Her gaze cut left, right . . . But he was gone. Vanished into the forest.

"Where is the commander?" Safi asked after gulping back four glorious mouthfuls of stale water. "He was hurt. You should check on him."

A metallic laugh echoed out from Lev's helmet. "I don't think so." More laughter, and after tying the water bag at her hip, Lev eased off her helmet.

The carmine light through the leaves showed a young face. Safi's age, at most. Short brown hair, a wide jaw that sloped down to a soft point. Pretty, actually, even with the puckered scars that slashed across her cheeks and behind her ear, as if someone had taken a razor to her face.

Lev grinned slightly to reveal crooked canines, and the scars stretched painfully tight. Shiny.

"Where are you from?" Safi asked. She already suspected the answer.

"Praga. In the Angelstatt." The northern slum, exactly what Safi'd expected with that accent—though of course, Safi's witchery stayed silent. No sense of truth or lie on the Hell-Bard's words.

Safi cracked her jaw, fighting the urge to ask *why* she couldn't read the Hell-Bards. It was possible they had no idea she was a Truthwitch. Yes, the commander called her Heretic, but perhaps only *he* knew exactly what she was.

Instead, Safi asked, "How did you become a Hell-Bard?"

"Same way as everyone else."

"Which is?"

Lev didn't answer. Instead, she made a sucking sound with her tongue, her pale green eyes running over Safi's taut rope and stretched arms. Then up Safi's face, like a Hell-Bard inspecting a heretic. Though what Lev saw, what she sensed, Safi couldn't begin to guess.

"It was the noose or the chopping block," Lev said at last. "And I chose the noose. More water?" She hefted up the bag, and at Safi's headshake added, "Suit yourself."

Safi observed absently as Lev hunkered nearby and began to inspect her weapons, crossbow first. Until her magic surged uncomfortably to the surface.

Lies. Happening behind her.

It was startling, that sensation. That ripple down her exposed arms. It had been so long since anyone had lied in Safi's presence—or that she'd been able to sense it—and it wasn't so much that the words lilting off the empress's tongue were false so much as the tone and drama behind them.

"You come from near the North Sea?" Vaness asked, her tone deceptively gentle and kind. "I also grew up near water. But not a cold sea like yours. A warm, sunny river." Her tone shifted to a faraway sound that rubbed, yet again, against Safi's witchery. "I was on my way back to that lake, with my family. Not by blood, but by Threads. By choice. We were almost there, you know. Perhaps a day or two more of sailing . . ."

A long pause, filled only with a katydid's refrain and a sighing breeze. Then: "Did you destroy my ship?"

"No," Zander blurted. Loud enough for Safi to hear. To feel him tensing with surprise. Vaness had lured him in with her sweetness.

"Liar," the empress proceeded, no more sugar to lace her tone. Only iron. "You killed the people I love, and you will pay

120

for it. I will bleed you dry, Hell-Bard from the North Sea. So I hope, for your sake, that you had nothing to do with it."

The empress's words sang with truth. A major chord of such purity, the intensity almost swallowed the promise's meaning.

Which made Safi smile. Her second for the day. Because she would do the same if it turned out the Hell-Bards had been responsible for the explosion. Even if they hadn't, she would *still* bleed dry the commander. The Chiseled Cheater who had ignited all this hell-fire and burned Safi's life to the ground.

She would make him pay.

She would make him bleed.

ELEVEN

Not now," Vivia said to the eight thousandth servant to approach her since returning to the palace. She was sweaty, she was hungry, she was late. Yet the sun-seamed gardener didn't seem to care as he scurried behind her through the royal gardens.

"But Your Highness, it's the plums. The storm took down half the fruits before they were even ripe—"

"Do I *look* like I care about plums?" She did care about plums, but there was protocol to follow for these sorts of conversations. Besides, the King Regent's inevitable displeasure at her tardiness was a lot more compelling than this gardener. So Vivia slanted her foulest Nihar glare and added, "Not. *Now.*"

The man took the hint, finally, and vanished into the shadows of said plum trees, which indeed looked worse for the wear. Then again, so did everything in Nubrevna.

Vivia had spent too long at the dam. Oh, it had taken her no time at all to sail her dugout over the northern Water-Bridge of Stefin-Ekart, and the ancient dam and its ancient splinter up the middle had quickly taken shape

122

against the evening sky. Up Vivia had ridden the locks—up, up, until at last, she'd reached the waters abovestream. There, she'd dunked her toes into the icy river, stretching, feeling, *reaching* until she'd sensed every dribble of water that entered the witch-controlled funnels of the dam. But all was as it should have been. The crack was still only surface level on the stones.

So Vivia had returned to Lovats, and *that* was when she'd lost all her time, stuck amid the ships carrying Nubrevnans into the city. The sun was setting by the time Vivia sailed into the Northern Wharf, and it was almost gone entirely behind the Sirmayans before she reached the palace grounds atop Queen's Hill, and finally, Vivia marched into a courtyard, surrounded on all sides by the royal living quarters.

The broken latch on the main door required three forceful *shakes* from a footman before he could get it open, and the hinges screamed like crows across the battlefield.

Into the entry hall, Vivia strode, where she ran—quite literally—into her father's youngest page. *Servant eight thousand and one.*

"Your Highness," the boy squeaked. "The King Regent is ready to see you." His nose wiggled, leaving his whisker-like mustache to tremble—and finally clarifying why all the other pages called him Rat. Vivia had always assumed it was because his name, Rayet, had a similar ring.

"I'm ready," she offered stiffly, brushing at her uniform.

Rat led the way. Their footsteps echoed off the hallway's oak walls. No more rugs to absorb her footfalls, no tapestries to muffle the *click-clack*. Twelve years ago, Serafin had removed all decorations that reminded him of Jana, throwing them into the storerooms beneath the palace, where they had rotted and where *real* rats had feasted upon the painted faces of long-forgotten kings.

So two years ago, Vivia had sold off each item. Piece by piece and on channels that weren't precisely legal. Dalmotti Guildmasters, it would seem, were quite willing to trade their food in secret if real Nubrevnan art was on the table.

When Vivia finally reached her father's wing, it was to find the inevitable darkness. Serafin's illness made his eyes sensitive to light; he now lived in a world of shadows. Rat scuttled ahead to open the door and announce her arrival.

Vivia swept past him the instant he'd finished. Twice as large as Vivia's own bedroom, the king's quarters were no less spare. A bed against the left wall with a stool beside the headboard. A hearth on the right wall, untouched and whooshing with winds. Closed shutters, closed curtains.

Vivia squared her body to her father. No bow. No salute. No word of greeting. *Save your energy for the council,* he would always say. *With me, you can be yourself.*

The king's gray head rested upon a pillow. His breath rattled in . . . out . . . and in again. He motioned Vivia closer. Somehow, even with his frail shoulders pointing from his night robe, and even with the pervasive stink of death that hung here like mist atop the morning tide, Serafin captured command of the room.

Once Vivia reached him, though, she almost recoiled. Her father's face, his eyes—they were ancient. Each visit was worse than the one before, but at least the king had seemed sharp when she'd come yesterday.

Cold pulled at the skin on Vivia's neck. This illness had

gone beyond frailty. His body was broken; his mind might soon follow.

"Sit," he croaked, one elbow sliding back. Bracing as if to rise. Vivia helped him, his ribs so sharp against her fingers. Once the king was fully upright, she sat on the stool beside his bed.

"You wear a captain's coat," Serafin said, voice stronger now and all acerbic consonants like Aunt Evrane's. "Why?"

"I was under the impression, Your Majesty, that *you* had taken over the position of admiral." He had said as much two weeks ago, during the same conversation in which Vivia had informed him of Merik's death.

So the admiralty returns to me, Serafin had said. But now he simply sighed.

"Do I look as if I can lead a fleet? Do not answer that," he added, a spark of his dry humor rising. "All day long, the healers tell me I improve—the liars. Sycophantic idiots, all of them." On and on he talked. About what the healers had told him, about how strong he'd been in his youth, about his years as admiral and king, and . . .

Vivia didn't know what else. She wasn't listening, and her frequent "mmm-hmms" and "hyes" were all a lie. She tried to listen—she truly did—yet all Serafin talked about was the past, rehashing the same stories she'd heard a thousand times before.

Noden hang her, she was a terrible daughter. This was a moment of triumph that she'd waited years to receive—he had just named her *admiral*—yet still, she couldn't seem to bring herself to listen.

She swallowed, quickly adjusting her cuffs while her

father prattled on. Now he was making jokes about the High Council, analyzing the vizers' copious flaws, and Vivia managed a shrill laugh in reply. It was so easily done, after all, and it always earned her an approving smile.

Even better, it sometimes earned her, as it did today, a snide, "We *are* just alike, are we not? Nihars to the core. I heard what happened in the Battle Room today. Your trick with the water was well done. Show them that temper."

Vivia's chest warmed. Then she summoned exactly what she knew he'd love most: "They are imbeciles. All of them."

He smiled as expected and then inhaled a phlegmy breath. Vivia's heart stuttered . . . But no. He was fine.

"What did the Council say today? Brief me."

"A hundred and forty-seven ships," she said crisply, "passed the Sentries this week. Most were filled with Nubrevnans, Your Majesty. The vizers are worried about food—"

"Food is coming," Serafin interrupted. "Thanks to our Foxes. We've accumulated a sizable supply beneath the palace, and those stores will keep us secure through this war. That treaty with the Cartorrans will help too, thanks to your brother using his brain."

Vivia's lungs tightened. *I use my brain too,* she wanted to say. *The Foxes were my idea and my hard work.* But she wouldn't say that to her father. He always insisted that they share the glory of any good decisions—and that they share the blame for any bad ones.

Guilt tidal-waved through her. She had never told her father about the mythical under-city or the underground lake, and though she insisted to herself it was because she'd been sworn to secrecy by her mother, Vivia's heart knew the

126

truth. She was a selfish daughter; she didn't *want* to share the glory if her hunt for the under-city ever paid off.

"And what of our negotiations with the Marstoks?" the king continued. "Another victory won by your brother that will keep us fed." As he said this, Serafin's eyes lingered on the mourning band at Vivia's biceps. The king had yet to don one, which had puzzled Vivia at first, since Serafin seemed to have nothing but praise for Merik—at least since Merik had moved back to Lovats and joined the Royal Forces.

Then the lack of a mourning band had pleased her, for surely it meant he loved her more.

Selfish daughter.

"Marstoks?" Vivia forced herself to repeat, shoulders inching toward her ears. There was the familiar sideways glint in the king's eyes. Serafin anticipated a specific answer, and he was waiting for Vivia to *fail* in giving it.

She wet her lips, puffing out her chest as she carefully offered, "We are still in discussions with the Marstoki Sultanate, Your Majesty, but I will inform you the instant an agreement is made—"

"Oh?" With a creaking lurch, he snatched a paper off his bed that had, thus far, been hidden in shadows. "Then why did I learn this morning that you canceled negotiations with them?"

Vivia's stomach hollowed out. The page he rattled at her was none other than the message she'd sent via Voicewitch to the Marstoki ambassador one week prior. How the *hell-waters* had Serafin gotten it?

"I did not think it a good bargain," she rushed to say, summoning a casual grin. When Serafin's stony expression didn't change, though, she shifted her tactics. Tried on a new mask—a snippier, angrier one. "A single glance at what the Marstoks proposed was all I needed to see Nubrevna would get the dung end of the shovel. Alliances are meant to serve our interests, *not* the Empire of Marstok's. There was also the tiny problem of Marstoki naval forces invading Nubrevna two weeks ago, Your Majesty."

"I only worry for your sake," he said, though his face still wasn't changing. "I would not want the Council to think you weak for not negotiating better."

Vivia felt sick. Her words tumbled out all the faster. "But Your Majesty, I thought surely *you* would never wish to treat with those flame eaters. You are much too smart for that, and if you'd only seen what they proposed in this deal! And of course, now with the empress possibly dead, I am certain they would have ended negotiations themselves!"

"But you could not have known the empress would die. Unless . . ." Some of Serafin's frost melted. Some of his humor returned. "There is more to her death than I realize."

Vivia's responding laughter was far too pinched.

He slouched against the headboard. "I told you, I only worry for your sake. *I* know you are strong, but the Council does not."

As the king devolved into more stories of his own prowess, Vivia tried to calm her heart. Tried to pretend she was listening, but the truth was that her hands trembled. She had to sit on them to hide it.

It was always this way with the King Regent. Whenever he was displeased, she would catch herself shivering like a bird—which was ridiculous. *Shameful*, for her father loved her. Like he'd said: he only ever worried for Vivia's sake.

Serafin was the good king, the strong leader, and Vivia could be too, if she would only act as he did. If she would only stick by his side. *Share the glory, share the blame.* So with that reminder—one she gave herself more and more these days— she settled her face and her posture into one of attentive interest. Then for the next two hours, she listened to tales of his feats, his brilliance, and his masterful navigations through Nubrevnan politics.

Outside the royal wing, Vivia met up with the palace steward and ten stiff soldiers. The soldiers saluted at Vivia's approach through the quad while the steward—a petite woman Vivia had known her entire life—smiled and bowed.

This was their evening routine: after briefing her father, Vivia and the steward would walk the palace grounds and battlements. Vivia would listen as the steward read all requests, all petitions, all complaints that had gathered during the day, and palace workers were allowed to approach.

Now was the right moment for that gardener to complain about his plum trees.

They set off at a brisk pace, a wind picking up around them. Rifling through the gardens as fresh clouds gathered on the horizon.

Once upon a time, these plants and gravel paths had been private, pruned, and purely for decoration. But eighteen years ago, Queen Jana had given the palace staff free rein. Within a few summers, row upon row of apple and pear trees had taken root beside the central fountain. Zucchini vines with fat yellow blossoms had crawled over the paths and around the rosebushes, while more heads of cabbage had sprouted in the western corner than there were actual heads in the palace.

Vivia's gaze flicked to the only spot in the royal gardens left untouched: a tiny enclosure on the northeast side, walled in by hedges and with a lily pond at its heart. It had been Jana's favorite place. Vivia had always assumed it was because the door to the underground lake waited within. Yet she wondered . . .

"Wait here," she murmured before cutting away. Moments later, her feet carried her beneath the overgrown archway, through the rusted gate, and into her mother's garden.

It looked exactly as it always had. Ivy grew wildly across the earth, hindered only by the pond and the cattails fluttering around it. A weeping willow reached long fingers into the water's edge, while blueberry bushes grew out of control against the farthest wall.

Every day, Vivia hurried down the gravel path—the only place ivy *hadn't* invaded—aiming for the trapdoor behind the blueberry bushes. And every day, she made sure there were no other signs of entry in the garden.

A lone bench stood several paces from the pond, and that was where Vivia strode now—for it was there that Jana had always sat. Vivia eased onto the bench, just as her mother used to do. Then she stared, just as her mother used to stare, at a cluster of bearded irises.

The flowers still held their own in a series of clay pots beyond the cattails. These were the only black irises Vivia had

130

ever seen. Most irises were blue or red or purple, but not these. Not the ones her mother had loved so much.

Jana would talk while she gazed upon them. Over and over, she'd recite one verse from "Eridysi's Lament," that song drunken sailors or the broken-hearted liked to sing. *Yet only in death, could they understand life. And only in life, will they change the world.* Then Jana would recite it again. And again, until anyone who was near her was driven just as mad as she.

For three breaths Vivia eyed those flowers, though her mind was lost in the past. In the way her mother would stare and croon. Infrequently at first, then once a week. Then once a day . . .

Then she was gone forever.

Vivia might be like her mother in some ways, but she was *not* that. She was stronger than Jana. She could fight this darkness inside her.

At that thought, Viva sprang off the bench and charged for the archway. There was nothing of value in this garden other than the trapdoor. Only madness and shadows lived here. Only memories and lament.

TWELVE

The Skulks.

It was the filthiest, most crowded part of the capital. Of all Nubrevna, even.

"Home," Cam said, as she led Merik through. It was the first thing she'd said since leaving Kullen's tenement, and she uttered it with such weight—as if it took all her strength to simply peel that word from her tongue—that Merik couldn't summon a decent response. Even in the dying Nihar lands to the south, there'd been space. There'd been food.

It didn't help that thunder rolled overhead or raindrops slung down every few minutes, weak but threatening all the same. Worse, the quake had left its mark. Collapsed gutters, crumpled tents, and white-rimmed terror in people's eyes. It could have been worse, though—Merik had heard stories of tremors that toppled entire buildings.

Cam moved smoothly through it all, her long legs adept at hopping puddles and looping around the inebriated, while Merik followed as best he could. Two lines from the old nursery rhyme kept trilling in the back of his mind as they walked. *Fool brother Filip led blind brother Daret, deep into the black cave.*

What Merik couldn't figure out, though, was if he was fool brother Filip or blind brother Daret.

Then he forgot all about it, for Cam was abruptly sidling left. In seconds, she'd disappeared down a shadowy alley, leaving Merik to scramble after. The stormy evening light vanished; his vision daubed with shadows.

"Here," Cam hissed, and she yanked him into a narrow strip of space between two buildings. There they stood, Merik gaping at Cam, and Cam with her scarred left hand clamped to her mouth, as if to muffle her breaths.

When, after a few moments, no one new appeared in the alley, her posture sagged. Her hand fell. "Sorry," she mumbled. "Thought someone saw us." Then she peeked her head around the edge of their hideout. Her posture drooped all the more.

It was, Merik thought, nothing like her easy twisting and hiding from earlier that day. And when he asked, "Who followed?" and she answered, "Soldiers," he wasn't entirely sure he believed her.

He didn't press the point. "Can we continue? The city needs us." *To stop Vivia,* he wanted to say. *To win more food, to win more trade.* He held his silence, though, for Cam didn't need to be scolded. Her face was already flushed with shame.

"Course, sir. Sorry, sir." She resumed her trek to Pin's Keep, though there was no missing how often she tugged at her hood or flinched whenever someone cut through their path.

Soon enough, though, Merik and Cam rounded a cluster of wooden lean-tos and the famous Pin's Keep loomed before

133

them. An ancient tower, it was older than Old Town. Older than the city's walls, and perhaps even older than the Water-Bridges of Stefin-Eckart. Merik knew by the stone from which it was hewn. A granite turned orange beneath the hearth-fire glow of sunset.

When Nubrevna had first been settled by men from the north, they'd carried black granite from their homeland, ready to beat this new land to their will. But over time, Nubrevna had become its own nation. Its own people, and they had in turn used the endless limestone that the local land had to offer.

Wooden planks and tumbled tents slouched against the tower's base, and the hacking sounds of sickness, the screech of crying babes carried over the clamor of the evening. Everything in the Skulks was louder than Merik remembered. Smellier too, and much more crowded. A line of people, some limping and limbless, some coughing and feeble, some barely out of swaddling, were strung out from the low archway that led into the tower.

Merik cursed. "Can we push in front of everyone, boy?"

Cam tossed him a knowing side-eye from the depths of her hood. "Find the entrance down below, sir. This way!" Just like that, the girl marched past the entire queue, then back behind the tower, and finally through a rusty gate. Here, the fat tower slanted against the matching granite of the city wall. Two steps through the gate, and the jagged cobbles of the alley dropped sharply, as if there had once been stairs.

"Wait over there." Cam pointed to a stretch of shadow, where the descending sun no longer reached. "I'll get the door open, and then you can slip inside when no one's lookin'."

Merik hesitated. He didn't want Cam inside—he'd only wanted her help getting this far, and then he'd intended to take the lead—yet the girl was already traipsing toward the door and lifting her hand to knock.

So even though a voice like Safi's slithered down Merik's neck, *I have a feeling I'll never see you again*, he did as Cam had ordered and huddled into the farthest corner.

As he stowed deeper into the shadows, the sunset's blaze hit the tower at just the correct angle to illuminate letters etched above the back doorway. First came a **P**, followed by a gap where rain, time, and bird crap had smoothed away letters. Then came **IN'S KEEP**.

Which answered a question Merik had held since boyhood: why the shelter was called Pin's Keep. Below the name, in smaller letters, he could just make out **DARKNESS IS NOT ALWAYS FOE, FIND THE ENTRANCE DOWN BELOW.**

So *that* was what Cam had been echoing.

She rapped once at the low door, and in seconds it swooped wide. Heat and steam billowed out. "Who's there? We have a line at the front, you know . . . *Cam!*" the woman on the other side shrieked. Then she yanked the girl inside, so fast Cam's loose coat flapped behind her like moth wings. "Varrmin! You'll never believe who the Hagfishes've dragged in!"

"No I won't," came the muffled reply.

"Camilla Leeri!"

The door began to close. Merik almost tripped over his own feet diving for it. He slid through *right* before it clicked shut. And only once he was inside, standing in a poorly lit, madly crowded kitchen, did it occur to him that the woman had said *Camilla*.

So not Cam—a name that Merik had never heard before—but rather Camilla. A solid Nubrevnan woman's name, if he'd ever heard one.

Well, that answered another question he'd been pondering.

After checking on his hood, Merik set off through the kitchen of Pin's Keep. A few workers glared his way, but otherwise no one paid him any heed.

He passed four people with Judgment Square tattoos below their eyes, and his chest warmed. His breath gusted. The assassin Garren *had* been sold here; this was the heart of Merik's sister's plans—he could *feel* it.

When at last Merik escaped the kitchen, a narrow entryway spanned before him. Low-beamed ceilings of dark wood brought to mind the belly of a ship, but instead of waves crashing outside, the waves crashed within.

Pin's Keep lived, it breathed, with crowds streaming into three different doorways. One group moved to a bright room mere paces away. A sickroom—there was no missing the workers in healer robes. Another group moved left, into a darker, quieter space, and the final current drove straight ahead toward the hum of laughter and voices.

Nothing distinct could be heard above these rough seas—no conversations, no individuals, no thoughts. The chaos of Pin's Keep filled every space inside Merik's skull.

His muscles relaxed. Some of the ever-present rage in his gut unwound—replaced by something softer. Something older. Something . . . sad.

Twice a week Queen Jana had come here, and twice a week Merik and Vivia had dutifully followed. Until, of course, the day that Merik's father had learned Merik's magic wasn't as strong as Vivia's. Until, of course, the day that Serafin had sent Merik to live with his outcast aunt in the south.

Merik's eyes shuttered. He wasn't here for himself. He was here for the wronged, for the wicked.

"Sir?" Cam's gentle grip settled onto his arm. At once recognizable and welcome. An anchor in the storm.

"I'm fine." Merik fidgeted with his sleeves. "I'm looking for an office or a private space, where records might be kept. Any ideas?"

"Hye." She tried for a grin, but it was tight. Furtive even.

Merik could guess why. *Camilla.* She must be worried that he'd overheard, so he made sure to say, with all the gruffness he could muster, "Which way, *boy*? No time to waste."

Her smile widened into something real. "Through the main room." She grabbed hold of Merik's cloak and towed him along as roughly as one of the mule-pulled boats in the canal.

With each step toward the tower's main space, the sensation of music grew louder. First a beat in his soles. Then a vibration spreading into his gut, his chest. Until at last he was through the door, and the song and the voices tumbled over him.

Merik and Cam were in a great hall, poorly lit yet boiling over with the stink of bodies spiced with the scent of rosemary. Of sheep's broth.

Merik's mouth watered. He couldn't remember the last

137

time he'd eaten a *hot* meal. It had to have been on the *Jana*—that much was certain. His stomach grumbled and spun.

Cam pointed to a spiral staircase in the farthest corner. "Used to be a closet at the top of those stairs, sir, but now it's an office."

Perfect. "Get some food," Merik ordered. "I'll return soon."

"I'm comin' with you." She tried to follow Merik as he twisted away, but he pinned her beneath his hardest, coldest stare.

"No, boy, you absolutely are not coming with me. I work alone."

"And then you get caught every time—"

"Stay. Here." Merik dipped into the crowds before she could follow. Once to the stairs, he peeled himself from the crowds and hopped up two steps. He paused here, to check on Cam. But the girl was fine, having slipped into the line for stew. Though she *did* keep glancing Merik's way, fretting with her hood.

With a long, shallow inhale, Merik curled his fingers. Drew in his power—just as Kullen had taught him to do more than ten years ago, two boys playing on a beach and trying to understand their magics.

Then he exhaled, sending a hot tendril curling up the stairs, into whatever room waited overhead.

His winds met no one. The room was empty.

So after a final glance to check on Cam, Merik hugged his cloak close and ascended.

*

138

An office *and* a bedroom. That was what Merik found above the dining hall of Pin's Keep. The attic between room and roof had been repurposed into a cramped living space.

When, though, was the question. After Jana's death, the running of Pin's Keep had fallen to Serafin, who had in turn passed it off to servants. The first Merik had heard of Vivia taking over had been when he'd moved back to Lovats three years ago. Yet this space was so unmistakably hers.

A couch sagged beneath an open window. The back, despite its moth-eaten corners, was covered in a neatly folded quilt embroidered with the Nihar family's sea fox standard. A matching curtain dangled from one corner of the window, suggesting that the poorly installed shutters did little to block the drafts.

Merik couldn't tear his eyes away from the curtains. They conjured the memory of another window, another space, just like this one but tucked in a forgotten wing of the palace.

Vivia had found it. Decorated it. And for a time, she'd allowed Merik to enjoy it with her. *My fox's den*, she'd called it, and he'd played with toy soldiers while she'd read book after book . . . after book.

Then their mother had died, and after setting the mourning wreaths aflame, tossing them off the water-bridges, and marching somberly back to the palace, Vivia had promptly locked herself in her fox's den.

Merik had never been allowed in again.

A moth flapped in on the storm's wet breeze, catching Merik's eye. Hooking him back into the present. It fluttered to the brightest corner in the room, where planks served double duty as wall support and shelving.

Merik crept over. He was careful to keep his pace slow, his gaze steady as he examined each spine. *Move with the wind,* Master Huntsman Yoris had taught Merik. *Move with the stream. Too fast, Prince, and your prey will sense you long before you reach 'em.*

Yoris had managed the Nihar men at arms, and Merik— and Kullen too—had spent countless hours tracking the lean soldier. Mimicking everything he did.

Merik mimicked him now, moving slowly. Carefully. Resisting an urge for speed. Until finally, he found a useful title on the highest shelf. *Judgment Square Sales, Year 19,* it read, and a smile built at the edge of Merik's lips. His smile grew when he found Garren's name inside.

Acquired Y19D173 from Judgment Square. Traded to Serrit Linday for farm labor, in exchange for food.

"Traded," Merik mouthed. "To Serrit Linday." He blinked. Read the name a second time. But no—it definitely still said Serrit Linday.

Which was not what Merik had expected to find. While he certainly hadn't anticipated finding a note that declared, *Sent to Nihar Cove to kill brother,* he *had* expected something to connect Garren to the attack on the *Jana.*

Instead, he'd found a completely new link in the chain. Hissing an oath, Merik snapped the book shut. Cam's words rang his ears. *What if it wasn't your sister who tried to kill you?*

But it was her. It had to be, for she was the only culprit that made any sense. Not to mention, the youngest Linday—a noble prick if ever there was one—had been Vivia's friend in childhood. This might be another link, but the chain still led back to Vivia.

By the time Merik had returned the book to its shelf, the moth had trapped itself in a Firewitched lantern. It was dead in seconds, and the stench of smoke briefly drowned out the sharp lemon.

For half a breath, Merik stared at the flame, burning brighter. At the smoke coiling off it from the moth. Then he forced his gaze to Vivia's desk. It was a table, really. No drawers to hide important messages in, no lockboxes beneath. All the same, Merik shuffled quickly through the stacks of papers. Checked between, behind, below.

Six stacks he flicked through, but there was nothing of interest. Just endless inventories and accounts in a tiny, slanted scrawl that was so neat it almost looked printed.

His eyes caught on a different stack, on the scribbled calculations and tallies and notes. Legible but so sharply slanted the numbers were almost horizontal.

And all of them crossed through. Scratched through with an angry pencil. The number of incoming people (by day) versus the amount of incoming food (by day, and with the palace's contribution subtracted), all underscored by the amount of coins being spent to pay for everything.

The numbers didn't add up. Not even close. The hungry and the homeless far outweighed the food and the funds coming in. Noden's breath, what a *huge* number it was. Sixteen new people came each day hoping for beds, and forty-four more people came looking for food.

If that was how many people made it to Pin's Keep for shelter, for meals, for healing, then how many *didn't*? Merik knew his homeland was in tatters—it had been for twenty years, and things had only sunk deeper into the hell-waters recently. But these numbers ...

They suggested a Nubrevna far worse than Merik had realized.

With a steeling sigh, he moved onward to the final stack on the desk. A large paper with creases down the center rested on top of it.

A map of the Cisterns, the vast network of tunnels below the city that carried water and sewage throughout. Merik leaned in, excited, for there was a spot on the map with a fat X atop it—as well as six times of day scribbled in the corner, one of which was circled. A meeting location and time, perhaps?

Merik eased the map from the stack and folded it along the already-creased lines. He was just tucking it into his belt when a chill settled over him. Ice and power and a voice saying, "Put it back, please."

Oh, Noden hang him. Merik knew that voice.

Stacia Sotar had arrived.

Merik swiveled his head ever so slightly, the hood blocking his face. All he needed was to get to the open window. A single jump, and he'd be free.

Or so he thought, until water surged up his leg. It snaked and coiled and constricted, freezing into a shackle of ice—because, of course, how could he forget? Stix was a full-blighted *Waterwitch*. It left Merik with only one choice: he gave in to the darkness.

He became the Fury.

His winds boomed out. The ice fractured. Merik yanked at his leg, ready to fly.

The ice melted. It steamed upward, scalding and searing into his ruined face.

Merik couldn't help it. He roared his pain before diving over the desk and dropping to the other side.

Ice shot above in a spray that beat the wall, sliced open Merik's scalp. His hood had fallen. Yet he was already moving. Crawling on all fours toward the window. He sensed Stix drawing in more magic. Easily, as if this fight had only just begun.

She slammed down her foot, and at once the water in the room turned to fog. Merik couldn't see a thing.

With a gust of weak winds, he puffed a path to the window. Mist coiled away. Merik pushed upright and ran.

Yet as he feared might happen, Stix appeared in his path. He spun right, his winds punching up to cloud her in her own fog. Before he could twirl past, her hand lashed out and grabbed his wrist.

Ice ripped across his forearm, locking her to him.

Their eyes met, hers dark as Noden's Hells—and widening. Thinning, just as her lips were parting.

She knows me. It was the worst possible outcome save for death. Being recognized would end everything Merik had planned.

Except that what left Stix's throat was not *Merik* or *Prince* or *Admiral.*

"The Fury," she breathed, and instantly the fog froze to snow. A flurry to drift harmlessly down around them. "You're . . . real."

A new cold—one from within—struck Merik in the chest. He was *that* broken. *That* unrecognizable. And though

143

he tried to tell himself she was nearsighted, she couldn't possibly recognize his face unless he was inches from her . . . He knew the truth. He was a horror to behold. He was the Fury.

But this pause was a gift. A moment he could use.

"I am the Fury." At those words, at that acknowledgment, heat frizzed down Merik's back. He tapped into the rage.

Power, power, power.

"Release me," he commanded.

Stix obeyed. Her hand snapped back; the ice retreated—though not before tearing open his sleeve. His skin too.

Merik lunged for the window. Headfirst, past shutters and lemongrass. Past shingles and guttering. Headfirst toward the ancient, narrow alley below.

His winds caught him. Cradled him so he could spin upright before hitting the jagged cobbles.

As soon as his boots touched down, he ran. Twice he looked back, though. First, to see if Cam was anywhere near, but the girl wasn't—and Merik couldn't exactly go back to search for her.

Second, he looked back to see if Stix pursued.

But she didn't. She simply watched him from the open window, haloed by candlelight and falling snow.

THIRTEEN

seult and Aeduan ate in silence. His jaw worked methodically. He hadn't spoken a word since leaving the bear trap.

Iseult hadn't expected him to. Never had she longed for Threads more, though. The world was so empty, so colorless without humans nearby, and weeks had passed with only distant plaits to brush against her. Now, when she was finally faced with a human again, he was colorless. Threadless. Blank.

Body language, expressions—these were puzzles Iseult had never had to decipher. Yet without Threads hovering over the Bloodwitch, she had to scrutinize every movement of his face. Every ripple of his muscles.

Not that he made many. *Cool as a Threadwitch*, her mother would say. Gretchya would mean it as a compliment, for of course Threadwitches were not meant to show emotion. It would sting like an insult for Iseult, though, since the phrase was never directed at her. Gretchya only ever used it for other people—the ones who were better at stasis, better at calm than Iseult could ever be.

The longer Iseult observed Aeduan, the more she sensed an emotion emanating off him. Distrust.

It was in the way he sat stiff and at the ready while he ate. In the way his eyes never left Iseult, tracking her as she moved about the small campsite. *He saved my life*, Iseult thought as he ate, *and he hates me for it.*

Iseult was accustomed to distrust, though, and to hate. And if those feelings could kill, then they would have slain her a long time ago.

"More?" She motioned to the campfire, to the final grayling staked to her spit.

The Bloodwitch cleared his throat. "Where are my blades, Threadwitch?" He stubbornly still spoke in Dalmotti.

So Iseult stubbornly answered in Nomatsi: "Hidden."

"And the rest of my talers?"

"Far away."

The Bloodwitch's fingers curled. He pushed to his feet. "I can force the answer from your throat if I wish."

He couldn't, and they both knew it. He'd lost all power over her by admitting in Veñaza City that he couldn't smell or control her blood.

Yet as Iseult matched his pose with her own chin high and her own shoulders back, she still found her heart running too fast. Thus far everything in her plan had gone as she'd estimated—as she'd hoped. But now ... Now was the final knot in her snare.

"I will return your coins to you," she declared, grateful her stammer felt leagues away, "only if you will hunt someone for me."

His entire body tightened like a snake's. For several

breaths, nothing happened. Distant thunder rolled. Wind gusted into the overhang, spraying them. Yet Aeduan moved not a muscle.

Until at last, he murmured, "So you . . . need me."

"Yes. To track Safiya fon Hasstrel."

"The Truthwitch."

Iseult winced at that word. The barest of flinches, yet she knew Aeduan saw. She knew he noted.

"The Truthwitch," she agreed eventually, marveling at how strange it was to utter that word aloud. The one word she hadn't dared say for six and a half years, lest someone overhear. Lest she accidentally curse Safi to imprisonment or death. "The Marstoks took Safi, but I don't know where. You, Bloodwitch, can track her."

"Why would I do that for you?"

"Because I will tell you where the rest of your coins are."

He eased two steps closer, circling around the dead fire. No blinking. No looking away. "You will pay me with my own silver talers?"

So the coins are his. Iseult didn't know how or why they had ended up in Mathew's cellar, but she would use that bargaining card all the same.

At her nod, Aeduan laughed. A sound that hummed with shock and disbelief. "What will prevent you from keeping my money? Once I find the Truthwitch for you, how do I know you will fulfill your end of the deal?"

"How do I know," Iseult countered, "that once you find Safiya fon Hasstrel, you won't try to keep her? Try to sell her off, like you did before?"

The Bloodwitch hesitated, as if quickly tracing several

options of conversation before choosing the one he liked most. Or the one that best served his purpose.

Cool as a Threadwitch.

"So it will come down to timing, then." He rolled his wrists. "Who betrays whom first."

"Does that mean you accept?"

He took another step toward her, this one long enough to close the gap between them. Iseult had to lift her chin to keep eye contact.

"You are not my master, Threadwitch. You are not my employer. And above all, you are not my ally. We travel the same route for a time, nothing more. Understood?"

"Understood."

"In that case," he continued, still in Dalmotti, always in Dalmotti, "I accept."

Iseult's fingers furled, fists to keep herself from reacting. From revealing how much relief ebbed through her.

I'm coming, Safi.

She turned away, waiting until the last moment to break eye contact and pivot entirely. Then she marched to a shadowy corner where fat mushrooms stacked downward on the limestone wall. A crouch, a grab, and her hands touched leather.

She was gentle with the baldric, careful to keep the knife hilts from scraping or the leather from dragging. Even as she crossed the wet earth, she kept the leather stretched long and the buckles quiet.

She offered it to him. "They need to be oiled."

No reaction. He simply refastened the blades across his chest, methodically and silently, before strolling toward the

148

overhang's edge. Rain misted over him, and for the first time since Aeduan had awoken in the forest, Iseult's lungs felt big enough to let in air.

He was going to help her.

He wasn't going to kill her.

"Are you ready to leave?" she asked, gripping her Threadstone. *I'm coming, Safi.* "There's no time to waste."

"We can make no progress in this weather, and darkness will soon fall." A yank at the buckle beside his shoulder; blades clinked in warning. "We travel tomorrow, at first light."

Then the Bloodwitch sank into a cross-legged position on the damp soil, closed his eyes, and did not speak again.

The Hell-Bard commander returned from the jungle, movements imbalanced as he shuffled to Zander's pack and rifled through. If he noticed Safi's gaze boring into him, he gave no indication.

Night was drawing near. Safi had hoped they might make camp, but Lady Fate was not favoring her thus far.

The commander withdrew dried meat, and after easing off his helm, he placed it beside the pack. A sunbeam broke through the forest's canopy. It flashed on the back of his neck, where blood crusted.

And where a white cloth peeked out.

He had gone into the woods to tend his wound. Safi would stake her life on that. He barely moved his left arm; his left shoulder looked a bit larger, as if bandages filled the space inside his leathers.

It's a bloody wound, then. Safi's lips twitched at this tiny stroke of fortune. She must've reopened the wound when she had pummeled him, and that meant he'd lost blood. *That* meant he'd grown weaker.

Her lips curved a bit higher.

The Hell-Bard noticed. "Don't look so smug, Heretic. You're the one tied to a tree."

You'll be tied up soon, she thought, although she did erase her smile. No sense giving away her tricks. "I was simply admiring the view, Hell-Bard. You look so much better without your helmet on."

A distrustful line crossed Caden's brow—and he was Caden now, without his helm. The Chiseled Cheater who had consigned her to a life on the run. To a life lived as prey.

Caden sauntered closer. Closer again until he was within reach, if had Safi not been bound.

He extended a strip of dried meat. "Pork belly?"

"Please." She fluttered her lashes. "And thank you."

The line deepened on his forehead, and he quickly examined Safi's bound arms and fettered feet. But she was still trussed up tight. "Why the good mood, Heretic? Why the nice manners?"

"I'm a domna. I can smile at even the ugliest toad and flatter him on his *perfectly* placed warts."

A huff of breath, not quite a laugh. Caden offered the pork; it hovered inches from Safi's lips, forcing her to extend her neck. To chomp down and tear. Demeaning. Weakening.

So Safi grinned all the more cheerfully as she chewed and chewed. And chewed some more before the salty toughness would fit down her throat. "It's . . . dry," she squeezed out. "Could I have some water?"

Caden hesitated, one eye squinting. A look Safi remembered from their night at the taro tables. A look that said, *I'm thinking, and I want you to see that I'm thinking.*

Then came a shrug, as if Caden saw no reason to refuse, and he untied a half-drained water bag from his hip. He held it to Safi's lips, and she gulped it back.

He let her drain the bag. "Thank you," she said after licking her lips. She truly meant it too.

He nodded and replaced the bag on his belt, a movement that his left fingers clearly didn't like.

"Hurt?" Safi chimed.

"Hell-Bards can't be hurt," he muttered.

"Ah," Safi breathed. "That must make it so much easier when you're killing innocent witches."

"I've never killed innocent witches." His head stayed down, still fumbling to lace up the bag. "But I have killed heretics."

"How many?"

"Four. They wouldn't yield."

Safi blinked. She hadn't expected him to answer, and though she couldn't read him with her magic, she suspected he spoke the truth. He had killed four heretics; it had been their lives or his.

"What about the entire ship of Marstoks you just slaughtered? Do you count them on your list of murders?"

"What ship?" The line returned between his brows. His gaze finally flicked up.

"The one you burned to embers. The one the empress and I were on."

"Wasn't us." He bounced his right shoulder, a vague

151

gesture toward Lev and Zander. "We've been tracking you since Lejna."

"Lies."

Another huff—this one undoubtedly a laugh, for a sly half smile crossed his face. "I'm glad to see your witchery still doesn't work on me, Heretic."

Safi's own smile faltered. She couldn't fake her way through this. She truly *couldn't* read him. So for once, she chose honesty. She let her grin slip away, and a frown bubbled to the surface. "Why? Why doesn't my magic work on you?"

"No magic on Hell-Bards."

"I know," she said simply. "Why is that?"

He scratched the tip of his chin, where the scar ran down. "I guess your uncle never told you, then.

He eased backward a single step. "Magic, witcheries, power. Those are for the living, Heretic. But us?" Caden patted his chest, clanking the brigandine's metal plates. "We Hell-Bards are already damned. We're already dead."

The arrowhead in Aeduan's pocket felt aflame as he scanned the dark pines and oaks around him. *Who would betray whom first?* An hour had passed since the agreement between him and the Threadwitch, yet Aeduan was still asking himself this question.

The rain had finally stopped. Not a gradual tapering like the rains at the Monastery but an abrupt *end*. Storm one moment. No storm the next. Southern weather was like that: all hard lines and nature waiting to pounce upon the off-beats.

The instant the rain ceased, the insects of the night were out. Cicadas clicked, moths took flight, and the bats that ate them awoke too. They swept and crisscrossed over a dull black sky. Eventually the clouds slipped away to reveal starlight, and Aeduan watched the Sleeping Giant rise—that bright column of stars that always guided north.

He watched it alone, for the Threadwitch slept. Shortly after their conversation, she'd settled into the driest corner of the overhang. Moments later, she'd been asleep.

Aeduan couldn't help but wonder at how quickly she had drifted off. At how miserable that sideways position must be. Or at how fearless she was to drop her guard so completely.

Fearless or stupid, and judging by her trick with the knives, it was the latter. Then again, she *had* deftly lured Aeduan into this insane partnership. *Who will betray whom first?*

All Aeduan knew for certain was that it was connected. The arrowhead. The Purist priest Corlant. And Aeduan's missing coins. It was all connected, even if Aeduan couldn't yet see how.

He released the arrowhead in his pocket and moved quietly, deliberately through the forest. There was a stream near; he needed a bath.

He found a spot on the shore where the canopy was less overgrown. Starlight poured down. Water burbled past.

Aeduan eased off his baldric, then his shirt. He hadn't had a moment since leaving the bear trap to check the old wounds. They had, no surprise, reopened. But a cautious dab revealed only dried blood.

Aeduan sighed, annoyed. His shirt and breeches were

ruined. While the forest wouldn't care, humans would. The Threadwitch would.

Doesn't matter. Blood was a part of Aeduan, and blood-stains had never slowed him before. He had come this far. He would keep going.

For some reason, though, he found himself bringing the shirt into the frozen stream. He found himself rubbing it, trying to get it clean. But the blood had set and could not be lifted.

Just as his wounds had set all those years ago. *Run, my child, run.*

It was, as Aeduan began to scrape at his chest, shuddering from the cold, that he saw something move along the opposite shore. At first, he thought it a trick of his eyes, a trick of the darkness, and an old song came to mind. One his father had sung back before ... everything.

> *Never trust what you see in the shadows,*
> *for Trickster, he hides in darkness and dapples.*
> *High in a tree or deep underground,*
> *never trust if Trickster's around.*

Aeduan shook his head. Water sprayed. He hadn't thought of that tune in so long. Another shake of his head, this time to clear the tricks from his eyes.

Yet the movement was still there. A subtle glow that seemed to pulse in clusters through the forest. The longer Aeduan observed, the brighter the clusters grew. The more solid and distinctly defined, as if clouds dispersed to reveal a starry sky.

"Fireflies," said a voice behind him. In a moment, Aeduan had her pinned against an oak by the shore.

They both stood there. Staring. The Threadwitch with her back to the trunk and hands at Aeduan's chest. He with his forearm to her throat, dripping water.

Two heaving breaths, and he released her. "Be more careful," he snapped, stalking away. Though if he spoke to her or to himself, he couldn't say. All he knew was that his heart juddered in his chest. His blood and his magic roared in his ears.

He hadn't smelled her coming. He *couldn't* smell her coming, so his body had reacted to a threat.

He'd have to get better at that. At least as long as she remained near him.

"I almost killed you," he said.

"Nomatsi," was her reply—which sent him glaring backward. Made him growl, "What?"

She stepped away from the tree, into the starlight, and like the fireflies in the forest, her face ignited. Ghostly white. Beautiful and burning from within.

Half a breath. That was all it lasted. Then the illusion passed. She was a plain-faced girl once more. *Never trust what you see in the shadows.*

"You're speaking to me in Nomatsi," she explained, brushing water off her chest, her arms. "And those glowing lights are fireflies. They're good luck in Marstok, you know. Children make wishes on them."

Aeduan exhaled. A long, hissing sound. She behaved as if he had not almost eviscerated her. As if discussing wishes or what language he spoke actually mattered.

"I will kill you," he warned, in Dalmotti once more, "if you aren't more careful. Do you understand, Threadwitch?"

"Give me one of your coins, then." She tipped back her head, emphasizing the way her jaw sloped to her collarbone.

And for the first time since she'd appeared, Aeduan realized his chest was bare. His scars were visible, and his skin rippled with chill bumps. His shirt, though, was nowhere to be seen—and he refused to turn away from the Threadwitch. "The coins have blood on them, right?" she continued. "That's how you found me. So give me a coin, and then you'll always sense me coming."

It was smart. A tidy, simple solution to a problem Aeduan wished she didn't know about. Yet she *did* know he couldn't smell her, and there was no changing it now.

Aeduan nodded. "In the morning," he said, fighting the urge to jerk away and dive into the stream after his shirt. "I'll give you a coin in the morning."

With a nod of her own, Iseult finally left the stream. The forest folded her in, fireflies lighting her way.

And Aeduan was instantly in the water, paddling fast and praying that the one shirt he owned wasn't too far downstream to find again.

FOURTEEN

A fog encased the night-darkened streets of Lovats while Merik watched the Linday family mansion. Like all vizerial city abodes, the house stood solemnly on the oak-lined road called White Street that traced up Queen's Hill.

No lanterns lit within the mansion, no shadows moved. Which left only one place a Plantwitch might logically go at night: his gardens.

It took Merik mere minutes to reach the Linday greenhouse. Vapor drifted into the gardens around it, veiling the structure of glass and iron that Merik knew waited within.

Thirteen years had passed since Merik had roamed the jungles of this greenhouse. He'd been a boy then, just seven years old.

It had also been daylight, and more important, he'd been invited.

Yet none of the clumsy guards noticed Merik stalking from one shadow to the next. Twice, Merik almost stumbled upon them, but twice, Merik gusted up a wall of mist to cloak him.

He spun around a bellflower hedge, its violet blossoms in

full bloom, and ducked beneath a cherry tree. Such a despicable waste of space, this greenhouse. This garden. And an even more despicable waste of magic. The Linday family could use their resources to feed the starving who crushed against their gates, yet instead they grew ornamental flowers of no use to anyone.

Perhaps Merik could add that to his list of conversation points with the vizer.

Onward Merik stole. Toward Linday, toward the truth about the assassin Garren. *Power, power, power.* It pumped through Merik, so easy to tap into. So easy to command, even as exhausted as he was.

Ever since Pin's Keep—ever since he had embraced the name *Fury*—his winds had come without protest, his temper had stayed calm. Easy.

And easy was good as far as Merik was concerned. Easy let ships sail without fear and crews reach home unharmed.

Easy, however, did not mean trip wires. Slung across the greenhouse's back entrance, Merik felt the string the instant it hit his shin—and he felt the vibration race outward like a plucked harp.

Oh, hell-waters.

His hands swept up; his winds shot out, a charge of power to counteract the moving line.

Merik watched, breath held, as it stilled. As the whole world stilled, shrinking down to that cursed string and his booming heart. It thundered loud enough to give him away.

Yet no alarm went off. No trap released, leaving Merik to carefully sweep his gaze over every leaf, every petal, every strip of bark in sight. The wire traveled into the shadows, to where iron beams held glass walls upright. Then up the string shot, ending at a brass bell.

Merik's breath kicked out. That had been too close, for though the bell might have been tiny, it was more than enough to alert someone of Merik's arrival. The only other sound was a burbling fountain at the greenhouse's heart.

While Merik wouldn't have been surprised to learn that young Serrit Linday was a paranoid bastard, there had never been guards or trip wires at the nobleman's mansion during their childhood.

Which suggested that Linday was meeting someone, and either he didn't trust that someone or he intended to betray that someone. Had Merik the time, he would've crawled into the nearby cherry tree and waited, watching to see who hit this backdoor trap. After all, learning whom Linday feared might be valuable information.

Merik hadn't the time, though, nor the patience. Plus, he'd abandoned poor Cam back at Pin's Keep. She was still out there, no doubt panicking over where her admiral had gone.

So after checking his hood was still firmly in place, Merik resumed his approach. Twice more, he found hidden trip wires, and twice more, he bypassed them. It was slow going, slipping through the leaves and roots, yet all the while using his winds to keep the jungle still. To keep the trip wires from activating.

At last Merik reached the center of the greenhouse, where the gravel of the outer paths gave way to sandstone tiles arranged in a complex array of sunbursts. The Linday family sigil. At the center was a fountain, also fashioned into a sunburst.

Before the bubbling water sat Serrit Linday. His frenetic energy clashed with the soft serenity of the scene. He swatted and swatted and swatted *again* at brilliant white lilies along the fountain's edge, while his finely slippered toe tapped the pristine grass into mush. Even the lamplight from the streets outside seemed too bright, too pure for Linday's antiquated black robe.

This was not the arrogant vizer Merik remembered from boyhood. This was a scared man—and scared men were easy men.

Easy was always *good*.

Merik slipped to the edge of the clearing, to where grass gave way to flagstones. Behind Linday and still out of sight. Then he lowered his hood and offered a rough, "Hello, Vizer."

The man's breath punched out. He deflated completely, spine wilting and shoulders dropping over his knees. For half a moment, Merik thought he'd fainted . . .

Until a weak, "I don't have it," whispered out.

Merik stepped from the shadows. "You mistake me for someone else."

At that, Linday tensed. Then his head swung around. His eyes met Merik's. Then he gazed up and down, clearly taking in Merik's scars, his ragged clothes. For half a skittering moment, Merik thought the vizer might recognize him from their brief encounters over the years.

But he didn't, and Merik almost smiled as warring expressions settled across the young man's face. Relief mingled with horror and confusion . . . before shivering back to relief.

Which was not precisely the end reaction Merik had hoped for.

He approached the fountain, and although Linday shrank back, the man didn't run. Not even when Merik gripped his collar and yanked him close.

"Do you know who I am?" Merik murmured. This close, the man's face was a mask of fine lines. He looked twice the age Merik knew him to be.

"No," Linday rasped. He was trembling now. "I don't know you."

"They call me the Left Hand of Noden. They call me the Fury." *Power, power, power.* "I'm going to ask you a few questions now, Vizer, and I want you to answer quickly. If you do not . . ." He twisted his fists, tightening Linday's collar. Cutting off the man's air.

Linday shook all the harder in Merik's hands, and *that* was more the reaction Merik had hoped for. "I'll answer, I'll answer."

"Good." Merik's eyes narrowed, his brow stretching. "You bought a prisoner from Pin's Keep. Garren was his name. I need to know what you did with him."

"I don't know."

Yank. Twist. Linday's breath slashed out.

"Don't lie to me."

"I must, I must." Linday's eyes began to cross. "I . . . *must*, or he'll kill me."

Fresh rage slashed through Merik. He wrung Linday's collar tighter. "By whose hand would you rather die, Vizer? His or mine?"

"*Neither,*" the man choked. "*Please*—the shadow man comes for me. Help me. Please, before they turn me into one of their puppets—please! I'll tell you everything you want—"

161

A bell rang.

A soft twinkle to fill the greenhouse.

Vizer Linday went limp, as if his knees could no longer hold him. Merik released Linday, who crumpled to the tiles.

A second bell tolled. Chills raced down the back of Merik's neck. His spine. He whirled around . . .

To find a wall of night slithering through the greenhouse. Approaching this way, it slipped and slid and coiled and gripped. Shadow hands that tendriled forward, over the ground, across the foliage, along the ceiling.

Instinct told Merik to run. Told his muscles to *flee*. Yet something else warred inside him—something hot and not to be trifled with.

Merik let his fury come. It roared to a fiery life right as the darkness scuttled across him.

The shadow man had arrived.

There was no other way to describe what prowled into the clearing—Linday had gotten the title right. Not because the man was made of shadows, so much as he was cloaked by them. Eaten alive by darkness.

The man, the *monster* towered before Merik, his features impossible to distinguish. What little of his skin was exposed—hands, neck, face—moved like a thousand eels skippering upstream.

Against all Merik knew to be wise or safe, his eyes closed and his arms shot up to block his face. He rocked back two steps, almost tripping over Linday.

The shadow man laughed at that. A sound so deep that Merik could scarcely hear it. He felt the thunder rumble in his lungs, though. Felt the man say, "I respect your attempt at stopping me, Vizer, but alarms and guards are useless now. Give me what I've come for, or everyone here dies. Your guards. This friend of yours. And you."

A whimper split the darkness, forcing Merik to lower his arms. To open his eyes and look at the shadow man, snaking closer. A creature with all the power in the room.

All the power in the world.

Merik made himself watch. Made his mind think, his muscles move, and his own power awaken. It was strangely weak. Strangely cold—a tendril of frost laced with darkness, as if the shadow man had stolen all heat in the room.

"Where is it, Vizer?" The monster's voice rippled and scraped. Scales rubbing against the sand. "We had a deal."

"I c-couldn't find it." Linday's teeth chattered, louder than his words. "I-I looked."

The shadow man laughed again before kneeling beside the vizer—and leaving Merik all but forgotten. Clearly he saw Merik as no threat.

Well, then, that was his mistake.

Immediately, Merik drew more magic to him, backing away as he did so. The wind was still frozen and off, yet it rose all the same. A subtle breeze to curl around him. To build. To expand while the shadow man reached for Linday's throat. It was an almost loving gesture, were it not for the death hissing between his fingers.

"This was your last chance, Vizer. Now we will be forced to enact the final plan. Your doing, Vizer. *Your* doing."

A root punched up from the earth and drove straight into the shadow man's chest. Linday's magic.

A scream—human and beastly, living and dead—tore

through the greenhouse. Unlike the spoken words, this sound was real. A physical thing, like icy winds, that smashed apart Merik's skull and flayed the flesh from his cheeks.

Merik had just enough time to lock eyes with Linday before the shadow man's fist squeezed.

He crushed the vizer's neck as easily as a grape. Darkness splattered from Linday's throat. Blood and shadows sprayed from his mouth. Burst from his eyes, and Merik knew, in that primal part of his spine he should have listened to before, that he stood no chance here.

With the little power he'd managed to grasp, Merik sprang backward. Ice carried him. Cold guided him. Winter *rushed* through him, both soothing and terrifying.

Branches cracked; leaves slapped; bell after bell rang out. The shadow man pursued, but he was hurt from Linday's root. Merik had a head start.

Merik reached a door. Not the one he'd come in, but an exit all the same that spit him into another part of the outer garden. Night air coursed over him, freeing. Empowering. And *finally* his witchery, hot and familiar, could truly unfurl.

He flew. Fast and high, winds bellowing beneath him. Yet just as Merik reached the peak of his flight, just as he relaxed his guard and risked looking back, the wall of shadows reached him.

Black erupted over him, frozen. Blinding. Like the explosion on the *Jana* but cold and darkness that erupted from the inside out. Too much power, too much anger, too much ice.

Then Merik's magic winked out. He fell. Spinning and choked by death. Until at last he hit something with such force it seemed to snap his bones. To snap his mind.

Yet even then, Merik didn't stop falling. He simply moved more slowly, sinking.

Water, he thought as his lungs bubbled full of it. Then he was too deep to know anything else beyond drowning and darkness and Noden's watery court.

FIFTEEN

You've been avoiding me, said a voice made of glass shards and nightmares.

Iseult was in the Dreaming again. That cusp between sleep and waking. A claustrophobic place where her mind detached from her body. Where she could do nothing but listen to the Puppeteer.

Esme was her name. Iseult had learned that in the last—and only—dream invasion since the night before the attacks in Lejna. Esme had plucked Iseult's location right from Iseult's mind, and then used that information to cleave, to kill.

Iseult had been completely helpless to stop it.

Admit it, Esme said, *you've been staying away from me on purpose.* Iseult didn't try to argue. She *had* been avoiding Esme. With every piece of her mind and her body, Iseult had been avoiding the other witch.

Which meant Iseult had scarcely slept in the last two weeks. It was the only way she could guarantee escape from the Dreaming. The only way she could *guarantee* the Puppeteer's nightly assaults did not occur.

Dreamless bursts of fitful sleep, plus a mind and body too

exerted to properly close down—those were the factors needed to evade Esme. But well fed and unafraid, it would seem, were not.

Don't do this. Iseult's dream-voice crackled out, a distant, fuzzy thing that seemed to echo inside the Puppeteer's skull.

Iseult sounded meek. Whimpering. She hated it, yet she couldn't seem to stop it—no more than she could stop Esme from raiding. She picked through Iseult's mind, like a rat atop the trash heap. *Don't read my thoughts tonight, Esme. Not now. Not ever.*

The girl seemed to tense up—a heated sensation that locked up Iseult's muscles in return. *I can't help it,* she defended. *I'm not trying to read your thoughts. They're just floating on the surface. Like that dead fish you saw this morning. And yes, I can see the fish and the cold stream and the Cleaved in the clearing. I can see that you abandoned the Cleaved, as well. Why, Iseult? They were there to help you.*

They were trying to kill me, Esme.

A jolt of horror flared through Esme—then across whatever magic she used to haunt Iseult's dreams. *No! I would never hurt you, Iseult. I sent them as friends.*

Now it was Iseult's turn for surprise. *I . . . don't understand.*

A pause. Esme was clearly debating how to reply. Then with a rush of warmth over their bond, she declared, *They had gifts for you, Iseult. One was a hunter whose gear I thought you could use. The others were soldiers. To protect you.*

Nausea spun up Iseult's sleeping throat. *I-I couldn't . . .* Iseult broke off. Goddess save her, she was stammering. She didn't even know she could do that in the Dreaming. *I . . .*

couldn't . . . tell, she forced out, *that they wanted to help. The Cleaved acted like they would kill me.*

But instead you killed them. A splash of flames from the Puppeteer. You led them onto a Nomatsi road and killed my Cleaved.

Iseult's nausea pitched faster. She hadn't killed those men . . . had she? They were Cleaved—already marked for death.

No, Esme said, her displeasure fanning into hot rage. *They were men I cleaved for you, since you foolishly intend to cross the Contested Lands. No one crosses the Contested Lands alone and survives, Iseult. But then you led my Cleaved astray, and they died.*

Iseult's lungs clenched tight. She didn't want Esme to know about the Bloodwitch; she didn't want Esme to know about *anything.* So she turned to the distraction of simple arithmetic. She could run through numbers on the surface, but inside her thoughts could run their course.

Multiplying. Iseult liked multiplying. *Nine times three is twenty-seven. Nine times eight . . . seventy-two.*

Iseult was too slow. Esme saw exactly what she'd tried to hide.

Threadless. The girl's surprise speared through Iseult. Such pure shock, Iseult could almost see turquoise Threads tinting the Dreaming.

Why is the Bloodwitch with you? Esme sounded frantic now. Her panic set Iseult's breath to choking off. *You don't understand, Iseult—he is dangerous!*

I know, Iseult squeezed out. *I need his magic, though. I need him to find my Threadsister.*

No, Esme cried. *I will help you, Iseult. I will help you! He isn't bound to the world as the rest of us are—you see it, don't you? He has no Threads!*

I . . . see it. Iseult could offer no other answer, for now shock of her own was winding through her dream-self. *You see that too?*

Of course I see it! And it means Weaverwitches like us cannot control him. It means he is dangerous, Iseult! You must run fast and run far! Wake up before he kills you in your sleep!

For the first time ever, though, Iseult didn't want to wake. She didn't want to be thrust out of the Dreaming. *What does it mean, Esme? Tell me. Please.*

Later, Iseult. Once he's gone. Please, I'm begging you—please, WAKE UP.

Iseult woke up.

Safi had never been more tired. Her knee ached where Lev had kicked it out. Her healing foot ached all the more.

The Hell-Bards had marched all night, a single lantern to light their way. The only breaks had been spent squatting in the woods while Lev kept her crossbow fixed on Safi's head.

The stars had risen while they trekked ever onward into a changing landscape. The jungle's canopy gave way to steamy marshes speckled by bursts of trees or lucent marble ruins that cut across the sky. Yet despite the openness of the swamps, Safi preferred the jungle. Here, the ground itself was lumpy, unstable. Grasses as tall as her waist razored and scraped at Safi's legs, while dark peat suddenly gave way beneath her, sucking Safi down.

She didn't complain. Not once. Even when the Hell-Bards asked how she felt, she squeezed out, "Fine," each time.

She wasn't fine, though. The throb in her knee compounded with each step. The linen-bound ropes at her wrists burned deeper, yet she wouldn't say a single rutting word about it. She wouldn't give the Hell-Bards the satisfaction of thinking they had won.

Vaness took the same approach. She never spoke. She never reacted, despite her heavy collar. Despite the mosquitoes that feasted on her more than anyone else. Despite the fat hives that welled up across her arms and legs from each bite.

Safi almost wept at the arrival of dawn, when the jungle took hold once more, and as soon as they reached signs of humanity, she found her chest truly expanding. Her eyes stinging with tears.

She no longer wanted to escape. She simply wanted to *stop*.

They were at a cluster of huts beside a sluggish river, over which a wood-slatted bridge stretched. Beyond, a full city waited, surrounded by marble ruins stained brown with jagged edges and cooking fire smoke reaching for the sunrise.

Safi wanted to enter that city. The Hell-Bards wanted to enter that city. The empress of Marstok, however, did not. She dug her heels into the dark road and barked, "You cannot take me there."

Her gaze swung back to the commander, even as Zander tried to yank her along. "That's Baedyed territory, and I will die if I enter."

A flick of the commander's wrist told Zander to stop

hauling the empress onward, and everyone paused at the boundary between nature and civilization.

"How do you know it's the Baedyeds in there?" The commander's voice was strained, drawing Safi's eyes to his shoulder. Yet if he felt any pain, his posture betrayed nothing.

Vaness glowered at a banner hanging atop the ruin walls. Green with a golden crescent—almost identical to the Marstoki naval standard . . . yet *not*. "The serpent around the moon," Vaness explained, "is the emblem of the Baedyed Pirates."

"Well," the commander mused aloud, "that's the only way I know into the Pirate Republic of Saldonica, so that's the way we will be taking."

"They will kill me on sight." Vaness's words, her face—they exuded panic and terror. Yet the truth grated against Safi's magic, prickling gooseflesh down her muddied arms.

The empress was lying.

Instantly, Safi was alert. The exhaustion, the burning muscles, the thirst all scurried away in a great upward rush of interest. The empress saw something, some chance for escape, and Safi tried to think back to all the lectures she'd endured on the warship. There *had* been something about the Baedyeds, hadn't there?

Hell-gates claim her. Mathew had been right all these years—Safi *should* have learned to listen better.

With a long inhale, Safi warped her face more deeply into exhaustion. She might not know what game was up, but she could still play along.

"Why should Baedyeds want you dead?" Lev asked.

"Because a century ago my ancestors were at war with

their ancestors. When the Baedyeds lost, they were forced to join the Marstoki Empire. Some of the rebels never stopped the fight, and they formed what are now the Baedyed Pirates. Ever since, those Pirates have had a kill order on my family."

For several long breaths, Caden's attention flicked from Vaness to the bridge to his Hell-Bards. Vaness, bridge, Hell-Bards. Then he sighed. "Gods thrice-damn me," he muttered at last. "I hate politics."

"Yet," Vaness said, standing taller, "that will not change the fact that the Baedyeds want me dead."

Lie, lie, lie.

"Nor," the commander shot back, "will it change the fact that this is the only entrance. The Red Sails are to the north, and they will kill us *all* on sight. Or they'll sell us to the arena, in which case we'll still die, just in a more painful manner."

"There is another entrance, sir." Zander's soft rumble was almost lost to the jungle's endless song. "It's a bigger bridge. More traffic. Easier to enter Baedyed territory unseen."

"That won't be enough," Vaness insisted. She puffed out her chest, tossing a wide-eyed look to each Hell-Bard. Pleading, scared, and absolutely false. "I am worth more to you alive than dead."

"You aren't the first person to say that." The commander breathed those words with such weariness that despite everything inside her, a flash of pity ignited in Safi's belly.

Until she recalled the meaning behind his words. He referred to *heretics*. Heretics he'd killed.

"But for once," Lev offered hesitantly, "it's actually true. She *is* worth more to us alive than dead."

"Fine. Fine. Good enough." A sigh from the commander.

"We'll take your way into the Republic, Zander, and then we can *finally* get on our ship and leave this place far behind. Lev, give the empress your helmet." Caden pivoted toward Safi, yanking off his own steel helm. "I will give mine to the heretic."

Caden plunked it over Safi's head before she could recoil. Heat, darkness, and the stink of metal and sweat crashed over her. Yet she didn't argue or protest, even as her vision was cut in half, even as the world took on a ringing, echoing quality. And even as Caden shoved her into a hard pace through the jungle.

None of that mattered, for Vaness seemed to have a winning taro card up her imperial sleeve, and when she played it, Safi had to make sure she was ready.

SIXTEEN

Vivia did not appreciate being awoken before the sun began its ascent.

Especially not by Serrit Linday.

It didn't help that her skull was pounding—or that her rib cage felt carved out and hollow. Three hours of broken sleep had done nothing to dull the darkness that had closed her day.

First, Vivia had gone to Pin's Keep to find her office in tatters. No one knew why. No one knew how. Stix had been there, they all said, yet no one had seen the first mate in hours.

So Vivia had waited for Stix. Well past midnight she'd stayed in her office, first cleaning, then checking records. Then simply staring out the window. But the first mate had never shown, so Vivia had shuffled back to the palace alone.

Each step had been worse than the last, for Vivia could guess exactly where Stix was. No doubt, the first mate had found someone to warm her bed. Yet again. And no doubt, that person was beautiful and charming and buoyant in a way that Vivia never could be.

Now, here Vivia was, tired and aching and following Serrit Linday through his family's greenhouse with twelve Royal Forces soldiers tromping behind. Magnolias shivered in the corner of her vision, so bright. So out of season.

The power of a Plantwitch, she thought, and fast on its heels came a second: *Why does Serrit have to be so selfish? We could use this space to grow food—we could use his magic too.*

Yet for all the lushness here, there was also no missing the damage. Entire hedges were smashed, and flowerbeds trampled to mush. Nothing at all like the last time Vivia had visited. Ages ago, it seemed, though it had really been only five years.

Serrit had confessed feelings Vivia knew he didn't have. She had seen in her own father just how men wielded lies and marriage to win power. Her friendship with Serrit had dissolved from there.

Vivia forced away that memory, squaring her shoulders and smoothing her captain's coat. Two paces ahead, Linday's feet limped unevenly over the gravel pathway that led to the greenhouse's center.

He glanced over his shoulder, fretting with the high neck of his robe as he did so. "I deeply appreciate you looking into this, Your Highness." Nothing in his tone sounded grateful, and he was being unusually whiny. "The princess herself coming here. What an honor."

Princess. Vivia felt the barbs on *that* word. A reminder that she was still not queen, for of course Linday and the rest of the Council wouldn't permit her to claim her rightful title.

She let frustration flash across her face. "Of course, my lord. I would do no less for any of my vizers."

"Oh?" Linday's eyebrows lifted. Warped, though, as if the muscles of his face wouldn't follow orders. A trick of the light, no doubt. "I thought perhaps you came because of your men's . . ." He lowered his voice. "Your men's *ineptitude*. For is it not their failures that have left this man called the Fury still out there?"

Ah, he was baiting her—and the soldiers behind too, for they certainly heard him. So Vivia ignored him.

Moments later, after rounding a bellflower, its violet flowers in full bloom, the greenhouse's central courtyard opened up before them. The fountain spat halfheartedly, its spout bent in half.

At its base was a dead man.

"There. Look at that." Linday pointed emphatically, as if Vivia couldn't see the mutilated body. His voice was abnormally high-pitched as he went on: "Look at what the Fury *did* to me!"

"You mean," Vivia countered, "what he did to *your guard*." She flipped up her hand, and the soldiers settled into a perfect waiting row. Then Vivia approached the corpse.

He was scarcely human now, with shadows crawling across his skin. "Vizer," Vivia began, smothering the bile in her throat, "why don't you tell me what happened here." She knelt.

Lines of darkness spread over the man's body, thin as a spider's web in some places and clotted together in others. His extremities had turned into shiny, charred chunks. Blackened fingers—only nine of them, Vivia noted absently—a blackened face, and a blackened, hairless scalp.

Behind her, his hands wringing with enthusiasm, Linday relayed how a scarred man had attacked while he tended the

176

garden. "A habit for those nights when I cannot sleep, as I'm sure you can understand."

"Hmmm," Vivia replied, listening about as closely as she listened to her father. She couldn't help it. There was something *alive* about the marks. When her gaze unfocused, they seemed to move. To pulse in a way that was sickly fascinating and viscerally familiar.

"Cleaved," Vivia murmured at last—although that wasn't *quite* it.

"Pardon?" Linday scurried in closer, his limp more pronounced, fidgeting with his robe's collar as if it wouldn't go high enough.

Vivia pushed upright. "Did the attacker—"

"The Fury," Linday cut in.

"—hurt you?" She waved to Linday's left leg, which he was favoring, and pretended not to have heard his use of the label *the Fury*. Naming the criminal after a saint, particularly in front of her troops, would only give the man power.

"The Fury did hurt me." Linday rolled back his sleeve to show blackened slashes down his inner forearm. "There's another like it on my leg."

Vivia's eyes widened. "What caused that? Magic?"

"Oh, certainly he was a witch. A corrupted Windwitch. Powerful."

Vivia's brow knit. A Windwitch did narrow down the pool of potential murderers—particularly since it would allow her to look at a registry. "Did he have a Witchmark?"

"I didn't notice. It was lost in all the scarring. *Scars*," Linday emphasized, "like those." He looked meaningfully at the dead body.

"So . . . you think the attacker was cleaved."

"It is a possibility."

Except that it isn't, Vivia thought. While cleaving would indeed explain why this corpse looked the way it did, it would *not* explain how the man posing as the Fury could hold conversations. Nor how he could live this long. Once the corruption began, it combusted a person's witchery in mere minutes.

"Did the attacker tell you why he came?" Vivia scooted a bit closer to Linday. Though holy hell-waters, was he always this sweaty? "Or did he make any demands?"

"He *did* make a demand," Linday oozed. "But forgive me, Your Highness, for you won't like what I have to say."

This was going to be good.

"The Fury said I must find the missing Origin Well."

Vivia stiffened. "Missing . . . Origin Well? I didn't realize one had been lost."

For several breaths, Linday held Vivia's gaze as if he didn't believe her. Then at last, he smiled lopsidedly. "And here I had so *hoped* you might know what the Fury was referring to, for he said if I did not find this Well, then he would kill me."

"Why exactly does this man think you can find it?"

A bob of Linday's crooked shoulder. "I cannot say, Your Highness. Perhaps I misheard. It *was* the middle of the night."

And it still is, you fool. But Vivia was intrigued. A missing Well. A man called the Fury. A body half cleaved . . .

"Vizer," she offered eventually, her tone bored, "would it be possible to get something to drink? I'm parched, yet I wish to continue examining this corpse."

Linday opened his arms. "Of course, Your Highness."

178

While he shuffled past the soldiers, squawking for someone to "bring her highness some refreshment," Vivia made her move and squatted roughly beside the dead man.

Spiders of all sizes scuttled across the grass. They were hidden within the blades if you weren't looking, but Vivia *was* looking.

Not just spiders either. Smaller mites and beetles too. They scuttled toward Vivia, then past, as if fleeing something in the greenhouse, deep in all the jungle-thick foliage.

It was just like what she'd encountered underground.

After a hiss for her men to wait where they were, Vivia followed the line of insects around a cherry tree. Then a plum. Moths—an ungodly number of them—took flight with each brush of her hip against the branches until at last she reached the source of the escaping insects.

A trapdoor. Wood, square, and stamped into the grass behind a massive frill of ferns. The wood was cracked at a corner, and from it crawled a trail of ants. A spindly harvest-man too.

Vivia's lips rolled together. This trapdoor looked strikingly like the one in her mother's garden. She cocked her head, waiting for Linday to leave the greenhouse entirely. Three heartbeats later, the sound of his screeching faded away.

Vivia heaved up the trapdoor. No protest from the hinges. *Well-oiled and oft-used.* More spiders crawled free, and she found herself staring into a black hole with a rope ladder dangling down.

She had no lantern, but she didn't need one. The smell of the damp air, the charge in her chest—they told her what was below.

179

The underground. *Her* underground, beneath the Cisterns and calling to her, *Come, Little Fox, come*, humming into her heels, her hands.

The ancient lake was that way. Blocked by hundreds of feet of limestone and darkness and tunnel, perhaps, but it was down there all the same. Dread unspooled in Vivia's veins. Jana had always insisted the lake remain secret. No one could know of it. Ever.

Yet somehow, Linday had discovered the underground passages leading to it. The question that remained was if he had found the underground lake too.

Then a new thought hit. *The missing Origin Well.* It couldn't be the lake . . . could it? Origin Wells were said to be the sources of magic—and Nubrevna already *had* one in the south. A dead Well, but there all the same.

Had Vivia's soldiers not been waiting nearby—if Linday hadn't been likely to return at any moment—Vivia would have scrambled down the hole immediately. She needed to know where it led. She needed to know how much Linday knew about the underground, and why he even cared in the first place.

Yet Vivia's men *were* here, and Linday too. Not to mention, the fifth-hour chimes were riding in on a honeysuckle breeze. This was the hour at which she normally awoke.

So with the sickening realization that this would have to wait, Vivia shouted for her men to begin clearing out the dead guard. Then she followed, once more, the ants and the spiders and the centipedes. Away from the trapdoor. Away from whatever frightened them underground.

*

Merik did not drown.

He should have, but somehow, the water—stark and cold—carried him ashore. He awoke with his back on a low lip of the Hawk's Way canal. He awoke to Cam's voice.

"Oh, come on, sir." She was shaking him. He wished she'd stop. "*Please*, wake up, sir."

"I'm . . . up," he gritted out. His eyelids shivered wide. Cam's dappled face swam into view, a gray dawn sky behind.

"Thank you, Noden," she breathed. And finally, *finally* she stopped shaking him. "You really should be dead, sir, but you've the blessing of Lady Baile on your side."

"That," Merik croaked, his throat more wasted and sore than it had been in days, "or the Hagfishes think I taste bad."

She laughed, but it was a taut sound. False. Then her words blurted out, too fast to stop. "I was so worried, sir! It's been hours since we went to Pin's Keep. I thought you were dead!"

Shame spun in Merik's chest, while she helped him to rise. "It's all right, boy. I'm all right."

"But I saw you go upstairs, sir, and I waited . . . and waited—just like you told me to do. But then that white-haired first mate went up, and I thought for sure you were in trouble. Except nothing happened. The woman came back down, and . . . you didn't." Cam thumped her stomach. "My gut was sayin' you were in trouble, but by the time I got up there, you were gone—are you sure you're not hurt?"

"I'm fine," Merik repeated, pulling his hood into place. "Just soaked through." It was true; he was drenched all the way to his small clothes. And cold—he was cold too.

"Why did I just fish you from the Timetz, then? Where'd

181

you go, sir?" She fixed him with an expression that was a cross between a glare and plea. As if she desperately wanted to be annoyed with her admiral but just couldn't quite bring herself to it.

"I'll explain once we're back at the tenement."

"Hye, Admiral," she murmured.

Merik's shoulders tensed for his ears. It felt like a lifetime since anyone had called him that. He didn't miss it.

Motioning for Cam to release him—he could walk on his own—Merik set off for the stone steps leading out of the canal. He owed the girl an apology. But not, he thought, an explanation. Stacia Sotar and the Fury, a shadow man with frozen winds, a dead vizer in the greenhouse—it wasn't a story easily relayed like one of Cam's melodic tales.

Besides, the less she knew, the safer she'd be.

As he walked, Cam scurrying behind, he re-created the greenhouse in his mind. He re-created the shadow man.

That creature had killed Vizer Linday as easily as Merik might crush a spider. If Merik hadn't fled when he did, he would have been next.

He hated that fact more than anything else, but there it was: he could not face that monster alone. He could not fight that dark magic, could not stop that *wrongness* alone. Yet his city, his people . . . They needed Merik to do something.

So what was left, then, beyond staying the current course? Only with an entire contingent of trained witches and soldiers could Merik possibly hope to face that shadow man. To gain an army such as that, he would need to gain the throne—or at least to keep Vivia off of it.

It was sunrise by the time Merik and Cam made it into

Old Town. The first beams of pink morning light glittered on puddles left from the night's storm. Water splashed up from Cam's steps, and Merik realized, his earlier shame doubling, that Cam was barefoot. She had been for weeks, and not once had she complained.

He'd noticed, of course, but there'd been so many other things to worry over. *Not an excuse.* Frowning, he fidgeted with his hood before ducking into the tenement. The halls were more crowded now, people off the streets seeking shelter for the night, and as he knew she would, always, always, Cam scampered just behind.

Upon reaching Kullen's low door, Merik kicked all thoughts aside and focused on tapping out the lock-spell. His knuckles hurt more than he cared to consider, and his fingers were pruned from all that time in the canal.

"Oh, sir!" Cam scooted in close. "You're bleeding again."

"Hye." Merik sighed. So tired. Stix's ice had shredded his right forearm, and who knew what injuries the escape from shadow man had opened up? He felt nothing, though. It was all old blood.

"I have an Earthwitch healer salve, sir. I got it at Pin's Keep."

Merik swiveled wearily toward the girl, with words of gratitude rising to his lips.

Cam misread him. Her mismatched hands shot up. "I didn't steal it, sir! My friends at Pin's Keep gave it to me!"

"Oh . . . I . . . thank you," he said at last, and he meant it. Though he hated that her first reaction was defensive—had he truly scolded her so much over the last two weeks that this was her first reaction?

183

After shoving into Kullen's apartment and hissing for the lanterns to ignite, Merik shuffled to the sagging table. The bread from yesterday had soaked up the water, and though by no means *soft*, now it was at least edible.

He bit off a chunk before removing the wet map from his belt and smoothing it across the table. Then he forced himself to say, "I'm sorry if I worried you, Cam. As you can see, I'm fine."

"You're alive," she accepted grudgingly, "but I wouldn't say you're fine. Water?" Her shadow stretched over the map, and a clay cup appeared before Merik.

"Thank you." He took it, only to glimpse Cam's wrist, puffy with fresh bruises. A cut stretched down her inner forearm. "What happened?"

"S'nothing, sir." She sidled away, and before Merik could follow, her shadow returned. This time, with a ceramic jar. "The salve, sir. For your face . . . and everywhere else too."

"You first." He pushed to his feet.

She thrust out her jaw. "I *said* it's nothing, sir. Just got cornered by the wrong sort near Pin's Keep. You, meanwhile, were only Noden knows where getting your face pummeled by only Noden knows *who*, so that you could then leap into a canal and almost drown. I reckon if anyone's owed a story here, it's me."

Merik hesitated, his fists tightening. Knuckles cracking. "Who cornered you?"

"You first," she countered.

Merik made the mistake of meeting Cam's eyes, where there was no missing the sharp stubbornness that burned

184

within—one he knew well from a different friend. A different lifetime.

Merik sighed and plunked himself into his chair. "Sit," he ordered. Cam sat. Merik downed the water she'd brought in two gulps and finally said, "What happened, Cam, was that I got caught because I'm a blighted fool. But Stix . . . that is to say, First Mate Sotar let me go once she realized I was the Fury."

Cam shivered and hugged her arms to her chest. The bruises were hidden in that position. "But you're not really the Fury, sir. If anything, you're a ghost who should be dead a hundred times over."

"The Hagfishes can have me," Merik murmured, staring into the empty cup, "if they'll release Kullen or Safiya or . . . any number of souls better than me."

"You might feel that way," Cam murmured, "but no one else does."

Merik knocked at the table, at the map—anything to change the subject. "I found this on my sister's desk at Pin's Keep."

"The Cisterns." Cam's tone was matter-of-fact, and if she noticed Merik's discomfort, there was no sign of it. Instead, she leaned over to tap the X. "What's this, though?"

"I was hoping you might know. Didn't you say you once used the Cisterns to travel the city?"

"Hye." Her face scrunched up, lips puckering to one side. "I dunno *that* place precisely, but I know vaguely where it is. This here"—she pointed to a wide tunnel that ran half the length of the map—"runs below White Street. We call it *Shite Street* 'cos it's where all the city's sewage collects."

185

"And these times?" Merik circled his finger around the list.

Instantly flags of scarlet raced up Cam's cheeks, splotching across the paler marks. "I know my numbers, sir, but I can't read them."

"Ah." Merik was struck by an embarrassed blush of his own. Of course most of his crew couldn't read. He'd forgotten it was a luxury he'd earned by simply being born into the right family.

"Well, there are six times listed," he said, "starting at half past the tenth chime and moving up in increments of half an hour."

"Oh hye, sir." A relieved smile. "That must be when the floods rush through. The tunnels bring water down from the river, see? Most of it goes into the city for plumbing and all that, but some goes down to Shite Street. It rushes through, picks up the sewage, and then flushes it back out again.

"It's cleaned in a big reservoir below the Southern Wharf, and then dumped back into the river south of the city. The floods run often on Shite Street, as you might guess, which is another reason people avoid it. But *maybe*," she said, drawling out the word, "there's a meeting going on. It happens all the time in other tunnels. The gangs are always gatherin' or fightin' or tradin' in any passages that the Royal Forces never enter."

"So my sister must be meeting someone at half past twelve." Merik smiled, if tiredly. "Well done, boy."

A visible gulp slid down Cam's long throat. She hastily ripped off another chunk of bread. "Breakfast?"

"Hmmm." Merik accepted a piece, before saying, "Now it's your turn, Cam. Tell me what happened."

"S'just one of the Skulks gangs." She chomped on the bread. Crumbs stuck to her lips, and through a full mouth she added, "I didn't know they'd expanded their territory, and I walked where I shouldn't've been walking. So, I went back to Pin's Keep, and they patched me up. Gave me that salve to use."

Merik tried to nod calmly—tried to hide the sudden fire now chasing through his veins. "What gang was it, Cam?"

"One you wouldn't know." More bread, more chewing, more stubborn resistance.

So Merik stopped pressing. For now. "They know you well at Pin's Keep?"

"Sure." She bounced a shoulder. "I used to visit before I enlisted, sir. When the streets or the Cisterns got too dangerous to sleep in ... Well, Pin's Keep is where I always ended up."

At those words, *the Cisterns got too dangerous to sleep in,* the heat in Merik's blood pumped hotter. "You ... slept in the Cisterns?"

Cam shrugged helplessly. "Hye, sir. It's shelter, ain't it? And you can live down there once you know the flood cycles."

"How many people live there?"

Hesitantly, as if realizing Merik wasn't going to bring up the gang again, Cam relaxed. Her posture regained its usual slouch while she tore into more bread. "Thousands, maybe?"

"Everyone knows this, don't they? I'm the one fool who doesn't." Merik folded his arms over his chest, leaning back. The wood creaked a protest. "Noden's breath," he said to the ceiling. "I know nothing about this city."

"You didn't grow up here, sir. I did."

187

So did Vivia. She'd grown up with the sailors and the soldiers. With the High Council and King Serafin. It gave her an advantage. One of many.

As a boy, Merik had thought he was the lucky one—living wild on the Nihar estate with Kullen at his side. Hunting and fishing and traipsing through forests half dead. While that had earned him loyalty and love in the south, here in Lovats, Merik was no one.

He could change that, though. He would make his amends. Be what the people needed him to be.

With a renewed sense of strength, Merik leaned over the map. "Can you get me to Shite Street, boy?"

"For this meeting, sir? Absolutely. But only so long as I can stay with you—because you *know*," she lifted her voice before Merik could argue, "that if I'd been allowed to join you at Pin's Keep, I could've whistled a warning before that first mate ever got upstairs."

"Then *you* would have been the one facing her Waterwitchery."

"A *Waterwitch*?" Cam's eyes bulged. "A full Waterwitch—not just a Tidewitch . . ." She trailed off as a yawn took hold. With her jaw stretched long and eyes squinting shut, she looked just like a sleepy puppy.

Merik's anger returned in an instant. He motioned stiffly to the bed. "Sleep, Cam." The command came out gruffer than he intended. "We'll brave Shite Street once the sun's a bit higher."

Cam's lips parted. She clearly wanted to obey—to sleep—but her blighted loyalty wouldn't let her abandon him so easily. "What about you, sir?" she asked, right on cue.

188

"I'll sleep too. Eventually."

Now came a cautious smile, and Merik tried not to smile back. Cam had that effect, though. A world of darkness, but she could still make a room glow.

In moments, the girl had curled onto the bed and was fast asleep. Merik waited until her chest swelled and sank with slumber before rising, quietly as he could, and tiptoeing for the door. He had two tasks to accomplish before he was allowed to sleep.

First, Merik had a pair of boots to find, though he had no idea where he might do so at this hour.

And second—the task that really mattered, the one that sent Merik hopping two steps at a time down the tenement stairs—he had a gang to find. One that lurked near Pin's Keep. One that thought preying on the weak was an acceptable way to live.

Why do you hold a razor in one hand?

"So men remember," Merik murmured as he stepped into the wet morning, "that I am as sharp as any edge."

And why do you hold broken glass in the other?

"So men remember that I am always watching." With that final utterance, Merik yanked his hood low and set off for the Skulks.

SEVENTEEN

The Pirate Republic of Saldonica was unlike anything Safi had ever seen. Oh, she'd heard stories of the vast city built into ancient ruins, with its factions constantly at war, their territories shifting and morphing. And she'd heard tell of the famed slave arena, where warriors and witches battled for coin—and where the rivalry between Baedyeds and Red Sails was deemed moot in favor of violence and wagers.

Safi had also heard how a person of any color or background or nation could not only exist in Saldonica but also could be bought or sold or traded. Then there were the legends of crocodiles lurking in the brackish waterways. Of sea foxes bigger than boats in the bay that would tow down men and ships alike.

Yet Safi had always thought those tales nothing more than bedtime stories for an unruly six-year-old *who didn't* want to *go to sleep yet, Habim, and couldn't he just tell her one more story about the pirates?*

Except it was real. All of it.

Well, maybe not the sea foxes. Safi knew—firsthand—that those creatures existed, but she had yet to see the Saldonican Bay, so she couldn't confirm if they resided there.

An hour of travel through the steamy foliage had spit the Hell-Bards, Safi, and Vaness onto a second road. Churned up and grooved down the center from hooves and wagons, it was at present packed with hooves and wagons ready to churn it up all the more. Everyone trundled northeast, and only three people gave Safi or Vaness a second look. Actual *help* or any real interest, though, the people seemed unwilling to spare.

Safi couldn't blame them. She *wanted* to blame them, but the truth was that she understood why others might keep their eyes on their own business. Zander alone, with his massive size, would have been enough to send a person running. Lev and Caden only added to the image of *People Best Left Alone*.

Besides, not everyone was selfless like Merik Nihar. Not *everyone* was a crazy Windwitch who would fly into fights, heedless of his own safety—or his own buttons.

Before long, the trees opened up to reveal a bridge. Here, the riverbank was scarcely higher than the lazy brown waters running beside it, and one good rain would submerge the wide bridge.

Crocodiles seemed to realize this, for the beasts lumbered and lounged on either side of the warped planks. Gods below, it was a lot of teeth. Caden didn't need to prod Safi to walk a bit faster.

At last, as the ninth chimes clinked on the breeze, the Hell-Bards led Safi and Vaness to a wide gate in an ancient, crooked wall. Dangling overtop was a massive standard, and this close, there was no missing the serpent looped around the Marstoki crescent moon.

Traffic bottlenecked, more people moving into the Pirate

191

Republic than shoved out. Until at last, Safi was inside—and found the Baedyed claim of Saldonica was *nice*. Shockingly so. Safi had imagined a slum of lawlessness and desperation, but instead there were roads and rainwater chutes, Fire-witched streetlights and gold-uniformed guards to direct traffic. There were even banners hanging from every lamp-post.

Yes, the buildings tumbled more tightly together as they progressed deeper into the lowlands. And yes, there were more people crammed here than most cities, yet nonetheless, the Baedyed-controlled part of Saldonica was undeniably *not* a slum.

Beyond the built-up streets of the Baedyed territory, a marshy delta spanned. On the left, thick, black jungle hugged the swampy landscape. On the right, the soggy earth gave way to a murky bay. Docks spanned for as far as Safi could see, crammed with ship after ship after ship.

It was as if every boat in Veñaza City had docked in one harbor. Never had Safi seen so many furled sails. Or circling sea gulls.

Cursed birds.

Yet what really drew Safi's eyes was the arena. There was no mistaking it. As soon as her helm-split gaze cast over the half-stone, half-wooden stadium, she knew what it was. The sheer size gave it away—larger and taller than any other structure in the entire Republic.

At this distance, though, it looked like some enormous ancient fortress that nature had tried to reclaim. Wooden scaffolding had been added, to fill in the missing half, and banners of all colors flapped from eight towers, giving it the look of a dirty bejeweled crown left behind for the crocodiles to enjoy.

Safi soon lost sight of the arena, of the marshes. Of anything at all but the people around her. Everywhere Safi's eyes landed, she saw people of all shades and histories. Even Nomatsis strutted cool as they pleased down the packed-earth Baedyed streets—as did Southlanders, Fareasters, and ethnicities Safi couldn't even recognize.

Atop the merchant calls and sailor shouts and *all* the sounds bombarding her, there were just as many lies—startling after so many days at sea and in the wilderness.

Quickly enough, though, as always happened, the truths and the lies blended into a familiar cascade in the background. One easily ignored, easily forgotten, even as the Hell-Bards led Safi and Vaness into an open market.

Here, billowy awnings traipsed outward for almost as far as the eye could see.

"Anything a man desires can be bought in Saldonica."

Safi twisted her stiff neck, glancing at Caden through the slits in her helm. He was pale, his face slick in a way that spoke of more than simple sweat from a summer's day. His wound wasn't doing well—and *that* made Safi happy.

He met her eyes with a slight bounce of his eyebrows. "And anything a man loathes can be sold here as well."

"Is that a threat?"

"I don't loathe you, Heretic. I simply follow orders—*shit*." In a burst of speed, he shoved ahead of Safi, but since he still held her ropes, she was jerked around. Her shoulders almost tore from their sockets.

Pain flashed. A scream split her lips. Then she was

dragging her feet, trying to keep up with Caden as he barreled forward.

He was too slow to stop it, though. The empress had fallen, knocked over by a passing cart. Not just any cart either, but one led by three men with the Baedyed standard on their gambesons.

Worse, Vaness's helmet had fallen, leaving her reddened, sweat-slick face exposed to the world. To the three Baedyeds. She ducked, as if to hide her features, but the way she moved *just* a beat too slow—and the way she angled her body *just* far enough for the pirates to see her Witchmark tattoo—rang false against Safi's senses.

Vaness wanted to be seen; she'd staged the entire accident, and now it was working. One of the Baedyeds was staring at her face, another at her hand, and the third was slipping away as if he had urgent business to attend elsewhere.

Urgent business that would get Safi and Vaness free from the Hell-Bards or urgent business that included *killing* the Marstoki empress, Safi couldn't be sure. And there was no time to mull it over either, for Lev was forging a path down a narrow string of stalls, Zander was lifting the unresisting, rehelmeted empress, and Caden was prodding Safi forward into a breakneck pace behind them all.

The first inn the Hell-Bards approached was full. As was the next one, and the next three after that. It would seem there was an important holiday in two days, and thousands upon thousands had swarmed the city for an arena fight that happened every year. *Baile's Slaughter*, they called it, and now the

Pirate Republic of Saldonica was crammed full and bursting at the caulked seams.

Safi took note of that information for later use—just as she tried to record how the Baedyed territory was laid out and how soldiers roamed, clearly on the lookout for the Hell-Bards. For Vaness. Yet with his height, Zander always saw them coming. He'd lift one hand, and the Hell-Bards would break off onto a side street, Vaness and Safi in tow.

The sixth inn was an old tower repurposed into something livable, each level a different style of stone and wood and shutters. There, the Hell-Bards found a space to hole up, though for how long they planned to stay, Safi had no hint.

The room they rented was small and four stories up. Scarcely tall enough for Zander to walk through without crooking his head sideways. Not that it mattered, for as soon as the Hell-Bards led Safi and Vaness inside, the giant departed.

Two against two. Better odds, but still not great. Especially since Safi was dust from the inside out, and since Vaness immediately curled up for sleep on one side of the lone bed.

It wasn't the fatigue in Safi's limbs or lungs that hurt most. Nor even the blisters that had torn open on her heels and toes and ankles. Even the aches in her knee and foot were mostly ignorable.

But the rope-shredded skin beneath the linens, the way Safi could *feel* every fraying fiber still stuck in her flesh . . . Each step had sloughed off more skin and spread the wounds higher, higher up her arms and legs.

Safi waited, silent, while Caden eased the helmet from her

head and the room's full scope came into view: a single bed with a tan wool coverlet and a low stool beside it. A table and washbasin against the opposite wall, with what looked like a Waterwitched tap. Two oil lamp sconces above, and finally a window, without glass but with the shutter slats wide enough to let in the day's breeze and sounds of revelry.

Nothing in the room was useful. At least not that Safi could spot through the exhaustion. There was, however, one interesting piece in the room, and that was a sign above the door that read ALWAYS, ALWAYS STAY THE NIGHT.

Safi had no idea what it meant.

As she stood there, a gentle pressure at her wrists drew her attention back to Caden. He was sawing off her ropes, and against her greatest wish, tears gathered in her eyes. Not from relief or gratitude, but from pain. A burst of it that clattered through her bones. "These need cleaning," Caden said, and although there was no command in his tone, Lev immediately hopped to.

She left the room. *Better odds.*

"Sit," Caden ordered, and Safi stumbled to the free side of the bed. It brought her closer to Vaness than she'd been since their capture. Hell-flames and demon-fire, the empress looked awful. Her shredded feet, her muddied legs and arms, and that colossal collar still locked around her neck.

Dizzy, Safi sank onto the bed's edge; the empress didn't stir, and it took all of Safi's energy to keep her eyes open until Lev finally returned with soap and fresh linen strips.

Then Zander returned too. With food—*real* food and *real* bread and *real* water to wash it all down. The smell seemed to rouse Vaness, and though the fish was too rubbery and so spicy it made Safi's tongue shriek, she didn't care. Neither did the empress. They wolfed down the meal, and then before Safi could even try to speak to the empress about, well, anything at all, Vaness was back on her side and asleep once more.

Meanwhile, Lev and Zander scampered off again, and Caden dragged the stool between the bed and the door. Then he removed his armor. Piece by piece. Layer by layer. Gauntlets, brigandine, chain mail, gambeson, and finally his boots. Each item he placed meticulously in a pile beside the washbasin.

The Hell-Bard commander shrank and shrank until he was half his former size and down to nothing more than his underclothes. Then even the undershirt was peeled off and added to the massive pile of gear, revealing someone Safi couldn't recognize.

Caden was not a Hell-Bard now. *That* person had been grim and terrifying and quick to attack. Nor was he the Chiseled Cheater, who was sly, charming, quick to quip.

This Caden was lean and scarred and muscled. He was duty, he was darkness, he was ... *heartbreak*. Yes, something about Caden seemed hollow. Lost.

Similar to someone else Safi knew. Her uncle.

With the full washbasin at his feet, Caden soaked a cloth, then scrubbed and hissed and scrubbed some more at the wound on his shoulder. All his blades remained sheathed but within easy reach. So though his pale chest was bared and his face screwed up with pain, Safi didn't doubt for one moment that he could kill her.

Lions versus wolves, after all.

197

What would Iseult do? Safi thought numbly. *Not get caught, for one.* But Iseult would also learn as much as she could. Food might have made Safi more tired, but surely she could conjure something useful from this foggy mind.

She cleared her throat. It hurt, and her next words tasted of black pepper. "What happened to you, Hell-Bard?"

"I was injured." Caden's chest shuddered as he dabbed at the bloodied gash on his shoulder. It looked deep, and there wasn't much depth on his frame to begin with. Ropy muscles were wrapped tightly to the bone.

It brought to mind a different chest on a different man. The first physical characteristic, really, that she'd seen of Merik as he flew through the air of a Veñaza City wharf.

Safi frowned, shaking away thoughts of the past. Of Merik's bare chest. Those memories wouldn't help her here.

"How did you get injured, Hell-Bard?"

"A blade."

"Oh?" Safi's tone was sharp now. The Hell-Bard commander was as good at dodging questions as she was at lobbing them. "And whose blade would that be?"

"My enemy's." For several long minutes, the only sounds were the splash of water when he dunked his bloodied cloth. The *drip-drip-drip* when he wrung it out. The huffing exhales when he cleaned a wound in need of more than just water to heal.

It turned out, Caden had more than just water. He pulled a clay jar from his pile of filthy gear, yet rather than apply it to his own wound, he soaked a fresh strip of cloth in the basin and crossed the room to Safi.

She refused to cower. Even when he trudged in close

198

enough to grab her. She simply thrust out her chin and braced her spine.

He looked, as he always did, unimpressed. *Or Unempressed*, she thought, doubting he would appreciate the joke any more than Vaness had.

"I know you think I enjoy this, but I don't." He dropped to his knees. "And I know you think that stubbornly ignoring pain is some kind of victory. But it isn't. Trust me. It will only injure you more in the long run. Now, let me see your feet."

Safi didn't move. She couldn't take her eyes off the glistening gash running beneath his collarbone. Red webbed out, a sign rot would soon be setting in. Yet that wasn't what surprised her—it was the scarring below that wound. And above it too, and all across his chest and arms. Jagged streaks, no whiter than his already pallid skin, yet raised and vicious. They covered every inch of Caden's body, identical to the ones on Lev's face.

"Your feet," Caden repeated.

Still, Safi remained frozen, her gaze trapped by the worst scar, at his throat. Just above the gold chain, identical to a chain Uncle Eron wore, this mark was as thick as Safi's thumb and circled all the way around Caden's neck.

"Good enough," Caden said at last. "If you don't want me to tend your wounds, I won't. The empress needs tending too."

"Yes." The word slipped out. Safi gulped, forcing her eyes away from the Hell-Bard's scars. "I do want them cleaned."

"Smart." He bowed his head, an almost gracious movement. *Almost.* "You know, I've been where you are, Heretic. All Hell-Bards have."

199

"Then let me go."

"So you can run away? Henrick wouldn't like that." Then slowly, as if he didn't want to frighten her, Caden reached for her ankles.

Safi almost fainted from the pain. A punch of heat and light. The world swam. She crumpled in on herself.

She wasn't stupid, though. She let the Hell-Bard clean her ankles because Caden was right that her stubbornness had served no purpose. It had only hurt her in the end. Though goat tits, it bruised her pride to admit that. Even to herself.

"Why did you run from the Truce Summit?" Caden asked as he dabbed at her wounds.

"Why," Safi hissed through the pain, "not? Would you want to marry an old toad who would use you for your magic?"

A chuckle from Caden, though if he smiled along with that sound, Safi missed it. "If you marry him, you could help Cartorra. You could help Hasstrel."

"They don't need me." She barely got the words through her clenched teeth. Caden had moved from her ankles to her soles, and somehow, they were worse. "Why do you even care about Hasstrel?"

"I grew up nearby."

"Then you should know how awful the Orhin Mountains are—and how small-minded its people. They love living under Emperor Henrick's yoke."

"And *you* should know how callow that sounds." A hardness laced Caden's words now. The first flare of anything close to emotion. *Good to know.* Yet none of his frustration affected his methodical washing of Safi's feet. "Cartorra has its flaws, Heretic, but it also has safety. Food too, as well as wealth, roads, education. I could keep going, for the list is long. Give me your wrists."

Safi did, her eyes screwing shut at that first slash of contact. Pain came. Pain receded. "But," she forced herself to say, clinging to the conversation, "you won't find freedom on your list, will you?"

"There are degrees of freedom. Complete freedom isn't always good, nor is the lack of it always bad."

"Easy for you to say when you're not the one being held against your will."

Again, the laugh, and Caden's eyes—bloodshot, thoughtful—lifted to hers. "You really have no idea, do you?"

"About what?"

But he had already moved on. "There are degrees of everything, Heretic, which I know doesn't fit well into your *true-or-false* view of the world."

"That's not how my magic works." *Not entirely.*

"Then tell me," he said.

Safi pinched her lips together, hesitating. She'd spent so long hiding her magic from the world. From the very man now kneeling before her ... Though she supposed there was no point in hiding her power now. Not when the emperor and the Hell-Bards had already won.

"Everyone lies," she finally said.

"I don't." He popped the cork from the healer salve, and with a clean linen, he scooped some out.

The instant it touched her wrists, the pain receded. Cold fizzed in.

"Of course you lie," she argued, eyes closing to savor the cool relief. "I told you, Hell-Bard. *Everyone* lies. It's in the way

201

we banter with our friends. It's in the mundane greetings we give passersby. It's in the most meaningless things we do every single moment of every single day. Hundreds upon thousands of tiny, inconsequential lies."

Caden's careful application paused. "And do you sense them all?"

She nodded, eyelids lifting just enough for her to meet his unflappable gaze. "It's like living beside the ocean. The waves eventually fade into nothing because you're so used to it. You stop hearing each crash, each swell . . . Until, one day, when a storm comes along. The big lies—I feel those. But the little ones? They ride away on the tide."

He offered no reaction, his face utterly still as if he was thinking through each sentence. Each word. Each pause. Yet before he could offer a response, a double knock came at the door.

"S'me, sir," Lev called.

Caden pushed to his feet, the duty and the focus instantly returning to the slant of his shoulders. He handed Safi the jar and the salve-covered linen before stepping to the door.

Lev strode in. "Zander and I finished checking the bath-house behind the inn, sir. It's safe for me to take the ladies for washing up." She swung a thumb toward the window. "Then you and Zander can set the wards and look for the ship while we're out."

"Good enough." Caden swooped up his undershirt and shrugged it on. "I'll help you escort the women down . . . what?"

Lev had her eyebrows high. "I was just thinking that . . . that maybe you and Zander could manage a bath today too?"

"I just washed off."

"Not well enough, you didn't. And *we're* the ones who gotta suffer through your stench."

It was too good for Safi to resist. "She means to say you smell like the inside of dead dog's bum."

"Noted," Caden declared at the same time Lev exclaimed, "Why, listen to that mountain accent. You sound worse than he does!"

A flush roared up Safi's cheeks. *Shit clogging up the storm drain.* It had been so long since she had spoken Cartorran. The Orhin accent must have crept onto her words, and now Caden was smiling while he fastened his sword belt to his waist. A real smile, like the Chiseled Cheater she'd met over a card game. Sly, private . . .

And reminding Safi that he was the enemy. That *he* was the reason her life had turned to ash. She couldn't let herself forget that. These people were her opponents, and escape was all that mattered.

EIGHTEEN

Iseult awoke to find her left hand completely numb. She'd slept in miserable spurts ever since her encounter with Esme, but the last spurt had melted into several awkwardly posed hours with her arm pinned beneath her hip.

She shifted her weight, using her right hand to move her left . . . and then to heft her body around. Gauzy pink light filtered into the mossy overhang that she and the Bloodwitch had shared. The air was moist with yesterday's rain, but warm, and Aeduan's soft, steady breaths puffed mere paces away.

Heat flashed in her chest. How could the Bloodwitch be sleeping? He should have woken Iseult so she could keep watch.

You traveled two weeks without anyone to stand guard, her conscience nagged.

Yes, she argued with herself as she massaged feeling back into her arm, *but I don't have to do that anymore.* She could use every resource available now, and the Bloodwitch was exactly that: a resource. A tool.

A gift.

Iseult shuddered, recalling Esme's words. The Puppeteer had killed those men to "help" Iseult, and not for the first time, Iseult wished she had someone to help her fight Esme.

Goddess, she would take anything at this point—surely someone out there knew about the Dreaming and Puppeteer-controlled Cleaved.

Weaverwitches like us, Esme had said—and Iseult rubbed her numb arm all the harder. She was not like Esme. She was *not* like Esme.

Stasis, she commanded herself. *Stasis in your fingers and in your toes.*

Once her arm felt human again, Iseult scooted out into the dawn, relieved she had a task to keep her occupied. After checking that her cutlass was strapped on and her salamander cloak—or rather, *Aeduan's* salamander cloak—was fastened tight, she slipped between the nearest groaning pines. While she walked, she clutched at her Threadstone.

I'm coming, Safi. For several breaths, while she gripped the ruby tight, the frost that lived in Iseult's shoulders melted. Crumbled beneath a wave of something warm. Something that expanded in her stomach and pressed against her lungs . . . *Hope,* she realized eventually. Faith that she and Safi would be reunited.

On Iseult's next footstep, a silver taler clinked against her knuckles, bound to the same leather cord as the Threadstone. Aeduan had poked a hole in the stained silver as easily as if it were paper, and the double-headed eagle was now warm against Iseult's fingertips. Her hand fell away. She walked faster, her footsteps squishing on the damp earth.

By the time she returned to the mossy overhang with a

rabbit from her snare, the Bloodwitch was awake and sitting cross-legged on the rock. His eyes were closed, his hands resting on his knees as he meditated.

Iseult had read about the practice in her book on the Carawen Monastery. The silence and the stillness allowed a monk to separate his mind from his body.

Iseult had tried it once, but with absolutely no success. She already fought so hard to separate herself from her emotions—if she got rid of her thoughts too, what would be left?

When Aeduan gave no indication he'd noticed Iseult's return, she slipped quietly into the overhang. She shrugged free of the salamander cloak and rolled up her sleeves, ready to start skinning the rabbit.

"No time."

Iseult flinched. She hadn't heard the Bloodwitch approach—yet unlike what *he* did when caught unawares, Iseult went very still. The bruise at her throat, just above the collarbone, was all the warning she needed to never startle him again.

When Aeduan had said he would kill her in Lejna, she hadn't believed him. When he'd said he would kill her last night, she had.

"It's easier to skin the rabbit while it's fresh—"

"It can wait a few hours." His Dalmotti was hoarse with sleep.

"The meat will spoil."

"Then you will catch another," he countered. "We need to get as far as we can before the heat of the day grows too intense."

"Why?" Iseult asked, but the Bloodwitch ignored her, and

in less than a minute, he had cleared the campsite. Everything was gathered, folded, and tucked neatly into Iseult's satchel. Then he swung it onto his back, ready to set out.

Iseult simply observed. He moved so fast. So efficiently, his witchery clearly propelling him to a speed and grace no man could match.

She itched to know how it worked. Itched to ask him how it felt when such power took hold—and if it was true that his magic was bound to the Void. Instead, though, she said nothing at all.

They hiked for hours, Aeduan always there, paces behind. He refused to walk in front, clearly expecting Iseult to stab him in the back. Or perhaps this was a test to see how much she trusted him.

Either way, Iseult went along with it. For now.

The Bloodwitch used single, hard words to guide her. One moment, they would be tromping through a mucky floodplain, and the next, he would order her to veer right and clamber back out.

"Due east," he would abruptly say. Or, "More south." Iseult never knew if the Bloodwitch changed his course because Safi had changed hers, or if Safi's scent came . . . and went . . . and then disappeared again, leaving Aeduan to follow as best could. He certainly stopped every few minutes to close his eyes and sniff the air.

Then, when his eyelids would lift, his irises would burn crimson for a breath. Perhaps two.

After half a day of ruddy bark and dark needles brushing past, the pines grew smaller, giving way to hardwood saplings. Oaks took hold, silver trunked and surrounded by ferns and white asphodel. The Amonra River, wide and dark, churned nearby.

Iseult knew from the map tucked in her satchel, as well as from her lessons with Mathew and Habim, that soon, the forest would give way entirely. The land would drop into a misty gorge filled with thick underbrush and thicker chimney-stack stones. The river would drop too at the towering Amonra Falls.

Here, the Marstoks had faced off against the Nubrevnans twenty years before. Here, fire had chased families from their homes, and Nubrevna had ultimately lost. One more nation to add to the list.

Before Nubrevna, it had been Dalmotti. Before Dalmotti, it had been Marstok. For centuries, this peninsula had changed hands, and for centuries, no one had ever fully won—or ever fully lost.

Beside Iseult, the Bloodwitch inhaled audibly, his eyes swirling red. "We have two choices," he said eventually, "either we descend beside the Amonra Falls, which is the safer route into the gorge. Or we travel northeast through the forests—and before you say 'Falls,' know that the path is slower."

"How far is Safi?" Iseult asked, squinting in the direction of the gorge. Birds circled above.

"Far."

"Can you be more specific?"

"No."

Iseult's nostrils flared. *Stasis.* "How do I know you are even taking me in the right direction, then?"

"How do I know that you possess the rest of my coins?"

He had a point—and they'd already established their inevitable betrayals. "How dangerous is 'dangerous'?"

"Very."

Iseult couldn't help it now. She sighed.

No change in Aeduan's expression, though he did say, "There is a settlement nearby. I can get you a horse. It will allow us to travel longer before you tire."

"How near?" Iseult could get herself a horse.

"An hour north at my fastest pace. I would return by late afternoon."

"And I . . . simply wait?" At Aeduan's nod, it took Iseult two stabilizing breaths before she felt able to continue. "And the hours lost are worth getting a steed?"

"Your friend is that direction." He pointed southeast into the Contested Lands. "She is many, many leagues away—and many, many days. A horse will help."

His argument made sense, as loathe as Iseult was to admit it. *Use every resource available.* Still, the thought of waiting several hours . . .

The Bloodwitch took Iseult's silence as an agreement. He extended his arm. "Return my cloak. Monks get better deals when bartering."

Iseult could hardly refuse. It belonged to him, after all. Yet she found herself resisting, moving extra slowly as she slipped it off her shoulders. Air washed over her, cool and exposing.

She swallowed, watching the Bloodwitch flip the white side outward and shrug it on with practiced ease.

"I'll be back soon," he said gruffly, already turning away. Already sniffing and tensing. "Stay out of sight until then.

There are worse things in the Contested Lands than Blood-witches."

A horse wouldn't save much time. Not in the overgrowth of the Contested Lands. While Aeduan certainly intended to find a steed for the Threadwitch if he could, it wasn't his main purpose for veering off alone.

Aeduan had caught a whiff of clear lakes and frozen winter. The blood-scent that had haunted him since Leopold's betrayal. The scent of whoever it was who had partnered with Leopold to stop Aeduan. The scent that had lingered where Aeduan had hidden his coins, the scent he could only assume belonged to the talers' thief.

How those coins had ended up in the Threadwitch's possession—that was just one more answer he would wring from this person's throat. And he would not be as generous with this person as he had been with Leopold at the Origin Well in Nubrevna.

Best of all, if Aeduan could find out who this ghost was and where he'd placed his coins, then Aeduan wouldn't need the Threadwitch anymore. He could leave her to rot in the woods and leave Corlant to rot in his compound.

That thought spurred Aeduan faster. The trees were thin, the ferns low. All of it easily navigated. The world blended around him. Green and granite and bark, shrouded in endless mist.

Soon he would have answers.

After painstakingly tracking the Truthwitch, who was hundreds of leagues outside Aeduan's magical range, this new hunt took no power at all. He used the extra magic to *fuel* his sprint faster.

Until, as it always seemed to be, Aeduan lost the smell. Between one bounding step and the next, it simply vanished. No frozen winters. No clear lake waters.

Aeduan slung to a stop, hissing, "Not again, not again," under his breath. *Every time*, this was what happened. *Every time*, Aeduan would get so close, only to lose the scent entirely.

As Aeduan stood there, one foot on a bed of pine needles and the other on a gnarling cypress root, he closed his eyes. He turned his mind and his witchery inward. Breath by careful breath passed. The forest awoke around him, trickling into its usual routine. A wary thing at first, with hesitant skylarks. A cautious pine marten.

If he could quiet his mind and still his body, then his witchery could rise to its maximum height.

At least that was the plan until a throaty cackle sounded to his left.

Aeduan's eyelids snapped up. His gaze connected with a rook's, whose black eyes and gray beak were perfectly still. Its scruffy feathers ruffled on the breeze. It didn't flee, didn't move. It simply considered Aeduan head-on.

Which made the hair on Aeduan's neck rise. He'd never seen a rook on its own. They usually flew in great swarms outside the forest.

Aeduan sniffed. From fish to fowl, all animals bore the same wild surface scent: *freedom*. Atop that scent rested . . . *forest fog*.

He coughed, a harsh burst of air that rattled through the

clearing. The rook blinked. Aeduan repeated his cough, and this time the rook took the hint. It hopped into flight, carrying its freedom and its fog away from Aeduan's as fast as its wings could go.

Except now a new blood coiled into Aeduan's nose. His witchery jerked to life. *Blood. Magic. Hundreds of people.* So many scents mingled together. All ages. All types. All of it straight ahead.

Pirates, no doubt. But which faction? And why this far inland? Both the Red Sails with their vast fleets, and the Baedyeds with their stealthier seafire attacks, kept their invasions close to shore.

Yet both slaughtered, both enslaved. Like war and rainstorms, there was no escaping the dominance men asserted on each other. There was, however, attempting to sneak past it, which was why Aeduan skulked onward. It was simple self-preservation. He needed to know whom he and the Threadwitch might encounter in the Contested Lands. He needed to know which route these pirates might be taking out of the valley beyond.

Especially if the Red Sails were involved.

So after reversing his Carawen cloak just as the Threadwitch had, he hurried around pines and saplings before finally clambering up a massive goshorn oak. There, he hunkered onto a branch to watch who passed the mud-trampled earth below.

It was not the Red Sails that came clipping into view. The advance rider wore drab clothes, but his auburn mare was strapped with a distinctly Baedyed saddle, a tasseled cloth style from their native Sand Sea.

212

After the first scout, two more Baedyeds on horseback ambled by. Then came foot soldiers—something Aeduan hadn't known the Baedyeds possessed within their ranks. Yet here they marched, man after man after woman in a long single-file line. Small steps, but strong. Sabers clanking at their hips.

And more than a few witches in their midst; Aeduan smelled storms and stones, fires and floods.

Aeduan sniffed harder at the air, just in case. But no, the clear waters and frozen winters were lost again. He should have known by now that hunting that ghost would never lead him true. A futile errand, every time. A distraction.

While Aeduan toyed with the idea of divesting one of these beautiful steeds from his Baedyed rider, he caught sight of twenty men on horseback clomping into the line. No order to their steps, no organization to their cluster. They had whips, and their horses bore open sores on flank and limb.

Red Sails.

Instantly, Aeduan's hackles rose. Though no man wanted his village or tribe hit by pirates, at least the Baedyeds followed a moral code. The Red Sails, Aeduan knew firsthand, did not.

What left Aeduan frowning—what sent him straining forward to gain a better view—was why these two factions were traveling together. They were enemies, constantly at war for more territory, more slaves, more coins. Yet here was an entire contingent of them marching as one.

An answer came moments later, for right as the Red Sails ambled below Aeduan's spying branch, a Baedyed trotted back to meet them.

"Where are the rest of your men?" The Baedyed spoke to the foulest Red Sail of them all.

Of all the wickedness below, this man delighted the most in the horror. It was there, in the furrows of his blood-scent. *Broken knuckles and torn-off fingernails.*

This man's blood marked him as a monster; his red saddle marked him as the leader.

"We caught wind of our bounty," the man said with complete disdain and disinterest.

Whatever alliance was happening here, it was not a strong one.

"Hell-fires scorch you," the Baedyed spat. His mare stamped anxiously. "We must reach the Purist compound by tomorrow. Do you expect us to wait?"

"If they do not rejoin us soon, then yes."

The Baedyed swore again, this time in a language Aeduan didn't recognize. But as he reined his horse back around, he spat, "The king will hear of this. I promise."

"And I promise he will not care."

Right after the Baedyed had cantered back toward the front of the marching line, another Red Sail appeared on horseback. *Burned hair and smoking flesh. Autumn pyres and mercy screams.*

A Firewitch. Aeduan's skin prickled. Fire . . . unsettled him.

The leader spotted the Firewitch too. "You are late," he called. "Go help the others. They are almost to the Falls, I want this Threadwitch caught today."

Threadwitch. Falls. The words solidified in Aeduan's mind, and a heartbeat later, he was moving. Scrabbling silently back across his branch.

Until something spooked within the leaves—a dark bird with enormous wings. The rook took flight, squawking into the sky.

The Firewitch looked up. His eyes met Aeduan's through a gap in the leaves. He smiled. He clapped. The goshorn oak caught fire.

From one moment to the next, the tree ignited, and within seconds, every inch of it crackled and popped and blazed. If Aeduan hadn't worn his salamander cloak, he'd have erupted too.

He *did* have his cloak, though, and he managed to leap to the ground. There, he fastened his fire-flap across his mouth, fingers shaking.

Run, my child, run.

He glanced back. A mistake, for the Firewitch approached, hands rising—and the flames building in response. All around Aeduan they licked and spat. A conflagration to bring him down.

Aeduan couldn't fight this. He could barely think, barely see, much less try to kill the Firewitch before the flames won. Already his legs trembled. Already it was too much like that morning all those years ago.

Without another thought or another glance at the Firewitch, Aeduan reeled about and ran.

NINETEEN

At the sound of the tenth chimes, Merik awoke to Cam tromping about the tenement in her new boots. Merik had placed them by the bed for her before crawling onto the other side and collapsing into a deep sleep of his own.

The girl moved like a newborn colt, stiff and jerky with her stride strangely long as she counted each step.

"Have you never worn shoes before?" Merik asked, his voice grating like a blade on the whetstone. "Or are those too small?"

"*Forty-eight, forty-nine.*" Cam gave a floppy shrug. "Right size, I think. And I've worn shoes before, sir. When I was younger. Just never had much of a reason to keep 'em."

"So what's the reason today?"

"Are you fishing for a thank-you?" Cam made a face, her nose wrinkling up—and Merik found himself chuckling.

Which made his throat hurt. And his chest. *And* his face. But at least his laugh earned one of Cam's wildfire smiles.

"Thank you for the boots, sir." She swept a bow. "I am now ready for Shite Street."

"I'm not." Merik pushed himself upright, muscles and new

216

skin resisting. The salve had helped, but his sleep had been restless. Filled with dreams of Lejna storms and fallen buildings and Kullen begging, *Kill . . . me.*

Merik was grateful when Cam slipped into her usual storyteller role over breakfast. He was grateful, too, that she didn't seem to notice the fresh scabs across his knuckles—nor the fact that he had snuck off while she slept.

"Best entrance to the Cisterns," Cam explained through a mouthful of too-juicy plums, "is by the Northern Wharf." On she babbled, as she so loved to do, about the best routes through the underground. The safest tunnels. The gangs that competed for space.

Merik listened, noting—not for the first time—that she rarely told stories about herself. He'd heard endless tales of things she'd seen or of secondhand histories from someone else, yet never narratives from her own life.

The longer he stared at her bright-eyed face, the more the old nursery rhyme sang in his skull.

> *Fool brother Filip led blind brother Daret*
> *deep into the black cave.*
> *He knew that inside it, the Queen Crab resided,*
> *but that didn't scare him away.*

Merik couldn't recall how the rest of the song went, and so that one verse kept chanting again and again, in time to each chomp of his plum.

By the time he and Cam, both hooded as always, set off into the streets of Old Town, the eleventh chimes were tolling. Late-morning traffic folded them into its currents, and they traveled east, with Cam leading the way.

A languid fog hung over the streets. Last night's rain, rising as the sun burned hotter, brighter. Before Merik and Cam had even passed the final decrepit homes of Old Town, sweat seeped from Merik's skin.

Cam aimed right at a butcher's bloodied front stoop and then crossed two more busy thoroughfares. As always, she let her gut guide them, swirling back to pluck Merik from traffic whenever soldiers came too near.

Soon enough, they reached the busiest wharf in Lovats. Here, not a single patch of water was visible between the boats. Had Merik wanted, he could skip clear across the harbor, stepping from pram to frigate to skiff and eventually onto a cobbled, shop-lined street a quarter mile away.

It was precisely the sort of challenge he'd have loved as a boy. He and Kullen both.

Kill . . . me.

Cam beckoned Merik onward to a slant of steps underground. Once, it had been a market, where goods fresh off the river were sold—Merik remembered visiting in boyhood. Before Jana had passed. Before Vivia had transformed forever.

While some brave merchants still attempted to hawk their wares, Merik saw more homeless and hungry than anything else as he followed Cam into the shadows. Almost all sconces affixed to the damp flagstones were empty, candles long stolen or lanterns long smashed.

The racket from above softened, morphing into higher voices. Children's. Women's. Merik's eyes adjusted, and families materialized in the gloom. Water dripped from the curved ceiling to gather in puddles underfoot that splashed as Merik and Cam marched by.

Unacceptable. This tunnel, these families, this life that they were all resigned to. *Help is coming*, Merik wanted to say. *I'm working as fast as I can.*

"This way, sir." Cam veered right. Two old men playing taro separated just enough for her and Merik to weave through. Then the girl vanished into a slice of darkness where no fire's glow reached.

They walked through the darkness for fifty-six paces (Cam counted, as she always did) before a pale yellow glow sparked ahead. Another fifty-two paces, and they reached it: a lantern, Firewitched, illuminating a sharp right turn in the tunnel. Then more darkness—this time for a hundred and six steps, with water dripping the entire way.

At last, though, he sensed a shift in Cam's step. The girl was slowing with a rustle, like fingers brushing a wall, before she vanished.

Just disappeared.

One moment, Merik heard Cam's tired breaths and clomping bootfalls. The next, there was nothing but the plopping of water droplets.

So Merik did as Cam had, skimming the tunnel wall with his palm and proceeding onward . . .

Power frizzed over him.

It lasted a single breath, the temperature dropping low. The air sucking from his ears and lungs. Then he was through. The light returned, uneven but bright. A low brick tunnel stretched side to side, while sounds rolled into Merik from all directions—men's shouts and thumping feet.

And the roar of waters channeling through some distant tunnel every few moments.

Cam fiddled with her hood for a moment, towing it so low her face was completely hidden. "Should've warned you about the old ward-spells. They're meant to keep people out, I suppose, but clearly they ain't working so well anymore. Oh, but pardon me, sir. Where are my manners?" She opened her hands wide. "Welcome to my second home, sir. Welcome to the Cisterns."

It was nearing midday before Vivia had a chance to return to the underground. Time was short; she had much to do. *Check the lake, search the tunnels.* The words recited, a beat to jog by. Her lantern swooped and sputtered. *Check the lake, search the tunnels.*

She was sprinting by the time she reached the lake, and she gave no thought to her uniform as she tore off boots and coat, breeches and blouse. There was something wrong—she could *see* it rippling over the shimmering lake surface.

"Extinguish," she murmured. Then in she dove.

Too much water. That was the first thing she felt as she kicked beneath the surface. There was water she'd never met before, twisting and twining through the rivers and into the Cisterns. Vivia needed to find out why. She needed to find out from *where.*

While yesterday's tremor might not have left significant surface damage, Vivia feared the same could not be said for below.

She hit the lake's center, where the crystalline waters were cold enough to grip. Where the rocks were keen enough to cut. But only here could she wholly connect with what the lake wanted, with what the lake felt.

Deep, deep beneath its waters, where the plateau's roots fed into the Sirmayans and grew up from ages past, Vivia sensed new water dripping in. It wasn't from the recent storms but from the tremor, and it wasn't limited to the plateau but rather had wormed its way under the valley and into the mountains.

There, currents leaked up from a crack in the earth. A new spring, icy and fresh, it was adding volume to these tunnels and to the River Timetz as well—abovestream. Above the dam.

Up, up, the water moved like bees humming in a hive. Out, around, and under too. If it wasn't diverted soon, the dam would overflow. The city would flood. It would be a slow thing. Months, perhaps even years, in the making, for these new springs were small. Mere fractures in the rock. Yet if these fractures ever became rifts, if another quake rattled through the Stefin-Ekart valley, then the water might expand too quickly to counter. The city could flood in days.

Or worse, if the dam finally broke, it could flood in hours.

At that thought, Vivia's latest Battle Room argument with Linday echoed out: *Our people could be safe, even beyond Nubrevna's borders, if the need arose.*

No. Vivia couldn't do it. Binding Nubrevna to the Purists was not a solution.

Yet . . . Serrit Linday. Why did everything keep circling back to him? Since the crack had first appeared in the dam three years before, *he* was the one who had resisted fixing it.

221

Now *he* was the one treating with Purists, and *he* was the one with a door to the underground hidden in his greenhouse.

That door was what had brought Vivia here today. She intended to find it from the underground, and she suspected it was just on the other side of the cave-in.

By the time Vivia dragged herself from the lake, she was frozen to the bone. Her breaths were harsh as she shivered back into her clothes. Yet as she turned to snatch up her dark lantern, a quivering glow caught her eyes.

Like a cloud rolling across the moon, the nearest stretch of foxfire blinked out.

Three of the six glimmering spokes were now dead.

Whatever happens over, happens under too. Fast on that thought's tail came another: *The Fury said I must find the missing Origin Well.*

Vivia swayed. No, no—Linday couldn't be right. Except . . . each Well had six trees around it, and here instead were six stretches of burning foxfire. Each Well was also a source of magic, and Vivia couldn't deny the immense power thrumming through these waters.

Long ago, Vivia's tutors had taught her that the five Origin Wells chose the rulers of the Witchlands. It was somehow connected to the Twelve Paladins, and though she couldn't remember precisely *how*, she did recall that the Water Well in southern Nubrevna was what had kept her nation autonomous for so long, even in the face of three growing empires.

Perhaps, though, the history books had missed something. There was, after all, one Well not accounted for. One well for an element no one believed existed.

The Void Well.

Vivia wasn't a Voidwitch, though—nor had her mother been, nor her grandmother before that—so how could their family's power stem from here? It couldn't be an Origin Well. It *couldn't*.

But if it was ... Then she could heal her father. That was the ultimate power of the Origin Well. The power to cure any ailment. Why, she could bring him down here to test it. If he healed, then she'd know.

At that thought, the empty space behind Vivia's breast-bone filled. Clogged. Almost as if she didn't *want* to bring her father down here.

No regrets. Keep moving.

Vivia grabbed the lantern, snapping, "Ignite," and squinting into the sudden light. There were too many questions, not enough time. She would have to mull all these ideas, all these possibilities while she searched—for the under-city wouldn't find itself.

Nor would the over-city *save* itself.

Alone.

Iseult was alone again and wondering what could possibly be worse than Bloodwitches in the Contested Lands. Aeduan had left her beside an overgrown gully. It was decent terrain, in case anything unexpected arose. The sight lines were good; the cover was better, with fat mossy trunks and thick upthrusting slabs of dark granite.

After finding a flat crag to stretch out upon, Iseult dropped her gear and finally turned her attention to the rabbit she'd caught that morning. All day, it had flopped limply from the satchel on Aeduan's back, and each time Iseult had glanced at it, its dead eyes had stared right back.

She stretched the rabbit across the stone. Its body was stiff and cold, exactly as she'd told Aeduan it would be. She just hoped the meat hadn't spoiled.

Only one way to learn.

She rolled up her sleeves. Aeduan's coat was far too big, and the wool itched. But she felt safer with it on. It smelled like smoke and old sweat. Not a bad smell, just . . . there.

After she'd rinsed her hands from water in the canteen, she freed her cutlass. While the blade was excellent for cutting off the rabbit's feet at each joint, it was not good for the second step: a tiny incision across the rabbit's back.

So absorbed was Iseult in not cutting too deeply and puncturing an organ (thereby *guaranteeing* that the meat would spoil) that she didn't feel the Threads approaching until they were almost upon her.

In fact, if she'd waited two breaths longer before reaching out to sense the world's weave, she would not have noticed the men until it was too late. But thank the Moon Mother, her habit was stronger than her attention on the rabbit.

Six sets of Threads crept toward her, purple tinged with steel gray. A hunger for violence, a desire for pain—and close. Mere seconds away.

Iseult's mind blanked out. No time to react, no time to plan. The only option before her was flight, so Iseult gripped her cutlass and leaped into the gully, where the substrate was flat and the undergrowth sparse.

The Threads flared with pink excitement and green determination. They moved faster too, launching into sprints

224

behind her. But why, why, *why*? Who were they and why were they hunting her? Unlike the men Esme had sent, these hunters were definitely not Cleaved. Their Threads were whole and thoroughly focused on hurting Iseult if they caught her.

She kicked her knees higher. Time blurred, the forest streaked. All Iseult saw and all Iseult was, was the gully's mud floor and the placement of ferns. Of stones. Of anything at all that might slow her.

A man behind her roared something in a language she didn't know. The Threads flared hotter. Hungrier. A battle cry to cow enemies.

It certainly cowed Iseult. She almost tripped, but somehow her balance prevailed. She punched her heels faster and gripped her cutlass tighter.

Ahead. Trees ending. Sky opening up. The thoughts slashed through her brain, one after another. Unbidden and with no time to examine. No time to plan.

She reached the end of the forest. Her feet pounded onto exposed stone, where water sprayed up. It was the Amonra River, foamy with speed, black with cold. The sort of rapids that even a Waterwitch would avoid—and there was no crossing it.

Iseult veered right. The shore was brutal, rocks and logs and undercut riverbank. She looked back.

A mistake. The men were closer than she'd realized. Close enough for her to see pockmarks and scars and toothless smiles. To see binding Threads oozing between them—a sign they all followed the same command. A sign they were comrades working as one.

Iseult pushed herself harder, her breath coming in short

fog-choked gasps. The Amonra Falls hummed ahead. First, a mere tickle at the base of Iseult's spine. A mist to linger on the horizon. It grew louder with each step, expanding into a heavy rumble in Iseult's gut, a rain that coated everything in fat droplets.

Stasis, Iseult! Stasis in your fingers and in your toes! But she couldn't reclaim it. She couldn't slow, she couldn't plan. She was against a wall, and it was made of violent men and violent rapids.

This was a wall that Safi would hurdle in a heartbeat, though. No preparing. No worrying. Just action. If Safi were here, she wouldn't wait. She'd see opportunity and she'd take it.

Stupid as it might seem, Safi had once told Iseult, *stupid is also something they never see coming.*

Yes, Iseult had answered at the time, *and it's also why I always end up saving your skin.*

But hey! A sharp Safi grin. *At least there's a skin to save, Iz. Am I right?*

She was right. Moon Mother save her, but Safi was right. Stupid was sometimes the best.

And sometimes, stupid was all that remained.

Iseult tipped her head left as she ran, letting her gaze shoot ahead to where river pounded against the shore. No debris rushed on that choppy surface, for the power of these rapids was too much. The Amonra yanked sticks, leaves, and life down; it did not spit them back up.

Goddess, it would be stupid to go in that river. *So* stupid.

Act now. Consequences later. Initiate, complete.

It was time. The hunters were lurching out of the trees.

226

Iseult initiated. Iseult jumped. As the muddy bank fell away and damp air kissed her cheeks, shouts clamored from the forest. Threads collectively brightened with turquoise surprise, crimson rage. Then Iseult reached the peak of her arc and began to fall.

A single sharp thought hit her in that moment. It wasn't a tangible thought, it wasn't carved in words to score across her mind, but rather it was a *feeling* that brightened every piece of her as the black river closed in.

You've been here before, the feeling said. *And you know what to do.*

Her hands moved instinctively to her wool coat. A tug of stiff fingers against the collar, then Iseult's feet hit the waves. Cold, cold, cold, cold—and *ripping* her under. Punching all breath from her chest. Tearing all sight and sound and senses.

The Amonra dragged Iseult down.

As she sank below, she wrestled free from the coat. It unfurled above, a distraction as well as a shield to hide Iseult while she flew downstream in a world without breath. A world without control.

TWENTY

After bathing under Lev's watchful eye, Vaness and Safi were forced to don their filthy, torn clothes.

Lev shot them each an apologetic look at the bathhouse exit. "Zander went to find clothes for you," she said, then she took up position behind the women and sent them marching back to their fourth-floor room.

They found Zander waiting inside, his face turned down to his toes. "I got several gowns. I wasn't sure what ladies like you might want to wear."

Safi didn't need her magic to feel the honesty shivering off Zander's proclamation. Against her better judgment, she caught herself smiling. "Thank you, Hell-Bard."

Then she and Vaness were left alone, while Lev and Zander began a hushed conversation in the hall. Caden was nowhere to be seen.

"Two against two," Vaness murmured in Marstoki as she glided for the bed. "Had I not this collar on"—she jiggled it, the wood darkened with water—"then there would be no contest."

Safi, meanwhile, shot for the window. The shutters were

open, and while four stories was undoubtedly a long drop, hell-flaming goat tits, she was willing to try.

She reached the window. The Pirate Republic spanned before her, the arena thrusting up in the distance. She tried to dip her head through . . .

A burst of warmth and light lashed out. Safi's forehead hit solid air—and her heart surged into her throat. Magic. *Wards*, Safi realized, although what they protected against or *how* Hell-Bards could even do magic, Safi had no idea.

She tried again, and again, but her skull simply smacked an invisible wall each time. Light flashed, shimmering along the edges with golden dust.

"So *that* is what the wards do," Vaness said from her spot at the bed. "It is good to know."

Safi grunted, scowling, and finally turned away from the sunny seascape outside. At the bed, she made quick work of her ruined gown, stripping it off in one move. Vaness, of course, was undressing more patiently, carefully removing her dirty gown and folding it neatly on the bed.

Safi's heart panged. It was such an Iseult-like thing to do. Such a familiar balance of Safi charging ahead, heedless and hurried, while her companion lingered, contemplated, gathered her thoughts.

Safi wavered, fingers gripped tight around a hunter green gown while her free hand moved to the Threadstone. The leather thong it was looped on now rested damp against her collarbone. She pulled it out.

And horror shoveled through her. The stone was blinking. *Iseult.*

"What does it mean?" Vaness asked quietly.

"It means my family is in danger." Safi's voice sounded so far away. She swiveled about, trying to gauge in which direction the Threadstone would lead. In which direction Iseult might be. "Somewhere . . . that way." She faced northwest.

All exhaustion was gone now. Safi wanted to move. She wanted to run.

The empress seemed to understand, for she said in Marstoki—and with a false layer of nonchalance overtop— "I have a plan to get us out of here."

Safi blinked, rounding on Vaness. "Earlier. You lied about the Baedyeds wanting to kill you."

"I did." Vaness eased a mustard gown from the stack and draped it against her body, checking the length. "Just before the Truce Summit, I came to an agreement with the Baedyed Pirates. I will return much of the Sand Sea to them, and in return they will become an extension of the Marstoki navy. So you see, they are not my enemies at all but are in fact my allies."

Safi's magic purred, *True*. "So they will help us?"

It took Vaness three yanks to get the neck of her gown past the wooden collar, and by the time it was on, Lev had poked her head in the room. "All ready?"

"Almost," Vaness trilled. Then, in a hurried whisper from the side of her mouth, she added, "Be ready, Safi. For soon, the Baedyeds will come for us."

"Good." Safi couldn't resist a dark, triumphant grin while she tugged on her forest green dress. It was loose in the bodice and the skirt barely made it mid-calf, but she preferred it that way. There was room to move. Room to fight.

I'm coming, Iz.

The door whooshed wide, and Caden strode in. He aimed straight for Safi, eyes flying over her gown—and chin dipping ever so slightly in approval. He too was clean and freshly clothed. His armor, however, was absent. No chain mail or brigandine, no gauntlets or steel helm.

Yet a sword still hung at his waist, and his shoulder appeared leagues sturdier than it had an hour before.

"Heretic," he said, coming to a stop before Safi, "don your boots."

Safi arched a cool eyebrow. "Why, Hell-Bard?"

"Because you and I are taking a little trip, and there's a reason the locals say the streets of Saldonica are paved with shit."

Though Caden didn't tie up Safi, he did keep a dagger out, and he forced her to march directly before him. Within grabbing distance, should the need arise.

The need *wouldn't* arise, for Safi had no desire to bolt. Her Threadstone might have stopped flashing, but that didn't change her need for escape—and her odds of survival were much higher with an entire contingent of Baedyed Pirates coming to her aid than all alone on the streets of Saldonica.

Which were indeed layered in shit and trash, something she noticed as soon as they left behind the clean corners of the Baedyed territory.

"Where are we going?" Safi asked, her head dipped back so Caden could hear. They were once more in the open market, but there was no missing the Red Sails' scarlet banners flapping ahead. "I thought you said the Red Sails would kill us all."

"They will," Caden said, pitching his voice over the noises of the afternoon. "They've a vow to kill all Cartorrans on sight, which is why we won't be speaking in Cartorran—and why we won't be staying long."

Staying long where? Safi wanted to press. *And why bring me at all?* But she didn't get the chance, for they were approaching a massive archway, where men waited, armed with more blades than they had teeth.

The men watched Safi and Caden saunter past. Bad men. Wrong men. The shivers against her witchery told Safi all she needed to know. At least none made a move to follow Safi and Caden into the world of torpid swamp that was the Red Sails' territory.

The Baedyeds might have cleared the land and established a proper city on their claim of the peninsula, but the Red Sails had left the jungle to its own devices. Theirs was a world like Safi had imagined, a world like Habim had described. Dilapidated huts sank against massive roots or nestled beside vine-covered ruins. Haphazard. No organization. And almost all of it built on stilts, as if this soggy earth flooded during storms.

Rope bridges were slung between buildings, and as often as Safi saw laundry dangling from a crooked window she saw corpses hanging as well. Some were bloated, fresh; others were decomposed all the way to gleaming skull.

This was what complete freedom allowed. *This* was what men did in the absence of rules or an imperial yoke.

Cartorra has its flaws, Heretic, but it also has safety. Food too, as well as wealth, roads, education. I could keep going, for the list is long.

Curse the Hell-Bard, for there was no denying the truth in his words. They sang, deep in Safi's witchery, a soothing, golden pulse beneath the erratic scritch of wrong that surrounded her.

Caden guided Safi up a narrow street that cut between ruins and trees. Muffled music, conversation, and sounds heard only in a whorehouse preceded a blossom-shaped sign that squeaked on the marshy breeze: **THE GILDED ROSE**.

Caden towed Safi to a stop outside the clapboard building. "There's an admiral inside whom I need to . . . *interview*. And you, Heretic, will be there to ensure she remains truthful."

"Over my grandmother's rotting corpse." Safi snorted. "I will never let you use my magic, Hell-Bard."

"You have little choice." He wiggled his dagger. Sunlight bounced off the steel.

"Oh, but you can't force me." She batted her lashes, hooking her arms behind her back. "As I believe I've mentioned before, I can smile at even the ugliest toad, and not once will he sense a lie."

Now it was Caden's turn to snort. "Oh, Heretic, you don't even know it, do you?" He eased his knife into a hip scabbard. "It wasn't my Hell-Bard protection that gave you away in Veñaza City. It was *you*."

Safi stiffened. Then against her better judgment, she took the bait. "What do you mean?"

"I mean," he said, closing the space between them, "that you have a tell."

"I do not."

233

"Oh, yes, you do." He smiled now. A Chiseled Cheater smile that made Safi's gut boil. Made her heels bounce. "So no matter what this admiral might say to me, I'll know just by looking at you whether she speaks the truth or not. Now . . ." He placed his hands calmly on Safi's shoulders, then twirled her around to face the Gilded Rose's dilapidated door. "Let's go inside and get this over with before we join those corpses hanging out to dry."

TWENTY-ONE

I t's not right," Merik muttered as he and Cam journeyed deeper underground by the light of an old torch. Two damp levels below the Cisterns' entrance, and still the squatters showed no sign of thinning out—nor did the rats, whose eyes glowed. "A man needs to see the sky."

"Didn't expect you to be scared, sir." Cam flung a mischievous smile across her shoulder.

"I'm not scared." Merik glowered. "There's no wind here, boy. No air. I feel . . . suffocated."

"Well, we've barely left the surface, so get used to it. Shite Street is much lower—and much smellier."

The girl wasn't exaggerating, and after circling six levels deeper, a stench began gathering in the air. Even as the ceilings lifted higher and the passages spread wider, the smell was soon thick enough to choke and sharp enough to burn.

It sent Cam doubling over, coughing, gagging, and spraying torchlight in all directions. "Shit," she said, and Merik couldn't tell if the girl swore at the stench or simply named its source. Either way, he agreed.

Three turns later in the tunnel, they reached the infamous

Shite Street. Cam clapped a hand to her mouth, hefting the torch high. Light glistened over a lumpy expanse of bodily fluids (and bodily solids). There was also something oily and dark dripping from a crack between ceiling bricks.

Worse than the sight of it, though, was the *ploop! ploop!* that each droplet made in the pool—and the bubbles that gurgled to life right after.

"Can't you fly us across, sir?"

Merik considered this, breathing through the edge of his hood as he did so.

But then he shook his head. "I need to summon winds to fly us. And though I could try, there's just not enough air to carry us far."

"S'better to fly halfway than walk through *all* of it," Cam pointed out. "The tunnel is almost full, sir! That line"—she pointed to the opposite wall—"is as high as the sewage gets before the floods come through to clean it out. That's as deep as our knees, sir!"

Merik held his silence while he contemplated just how badly he wanted answers about his sister's enterprises in the Cisterns. Except ... it didn't matter what *he* wanted. The city's people needed his help.

Merik set his jaw. The X on the map was straight ahead, and so straight ahead he had to go.

"Did you hear me?" Cam demanded. "The sewage is almost to our cursed knees, sir! That means ..." Somehow, she managed to look even more sick. Her eyes screwed shut. "The floods'll rush through at any moment."

"Shit," Merik said, and *he* meant the swear. "Cam, I want you to wait nearby. In a safer tunnel."

She bristled. "I'm not leaving you. I know I'm moanin' a lot, but this is my fault, see? I said those times were the floods, but I was thinkin' it meant when they'd *end*—not arrive!"

"Don't blame yourself, boy." Urgency hardened Merik's tone. "I'm the one who thought it was a meeting time—and it might still be. But it isn't safe for you to go any farther."

"S'not safe for you either," she retorted. "And besides, if I don't go with you, you'll end up doing something stupid." She pushed out her chest. "You can't stop me, sir."

A tense pause. Cam looked so small in this light. So blighted obstinate too.

> Fool brother Filip led blind brother Daret
> deep into the black cave.
> He knew that inside it, the Queen Crab resided
> but that didn't scare him away.

"If you get hurt..." Merik began.

"Won't happen."

"...you'll ruin your new boots."

"Never did like shoes anyway."

"Fine," was all Merik said, and Cam's teeth flashed in a victorious grin. It marked the end of the argument, though Merik almost wished otherwise, for now there was nothing left to do but trek through human excrement.

Hell-waters claim him, he had never imagined that hiking through underground sewage would one day be his life. Of course, he also hadn't thought he'd be a dead man on the run from his own family.

When at last a wall came into view, when at last Cam exclaimed, "The meeting place is up those steps, sir," Merik almost whooped with relief. Here, a fork in the tunnel sent sewage splitting in two directions, and here a low archway was carved into the wall and lit by pale torchlight. Merik hauled himself onto a waist-high landing before helping Cam scramble from the clutches of Shite Street.

They were both disgusting, coated in muck that was too slimy for Merik to examine without gagging. Though both he and Cam stomped and tried to shake off the dung, it wasn't much use.

Soon, they crossed under the archway, with a hiss of magic to graze over them, just like when they'd entered the Cisterns.

It would seem, Merik realized, that the spells weren't simply to keep people out; they also were to keep the flood-waters *in*.

"Do people ever get caught in the floods?" he asked.

Cam shrugged one shoulder, finally towing back her hood, "Course they do, sir. Course they do." Then she jerked her head up the fire-lit stairs, and without waiting to see if Merik followed, she marched off.

Vivia was crossing through the plum trees of the palace gardens, having just changed into the fresh uniform she always kept tucked behind the blueberries, when a commotion caught her ear.

She slowed, turned back and found the king headed for the queen's garden. Guards and servants trailed behind, as well as two healers in standard brown.

Now *this* was odd. The king rarely left his rooms, and he never entered the queen's garden.

Never.

By the time Vivia had hurried to the ivy-strewn walls, each member of the entourage had taken a spot before the ivy-strewn walls. The king and his chair, pushed by Rat, had rolled inside.

Rat was just scuttling back outside the gate. He avoided Vivia's gaze while he popped a gruff bow, and she avoided his while she sped inside.

The king faced away from her, seated in his rolling chair before the garden's pond. The nimbus of his hair barely covered his skull, and he still wore his night robe—something Vivia couldn't believe he did where so many people might see. It was exactly the sort of thing he used to scold her mother for.

Vivia kept her spine mast straight as she approached Serafin. *This is normal,* she wanted her body to say. *I see nothing here to be alarmed by.*

A lie. Her body was a lie. Her mind raced, running over every step she'd taken since leaving the underground mere minutes ago. Had she closed the trapdoor all the way? Were the blueberries arranged as they ought to be? And irises, she hadn't accidentally trampled any, had she?

"Rayet?" came the king's reedy voice.

"No, Your Majesty," she called. "It's Vivia."

"Oh, a nice surprise." The king's head listed sideways, just enough for her to see the edge of a ragged ear. "Help me rise."

"Sir?" She tumbled forward, praying he wouldn't attempt

239

to stand on his own. She reached his chair. "Are you sure it's wise?"

He looked up at her.

She barely swallowed her gasp. In the darkness of the royal wing, she'd missed how sallow the king's skin had grown. How sunken his eyes.

"I wish to sit on Jana's bench," he explained. But when Vivia made no move to help, he snarled, "*Now.*" His body might be ailing, but his mind still held the Nihar rage.

Vivia slipped a hand behind him. He hissed with pain, eyes thinning. *A skeleton*, Vivia thought. Her fingers gripped nothing but bone.

Fresh shame fired through her. The answer to healing her father might be directly below them. She *couldn't* withhold that from him.

She would tell him about the lake. Of course, she would tell him.

Four uneven steps later, they reached the bench. It was filthy, but when Vivia tried to brush away dirt and pollen and seeds, Serafin murmured for her to leave it.

Once he was seated, though, she caught sight of his expression. Of his lips curling back, nostrils fluttering.

At first, Vivia thought the bench was still too dirty. Then she realized his eyes were rooted on her navy jacket. "Still no admiral's coat?"

"I haven't had time," she murmured. "I'll find a gray coat tonight."

"Oh, *I* do not mind." He lifted a sharp shoulder. "I only worry for *you*, Vivia. The vizers will call you grubby, and the

240

staff will say you look like your mother. We would not want that, would we?"

"No," Vivia agreed, though she couldn't help but think that he was the one who looked truly grubby—and *he* was the one who looked slightly deranged.

"Any word on Merik's death?" he asked, finally bending his gaze away from Vivia, toward the pond. "Surely it is not so difficult for our spies to find out who killed him."

Vivia *had* received news, but it had been a jumbled mess that had led right back to Nubrevna. To a culprit tucked somewhere in their midst, and she wasn't ready to share *that* information with her father.

Not yet, at least.

So all she said was, "No new leads, Your Majesty, though it does sound as if the Empress of Marstok was killed in the same way."

"Now there was a strong leader. Vaness, as well as her mother before her."

Vivia gulped. *I can be strong.*

"Jana was always too gentle. Too meek." Serafin motioned for Vivia to sit beside him. "Not like us."

Vivia sat, though she couldn't keep her hands from shaking. She had to ball them into fists atop her thighs. *Sitting still is a quick path to madness,* she reminded herself—as if this might explain the trembling.

However, the more her father criticized and nitpicked at Jana, the more Vivia wondered if perhaps it was something else that sent heat slicing down her shoulders.

Oh, Vivia was used to the insults against others by now. Normally, she could even revel in the fact that although

241

Serafin hated everyone, he still seemed to love *her*. Today, though, she was finding it harder to smile and laugh.

"Idiots," he said, and it took Vivia a moment to sort out whom he currently railed against. *The healers*, she realized soon enough.

"They do tell me I am doing better, though." Serafin smiled. "It is the Nihar blood, you know. You are lucky to have such strength running in your veins."

"I know," she replied, yet her gaze lingered on his skin, fragile as a snake's shed scales.

"The royal line sorely needed the Nihars in it," Serafin continued, warming to the subject. "Until I came along, Jana had no respect. Not from the civilians, not from the Forces, and especially not from the Council. I earned that for her, you know."

"I know," Vivia repeated.

"And I will earn it for you too." He smiled tenderly, his watery eyes disappearing in the folds of his skin. "Once I am well again, I will march into that Council and tell them to put that crown upon your head."

"Thank you." She smiled tenderly back—and it was real, for Noden only knew what Vivia would do without her father by her side. Or without that Nihar blood in her veins.

Join her mother, she supposed.

"I only want what's best for you, Vivia." The breeze kicked at his wispy hair. "And I know you only want what's best for me."

Vivia stiffened, the shame roiling hotter. Her father was *so* frail. No matter what the healers might say, he was on the verge of death.

So of course she would try to heal him. Of *course* she would tell him about the underground lake. Yes, something spidered down her spine at the thought of it—and yes, her mother had said to keep it secret, but that was before Jana had leaped to her death and left Vivia all alone. It was before she'd decided her own melancholy meant more than her daughter.

Serafin had stuck by Vivia through everything. He was a good father, even if Vivia was not worthy of it.

She sucked in a breath, ready to point out the blueberries and the trapdoor, when a bell began to clang.

The palace alarm.

Instantly Vivia was on her feet—and instantly she was hollering for the guards to gather around the king. Then, with nothing more than a breathy warning for her father to remain calm, Vivia sprinted out of the queen's garden. Halfway down the row of zucchini vines, she encountered Stix.

"What is it?" Vivia shouted over the alarm, trying not to notice how disheveled and puffy-faced Stix was. As if the girl had spent the entire night out.

"The storerooms," Stix hollered back, waving for Vivia to follow her. "Someone's gotten in there—and, sir, I think it might be the Fury."

After the deafening churn of the floods, the silence of the rising tunnel was unsettling. How so little rock could muffle the thunder below, Merik didn't know. Especially when he still felt the quake in his feet, in his lungs.

The smell here was only marginally better, for though

Merik and Cam had abandoned Shite Street, they carried the shite with them.

Forty-four steps passed, with Cam counting softly the entire way, before Merik and the girl reached a brick wall with a jagged crack slicing down. The rift looked accidental.

It also looked recent, the edges sharp. The rubble fresh.

But clearly this was what Merik and Cam had come for, so they slipped through the crack. Merik went first, only to end up behind a shelf of damp cedar. A shuffle sideways and he found himself in a cellar.

The royal storerooms. They looked exactly as Merik remembered: uneven shelves filled with boxes and sacks and blankets and bottles—any supply that might be needed for running the palace.

For several long breaths, Merik waited, listening. Feeling for breaths in the stale air, squinting for figures in the weak light that flickered from magicked lamps.

Merik heard no one; Merik saw no one. The only sound was water dripping into a puddle nearby. Condensation off the weeping granite walls, and perhaps a leak in the foundation too.

"We're on the lowest level of the royal storerooms," Merik murmured to Cam at last.

Her breath kicked out with surprise. "Well, that was easy to get in."

Merik agreed, and he couldn't help but wonder if perhaps the X on the map hadn't indicated a meeting at all—but rather a hole in the Cisterns that needed repair.

Here they were, though, and Merik intended to look around. Particularly since this was the first time he had ever seen supplies on the lowest level. The upper two floors were usually well stocked, but the lower four were always empty. *Always.*

Merik had entered these storerooms two months before. He'd descended to level two, seen nothing but mice, and gone straight to his father to request a trade envoy be sent to Veñaza City before the Truce Summit.

Serafin had agreed.

Then Serafin had appointed Merik to that task—and not just the task of reopening trade but also of representing Nubrevna as Admiral of the Royal Navy at the Truce Summit.

The holiest always have the farthest to fall.

"Come." Merik cocked his chin, beckoning Cam onward. The storeroom's shelves crisscrossed toward a central intersection where a stone staircase circled upward six levels.

Row after row they passed, each shelf crammed full of supplies.

"What's that say?" Cam whispered, pointing to a fat sack. They were halfway to the room's center, and supplies were thinning out. "It doesn't look like Nubrevnan letters."

"Because it's not," Merik answered. He toyed with his filthy sleeves. "Those are Dalmotti words. That one says *wheat.* The other says *barley.*" He motioned to a crate with red paint on the side. "That crate has dried dates in it from Marstok. That one of over there says *walnuts* in Cartorran."

Cam's lips pinched sideways. "But, sir . . . what are foreign foods doing here? I thought no one would trade with us."

Merik was wondering the same, though he could make a guess. One that conjured Marstoki weapons, miniature ships, and violence at sea.

Heat spindled down Merik's arms.

The amount of stores here was far more than two weeks of piracy could provide though. Vivia must have started the Foxes months ago—long before she'd betrayed Merik at sea and left him to die.

Merik's certainty of that grew, as did his rage, the closer he and Cam came to the cellar's heart, where the stairwell waited. Here, all shelves were empty, as if whoever had stocked this space wanted the wares to be hidden.

"Up," Merik ordered. He had to check the fifth level. He had to see if there was more of the same.

There was, and Merik's lungs fanned hotter. The fifth floor was even more crowded with supplies than the sixth, none labeled in Nubrevnan.

And all of it *here*, where it could do no one any good.

This food should be feeding Pin's Keep or the homeless in the Cisterns—or, hell-waters, the people of Nihar would take it. Instead, though, it sat here and served no one. Except, perhaps, Vivia.

Enough—Merik had seen enough, and it was time to leave the way they'd come. There was no meeting here. Only a hole in the Cisterns wall that needed fixing.

Merik and Cam were halfway back to the stairwell, though, when a groan drifted toward them. "Help."

Merik froze midstride; Cam halted beside him. The groan repeated, "Help," and Cam clutched at her stomach.

"We need to go check, sir."

A snap of Merik's head. *No.*

"Someone's hurt, sir."

Another snap, harder this time. Something icy was rising

246

in Merik's veins. Something powerful and dark, made of Hagfishes and shadows. *Leave while you still can*, Merik's instincts screamed. *This place is not safe for you!*

The shadow man was here.

Merik grabbed Cam's cloak, still damp and filthy, and towed her toward the stairs. They made it three steps before they reached the source of the groans.

A man stretched across the flagstones with a sword in his belly and intestines glittering on the floor. Pain shook in his eyes, while lines as dark as the sea's blackest depths webbed across his face.

It looked so much like a different death. A different murder—one that Merik had committed. *Leave while you still can, leave while you still can.*

Cam yanked herself free from Merik's grip and dropped beside the man. "I'm here," she crooned in an attempt to comfort. "I'm here now."

The man's eyes swiveled to Cam, and something almost like recognition flashed there. He tried to speak, but blood burbled from his mouth. From the hole in his stomach too.

The guard could not possibly survive this injury, yet Cam was right. Even dead men deserved compassion. So though every fiber in his body screeched at Merik to run, he made himself crouch beside the girl. That was when he saw it.

The man was missing a finger—his left pinkie, just like the assassin Garren.

It was like that night on the *Jana* all over again. How, though? Who was this man? It couldn't just be random coincidence.

Before Merik could put these questions to the dying man,

everything stilled in his body. Even the storeroom and the dust motes seemed to pause.

Dead. The man was dead.

Merik's throat cleared, ready to order Cam onward. Except that at that moment, a rasp scuttled through the cellar. It crawled over Merik's skin like a thousand sand fleas.

> *"Fool brother Filip led blind brother Daret*
> *deep into the black cave.*
> *He knew that inside it, the Queen Crab resided,*
> *but that didn't scare him away."*

Cam rocked back, falling onto her haunches. Merik simply gaped at the corpse. The man's dead mouth didn't move, and his eyes stayed stiff and glassy ... Yet there was no denying the words came from his throat.

Impossible, impossible.

Cam scrabbled back on all fours, hissing, "Sir, sir," while the corpse continued to whisper.

> *"Said blind brother Daret to fool brother Filip,*
> *does Queen Crab no longer reign?*
> *I have heard she is vicious, and likes to eat fishes.*
> *It's best we avoid her domain."*

"Sir, sir, sir." Cam grabbed for Merik.

A bell began to clamor. Ear-splitting in volume and brutal in intensity, it was the palace alarm.

Merik moved. Hand in hand with Cam, he bolted for the

248

stairs—even as the rest of the song slithered out around them.

"Answered fool Filip to his brother small,
have I not always kept you safe?
I know what I'm doing, for I'm older than you,
and I'll never lead you astray."

Impossible, *impossible*.

Guards charged downward from the surface now. Merik felt their footsteps hammering behind them on the stone steps. He sensed their breaths skating down the stairwell's air.

He and Cam reached the lowest level and sprinted into the rows of shelves. Somehow, though, the guards still closed in from behind.

It's the smell, Merik thought vaguely. *The guards can follow the smell.* Yet there was nothing to be done for it except to keep running. Shelves went hazy at the edges of his vision. His breath, and Cam's too, came in short gasps.

They reached the back wall. Merik thrust Cam behind the cedar cases as light tore over him. Ten guards with torches in hand careened closer.

"The Fury!" one shouted. "Shoot him!" barked another.

Merik heaved into the Cisterns after Cam. She had waited for him—fool girl—and he gripped her once more. Held fast to her arm as they barreled down the dark tunnel.

Shadows, shouts, shit—it all bounced off the limestone walls. Then came a bark from Cam—"Crossbows!"—and a burst of wind in Merik's chest.

No, not wind. That charge, that thunder—it was the flood.

The soldiers hollered for Merik and Cam to stop. But they didn't. They *couldn't*. That sound, that tempest approaching...

Merik and Cam had to get past Shite Street before it hit.

They reached the sewage. Cam plummeted in, and Merik fell with her, knees buckling. Hands and chest submerging. Yet the roar, the flood—it pushed Merik and Cam onto their feet once more.

They ran. A crossbow bolt sang past their heads. A second shattered the nearest lantern, swathing them in darkness and leaving only the soldiers' approaching torches to see by.

The flood didn't care. It still approached, so loud now it was like Lejna. Like Kullen's cleaving death. *No escape. Just the storm.*

Merik kept running, his eyes blanketed by black. His hearing consumed by tides. Ahead, ahead—he just had to get ahead.

Orange light flickered. New lanterns. New tunnels. The end of Shite Street was so close now with a glistening ramp visible beyond. Merik ran harder. Four steps.

Two.

He launched onto the landing, only to lurch around and see Cam, still ten paces back and chased by a mountain of charging water.

Without thought, Merik lashed out with a *whip* of power. The winds snapped around Cam. Tiny but strong. Just like she was. A coil of air that carried her the final steps to safety.

The girl collapsed on the ground beside Merik, breathing

heavily. Body shaking. Coated in dung and only Noden knew what else while water frothed past in a perfect, bewitched funnel.

Worried, Merik reached for her. "Are you," he gasped, "all right?"

An exhausted nod. "Hye . . . sir."

"We can't stop."

"Never," she panted, and when Merik offered her his hand, she smiled wearily. Then together, they left the ferocity of Shite Street behind.

TWENTY-TWO

Aeduan stormed down the riverside path, his magic on fire. His body moving too fast to stop, too fast to fight. Straight through the Red Sails hunting the Threadwitch, he drove.

They withdrew blades in flashes of steel and bellows of ire. Yet Aeduan had no plans for combat. Not today.

One saber hissed out, setting Aeduan's instincts alight. He ducked, rolled forward, and broke from the trees to face the Amonra.

Threadwitch, Threadwitch—where was the Threadwitch?

He spotted her. Not far ahead, on the shore. He could reach her if she would just stop running.

She didn't stop but rather made a move of such vast stupidity that Aeduan had to wonder if she had a death wish. For he'd seen her make this move before, on a cliffside road north of Veñaza City. This time, though, Aeduan wasn't letting her get away.

This time, he would follow her over the edge.

A blood-scent that stank of torture and splattered guts hit Aeduan's nose. He twirled backward just as the man attacked. Aeduan kicked, a hammer to the side of the man's knee.

Bone cracked. The man fell, but Aeduan was already out of the way. Already running, ready to dive into the river as planned . . . But he froze. A beige coat—*his* coat that he'd left with the Threadwitch—was now coursing down the river at a speed no man could match.

No man except Aeduan. He hurtled into the magic-powered sprint. In seconds, he caught up to the coat. It flew downstream, within reach of the shore.

Aeduan shot ahead, faster now and aiming for a riverside tree. The bank beneath it was undercut, exposing roots and offering the perfect handhold.

Soil rained as Aeduan scrambled down and hooked his arm into the roots. Water sprayed, frost to flay his cheeks.

The coat was almost to him. He stretched. He reached . . . He was too far. His hand gripped only icy water. So without another thought, he thrust off the bank and dove into the waves.

But no Threadwitch was waiting beneath the wool. Nothing save the cold and the sheer rage of the Amonra.

Iseult had no idea how she was still alive.

By all logic and physics, she should not be. The Amonra was indomitable. It spat her up and then kicked her down. Light, gasps. Darkness, death. No sound, no sight, no breath, no life. For a century—or perhaps only moments—the current possessed every piece of Iseult's being.

She hit boulders, she hit substrate, she hit waves so hard they felt solid. Her ankles snagged on rocks, on branches. A thousand unseen claws in the riverbed. Each time the foamy rapids spat her out so she could gulp in air, they instantly sucked her down again.

Until Iseult hit something that hit *back*. The world punched from her mind. Then her body snapped around backward. All wrong, yet held fast by something.

Iseult snapped open her eyes, fighting the river's pound against her face. She saw nothing, but she felt hands. Arms.

Him. It had to be. No one else was Threadless.

No one else was this strong.

The Amonra was stronger yet. *Always* stronger. It yanked the Bloodwitch—and Iseult with him—onward. Lifted them to the surface . . . and smashed them back down.

Air, Iseult thought. It was the only thought she could manage. Stars flashed, stars burst. A booming to fill her skull.

But something else was wriggling into her pinpointed awareness. Something rumbling, something violent.

Something she and the Bloodwitch absolutely could not survive: the Amonra Falls.

When her numbed toes hit gravel sediment, Iseult dug in. The river heaved at her, but she pressed deeper. Behind her the Bloodwitch realized what she did and imitated, heels shoveling down.

He blocked her from the current's teeth, and Iseult reached with ice-block hands for anything to grab on to. Frantic now. *Air, air.* Her knuckles grazed stone. Distantly, she felt the skin tear open—and she also felt the Bloodwitch lose his grip. The river would reclaim them soon.

Air, air.

Whatever had cut her knuckles was a protrusion on a tall column of stone. She grabbed hold with frozen fingers. Just

254

in time. Aeduan's hold on the sediment gave way; the river *snapped* him onward.

He held tight to Iseult, though, and Iseult held tight to the rock. Her muscles screamed, her sockets popped.

Aeduan clambered around Iseult. One hand, large and rough, closed over hers—locking her grip in place, and anchoring him too, as he grabbed at the same stone.

Air, air.

He found another handhold. He pulled; Iseult pushed; and up they moved, inch by inch. Iseult anchoring. Aeduan grappling. The river towing.

Until at last the Amonra released them both. Until at last they broke the surface, and air, air, *air* coursed over them.

Iseult had just enough time to glance around—craggy outcropping, waterfall below, coughing Bloodwitch beside her—before she collapsed to the wet granite and the world went blessedly quiet.

For what had felt like hours, Aeduan simply lay on the granite, breathing, while the river churned past and the Amonra's icy bite faded from his bones. The Amonra's roar, however, never died.

Eventually, the Threadwitch sat up, so Aeduan sat up too. The Red Sails who'd hunted them were gone. No scents lurked nearby—theirs or anyone else's.

"Wait here," Aeduan said, his voice waterlogged. "I'll be back soon."

At the girl's silent nod, Aeduan stretched his magic to its maximum reach, and then he scouted the area for a safe place to hide. For a spot where no human blood hit his nose, where no man had walked for ages.

What he found were ancient ruins. Built into the cliffside, more forest than fortress, whoever had left these granite walls and columns, they were lost to time now. Old carvings had eroded to inscrutable grooves. Floors and roofs had been replaced by roots and branches, tiles and mosaics had been replaced by lichen and fungus.

But it was defensible, hugging the cliff as it did, and it was hidden. A thorough sniff around the place yielded nothing but animal scents. The rook had passed this way, but not men. Not slavers.

When Aeduan returned to the slick granite, he uttered only the words, "This way," but she understood. She followed. Away from the waterfall, away from the river, away from any blood-scent belonging to men.

Descending the steep hillside was slow. A constant back-and-forth in the only way the terrain would allow. Finally, the first monoliths crooked up from the earth, and the ground flattened into narrow, overgrown steppes. Here, men had carved the cliff to their liking. Here, enormous cypresses had taken root unimpeded.

The Threadwitch never spoke on the hike. Her breath came in curt gulps. She clearly needed rest; she clearly needed food. So though Aeduan's muscles sang with the urge to move faster, he kept his pace slow. Manageable.

Until they finally reached the heart of the ruins. It was the only space with four walls still standing. Admittedly, vines and mushrooms had laid claim to the granite and there was no roof to top it off, but walls were walls. Most people liked them.

Then again, the Threadwitch wasn't most people.

She sank to the stone and mud-earth and hugged her knees to her chest. Despite the heat sweltering here, she shivered.

"Why does he hunt you?" Aeduan's hoarse words split the living silence of the place.

"Who?" the Threadwitch asked, her voice haggard and muffled by her knees. She lifted her head. There was a cut on her brow that Aeduan hadn't seen before.

"The Purist priest," Aeduan answered. "Corlant."

To his surprise, her breath hitched. She clutched at her right biceps, and something like fear flashed across her face.

It was the most expressive he'd ever seen the Threadwitch. A sign her careful control had crumbled beneath exhaustion. Aeduan hadn't known it was possible.

This girl had fought Aeduan—tricked him and broken his spine. She had battled city guards and faced cleaved Poison-witches head-on, yet never had Aeduan seen her show fear.

"You know him, then," Aeduan said.

"*How*," she clearly had to concentrate to get that word out, "do *you* know him?"

Aeduan hesitated. For several moments, there was no sound beyond the distant waterfall. No movement beyond the breeze towing at the branches overhead.

Aeduan hovered under Lady Fate's knife. The question was, which side of the blade would hurt less? To tell Iseult the truth about Corlant and the arrowhead would mean that any betrayal Aeduan might have had planned would be impossible.

Yet to keep the arrowhead a secret would guarantee that more men like the Red Sails would follow. Aeduan couldn't spend every moment by Iseult's side, and if one of Corlant's other dogs caught up again—if he lost her to the Red Sails . . . to that Firewitch—then he would lose his silver too.

He pulled the arrowhead from his pocket. "Corlant hired me," he explained brusquely, "before I encountered you. He wanted me to find you and bring you to him. Alive." Cautiously, Aeduan inched toward the Threadwitch, expecting her to cower.

She didn't. Of course she didn't. She merely rubbed her biceps, and once Aeduan was close enough, she plucked the arrowhead from his waiting hand.

"Why are you telling me this?" she asked.

"Because my silver talers are worth more to me than what the priest is offering. And because I am not the only person Corlant has hired to find you. Those men work for him, and I assume there will be more."

Iseult stared at Aeduan, posture swaying. Face crumpling. Then she began to laugh.

It was unlike any sound Aeduan had ever heard. Not a pretty twinkle like the wealthy wives in Veñaza City, who kept amusement contained and wielded it like a weapon. Nor a raucous guffaw from someone who laughed freely, openly, often.

This was a shrill, breathy sound, part warbling trill and part frantic gasp. It was not a pleasant sound; it did not invite others to join.

258

"Dumb luck," she choked out. "That's what keeps saving me, Bloodwitch. Pure. Dumb. *Luck.*" For the first time since partnering with her, the Threadwitch slipped into Dalmotti. "Goddess above, it's right there in the phrase, isn't it? 'Dumb luck.' Choose the stupidest option, and Lady Fate will reward you.

"I should be dead, Bloodwitch. I should be shredded upon the stones or pummeled beneath the waterfall. But I'm not. And Corlant? H-he tried to kill me before. With this arrow." She held it up, eyes fixed on it. "And he cursed it too. So if the wound didn't kill me, the c-c-*curse* would. Yet somehow, I survived."

Iseult's laughter weakened. Then rattled off completely. "You've been there all along, Bloodwitch. Somewhere, l-lurking. *You* are the reason I had to go to my tribe—which means *you* are the reason Corlant c-c-could attack. So if I had never met you, then would I even be here right now?"

Aeduan's eyes thinned—not because of what she said but rather how she chose to say it. She was blaming him for the Purist priest Corlant. Blaming him for everything, yet it wasn't as if he had asked for this either.

"If I had never met you," he countered coolly, "then my spine would never have snapped, and Leopold fon Cartorra would never have hired me. Monk Evrane would not have almost died, and I would not be forced to work for—"

"Monk Evrane lives?" The Threadwitch pushed to her feet, a new expression washing away her hysteria: eyes huge, lips parted. *Hope.* "I thought the Cleaved had claimed her in Lejna. But . . . she lives?"

At Aeduan's nod, Iseult's head tipped back. Her eyes

closed. When she spoke again, it was in Nomatsi once more and with no stutter to trip her words. "Whatever has happened between us," she said evenly, "whatever events have passed to lead us here, they cannot be undone. And now I owe you my life. Twice."

Aeduan stiffened at the mention of a life-debt. She wasn't finished, though.

"In Lejna, you promised to kill me if we ever met again. You said your life-debt had been repaid. By your own accounting, I owe you once for not killing me last night. Twice, for saving me from the Amonra. Maybe even three times, for warning me against Corlant." She laughed, that same hysterical sound—but gone in an instant, her face cold and somber as she said, "I don't know how to repay you, Monk Aeduan, but I know the Moon Mother would want me to try."

Aeduan's jaw muscles twitched at that. He spun away from her with too much force. "I'm not a monk anymore," was all he said before striding out of the ruins.

Someone had to salvage their forgotten supplies.

His careful walk soon became a jog. A gallop, with ferns to snap against his calves. Branches to scrape his skin.

Someone owed Aeduan a life-debt. It was . . .

A first.

A first that he didn't know how to swallow. The Threadwitch Iseult was alive because he had made it so. She could breathe her current breaths and could taste the river's water because he had saved her life.

Though she had also, in a way, saved his. First, she had not killed him while he lay unconscious in the bear trap. And second, *she* had been the one to hook them to that stone before the Falls.

But Aeduan decided not to mention any of this, for if the Threadwitch believed she owed him three lives, then that gave him an advantage. *That*, he could use. He didn't know how, he didn't know when, only that he absolutely would.

TWENTY-THREE

Despite its dubious exterior, the Gilded Rose catered to the richest of Red Sails. It was the slaves that proved it—their clean faces, their tailored clothes.

The air seemed to tighten as Caden and Safi entered, and Safi's magic instantly stirred against the back of her neck. There was some sort of glamour at work here. A spell to smooth away flaws, soften the truth, and leave everyone awash in an unnatural but flattering glow.

False, false, false.

The couples on the low sofa and the people dining at the tables all looked as if they'd stepped from a painting.

Beauty, Safi realized as she followed Caden toward a curtain-covered doorway in the back. Whatever spell was at work here, it gave *everyone* beauty.

Though not Caden. The glamour of the room didn't sparkle over him, and whatever beauty he possessed—Safi couldn't deny it was there—was all nature's doing. Then they were through the curtain, where knee-high tables were spread evenly over the elaborate rugs and floor pillows. Every table was crowded with cards and coins, while thick smoke from pipes curled over the bare flesh of Gilded Rose slaves.

Safi's magic grated and scratched as they crossed the room. *Wrong* didn't even begin to describe what this place was. What the Red Sails were.

Caden motioned to a table in the farthest corner, where a woman sat alone. Her gray hair was piled atop her head, and like everyone else in the establishment, her black skin glowed with perfection. Winnings and cards lay scattered before her, and a self-satisfied grin implied she'd just sent some taro losers running.

So absorbed was the woman in counting her coins that she didn't notice Caden or Safi's approach until Caden was dropping onto the bench beside her.

A frown. "Who are you—" She cut off, the frown deepening. "Is that a knife you have poking into my kidney?"

"It is," Caden replied, speaking in Dalmotti as the woman had. "I have only a few questions to ask, Admiral Kahina, and then my companion and I will leave you to your card game."

"And if I don't answer ... then what? You'll gut me?" With an indifferent flip of her wrists, she drawled, "Oh, no. Someone protect me from the bad man with a knife."

Instantly, Safi liked the woman.

"You do realize," Kahina went on, "that I run the largest fleet of Red Sails in the Jadansi? If you were *actually* stupid enough to put that knife in my back, you'd be dead before you could even reach the door."

"Then if you prefer," Caden offered, his expression unchanged, "the two of us can continue this conversation at the bottom of the hell-gates. I've heard kidney wounds bleed fast. We could meet there before the next chimes even toll."

Kahina eyed Caden for several long breaths, her fingers tapping against the table. On her right thumb was a fat jade ring that clacked and clacked against the wood. Then a smile curled over her face. "Who *are* you? I'm not used to men who have tongues as sharp as their looks. And you"—her gaze swung to Safi—"sit down, girl. On my honor, I won't bite."

There was no missing the truth in that assertion, so Safi did as she'd been ordered, claiming the seat on Kahina's other side. Up close, the taro deck was on full display across the table. Teal backs, worn edges.

Safi's hands started drumming against her knees, itching to shuffle. To play. But she forced herself to look away and examine Admiral Kahina instead—whom Safi could now see through the glamour's magic. The Admiral, though naturally dazzling, was no youth, and her teeth had stained to muddy brown.

Safi realized why when Kahina said, "Hand me that pipe, girl."

Safi handed her the pipe; Caden glared. "We aren't here for pleasure, Admiral. We're here for a ship that you took hold of three days ago."

"Ignite," Kahina murmured to the pipe before sucking in a long inhale. Pale smoke slithered out between her teeth as she purred, "You'll have to elaborate. I do take so many ships. Did I mention I have the largest fleet in the Red Sails?" Kahina leaned seductively toward Caden.

To Safi's shock, he leaned seductively right back. Before her eyes, Caden transformed into the Chiseled Cheater. It was amazing how stark the contrast—and how quick the change. The Hell-Bard named Caden, so duty bound and intense, relaxed into the Chiseled Cheater, all charms and sweet smiles.

He flashed such a smile now, and heat swept over Safi. Furious heat. Attracted heat. *Confused* heat. For it was that perfect thrice-damned grin that had gotten her into so much trouble in Veñaza City.

"The ship I'm looking for is a naval cutter. Crewed by men in green."

"Marstoki green or Cartorran green? Oh, but how silly of me." She dragged on her pipe, before shifting her attention to Safi.

Safi's fingers tapped faster.

"I have never seen two people who looked more Cartorran in my life. That fair hair and those *freckles*. You are lucky no one in our little territory has skinned you yet."

"Answer the question." Caden's voice was stonier now, his charm already wearing thin. "Where is the *Cartorran* cutter?"

"At the bottom of the bay."

Well, *that* was a lie—and the perfect time for Safi to step in. After all, she could play this game too. "Is that also where you hid your beauty and youth?"

Kahina choked on a lungful of smoke. Then laughed. "The two of you," she said between chuckles, "are much more fun than my usual company." She chomped on the pipe stem, holding it in place, and then gathered up the deck of taro cards. "You do realize that even if this ship were nearby, you would never be able to sail her out."

"Which is why you'll be telling us where the crew is too."

Kahina sniffed dismissively. "It is Baile's Slaughter tomorrow." At Safi's and Caden's confused frowns, she added, "Lady Baile—you do not have her in Cartorra, I suppose. But in these parts, she is the patron saint of the seas, and sailors take her rules very seriously."

"Rules?" Safi asked, even though Caden was glaring in a way that said, *Don't indulge her.*

"Three rules has she," Kahina sang, shuffling her cards, "Our Lady of the Seas. No whistling when a storm's in sight. Six-fingered cats will ward off mice. And always, always stay the night for Baile's Slaughter Ring."

Well, Safi thought, *that explains the sign at the inn.*

Kahina wasn't finished. "So don't you see, lovelies? No ships are even *allowed* to leave the harbor until after the fight at the arena. Even then, very few will actually do so. Everyone will be drinking heavy tonight, and twice as heavy tomorrow. 'Tis the biggest fight of the year, after all." With a smile, she fanned the cards, a showy movement to draw the eye.

Neither Caden nor Safi fell for it. In fact, Caden dug the knife in a bit harder and said, "Admiral, my patience is fading fast. Where. Is. The Cartorran cutter?"

Kahina pouted. "Oh, the two of you are so dour. How about this . . ." She offered the cards to Caden. "I'll tell you where that ship is if you can win at taro."

"No, Admiral," Caden said. "You'll tell us now."

"One round is all I ask. Best hand wins."

"I'll do it." The words popped from Safi's mouth before she could consider them. Before she could even gauge what sort of opponent Kahina would be. She simply knew that

Kahina had spoken the truth: she *would* tell them about the missing ship if she lost.

And Safi also knew that the instant the deal had been made, her fingers finally stilled.

The Red Sails Admiral smiled. Smoke twined between her brown teeth. Then, in a flutter of cards, she shuffled twice and dealt out four cards for each of them. Her ring glinted and flashed.

"Flip," she commanded.

Safi flipped. It was a good hand, and though she was absolutely certain she had no tell, she still paid extra care to keeping her face inscrutable.

"Trade?" Kahina asked silkily. Her nostrils flared, an expression of victory.

It was a bluff. A lie. Safi could feel it scratching with only a single glance.

"Two cards trade." Safi slid over her worst two before snagging more off the deck. The Empress and the Witch. An *excellent* combination.

Yet when Kahina traded only one of her cards, dismay jolted in Safi's heart. Had she been wrong? Was this Veñaza City all over again? Was she misreading and falling for a trap—

"Reveal."

At the command, instinct took over. Safi revealed her cards as Kahina revealed hers.

Safi had won. *Barely.* Kahina's Nameless Monk card doubled her own hand's strength—but Safi's combination of Witch, Empress, Sun, and Birth were a win in the end. And Safi finally allowed her eyes to flick Caden's way.

His eyes shone, and when he dipped in toward Kahina, it was with a smile and a fresh surge of energy to his movements. "Now about that ship, Admiral."

"*Fine.*" A dramatic sigh. "I adopted her into my fleet, as anyone with half a brain would do. She's a fine, speedy creature, and I do so hope that you don't want to take her back." She paused to draw in fresh smoke. Then the words sifted out on a smoggy exhale: "And as for her crew, I sold them to the arena. Any witches will be in tomorrow's fight, and all the others, well ... Every good skirmish needs sheep for the slaughter."

True, true, true.

Yet even as the warmth of truth settled over Safi's skin, her stomach flipped.

Caden seemed to feel the same, for his expression had turned glacial. No more Chiseled Cheater, only cool Hell-Bard intent. He pushed to his feet; Safi pushed to hers.

Admiral Kahina smirked at them both. "I do so hope I see you again."

"You won't," Caden promised, reaching for Safi. He didn't touch her but simply motioned for her to move in front so they could make their way back to the door.

"But what about," Kahina trilled after them, "our meeting at the bottom of the hell-gates? I was looking forward to it."

Neither Safi nor Caden looked back. They didn't need to, for the pirate's mocking laughter followed them all the way to the exit.

TWENTY-FOUR

Vivia examined the hole in the royal storeroom wall. She kept her forehead scrunched into the famous displeased Nihar frown—the one Merik had always managed so easily—while her fingers pinched her nose tight.

Everything stank of excrement.

Beside her, a pretty guard babbled on and on about how she hadn't known there was a crack in the foundation. "We'd have fixed it long ago, had we known," she insisted.

To which Vivia simply had to nod and look suitably irate. The truth was that Vivia had known this hole was here. In fact, she'd *put* this hole here, knowing the floods and the filth of Shite Street would keep intruders out. Until now, it had been a perfect solution for getting Fox goods into the storeroom unseen. Either Vivia or Stix would sweep a fresh flood through to clear out the tunnel, then, one by one, the stolen wares were loaded in.

The girls had attempted this trick fifty times, and each time it had come off without a hitch.

Until, of course, right now.

"Blighted Fury," Vivia spat, and genuine venom laced the

words. Not merely because the man had killed a royal guard, but because now Vivia's plan was unraveling. Too many people had seen the secret, undeniably foreign foodstuffs hiding in the lowest levels, and this method into the store-rooms had been *her* idea—one her father had opposed.

Oh, Serafin was not going to be happy.

Vivia turned to go. The guard called after, "Should we fix the hole, sir?"

"Leave it," Vivia called. "For now, I want it guarded. Ten men, all hours." A curt agreement, and Vivia left the guard behind, aiming for the stairwell. She wove around servants and soldiers and officers, each searching for more cracks in the palace. For more areas where more criminals might get in.

It was too many people, Vivia thought as she hit the stairs. There was no way she could expect them all to keep the Fox secret quiet. One person—that was all it would take. He would blab to his friend over ox tea at the Cleaved Man: "I saw Marstoki grains in the storeroom!" Then that friend would prattle to his mother, and then on the story would move, until everyone knew about the Foxes before Vivia or Serafin was ready to share. The High Council would deem it a wild risk, a *mad* risk, and then Vivia would never win her mother's crown—

"No," she hissed at herself, bounding up two steps at a time. "No regrets. Keep moving." She reached the next level's landing and hopped off. Stix's white head buoyed above the rest of the guards, all of them circled around the corpse.

Vivia had only glanced at the body, but a glance was all she'd needed. The man was an exact match for the corpse in

Linday's garden. The Fury had indeed been here; the Fury had indeed killed again.

Yet now an officer, bald and baritone, was cutting in front of Vivia. His head wagged. "It's not one of ours, sir."

Vivia blinked, confused. "What do you mean?"

"I mean, he isn't a royal guard." He elbowed a path to the body until both he and Vivia could stare down at it. "That's not our uniform, sir. It's hard to tell with all that tarry blood on him—or whatever it is." He cringed. "But underneath, it's a different outfit entirely. Also, notice he's only got nine fingers."

With a hand over her mouth and nose, Vivia bent forward. Sure enough, nine fingers. *Just like the body at Linday's.*

"Are you suggesting," Vivia asked, straightening, "that he was part of the Nines? I thought that gang had dissolved years ago."

"Maybe not." The officer shrugged. "Or maybe he just *used* to be part of the Nines. It's not like you can grow back a pinkie."

"Right," she murmured, and now her Nihar frown was a thoroughly real one. None of this made sense. Nines in the storerooms—or Nines guarding Linday's greenhouse.

"Sir," Stix said.

Vivia pretended not to hear and instead marched back to the stairs. She *knew* it was petty of her, but there was already so much going on. She wasn't sure she had the strength to keep staring at Stix's ruffled hair or wrinkled uniform.

Too good for me.

"*Sir.*" Stix clamped a hand on her biceps. On the mourning

band. "The Fury has a companion—and I know where the boy lives."

Now Vivia heard. Now she ground to a halt, three steps up. She twisted back, her eyes level with Stix's. The first mate had paused a step below.

"Last night, it was the Fury who ruined your office. I didn't have time to clean up—or wait for you—because I followed him."

Vivia exhaled, hating how much relief slackened in her belly. For though Stix hadn't spent the night out with a lover, it still didn't make her a suitable match for Vivia.

"Followed him where?" Vivia asked tightly.

"To Vizer Linday's greenhouse."

Noden hang her. Vivia lurched back into an ascent. "Why didn't you stop the man? Why didn't you arrest him? He's killed two men, Stix!"

Stix flung up her hands. "I didn't know he would kill! I thought maybe he was working with Vizer Linday, so I waited outside, hoping he would reappear. When the man didn't, I returned to Pin's Keep—where a *second* person was in your office."

They passed the fourth-level landing, both girls taking two steps now.

"A boy," Stix went on. "He was skinny with two-toned skin, and he was clearly looking for someone. So I let him search . . . Then I followed him. First to a Noden's Temple on Hawk's Way, and finally to a tenement house in Old Town."

The third landing smeared past. "Did you follow him inside? Did you see which room he went into?"

"No. I couldn't get close—he's got incredible reflexes. The kind you only see in kids from the Cisterns."

Second landing, and Vivia was practically running now. *Keep moving, keep moving.*

"I could send soldiers to search the tenement, sir."

"No," Vivia panted. "I don't want to risk spooking this man. If he's got the power to kill like ... like *that*"—she motioned down—"then we can't put all those civilians at risk. But I do want eyes on the house. If the boy shows up, I want him followed. If we can arrest him, then maybe we can lure out this beast calling himself the Fury."

"Hye, sir!" Stix popped a rough salute as they jogged onto the highest landing. Yet Vivia made it only ten steps before her feet slowed. Before she had to stop and bend and catch her heaving breath.

For a sickening thought had just set the hairs on her arms to rising. "Stix," she huffed. "If that corpse ... down there ... wasn't a guard"—she paused, gulping in breaths—"and he was in fact one of the Nines, then what was he doing here? And what was the *Fury* doing here?"

Stix tossed up her hands, a helpless gesture. "I ... I don't know, sir. Did you check the stores?"

"No ... Curse me, *no.*"

As one, both women dove back for the stairs. Down they sprinted, twice as fast as they'd come up. Then Vivia was at the fifth level and shoving past guards, Stix right on her heels as they aimed for the closest bags of foreign grain.

Vivia knew what she'd find, though. She felt it roiling in her abdomen. A certainty that sickened, a certainty that hurt.

She tore open a sack of Dalmotti barley.

Black, all of it—coated in the same shadowy, charred oil that coated the corpses. Completely inedible. As was the next sack and the next sack after that.

Everything Vivia had worked for was gone. Months of secret piracy without sufficient weapons to protect her men...Months of furtive loading and unloading into the storerooms...And *months* of hiding and lying and praying it would all pay off. But for what? So all of it could be ruined by the foul taint of corrupted magic.

She should never have listened to her father. She should have trusted her own instincts and used this food at Pin's Keep.

And she should have never, *never* gotten those thrice-damned weapons from the thrice-damned Marstoks and left Merik behind.

Vivia couldn't help it. Even though Stix stood right there and another hundred soldiers too, even though she knew this tale would get back to the High Council, Vivia clutched at her head and screamed.

In the furnace-like heat of midafternoon, Cam ferried Merik through back alleys and side streets to a public bathhouse in Old Town. It was as run-down as everything else in the area, but at least the waters inside were clean.

Better yet, no one visited it at this time of day, and the attendant within scarcely roused from her nap to take Merik's coins. If she noticed their stink or their grime, she gave no hint of it.

"We need new clothes," Cam blurted, mere seconds after

entering the dark wooden hut. "Leave it to me, hye? I'll bathe when I get back!" She didn't wait for a response before hastening back into the sunlight.

Merik let her go. He understood her need to protect the *Camilla* secret, and in the end, she was right. They *did* need new clothes.

Merik bathed alone, reveling in the pain of the soap against raw skin. In the hot, magicked waters sweeping past his waist. How much scrubbing would it take, he wondered, to clean away the rage?

Or to clean away the shadows.

He had hoped that he'd imagined the lines at dawn, when he'd applied the healer salve—that the streaks on his chest had been illusions of the light. But now ... there was no ignoring the black lines that radiated from his heart like shattered glass.

Were this a month ago, Merik would have asked his aunt what the hell was happening to him. As it was, though, Merik had no one to turn to. Only Cam, who knew less about magic than a frog in the well knows the sea.

As if summoned by his thoughts, the room's wood-slatted door rasped open. Cam's dark head popped through. "Clothes, sir." She dropped them to the floor, along with a pair of rough leather boots. Then she backed out, the door squeaking shut.

"Boy!"

The door paused.

"Are the wind-drums still pounding?"

"Hye, sir," came the taut reply. "But no soldiers in Old Town." *Yet*, Merik thought before the door closed entirely. He rushed through the rest of his bath. Shadows and dead men—he'd deal with it all later.

By the time he found Cam in the bathhouse's entryway, counting planks in the wall, the girl's skin shone, her black hair looking downy as a gosling's. Like Merik, she wore a plain white tunic and baggy tan pants, but they were huge on her, even rolled up and belted. Unlike Merik, she lacked shoes or a hooded cloak, but then again, Merik supposed she didn't need them. Her face wasn't lined by scars, and she wasn't the one for whom the wind-drums sang.

"I think," he said, coming to her side, "I still reek of sewage. And I am certain it's burned in my nose forever."

Instead of the grin he'd anticipated, all Merik earned was a grunt. It was so unlike the girl that he gave her a double take. She had already turned away, was already planting a hand on the exit.

The city stewed with humidity and humans and heat, but Cam had no commentary on that either—nor on the soldiers she had to rush Merik past. Nor even on the massive puddle of only Noden knew what that she planted her clean heels directly into.

The grim slant to her lips never parted. The furrow on her brow never smoothed away.

It wasn't until she and Merik were firmly back in Kullen's tenement that Cam's silence finally broke.

She stalked to the window's hazy glass, gazing outside for two breaths, and then rounded on Merik. Her cheeks flushed with what Merik hoped was heat but suspected might be anger.

"I've thought long and hard about it, sir, ever since we left those storerooms. I've decided that we need help."

"Help," Merik repeated, easing off his new cloak—much too large—and draping it across the bed. "With what exactly?"

"Dead men comin' back to life." She thrust out her chin, as if preparing an argument. "Whatever that was—whatever we saw in the storerooms, it wasn't right. It was . . . *unholy!*"

"And I'm sure the guards will deal with it."

"What if they don't? What if they *can't?* Or what if they didn't even see what we saw? Someone needs to know there's dark magic happening in the Cisterns, sir."

"Someone?" he asked carefully, though he already saw where this was headed.

"The Royal Forces. Or . . . or the High Council."

"Ah, right." Merik laughed a dry, cruel sound. "You mean the Royal Forces and the High Council that are led by my *sister.* Who, in case you've forgotten, tried to kill me."

"We don't know she did that. Not for certain."

"Don't we, though?" A hot, charged breeze scraped through his chest. Merik fought it. He wouldn't let it loose—not on Cam. "We know she left us for dead at sea."

"She did that for the Foxes, sir. I ain't saying it was right, but she got those weapons for the Foxes, and we just saw, plain as rain, that her piracy is working."

For half a shallow breath, all he could do was stare at Cam. Then, with lethal slowness, he said, "What we saw was Vivia hoarding food. For herself. Are you taking her side, Cam?"

"No!" Cam's hands shot up. "I just . . . we can't face corpses

277

that wake up, sir! Not on our own! And what if," she pressed, "the princess *didn't* try to kill you? What if it was . . . well, what if it was someone connected to that dead man in the storerooms?" She stumbled two steps toward Merik.

But he turned away. He couldn't look at her. The one person he'd trusted, the one person who'd stood by him through everything . . . Now she was turning on him too.

He fixed his eyes on Kullen's books. On *The True Tale of the Twelve Paladins*. His lungs were expanding, pressing against his ribs with a rage that begged to be used. To pummel and break. To go head-to-head with his sister, once and for all.

"Vivia," he forced out, "is the one who tried to kill us."

"No," Cam snarled. "She ain't. *Look* at me, sir."

Merik didn't look at her, and his winds were spinning now. Small, turbulent chops.

Cam stomped in closer, her shirt flapping like sailcloth the instant she got close. "Look at me!"

"Why?" Merik had to pitch his voice over the building winds. The cover of *The True Tale* popped wide open. "What do you want from me, Cam?"

"I want you to see the truth! I want you to *face* it, sir. I ain't blind, you know—I've seen the marks on your chest, and on your arms! Just like the dead man in the cellar. We need answers, sir, and I think I know where—"

"And *I* ain't blind either, Cam." Merik finally turned toward her. "I can see blighted well that you're a girl."

For half a windswept breath, she gawped at him. Surprised. "Is that what you think I am? All this time, and you *still* haven't sorted it out?" Then she barked a hollow laugh.

278

"Why am I surprised? You didn't notice me when we were on the *Jana*. You couldn't even remember my name back then, so why should I expect you to understand—to *see* me for what I am now!"

Cam thrust in closer, until there was nothing but her face mere inches away. Too close for Merik's hot winds to even spiral between. "You think you're so selfless," she spat. "You think you're working to save everyone, but what if you're going about it all wrong? At least when I live as a boy, no one gets hurt. But you pretendin' to be a martyr? Pretending to be the Fury? That hurts everyone."

Too far. Merik's winds launched up, sweeping between them. Knocking Cam back and kicking books in all directions. But she wasn't finished. She wasn't even fazed.

She just stretched to her fullest height and roared, "Stop seeing what you *want* to see, Merik Nihar, and start seeing what's really here!"

Then she launched past him, aiming for the door. It slammed, leaving him alone with his winds, his rage, and books scattered everywhere.

TWENTY-FIVE

The Dreaming was different tonight. Vastly so.

Iseult found herself in Esme's tower, a decrepit, crumbling thing in Poznin that she'd seen once before—except that the last time, it had been through Esme's eyes.

This time, Iseult saw the tower through her own. She was in Poznin, in her very own body, and staring at the back of a girl she could only assume was the Puppeteer.

Iseult had no idea how she was here. She had drifted off just a few moments earlier, while the Bloodwitch stood guard nearby. Then she had awoken—if it could even be called that—in this tower. Her vision had been fuzzy at first, the bricks of this top floor blurring into a gray mass, the darkness of the night outside like a black blob in the middle. Iseult had recognized it anyway.

She had recognized the Puppeteer too, even though she'd never seen the girl. Esme sat on a stool, facing a desk on which books were piled. Candles shimmered on the desk, on the windowsill, on jutting stones in the wall, casting the entire space in a flickering warmth.

Esme's long black hair was divided into two braids, and as

280

Iseult's vision cleared, she realized the bright bursts of color within Esme's hair were actually strips of felt. Strings of beads. Dried flowers too.

When at last the girl turned, it was clear from her soft cry and widening hazel eyes, that she hadn't realized anyone was present.

Then her pale Nomatsi face lit up. "It's you," she whispered, before racing across the uneven floor toward Iseult.

Iseult's dream-body reeled back two steps. The room turned foggy, unraveling around the edges. Esme reached her. Everything sharpened to a perfect, crisp focus as if Iseult were truly standing in the room.

Except that when Esme reached for Iseult, her hands cut right through.

The girl laughed, an easy, lilting sound. "It's as if you're standing here with me! You look so clear. How?" She scurried left, circling Iseult. Her eyes raking up and down.

"I . . . I don't know." Iseult's dream-tongue felt fat. Her throat too tight.

"You're taller than I thought you'd be," Esme chimed, clapping her hands. "And more muscled." She grabbed for Iseult's biceps, but of course, her fingers whispered through.

Another delighted laugh. She pranced back in front of Iseult, and this time her attention fixed on Iseult's face.

A frown knit down her forehead. "You have a scar beside your eye. Like a red teardrop. When did that happen?"

Lejna, Iseult wanted to snap. *The Poisonwitches that you cleaved.* But she swallowed her dream-words. If Esme had been angry about Iseult's treatment of those Cleaved on the

Nomatsi road, how would she feel about the ones Iseult and Aeduan had decapitated in Lejna?

Fortunately, Esme didn't noticed Iseult's silence. Instead, she was opening her arms and asking, "Do I look as you expected?"

Iseult forced herself to nod, even though it wasn't true. The Puppeteer was much prettier—easily the most beautiful Nomatsi woman Iseult had ever seen, with her delicate jaw and lucent white skin. The flashes of color in her long hair enhanced the beauty, as did the dimple in her right cheek that flashed whenever she smiled.

"You're . . . smaller than I imagined." That, at least, was true. Esme's petite stature simply didn't align with the enormous magic she controlled.

"What a wonderful surprise to have you here." Esme's dimple sank deeper. "I was studying, as I always do at this hour. Night is the only time I have for myself." The dimple vanished—but just for a moment. Then her grin rallied, and she traipsed off toward the desk.

"You must be in one of the old places," she called over her shoulder. "Somewhere like my tower, where the walls between this world and the Old Ones is thinner. But which place, I wonder?" She grabbed a ragged tome off her desk, setting the nearest candles to guttering.

Then she spun toward Iseult. "OPEN YOUR EYES."

The strength of the command—and the surprise of it— slammed over Iseult. She couldn't resist, not before the tower scene dissolved and the ruins where Iseult slept coalesced.

Esme exhaled more glee. Somehow, she stood beside Iseult, her book clutched tight, and Iseult was hovering above her own sleeping body. Ice splintered through Iseult's dream-self. She'd never seen magic like this. Never *heard* of it either.

Esme didn't notice Iseult's distress. The Puppeteer was, for once, fully separate from Iseult's mind. No reading of Iseult's thoughts, no stealing of Iseult's secrets.

"This is definitely a palace from the old days. Those statues give it away. But are they owls or are they rooks?"

Owls? Iseult looked to where Esme motioned. Starlight poured over the eroded monoliths in each corner of the room; they looked like nothing but stone slabs covered in yellow lichen to Iseult. Not owls or rooks or anything else.

"And of course," Esme continued, "the ease with which we can speak also shows this place for what it is." She was talking to herself now, and after kneeling at the center of the room, she opened the book. There was no light to read by, but Esme didn't need it. It was as if the candles in Poznin transferred here.

Iseult crept closer to Esme, her eyes bouncing from whatever it was the Puppeteer inspected to her own sleeping self. *Wrong.*

Iseult's body never stirred, and Esme's pages made no sound. *Wrong, wrong.* In fact, nothing but Esme's voice carried here.

"I don't see this place," Esme said, sitting cross-legged. "Eridysi's notes don't mention it."

"Eridysi?" The name blurted out before Iseult could stop it. Before she could even let the name sink in—for of course Esme couldn't be referring to Eridysi the Sightwitch who'd written the famous "Lament" centuries before. Just as Iseult's

283

old rag doll hadn't been named after *that* Eridysi either but had merely been a name she'd found pretty as a little girl.

Except that Esme did indeed mean the famed Sightwitch. "Yes," she said simply. "Ragnor gave me the old Sightwitch Sister's journal a few years ago." She tossed a sideways smile at Iseult. Almost coy. "Everything I know is from these pages. From cleaving to reanimating to binding puppets to the Loom. And you can learn it all too, Iseult."

Or maybe I could unlearn it. Before Iseult could ask how to avoid this . . . this dream-walking, Aeduan entered the room.

He prowled like a caged animal, passing directly through Esme. His nostrils fluttered as he sniffed, yet whatever he might have sensed, it was obvious that he could not see Esme or Iseult hovering like ghosts in the middle of the ruins.

Esme pushed to her feet, glaring knives at Iseult. "You're still with him. I *told* you he was dangerous, Iseult."

"He saved my life." Iseult scarcely heard her own words. Her attention was captured by the Bloodwitch—whose attention was captured by the sleeping Iseult.

No sniffing. No prowling. Just staring at her, expression unreadable.

"He saved your life from what?" Esme demanded. She pushed in front of Iseult, blocking the view of Aeduan. When Iseult still didn't answer, she repeated, "Saved your life from *what?*"

Esme's free hand swept up, fingers splayed, and she charged it into Iseult's skull.

The Dreaming took hold. No more ruins, no more shadow selves, no more Bloodwitch. Iseult was trapped, and Esme controlled her mind once more.

Nothing was private. In seconds, Esme had the memory she sought. *Oh, goddess bless me.* Her words echoed within Iseult's skull. *Those men almost caught you—and the Bloodwitch did save you.*

More rummaging. Worms in Iseult's brain. *Nine times four, thirty-six. Nine times fifteen, one hundred and thirty-five . . .*

Iseult's multiplication didn't stop Esme.

These men work for . . . Corlant? Who is he? A Purist priest, but . . . Esme trailed off, and hints of blue understanding lanced through the Dreaming. *I know that man,* she continued at last. *But by a different name. If he hunts you, Iseult, then that means you . . . It means he . . .* Esme's surprise kicked over Iseult. *Oh, this is unexpected. And surely a mistake! You cannot possibly be the Cahr Awen, can you?*

NO! Iseult squeezed out. With far too much emphasis. But striking a balance was always so hard in the Dreaming. Especially after the ease of the ghost ruins.

A long pause settled then, suggesting Esme pondered and mused. The seconds blended into minutes, and all Iseult could do was wait. Alone. In a world of endless, choking shadows.

Until at last, Esme spoke again—and Iseult's traitorous dream-lungs shuddered with relief.

Perhaps you are the Cahr Awen, Iseult. Or perhaps you are not. Either way, you should not need the Bloodwitch to save you anymore. Four men is easy for the likes of us. Simply cleave them and be done.

Look, I will show you how.

A flash of light. Then they were back in Esme's tower, but

this time Iseult was trapped in Esme's mind. Forced to see through Esme's eyes.

The girl was at her window, seemingly unconcerned by the candle flames winking so near or the wax melting onto her gown. She pointed into the darkness, squinting until the rows of the Cleaved—the same rows Iseult had seen two weeks before—came into focus. Shady silhouettes in the darkness.

"There is a man in the front," Esme said. "Do you see him, with the apron? He used to be a blacksmith."

Iseult did see the man—there was no way to avoid it when Esme fixed her eyes on him. The man's gray apron was stained black with blood.

"He was a weak Ironwitch," the Puppeteer explained, her voice quite cool. Quite calm. "In his village, he had a Thread-brother. An elementally powerless man. When I cleaved the blacksmith, the Threadbrother tried to intervene. I don't know what he *thought* he could do. When a man is cleaving, there is little to heal him save the Moon Mother ... and me, of course." Esme spoke matter-of-factly—no sign of vanity as she declared her power equal to that of their goddess.

"For some reason, though," Esme continued, fatigue creeping into her tone, "I didn't let the blacksmith attack his Threadbrother. I suppose I still felt generous in those days, and I called the blacksmith away before he could kill anyone. But look—do you see the pink Threads? They shimmer inside the Severed Threads. They still remain even when all other Threads have vanished." Esme scrutinized the Threads spinning over the cleric's body, waiting for Iseult to answer.

So Iseult made her Dreaming self say, *Yes, Esme. I see the Threads of friendship.*

"That is how I control them. I sever all their Threads save one, then I bind that final Thread to the Loom. But that is complicated. A technique I will teach you another night. For now, all you need to know is how to *kill them*."

With that declaration, the Puppeteer's hands lifted, her wrists so fine, her forearms so fragile. This close, though, there was no missing how similar her fingers were to Iseult's: thin to the point of knobby, and widely spaced when flexed.

The Puppeteer reached out, fingers curling and stretching like a musician at the harp.

Or a weaver at the loom.

The blacksmith's Threads—the sunset-colored strands that still bound him to his distant Threadbrother—floated ever so slowly toward Esme's hands, stretching thinner and thinner as they moved . . . then sliding into the gaps between her fingers.

Once the Threads had strained so thin as to be almost invisible, and had gathered so thickly around Esme's fingers that they looked like a glowing ball of pink yarn, she drew her hands to her face. "Now all it takes is a little snip."

Esme's face dipped forward, and Iseult had the sensation of her mouth opening, of her teeth baring and the Threads slipping between . . .

Esme snapped her jaw shut. The Threads cracked like a misstep on a frozen lake. In a flash of light, the strands shriveled inward, shrank backward, vanished entirely.

The blacksmith started convulsing. He fell to his knees as fresh pustules rippled and popped across his body. Then Esme turned away from the window, and Iseult lost sight of him.

287

"The cleaving will burn through him completely now." Esme dusted off her hands as if bits of Thread still clung. "He will be dead in seconds."

Iseult had no response. Heat was rising in her chest. Boiling in her throat. This was not Thread magic. This was not Aether magic. This was *not* something Iseult could do.

She was not like Esme. *She was not like Esme!*

"What is wrong with you, Iseult?"

N-nothing, she tried to say. She needed to escape. She needed to wake up. *I . . . want to try what you showed me,* she lied. Anything to escape the Dreaming.

It worked. Esme smiled—Iseult *felt* the smile spread across a face that was not her own. Then Esme nodded, sending the view of the tower lurching. "Good, Iseult. Practice, and before long, we will be together."

Esme clapped her hands.

The world went black, and Iseult finally toppled into true, dreamless sleep.

The Threadwitch made too much noise.

Aeduan never would have expected it from her. She was so stoic, so hard. Yet here they were: Aeduan attempting to finish his morning routine, and the Threadwitch constantly interrupting.

He had moved from the inner rooms of the ancient fortress at first light, finding an open area on one of the higher steppes. Fire had burned through here, recently enough to have cleared away saplings and underbrush in a storm-struck burst of flames. It happened often in the Contested Lands, almost as if the gods swooped through from time to time, clearing out the old. Making space for the new.

It was like the Nomatsi skipping rhyme.

> *Dead grass is awakened by fire,*
> *dead earth is awakened by rain.*
> *One life will give way to another,*
> *the cycle will begin again.*

That was the tune the Threadwitch sang this morning. She crooned wildly off-key, and it was wildly distracting for Aeduan, who meditated cross-legged atop a fallen column.

She cut off once she'd realized he was there, but it was too late. His concentration had been disrupted.

He would have cursed at the girl if he'd thought it would make a difference. It wouldn't, though, and the instant he rose and slipped free of his Carawen cloak, she resumed her tune—a soft humming while she assembled a campfire with practiced ease.

Aeduan attempted to begin his morning warm-up instead, rolling his wrists and swinging his arms, but he couldn't focus. Not with all her noise.

"Quiet," he snarled at last.

"Why?" she countered, defiance in the lift of her chin.

"You distract me."

The defiance expanded, moving from her face to her shoulders. She straightened. "I thought you were a monk no longer. So why are you meditating or ... whatever this is?"

Aeduan ignored her and shifted into warming kicks, his legs loose as he flung them high.

289

"What was it like, being a monk?" She stepped closer.

Three more kicks, and he moved to squats. *One, two—*

"Anyone can become a monk," she went on, striding in front of him now. "Regardless of their background or their" —she waved at him—"witchery."

"No." Aeduan knew he ought to leave this conversation and the Threadwitch alone, but he couldn't let her words— false as they were—hang between them. "Trust me, Threadwitch," he huffed between squats, "monks can be as cruel as the rest of humanity. They simply do it in the name of the Cahr Awen."

"You left because of cruelty?"

Aeduan paused at the top of his next squat. The girl's face was blank, and even her expressive nose was completely still.

He sighed. "Simply because I have lost faith in the cause doesn't mean the training has lost all of its usefulness."

Her head tipped sideways. "And why don't you believe in the cause?"

What had Aeduan stepped into? One question begat another hundred, and now the girl had landed on the last subject Aeduan wished to discuss. Ever.

"Enough." He turned away from her. "Leave this area or be quiet."

He moved for a shaded patch in the clearing, where the grass was the shortest and no crumbling fortress could get in the way. Where he could spin and roll, kick and curl.

For some unfathomable reason, the Threadwitch followed.

"You can avoid answering me for now, but I intend to keep asking." There was an urgency in her voice. Not a stammer, like he'd caught slipping in a few times. This was a hot intensity.

And she was standing much too close. Entering his personal space in a way no one ever dared. "Back away," he warned, "or I'll assume you wish to join the training."

"I won't leave until you answer." She moved another pace, and the challenge was there. In her eyes, in her stance, in her jaw.

A thrill rose in Aeduan's gut. Then he swept her legs out from under her.

She saw it coming—she was ready for it—but Aeduan was too fast to stop. His foot swung out, and she fell.

Yet before her back could hit the grass, Aeduan caught her and eased her down. She grabbed his shirt in two white-knuckled fists as her back settled onto the dewy earth.

"You shouldn't waste energy," she said flatly, "on showing off." No fear in her yellow Nomatsi eyes, just a slight flush on her cheeks.

Aeduan almost laughed at those flags of color—and at her words too, for this was not showing off. This was merely the most basic of Carawen training. To prove that point, he gripped her wrist with his opposite hand, dug his fingers into her tendons, and twisted inward. Her joints had no choice but to follow.

She released his shirt, but to his surprise, she didn't shrink away or buck her hips in panic. She simply kicked her feet wide, hooking with her heels. Trying to pin him to the grass. Too slow, she was too slow. A beginning grappler facing a master.

Aeduan squeezed tighter, twisting harder and forcing her

to roll sideways. In half a breath, she had pivoted completely onto her belly, her head swiveled back. Now there was no missing what burned in her eyes. No Threadwitch calm remained.

She had asked him for this; she knew it and she was furious.

"Why do you care," Aeduan said, "if I left the Monastery?"

"I don't ... care ... that you left." The strain was back in her words, a sound Aeduan was a beginning to recognize as a sign she fought off a stutter. "I care ... why. Do you not believe in the Cahr Awen anymore?"

Aeduan hesitated, caught off guard by her pointed question. Then he remembered.

"Ah. Monk Evrane has filled your head with nonsense, and now you think you are the Cahr Awen." He released her, rolling off her back and hopping to his feet. He offered her his hand.

She didn't take it. Just pushed onto her hands and knees, staring down at the grass. "Why ... is it nonsense?"

"You are not a Voidwitch." His words were inflectionless, yet they seemed to hit her like stones.

She flinched. Then said, "B-but ... I ... *we* healed the Well."

Aeduan's head tipped sideways. He inhaled a long breath of the humid, morning air while crickets whistled from the forest and, again, distant thunder rolled.

"Yes," he admitted eventually, "someone healed it." He had seen the waking Origin Well himself, yet it had not seemed fully intact—nothing like the Aether Well that Aeduan had spent most of his childhood living beside.

292

He said as much, adding, "It was as if the Well was only partially alive. As if only half of the Cahr Awen had healed it, and I do not think, Threadwitch, that you were that half."

Now it was the girl's turn to exhale, "Ah." She scrabbled upright. Her body wobbled, her gaze jumpy and unfocused.

Aeduan could see right away that he had made a mistake. He should have said nothing. He should have let her keep hoping for a pointless, fruitless fantasy.

After all, an unhappy Threadwitch would only slow them.

"First lesson of a Carawen novice," Aeduan offered, acting as if nothing had just passed between them. "Do not challenge someone more skilled than you."

Iseult's nostrils twitched. Her face hardened. The defiance, the determination—they were back, and against his will, Aeduan's lips twitched upward.

"I didn't challenge you," she said coolly.

"Getting too close is considered a challenge in most cultures."

"Then teach me."

His eyebrows lifted.

"What you just did, pinning me like that. Teach me, so I won't make the same mistake again."

"We don't have time for that." He shook his head, and then with great deliberation, he turned his back on the Threadwitch.

She attacked.

And Aeduan smiled.

TWENTY-SIX

Despite her strongest attempts not to, Safi had fallen asleep. All through the night and into the next day, she'd slept. Food, a bath, *and* a taro game—it had been too much for her body, and she'd curled up beside Vaness on the bed. Her eyes had seared shut. Then the Hell-Bards and the empress and the Pirate Republic of Saldonica had drifted away.

Until the knock sounded at the door.

That jerked Safi awake so fast that she fell from the bed. Her limbs tangled in the new silk-wrapped ropes that Lev had, quite apologetically, tied around her ankles after the trip into Red Sails territory.

The Hell-Bards had knives and hatchets drawn before Safi could right herself, and by the time she did struggle to her feet, Lev—the only one in full armor—was creeping toward the door with a blade outstretched.

A second knock. Efficient, determined. Safi glanced at the empress, who sat calmly near the close-slatted shutters. Hands folded upon her lap, posture perfect atop the lone stool.

"You should not have come here!" shouted a man in Marstoki.

The empress's nostrils flared with a poorly concealed smile—which meant this must be part of her plan. If Safi only knew what it *actually* entailed.

The Hell-Bards were clearly as lost as she, for Lev and Zander ogled Caden, waiting for a command that wasn't coming.

"Do you speak Marstoki?" the empress asked, so prim. *Too* prim. She pushed to her feet, the collar at her neck seeming light as dandelions for all it slowed her rise. "They said that we should not have come here."

Caden lifted one hand, a knife flashing. Then he sniffed at the air, his narrowed eyes fixing on the window. "Smoke," he said.

As one, everyone's heads yanked toward the shutters, where sure enough, gray was just starting to trickle through.

"Hell pits," Lev swore at the same moment Zander rumbled, "I warded against Firewitched flames!"

"Yes, but these are not magic flames," Vaness inserted, beaming now. A hungry smile. "They are alchemical, for that is Baedyed seafire."

"But we're not at sea," Lev muttered. "And why burn the entire inn? I thought they wanted only you." She threw a look at the empress.

"Do you not want the Empress of Marstok?" Caden shouted, still using Cartorran. "She will die if you do not let us free."

"She deserves no less!" came the muffled reply. Then an

impassioned, "Why should we take only pieces of the Sand Sea when we could have all of Marstok instead?"

A moment of crackling silence while the blood seemed to drain from Vaness's face.

Then a choked cry split her lips. She lurched from her stool and to the window. Before anyone could stop her, she had the shutters yanked open. "*Stand down!*" she shrieked as smoke billowed in. "As your empress, I order you to stand down!"

"*For the Sand Sea! For the Sand Sea!*"

A flash of light tore through the room, rushing over Safi in a burst of magic. Three more flashes, and then Zander was hauling the empress away from the window. Squinting through the bright onslaught, Safi realized crossbow bolts flew against the wards and ricocheted backward.

The protective magic was working—at least against the attack outside. Smoke, though, was coiling in. Hot, choking, and all too familiar. Too recent and too fresh, it set Safi's throat to tightening. *Smoke. Flames. Death.*

"Expand the wards against real fire," Caden barked at Zander. He turned next to Lev. "We need to keep the smoke out as long as possible." Then together, he and Lev tore the wool coverlet off the bed and with a practiced speed set to billowing it like a topsail.

White light cracked through the room, and smoke burned in Safi's tear ducts. She dragged herself to the wall where Vaness cowered.

None of the empress's perfect mask remained now. Through the haze and the blasting lights, Safi found a wide-eyed empress. Her fingers were white-knuckled around the collar as she tugged it, arms shaking. *Everything* shaking.

"They betrayed me," she mumbled, her quivering eyes fixing on Safi. "They betrayed me." It was all she would say, over and over again, "They betrayed me."

Abruptly, the flashing light stopped. No more bolts cracked against the ward, and Caden and Lev had reached the window with their waving banner. Safi hardly noticed, for now Vaness was wrenching at her collar with such desperation that her nose had begun to bleed. A downward seep from one nostril.

"Stop." Safi scuttled in close, grabbing the empress's wrists. "You can't break through this."

Vaness's eyes flicked up, thinning into violent slits. "Do you not see, Safi? The Baedyeds have betrayed me. They were the *rot* in my court all this time—and *they* were the ones who destroyed my ship and killed my . . ." Her voice broke, and she pushed unsteadily to her feet. "Free me," she flung at the Hell-Bards in Cartorran. Blood trickled from both nostrils now.

"Our wards will hold," Caden answered. Yet as soon as that statement fell, stony and unyielding, Zander turned away from his spot at the door and said, "I can't expand the wards, sir. Not while we're under attack—the flames below are rising too fast."

Lev swung toward Vaness. "How would you get us out?"

"I can snuff out the flames. I have done it before."

"She has," Safi offered, scrabbling upright. "It's how we survived the attack on our ship."

Caden anchored his gaze to Vaness, and his two Hell-Bards anchored their gazes to the commander. Waiting.

Until at last Caden asked, "How do we know you will not turn on us, Your Majesty?"

"Because there is no time," Vaness said. Yet even through the madness hitting the room, even through the heat now rising against the floorboards, Safi felt the lie in her words.

"We can't be killed by your magic," Caden continued, sheathing his knife. A cautious movement, as if he still debated what to do. "There is no point trying."

"Your death," Vaness flung back, faster now, "will not help me. Seafire burns much faster than natural flame, and we are out of time!" She slung a pointed finger toward the door, where smoke now coiled in through the cracks.

Zander swore; Lev grabbed for the wool blanket; Caden's hands settled on either side of Vaness's collar. His mouth moved silently until a click rippled through the room. The wooden collar cut wide.

Instantly, Vaness was moving. Out of the collar, which fell to the ground in a plank-trembling *thunk*, she grabbed Safi and shot for the door. "Pull down the wards," she ordered Zander. "We cannot exit while they still stand."

Zander looked at Caden. The commander nodded. "Do it."

The giant's arms rose, and he muttered softly. The room flickered and hummed, and power unwound strand by strand in a way that made no sense to Safi—Hell-Bards doing magic?

Then silver and darkness erupted, blurring streaks as Vaness called every piece of iron in the room to her. Two chunks reshaped themselves into blades, effortlessly slicing through Vaness's and Safi's ropes, before spiraling up into thin rapiers to be plucked from the air. One for the empress, one for Safi.

The ward fell. Safi felt it in a great eruption of noise and a violent battering of crossbow bolts against the outside walls.

"Get us out of here!" Caden barked at Vaness.

"No," she replied. Her hands rose. The Hell-Bards' blades turned on them and drove straight for their skulls.

Like minnows through a stream, the iron simply sizzled through and flipped out the backs of each Hell-Bard's head—and the chains at the Hell-Bards' throats glowed red.

Vaness seemed to know this would happen, though. She seemed to *want* it for the brief distraction it gave while she turned her magic to the door.

A groan of metal sent Safi spiraling away from the Hell-Bards. The door's hinges were peeling back. The latch was releasing, reshaping. Then, before any of the Hell-Bards could stop her, Vaness's arms flew straight up.

The door swung past Safi and Vaness. A blast of air and smoke and heat. It spun sideways before crashing into all three Hell-Bards. It flung them back against the wall, as easy as a flyswatter to three flies.

"We were only following orders," Caden shouted. With smoke rushing over him, he looked ghostly. Skeletal. "We were only doing our jobs."

"And I," Vaness growled, her face striped with blood, "am only doing mine." She spun for the empty doorway.

Safi didn't chase after, though. She was staring at Caden on the left. At Lev in the middle. At Zander on the right. She didn't trust the Hell-Bards, she didn't like the Hell-Bards, yet that did not mean she could leave them to die.

"Wait!" she hollered at Vaness, and the empress paused at the door. Behind her, a wall of iron scuttled upward, plucked from hinges and nails and anything her Ironwitchery could grasp. "Let them go."

"They will try to capture us again."

"No!" Lev cried. The scars on her face flickered and glowed. "We will help you!"

"We cannot trust them," Vaness insisted. She reached for Safi's arm. Blood dripped from her chin. "We have to go, Safi. *Now.*"

"You can trust us." This came from Zander, his face drawn tight as the door squashed him harder, harder to the wall. "We can prove it. Just let me remove my noose—"

"I already did."

All eyes snapped to Caden, whose fingers poked above the door, a gold chain woven between his knuckles. It was the necklace all Hell-Bards wore, including Safi's uncle. And it was, Safi realized, what they'd all meant when they referred to the noose.

"On our honor," Caden croaked, the words seeming to take great effort—and to cause great pain—"we won't hurt you."

It was the first assertion from a Hell-Bard that rang against Safi's magic, and it was *true.*

"We won't capture you again," he went on, his face screwed tighter. "We'll all escape together."

Still true, true, *true*—there was no denying it. Safi's magic was alight with the honesty in his words, and though it made no sense to her, she couldn't deny what she saw. What she felt.

"Free them!" she shrieked at Vaness. "He speaks the truth—we can trust them. They'll *help* us."

A pause took hold of the world. Smoke, heat, sparks. It all melted back while the empress considered.

"Hurry!" Safi tried to scream, but at that precise moment, the entire inn *cracked!* Then sagged sharply down.

Time was up, and the empress knew it. With a snarl, she let the door fall. Caden fell into Lev, who instantly helped him refasten the noose. Meanwhile, Vaness claimed all iron from the door, strips of black to fill the air. To expand her shield before they all tromped off into the corridor with a wall of iron to press back the smoke, the flames.

It protected them step-by-step, Safi and Vaness at the fore, three Hell-Bards staggering behind.

It was right as Aeduan and Iseult were gathering their things from the ruins that a *boom* split the air. A distant sound, like a cannon fired off leagues away.

Iseult met Aeduan's eyes. "People," she said.

He nodded.

"We should check," she said.

He nodded again. "Stay here."

She didn't. And he sighed—something he found himself doing more and more often around her. He didn't stop her, though, and in minutes they'd threaded their way back to the same steppe they'd sparred upon.

The grass remained trampled where he'd pinned her again and again. Aeduan had never hurt her—he'd been careful to always stop, to always watch her face for pain—but he also never let her win. Just as Monk Evrane had never let *him* win.

From the steppe, they ascended, zigzagging up the forested cliff until they reached an opening in the oaks and pines.

Until they saw the boats drifting up the Amonra.

Aeduan exhaled sharply; Iseult's nose twitched. "Red Sails," he guessed. "Baedyeds too. With the Twenty Year Truce over, I suspect they've allied for an attack." Quickly, he explained who the two pirate factions were and how whatever alliance they'd formed hovered beneath the tip of Lady Fate's knife.

As he spoke, Aeduan eased a bronze spyglass from his baldric and scanned the view. Each ship was packed with soldiers, and each soldier was well armed. People teemed along the shore too. Almost invisible, but if he fixed on one spot long enough . . . There. Movement. Horses. More soldiers.

"Where are they going?" Iseult asked once he'd finished his explanation.

"Upstream."

Now it was Iseult's turn to sigh, but she didn't say anything. In fact, the silence hung so long that Aeduan finally lowered his spyglass.

And found that she was watching him, her body still. For once, though, her face was not expressionless. It was tight with pain, her lips pinched and nose scrunched. Aeduan swallowed. Perhaps he *had* hurt her. Grass stains covered her shoulders, her knees, and a bruise purpled on her cheekbone.

But no. The longer he held her hazel gaze, the more he discerned. This wasn't pain—this was grief. For the second time that morning, he wished he had said nothing about the Cahr Awen.

He angled away, returning the spyglass to his baldric, and cleared his throat. "They will have to disembark before the Falls, Threadwitch. We need to be gone before that happens."

"Then let us leave," she said, voice flat.

"We will need to move fast. Are you up for that?"

She snorted, and when Aeduan glanced back, he found her face had softened. The slightest—almost imperceptible—glint of mischief hovered there now.

"I think we both know the answer to that, Bloodwitch." She stalked past him, her chin high. Challenging. "The question will be if *you* can keep up."

Then she broke into a run, Aeduan broke into a run after her.

TWENTY-SEVEN

Cam hadn't returned by morning of the next day. Merik had combed the streets of Old Town and the streets beyond—even the Cisterns too—but had found no trace of her.

Stop seeing what you want to see, Merik Nihar, and start seeing what's really here! Her last words grated within his eardrums. Over and over. Laughing. Taunting. A ghost that wanted release. *Stop seeing what you want to see!*

What Merik *wanted* to see was Cam, the friend who had stood by him through floods and hell-waters. Over Shite Street and back.

Before he'd pushed her away.

All Merik could figure was that Cam had gone out to search for answers on the dead man in the storerooms . . . And then she had stumbled upon something she couldn't fight. Like the shadow man.

Merik heaved his hood lower, streaking faster down Hawk's Way. *Stop seeing what you want to see!* The attack pounded in his chest, in his eardrums. Inescapable and all too true.

Merik had seen potential trade for Nubrevna where there

was none. He'd seen a navy that had "needed his leadership" when it hadn't. He'd seen a selfish domna in Safiya fon Hasstrel, a frustrating Threadwitch in Iseult det Midenzi, and then an inconsequential ship's boy in Cam—yet none of those presumptions had proved true.

Worst of all, in all of his holiest of holy conceit, Merik had seen a throne he thought he should sit upon—that Kullen had implied he should one day claim, even though that "greatness" was his sister's right by birth.

Merik jostled forward, slow. Too slow. Carts and refugees and thrice-damned mules everywhere he tried to step.

A man stumbled against Merik's back, and when Merik didn't budge, the man shoved. "Stand aside—"

Merik had the man's wrist in an instant, twisting until he felt the ligaments and bone strain. Another inch, and they would snap. "I will kill you," was all Merik said.

"Please," the man stammered.

Merik released him. Flung him away. He wanted to roar. *I am dangerous!*

But the words never came, for at that moment, a cool wind spiraled against Merik's flesh. A breeze that sang to his witchery.

Death. Shadows. It called him . . . south. Farther down Hawk's Way. The same icy darkness that had spoken to him in the storerooms—the same frozen curse that he feared might have claimed Cam.

Merik abandoned the quay, hurtling into a dark alley. There, he sprang up, foot by foot. Leaping one wall to the other, a wind to punt him higher. Side to side, until finally he hit a shingled roof.

Sunlight burned down. He dropped to a crouch and flexed his fingers, watching as dust coiled outward, carried by his winds. He reached for anything his charged air connected with.

There. Straight ahead.

Merik set off, cloak flying around him. His hood fell back. His boots slammed onto shingles, knocking them. Cracking them. Shattering more than a few.

He reached the end of the building. Gathering his breath and his power, Merik bounded over a strip of black alley. Rooftop after rooftop, the gap between Merik and this darkness—a shadow that *sang* to his blood—shrank with each gusting bound.

Until the rooftops ended, forcing him to stop. The Southern Wharf spanned before him, and beyond it, the water-bridge thrust across the clouded valley toward the Sentries.

So crowded. Boats crammed bow to stern, leaving no water visible. No gap in the people arriving.

Merik sank flat against the sloped shale and snaked to the edge. Instinct sent him grabbing for a spyglass in his admiral's coat . . .

But of course, he had no coat. No spyglass. No weapon.

No matter. He didn't need that—not when his blood *hungered* for that shadow wind.

A quick scan of the wharf showed ethnicities as varied as ages, as voices, as degrees of desperation. These were not only Nubrevnans but people from outside the borders as well. People from the Contested Lands or the unstable Sirmayans.

Merik's eyes snagged on a bald man hovering where the docks jutted into the man-made harbor. He was as badly scarred as Merik, at least on his scalp—as well as on the hand he now lifted overhead.

A hand with no pinkie.

Chills lifted across Merik's neck and arms as he wondered if it could be another man like the one from the storerooms. Then the man turned, and it was Garren. The assassin from the *Jana*.

For several booming heartbeats, the wharf seemed to fall away. All Merik saw was the assassin, and all he heard was his blood thumping in his ears. No wind reached his cheeks, no voices hit his ears.

The entire world was a dead man walking.

That night, in the darkness of his cabin, Merik had thrust a cutlass through Garren's gut. Blood had sprayed; innards had fallen. Yet here the man now stood.

Merik squinted. Sunspots speckled his vision, but he could still make out the jagged black lines throbbing down the man's neck.

Marks like Merik's.

Marks that called to him.

He hadn't known what those lines meant earlier. He didn't know what they meant now. He simply knew that Cam was right: they were bad.

And Merik knew that if following Garren might lead him to Cam, then he couldn't stop now.

Garren shuffled away from Merik, pushing steadily through the chaos. He aimed for a bar called the Cleaved Man that hugged the canal. A large stone building filled with sailors and soldiers and those who needed a cheap drink.

In moments, Merik was off the roof and approaching the

ramshackle tavern. The crowds settled into cursory background noise, vague colors of no import.

Then he was there, at the Cleaved Man and staring at the sign creaking on the breeze. The blackened eyeball painted on the wood felt a little too familiar. A little too ... *real*.

The door swung wide. Merik ducked his head as two sailors staggered into the day, drunk even at this hour. Behind them, though—that was what interested Merik. For somewhere within, darkness slithered and dead men walked.

Merik found the entryway just as he remembered from past visits, half the lamps unlit, the blue rugs muddied to brown, and everything coated in the sheen of ox tea. The Cleaved Man brewed many varieties of alcohol in the basement, but their most famous was ox tea, which was neither tea nor related to an ox.

But it got a man drunk. Fast. And in a world torn apart by enemies and empty stomachs, patrons wanted to get drunk. Fast.

Merik reached the bar's main space. It spread before him, candles flickering from fat chandeliers. Wax dripped onto people at the dozens of rickety tables. Merik was halfway to a door in the back corner, when he realized a hush had wrapped around the room. The revelers had stopped reveling, and at the nearest table, a sailor sat immobile with a flagon of ox tea halfway to his lips.

A nudge from his neighbor. A cough from nearby. Then all at once, wood groaned, vibrating through the floor as every person who sat abruptly decided to stand.

"I told you he would come." A man's voice, greasy and familiar, snaked through the silence.

Merik whirled toward the bar, to where a sweaty Serrit Linday held his arm outstretched.

For the briefest fraction of a moment, the world slowed. Stopped entirely. *I saw you die*, Merik thought. Yet here Linday stood, a second dead man walking—and now speaking too, with almost giddy delight, "Arrest him, soldiers. Arrest the Fury."

Safi, Vaness, and the Hell-Bards burst out of the inn mere minutes before it crashed to the ground in a cacophony of black seafire. They bolted through the bathhouse, using plumes of smoke to hide themselves, before tumbling into a scalding midday that had no business being so sunny, so blue.

Zander led the way, though as far as Safi could tell, every street looked the same. More buildings cradled in ruins from a forgotten past. The blood from Vaness's nose gushed at a rate that no body could sustain, much less while sprinting at top speed through a hostile city. With Lev on one side and Safi on the other, the empress managed to maintain at least a stumbling jog onward.

Caden kept the rear, an iron longsword—created by Vaness from the two rapiers—in hand.

As Zander led them into a five-way intersection, elm guttered and Baedyed bannered like every other in the district, Vaness planted her heels. "Must . . . stop," she panted, doubling over.

Safi circled back with Lev, and horror pummeled through her. Blood from Vaness's nose streaked behind them, a trail

309

that any idiot could follow. *Think like Iseult, think like Iseult.* First things first: the blood. They had to stop it from falling.

But Lev was already tearing fabric from her sleeve. "Here." Crouching, Lev pressed it to the empress's nose. "We have to keep moving."

"I know." Her voice was thick beneath the dark cotton. "I'll manage. Just let me breathe . . . for . . . a moment—"

"We don't have a moment!" Caden rushed in. He pushed Lev aside and hooked his much larger, much stronger arm behind the empress. "The Baedyeds are right on our tail. We need to *move.*" As Safi released Vaness, he lugged the empress back into a jog.

Just in time, for a man wearing Baedyed gold was most assuredly sprinting their way. *Fast.*

But Caden was already gone, already ducking low and wrenching Vaness down the narrowest of the five streets. "Meet you around!" he shouted, leaving Safi with no choice but to ratchet her legs faster after Lev and Zander.

Except that they were gone too, lost in the crowds, and now a second Baedyed was barreling right for her.

"Muck-eating bastards!" Safi screeched, running for the only route left to her: straight ahead. As her heels pounded hard on the packed earth, her temper flared straight up from her toes. The shit noggins had left her! And *meet you around* where, precisely?

Safi hooked left, into a clump of men bowed low beneath creaking laundry baskets. As they angled onto another road, Safi angled too. She shoved at the nearest man. He tripped, his basket fell, laundry bursting forth to trip the men behind him. Traffic halted, but Safi was already through.

At the next intersection, Safi ran smack-dab into Caden and Vaness. Oh, and there was Zander and Lev too, hurtling ahead and clearing a way through traffic.

She amended her estimation of *muck-eating bastards.* Though only slightly.

The road ran downhill now, offering a view of the open market, with its seascape of tents rippling on the breeze. Alarm bells rang—when had that begun?—and it meant either more Baedyeds waited ahead or the fire at the inn had spread.

Probably both. Yet no one slowed. Not even Vaness, whom Caden practically carried now. Down they sped, Hell-Bard and heretic and empress alike. Intersections and people streamed past.

Until sure enough, precisely as Safi had feared, they all sprinted into the market and were swarmed by flashes of green and gold. It swam in from all angles. Baedyeds. *Angry* Baedyeds.

They skirted behind a series of tents, Zander in the lead, Safi at the rear. For the moment, no one followed. This little alley—if it could even be called that—was empty.

What would Iseult do? What would Iseult do?

Then Safi saw, and Safi knew. She couldn't help it—a smile tore over her face. "Ahead!" she bellowed. "*That carriage at the end of the tents!*"

Zander needed no more guidance. A carriage was stuck in the crowds, its shadow sweeping into the alley.

And its door quite unlocked, as Safi saw when Zander yanked it wide. The woman inside opened her mouth to scream, but Lev had a knife against her throat before the slightest peep could squeak out.

Then Caden, Vaness, and Safi were crawling inside behind the other two Hell-Bards. They toppled onto the benches, as Safi slammed the door shut.

One ragged breath passed. Two. Three. But if the carriage driver noticed new arrivals in all the chaos outside, he gave no indication.

What followed, Safi would remember for the rest of her life as one of the most peculiar half hours she ever spent. The elegant silence within the rocking carriage clashed with the traffic and alarms outside, while the tasteful blue-felted walls and crimson-curtained windows felt completely incongruous against the five unwelcome visitors, all panting and reeking of smoke.

Not to mention their unwilling hostess, a grandma with eyes of Fareastern descent, who seemed thoroughly unperturbed by the blade Lev held to her neck.

The only thing missing from this absurd tableau, Safi thought, *is a waltz humming in the background.* Then it could have been a scene right out of the stage comedies Mathew loved most.

"I'm . . . sorry," Caden offered to the woman eventually, still trying to catch his breath. "We need . . . a place to hide."

"We also need help for Vaness." Safi twisted to the empress beside her, who seemed barely able to cling to consciousness.

The Fareaster noticed the same, and without moving her arms, she pointed a single finger to a trunk beneath Safi's bench.

"A healer kit," Zander said, and the giant—already stooped to fit inside—stooped even more to tug it out from between Safi's legs.

"Careful," Caden warned, though his attention was on the empress. On keeping the cloth pressed to her gushing nose. "This woman is a slaver. She can't be trusted."

"A slaver?" Safi scoffed. "I don't think so. *Look* at her."

The woman's eyes shot side to side. Confused by the Cartorran language, perhaps, but not afraid.

"I am looking," Caden shot back. "At that healer kit. It's what slavers bring to the arena, since so many of their contestants come out of the fights half dead."

"He's . . . right," Vaness croaked—and Safi's magic hummed, *True.* Yet even as she held the old woman's dark gaze, she didn't see *how* it was possible. This slight grandma looked so kind and compassionate.

There are degrees of everything, Caden had said the day before, *which I know doesn't fit well into your* true-or-false *view of the world.*

Carefully, and with his enormous muscles bracing for a trap, Zander opened the trunk. No fires erupted; no poisons sprayed. Instead, they found exactly what was promised: a healer kit.

"May I?" Zander asked the woman with painstaking politeness—one more absurdity to add to the scene. But the woman was already twirling her hands toward Vaness as if to say, *Hurry, hurry!*

Zander hurried, rummaging through to find a blood-thickening tonic. Safi hurried, grabbing the bottle from the giant. Then Caden hurried too, ditching the soaked cotton

313

and tilting up Vaness's chin. A thick, syrupy tincture the color of old blood slid into her mouth.

Then everyone in the listing carriage stared—hard and relentless—at the Empress of Marstok.

She sucked in a breath, coughed once, and lowered her head. No blood poured from her nose. Her eyes, though red-rimmed, were open and alert.

As one, Safi's and the Hell-Bards' postures deflated. Their breaths collectively whooshed out.

Vaness, meanwhile, dragged her gaze over each Hell-Bard in turn. Zander, Lev, then Caden. "Thank you."

"Don't thank us yet." Caden inched aside the curtain, squinting into a sliver of sunlight. "The alarms are still clanging, and we're surrounded on all sides. It's only a matter of time before they start searching carriages."

"What about the Red Sails' territory?" Safi asked. "Couldn't we go there? Hide until this passes?"

Though Safi directed her question at Caden, it was the Fareaster woman who spoke. "They are united now." Her voice was a husky, rounded thing. "The Baedyeds and the Red Sails have allied under the Raider King's banner. He has promised them all of Nubrevna and Marstok in return."

Caden glanced at Safi, but there was nothing she could do beyond nod—for the grandma's words shivered with truth.

"Hell pits," Lev muttered at the same time that Caden groaned.

Vaness scooted forward, steel in her posture. "Why do you tell us this?"

"It is bad for business." The old woman's nose wrinkled and her tone turned frosty with condescension. "If the two sides become one, then trade is no longer controlled by supply and demand."

"You mean the *arena* is no longer controlled by it," Caden countered, and the woman simply bounced a single, unimpressed shoulder. As if to say, *Same idea.*

All the while, the carriage trundled on.

"Do you go there now?" Lev asked. "To the arena?"

The woman's nod sent Caden slouching back. "Good enough." He flashed a Chiseled Cheater grin at Safi and Vaness. "Our men are at the arena. Once we free them, we'll leave this festering swampland far behind. Together. Just as promised."

TWENTY-EIGHT

I t took several hours to descend the cliffs beside the Amonra Falls. The humidity and heat were suffocating, rising up from the gorge below.

Iseult never uttered a word about it, and of course, Aeduan didn't either.

He walked in front now, as if Iseult had passed whatever test he'd issued the day before. Or perhaps he'd just forgotten not to trust her. She suspected both. He'd also given her the salamander cloak and reclaimed the bland coat she'd first found him in.

It meant something—giving her that cloak for a second time. And though Iseult didn't know *what* precisely, she did know it felt good to be back beneath its thick fibers.

Especially since something fundamental had snapped inside her.

Hours after the fact and miles away, she finally understood it must have been her heart. That when Aeduan had told her she was not the Cahr Awen, she had felt a grief so rough, it had bowled her over and dragged her down. But at

316

the time, all she had known was that this was her confirmation. This was her proof.

She was broken. She was useless. She was the pointless half of a friendship. The one who would live forever in shadows, no matter what she did. No matter whom she fought. Never had Iseult asked for anything. Not since learning as a little girl that rusted locks on a door were the best she could ever hope for.

Then she'd met Safi, and secretly, silently, so deep no one would ever find it, Iseult had started to hope that her life might turn into something. Little dreams weren't so bad. Iseult could brush against them from time to time, and no one would ever be the wiser.

Only now, now that she couldn't have this one huge dream that she'd been whispering to herself couldn't possibly be true ... That *she* was part of the Cahr Awen. Only now did she realize how hungry she'd actually been for it.

All along, since she was a little girl.

Fanciful fool.

Attacking Aeduan had felt good. Too good. Iseult had lost herself in the sparring. In the grappling. In the bright bursts of pain each time Aeduan landed a blow.

She'd been soaked in sweat by the end, her chest heaving long before her body had given up; Aeduan had been too. Though Iseult's form had grown ragged, erratic as the sparring went on, and though he'd thrown her, strangled her, blocked her every punch, the Bloodwitch had never eased up or backed down.

Then racing him through the forest—that had felt even better. More fun than Iseult had had in a long time. A long,

long time, and she was grateful for it. Even now, with welts and bruises and aching calves. Perhaps, once the sore muscles fully took hold and she was too stiff to walk, Iseult would change her mind. But she suspected not.

After all, pain was her lesson for dreaming too big.

The valley beyond the Falls was blessedly cool. Ferns shivered on the breeze here, along with white- and yellow-petaled asphodels. Trees were rare, replaced by massive stone pillars that grew up from the earth, chiseled and striated by a river's changing course. The columns were all widths, all heights, all colors.

And always silent. No men traveled here.

Eventually, Aeduan led Iseult outside the narrow gorge, where the land opened into flat floodplains. Oaks reappeared, as did full shade against the sun.

Signs of humanity reappeared as well, but not of the living men who waited ahead. These were battlefields from a time long past, long forgotten.

Rusted helms and chest plates. Swords, spears, arrowheads. Signs of death were everywhere Iseult's gaze landed, some pieces so ancient, the earth and ferns had laid claim. Iseult would discover them only when they crumbled beneath her feet. Other remnants were new enough to shine, untouched where they'd fallen, left to cook beneath a boiling sun.

There were skeletons too, most shrouded in moss. Though not always.

"Why is this here?" Iseult asked eventually. "Why did no one bury or burn their dead?"

"Because there weren't enough survivors left to do so." Aeduan dipped right, drawing Iseult south. Closer to the

318

Amonra. Huge, smooth river boulders disrupted the soft soil here and saplings groped for the sky at odd angles.

The forest was eerily quiet, as if even the animals knew this place was damned. As if they knew pirates approached by boat.

So Iseult kept her voice low. "Why so much fighting? Is the land valuable?"

"There is nothing of value here." Aeduan also spoke softly. "Yet men have always believed that they know better than those who came before. That *they* will be the ones to claim the Contested Lands."

He hopped a stony rise and reached back, offering Iseult his hand. She took it, glad for the help even if her sore knuckles protested. His fingers were warm against hers.

"At the Monastery," he went on, releasing her, "they taught us that when the Paladins betrayed each other, they fought their final battle here. Their deaths cursed the soil, so no man can ever claim the Contested Lands. I think it all a lie, though."

"Why?"

He took a moment to answer, his hand flexing, as if she'd squeezed too tight.

"Because," he said eventually, the slightest frown marring his brow, "it is always easier to blame gods or legends than it is to face our own mistakes. This land is no more cursed than any other. It is simply steeped in too much blood."

With that statement, Aeduan resumed his forward hike, and Iseult followed. For another mile, they encountered no signs of human life. Only ancient, forgotten blood. Until Aeduan abruptly froze midstride.

"Red Sails," he murmured, crouching. Sniffing. "The ones who hunted you. We must circle north." He made it only three steps, though, before he paused a second time. Now his eyes shone crimson from rim to rim.

He abruptly turned to Iseult, his coat flicking like a cat's tail. "Wait here," he commanded. "I need to check something."

Iseult had no chance to speak before he had disappeared back into the forest. Her nose wiggled, but she made no attempt to follow. The Bloodwitch had guided her true so far, and only stasis would serve her well.

Or so she told herself as the heartbeats shivered past— and as the earth began to shake. Just a soft jolt. Almost imperceptible, save for how it sent Iseult's ankles rolling. Sent moths zipping up around her.

Then the earth trembled again, and this time, more than mere moths spun free. A giant swarm of starlings abandoned their branches and swooped above the trees.

A third quake shivered through the land. A great kick of the earth that sent Iseult tumbling to the ground. She immediately shoved back upright, pulse beating faster, but the ground still moved. Branches shook; leaves fell; squirrels and martins and thrushes now raced past.

A shadow swooped over the forest. Massive. Winged. And throbbing with bright silver Threads. Only once had Iseult seen Threads like those.

On sea foxes.

There are worse things in the Contested Lands than Blood-witches.

Iseult had assumed Aeduan meant worse *humans* than Bloodwitches—men like the Red Sails. Yet as the shadow streaked closer, silver Threads sparkling along its heart, she realized Aeduan hadn't meant humans at all.

He'd meant mountain bats, those massive serpentine creatures of myth. Those ancient scavengers of the battlefield.

Iseult scrabbled to her feet and ran.

There was only one reason Aeduan stalked toward the armies ahead—and he was certain there were armies.

He had smelled broken knuckles and torn-off fingernails, a stink that stood out against all the others. A sign the leader of the Red Sails lurked somewhere nearby. Yet it was the scent lingering beneath that wretchedness that hounded Aeduan. That propelled him ahead, the Threadwitch completely forgotten.

Rosewater and wool-wrapped lullabies. A child.

Cold spread through Aeduan's gut. Into his lungs, into his fists, it boomed in his eardrums. Only twice in the past decade had this feeling—this memory—been summoned fully to the surface. Twice, Aeduan had looked it directly in the eye and said, "Yes. Today, you can come out."

Both times, people had died at Aeduan's hands. Both times, he'd felt an inescapable need to even a life-debt for somebody else.

Today would mark number three.

Run, my child, run.

He moved with extreme care through the terrain, sandy and soft with the river so close. His muscles—his witchery—screamed to ignite. With speed. With power. But blood lived in the air here, saturating the floodplain like the stink on a mosquito-infested pond. Aeduan forced his feet to creep onward with agonizing slowness.

He reached the river and stopped beside a peeling silver birch. The scents Aeduan followed—the child and the Red Sails leader—trailed off to the north, away from the river. Aeduan followed, his witchery coursing through his muscles. Creatures cleared from his path. The earth shook, a distant distraction.

All Aeduan felt was the cold in his fists, the murder in his veins.

Then he was there, at a campsite beside a trickling creek. It was so familiar. So similar to that day fourteen years ago.

Seven men lingered here, most waiting within a well-made tent with golden stripes circling the edges. The sort of tent Aeduan had seen wealthy families take on picnics.

These were the men Aeduan had encountered the day before. The men who had hunted the Threadwitch.

Aeduan stepped into the clearing, distantly pleased when the earth chose to tremble not two breaths later. The lone guard outside spotted Aeduan. His beard was greasy, while his fine, oiled cloak had clearly been claimed off the back of a traveler. He threw anxious glances at the sky before advancing on Aeduan.

But the idiot didn't draw his weapon. Then again, neither did Aeduan.

The man stomped forward, silicate gravel crunching underfoot as his gaze swept over Aeduan. Whatever he saw, it didn't impress him.

Which was good. The closer he came to Aeduan, and the

farther he stepped from that tent, the easier this fight would be.

"You should not be here." The guard was close enough now to be heard over the earth's quaking, the forest's creaking. His beard was trimmed to a long point like men in the northlands favored. "Turn around and leave."

Again, a sharp look at the sky. Then a shadow hurtled over, swooping up winds and drawing Aeduan's gaze too.

A mountain bat soared overhead. Distantly, it occurred to Aeduan that he'd never seen such a creature before. It was both larger and leaner than he'd expected, and with a long tail whipping behind. Otherwise, though, the monstrous bat looked exactly like the smaller fruit bats in the jungles to the south.

Aeduan supposed he ought to be afraid.

He wasn't. The cold in his blood needed release, and the child trapped inside that tent needed help. *That* was all that mattered now.

He twisted back to the slaver, who was clearly at a loss for who posed more of a threat: Aeduan or the mountain bat. To Aeduan, the answer was obvious. "You should run now," he warned the man. "Or I will kill you."

The man's lips curled back. "Seven of us and only one of you." He grabbed Aeduan's shirt.

"Exactly," Aeduan said. "Which is why you should be running." Then, with a speed that no man could match, he clutched the man's hand to his chest, and punched up. His fist connected just above the elbow, breaking the joint and snapping the humerus in two.

Bone tore through flesh; the man screamed.

This was only the beginning. With the man's arm angled in a way it was never meant to be, Aeduan *thrust* the limp elbow toward the man's neck. The jagged tip of bone that had erupted outward now pierced soft throat.

The man's beard was instantly red, and with a soft flick of his wrists, Aeduan pushed the body over.

After that, everything was a blur of shaking earth and screams and blood. Of terror that expanded in men's pupils when they realized that they were going to die.

Six more men. Aeduan killed each one in less time than it took him to tie his boots. But the last man, the leader who stank of broken knuckles, Aeduan took his time with that one.

Or that was the plan, but as Aeduan pinned his knee in the man's back, the creek lapping over the gravel around his face, as he grabbed the man's hair and snapped back his head to expose a pocked chin speckled with open sores, the human filth began to speak.

"The king," he rasped, "is waiting for us."

"I doubt that." Aeduan unbuckled a knife. The first weapon in this fight, and he rested it against a pressure point just behind the ear.

The man shivered, though not with fear. A monster like this had no capacity for fear, and Aeduan could smell pleasure pulsing in the man's veins. He seemed to relish how the knife tip slowly pierced the skin, how it buried into a cluster of nerves that sent pain shrieking through his entire body. "The king . . . in the north. Ragnor."

At that name, Aeduan's blade stilled.

"Ragnor," the man repeated. "He's . . . the Raider King, and he's waiting for us. For our cargo."

324

A long moment passed. The mountain bat was coming this way, kicking up wind and leaves and branches.

Yet Aeduan stayed still, watching the slaver's blood slide down his neck to mix with the creek.

Then Aeduan shoved the knife in all the way. One puncture, in and out. Blood spurted. The stench rushed over him.

Before standing, Aeduan carefully wiped his blade on the man's back. The darkness in his gut was colder now.

Run, my child, run.

Aeduan glanced at the sky, sheathing his knife. The mountain bat was headed this way, its membranous wings almost transparent.

It shrieked, setting Aeduan's teeth to chattering. But he couldn't run yet. Not without the child who'd drawn him here in the first place.

Aeduan spun for the tent. The girl—for that was what he sensed amid the roses and the lullabies—was inside.

The space within was cramped with supplies and crates. Tucked behind one such box was a tiny figure curled into a ball. Her Nomatsi-pale hands were tied, a sack wrapped over her head.

Aeduan dropped beside her, his fingers flying to release his smallest blade. While he cut the ropes at her wrists, he spoke to her in Nomatsi. "I won't hurt you. I'm here to help, Little Sister."

Overhead, the mountain bat screamed again. Wind billowed against the tent, shaking the sides with rhythmic beats, as if the creature hovered directly overhead.

It wasn't attacking, though, so Aeduan ignored it.

The girl's flimsy sage-green gown was soaked from the

muddy floor. Her skin was ice, her bare toes almost blue. She shook, but didn't fight as Aeduan turned to the sack tied over her head.

She was even younger than he'd expected—and grimy too, her black hair wet and matted.

Whatever tribe she'd come from, she had been captured by the Red Sails at least a few days before. Which made no sense to Aeduan. Surely, his father wouldn't work with slavers. Not after everything.

Run, my child, run.

"I won't hurt you," Aeduan repeated. The language came so naturally to his tongue yet sounded so strange in his ears. "I'm here to help."

The girl gave no reaction. No indication that she'd heard his words at all. When he tried to guide her toward the tent's exit, though, she let him. And when he said, "I'm going to carry you now," she didn't resist.

Aeduan bundled her up and stood. She was so light, so fragile. A bird in his demon arms.

Outside, the mountain bat's cries abruptly ended. The tent shook less and less . . . then not at all.

The creature had flown away.

"Close your eyes," Aeduan told the girl as they neared the tent's flap. He didn't want her to see the death he'd left behind.

But she refused. Like Moon Mother's littlest sister who wouldn't close her eyes when Trickster betrayed them all, this little Owl kept her lashes held high.

That was her choice then, Aeduan decided, and he stepped back into the slaughter.

TWENTY-NINE

Well, Merik had walked right into this trap. He'd seen what he wanted to see—the dead assassin—and sauntered directly into a room full of Royal Forces.

In a breath, Merik counted twenty soldiers blocking him from the bar's exits, with at least as many blades among them all.

Excellent odds. For the soldiers.

But Merik had one advantage: his magic. A single breath, and the heat was alight. A second breath, and he was moving, spinning into a backward kick at a cup of ox tea steaming on the nearest table with burst of winds, of rage, the boiling alcohol launched through the air.

A hissing rain of ox tea seared into the oncoming soldiers.

One man was clearly ready for this trick. He had dived low and was now zooming in close, ready to tackle.

Merik let him come. When the man collided, Merik rolled onto his back and grabbed tight. They somersaulted, the man's momentum carrying them over...Where Merik instantly fishtailed on top.

One punch to the nose. Blood erupted. A second punch

to the ear with Merik's winds looping in along for a wind clap. The man's eardrum ruptured; he screamed.

Good. The word tingled in Merik's fingers as he snatched the officer's cutlass free. This felt good. Vicious. Vengeful.

Merik turned. His blade arced up and clashed against a matching naval sword. He swiveled his pommel around this new soldier's wrist. A single tug, and the man tumbled down. His cutlass fell, and Merik retrieved it easily.

Now he had two swords. His odds were improving.

Except, of course, for the crossbows that several soldiers now aimed his way.

Down charged Merik's foot. *Crack!* went a table, toward the floor, and out flung two more cups of ox tea. Then Merik dropped behind the overturned table as bolts twanged loose. The table crunched, flagons shattered, and a flash of heat and light ignited.

One of the candles had fallen off the chandelier, sparking nearby ox tea. A wall of fire would soon erupt between Merik and the soldiers.

Which meant *now* would be a good time for Merik to dive for the bar. He dropped both cutlasses before flipping behind the counter, just in time to feel the heat and hear the sound as true fury let loose.

In seconds, the Cleaved Man was aflame.

Squinting against the smoke and the fire, Merik searched behind the bar for any sign of Garren. In the corner of the Cleaved Man, the dark door still called to him. Shadows still sang.

At that thought, the full expanse of Merik's power awoke. Air funneled in, carrying sparks. He launched out from

328

behind the bar. As fast as muscles and magic could carry him, he dove toward the four soldiers, all that stood between him and the door at the back corner.

One solider tried to run. Merik snapped his winds like a whip. Two men toppled over.

Merik's odds improved again. He couldn't resist grinning, sending thick, scorching air down his throat. Light, smoke, flame—these were his elements. His friends. He'd been born from them, a creature of half flesh, half shadows. And to these elements he would return.

Sharp as any edge.

The last two men charged, firing their crossbows. Too fast for Merik to dodge, the bolts hit his stomach, his thigh. But in a flash of power that rippled through him, shadows coalesced in his veins.

Merik had just enough time to think, *No pain*, before he yanked out both bolts and kept moving. Then he strode through the corner door, made almost impenetrable by fumes and fire.

The Fury was coming.

Vivia sat at her desk in Pin's Keep, recalculating numbers she'd logged a few days before. The formerly bleak, negative totals would soon be gloriously positive. While yes, her stomach panged a bit at the thought of hiding the latest Fox shipment from her father, the warmth building in her chest quickly drowned out the guilt.

After all, hiding supplies in the storeroom had been a

massive loss in the end, so Vivia saw no reason to continue hoarding. Pin's Keep was starving *now*. End of story.

With a satisfying *scriiittttch*, she marked through the amount of incoming supplies. Then she wrote in the new total.

Footsteps beat on the stairs, fast and leaping. Then Stix rushed in. "Sir!" She was panting. "I followed the boy—the Fury's companion. You need to come. Now."

Vivia sprang to her feet. Papers scattered. "Where is he?"

"Here. Inside Pin's Keep." She didn't wait for Vivia to follow, and her white head shot from sight before Vivia could even scrabble to the door. By the time Vivia hit the bottom of the spiral stairs, Stix and her long legs were already almost out of the hall.

Vivia half walked, half ran after her, catching up as Stix ducked into the kitchen. Steam and heat and the dull *clack-clack-clack* of knives washed over Vivia. People paused to smile at their princess, to bow or curtsy or salute. Stix wasn't slowing, though, so Vivia didn't either.

They passed the billowing stoves, then the racks with the day's supplies. Then, finally, they reached the cellar door in the darkest corner. Two soldiers stood sentry.

"Has the boy come back out?" Stix called.

"No, sir!" barked one, while the other shouted, "No one's come through, sir!"

"Good." Stix bent through the archway. Vivia followed, the stones grazing atop her hair. Shadows blanketed her eyes.

"The boy went down here," Stix whispered as they crept, quieter now and slower too. "Might be we can corner him.

330

Use him as bait for the Fury... There's no one here." Stix hopped off the final step. Then spun. "No one at all."

She was right. The square lantern-lit cellar was empty, the space too small for anyone to hide. There was nowhere on or behind the shelves sagging against the walls that could possibly fit a person.

"I swear," Stix hissed, more to herself than Vivia, "that the boy came down here. My men must've missed him." She lurched back for the stairs.

"Wait." Vivia walked, neck craned, toward a shelf straight ahead. It was tipped askew, and in the crack between it and another shelf, spiders crawled. One by one. A centipede too.

In seconds, Vivia had her fingers wedged behind the wood. She yanked. The case slid easily forward—too easily. As if small wheels were tucked beneath its pine planks.

An archway yawned wide in the stones, water dripping from its ancient keystone. A roach scuttled out.

"Holy hell-waters," Stix whispered, moving to Vivia's side. "Where do you think it leads?"

"Darkness is not always a foe," Vivia murmured. "Find the entrance down below."

"Entrance to ... where?"

Vivia didn't answer. She couldn't, for at the moment something burbled in her chest. Something hot that might have been a laugh, might have been sob. For of *course*, the answer to the under-city would be here. Right under her blighted nose—and right under her mother's blighted nose too. All these years, they had believed the city was lost, and all these months, Vivia had wasted her time searching.

Tears prickled, but Vivia ground her teeth against them.

She could laugh, she could cry, she could *feel* all of this later. For now, she had to keep moving.

"Grab the lantern," she said thickly. Then she entered the darkness.

Vivia led the way, though Stix held the lantern behind. Vivia's shadows drifted long across the limestone tunnel, which ran in a single direction: down.

Aside from her first questions, Stix—ever the perfect first mate—asked no more, and Vivia offered no explanations.

Each step they moved deeper, the more a familiar green glow took hold. Until Vivia and Stix no longer needed their lantern. Foxfire illuminated everything, trailing ever onward, a constellation to track across the sky. Then the tunnel ended and a stone door waited, cracked ajar.

Hewn from the glowing limestone, six faces peered out from the door's center. One atop the next, smoothed away, yet unmistakable all the same. Noden's Hagfishes.

Vivia paused here, swallowing and breathing and swallowing again, for a black whirlpool had opened in her belly.

All she had to do was push through. Then she could have her answers. *Then* she could have what she'd been hunting for all along.

A steeling breath. Vivia pushed through. The stone gritted against its frame, the faces darkened as the green glow fell away.

Then she was there. *The under-city*. It spanned in the cavern before her, narrow roads radiating outward, with buildings—three stories tall—rising up on both sides. Some

332

jutted out of cavern walls, others rooted up straight from the limestone floor. Windows and doorways gaped empty, save for the cobwebs strung inside.

All of it was lit by foxfire. The fungus climbed cavern walls and the jagged ceiling, wound up columns, and fanned over doorways. Some even shimmered from within the empty homes.

Empty. Habitable. Vivia could fit thousands—tens of thousands—of Nubrevnans in here. The spinning in her belly resumed. Twice as fast. A happy pain that swelled in her lungs and pressed against her breastbone.

Stix clapped a gentle hand atop her shoulder. "What is this place, sir? It's as big as Hawk's Way."

"It's bigger." Vivia gripped Stix's hand, towing her forward. "Come on." She *had* to keep moving. She *had* to get answers.

They explored further, passing signs of life. Footprints through dusty webs or smears in the foxfire, as if people had dragged clumsy hands through. The houses were all the same, one after the other. Tenements built identically to the oldest structures aboveground. So much space—finally, *finally*.

Yet just as Vivia and Stix crept through an intersection, a *clank!* sounded through the city. Like iron on stone. Like an old blade fallen to a distant floor.

Vivia tensed. Stix froze. There they waited, breaths held, while green light and cobwebs whispered around them.

Then came a voice. Yelling and near—much too near. Vivia and Stix dove for the nearest house. Just in time, for the shouting speaker was soon dragged past.

Vivia peeked around the ancient doorway she and Stix hovered behind. A boy, short-haired and lanky, fought against the two people who hauled him down the road. He was bound at the wrists, yet he kicked. He pulled. He spat. And over and over he hollered, "It doesn't have to be like this! It doesn't have to be like this!"

Vivia met Stix's eyes in the dark. "Is that the boy?" she mouthed.

Stix nodded.

One of the men, a bearded beast of a Nubrevnan, finally lost his patience with the boy. He gripped him by the collar and punched him hard across the nose.

The boy coughed—and coughed some more, but it quickly melted into a frenzied laugh. "You'll . . . regret this," he said between gasping chuckles.

"More like *you'll* regret it," the beast snarled. "Comin' back here was the stupidest thing you could've done, Cam. He'll make you pay, you know."

"That'll be fun to watch," said a second voice. Female and gruff. "This time I doubt he'll let you leave."

"Who are you working for?" the boy demanded, all laughter gone. "Who hired you to kill the pr—"

Crack! The boy's voice broke off. A thump sounded, as if his knees had given way.

"Be a good girl, Cam," the enormous man said, "and shut your blighted mouth."

No response, and when Vivia peered out once more, the huge man was hefting the limp *girl* onto his shoulder.

Vivia waited until they were out of sight before turning to Stix, who murmured, "Did you notice something about their hands?" At Vivia's pinched brow, Stix wiggled her left hand. "No pinkies."

Vivia's forehead relaxed. "Just like the corpses the Fury killed. I guess the Nines *are* back."

"*Or*," Stix said pointedly, "they never left. They might've been hiding here all this time . . ." She trailed off, eyes widening. More voices approached. More light too, orange in the way that only lanterns' fire could produce.

People. *Lots* of them. In Vivia's city, and presumably working with the Fury.

So Vivia made a decision. She scooted close to Stix. Close enough that no one else could possibly hear as she said, "Go back to Pin's Keep. We need soldiers."

"What will you do?"

"Nothing foolish."

Stix regarded Vivia, her face drawn. "I don't believe you. You seem . . . different today."

Vivia's eyebrows bounced with surprise—then she realized what Stix meant. She *was* different today. She'd been so preoccupied, so focused, she hadn't bothered to be a Nihar.

For some irrational reason, this made her smile. Made a strange exultation build behind her ribs. "Go on, Stix," she nudged. "I'm just going to watch the Nines. See what I can learn."

"All right," Stix said, though she still made no move to leave. Her frown deepened, as if she were trapped in indecision . . .

She decided, leaning in until her lips brushed against Vivia's cheek. The softest of kisses. "Be careful."

Then Stix was gone.

For several erratic heartbeats, Vivia could not breathe. Stix had seen through her mask, yet she hadn't run. She hadn't judged. She hadn't hated.

Hell-waters, what might have happened if she'd shown her true self years ago? Maybe she and Stix could have . . .

No. Vivia rubbed her eyes. *No regrets.* She could analyze and replay this later. For now, she had to keep moving.

After a moment to regain her bearings, Vivia scouted onward. Alone. The noises ahead grew louder—at least ten people—as did the glare of too many lamps in one space.

She reached the crowd gathered in a wide square. She cut into a house that faced it. Up she wound, floor after floor until she hit the top. Here, Vivia found the perfect view. Here, she could linger in a shadow and watch the Nines below.

For Stix was right. These *were* the Nines. She knew that man in the center—she'd *hired* that man in the center. Garren Leeri, from Judgment Square. He'd slacked so much on the job, though, that she'd traded him off as soon as she could.

He looked *awful.* Skin and bones now. Black scars everywhere.

"Back off," he squawked. "Give my sister space!"

The people backed off, giving Vivia a clear view of the girl just awakening. "Garren," she mumbled, a surprised sound.

Then suddenly, she was a cyclone. She wriggled, she pummeled, she spun. Trying to rise, trying to fight her ropes. Until Garren eased a cleaver from a sheath at his waist.

Cam stilled, but she did not stay quiet. "You used me." Her words bounced off the limestone, loud enough for everyone in the square to hear. "I trusted you, and you *used* me."

"I only collected what I was owed, Cam, since you left us

without paying your dues." He wiggled the blade at her. "Can I cut you loose? Will you behave?"

Her lips pursed sideways. She nodded.

Garren sliced through the ropes, a surprisingly tender gesture. As soon as the final fiber snapped, Cam scrabbled away. "What *are* you?"

"I could ask you the same." He laughed, and two other Nines laughed with him. "Boy, girl—have you made up your mind yet, Cam?"

She was having none of that. Her lips snarled up. "I *saw* you die, Garren."

"Hye. And you saw your prince die too. But death—it isn't a boundary for me anymore. It needn't be for you either, Cam. Now give me your left hand. We have to finish what we started before you ran off."

"No." Cam tried to bolt. The bearded man grabbed her, thrust her back. "*No!*" she shrieked. "*NO!*"

Vivia stood. She was outnumbered, and she only had this blade to protect her since no water was near. It didn't matter, though. This girl was threatened; Vivia would help.

At the same instant that Vivia pivoted to race back for the stairs, she caught sight of another figure. Cloaked in darkness, he waited atop the building opposite her. A wind eddied around him. His clothes flapped. Shadows twined.

Then he leaped into the square, and light washed over his face.

It was Merik.

It was Vivia's brother.

*

Merik had found the enemy: fifteen people, with their eyes on Garren and Cam at the center of the square. *The Nines*, Merik now knew, and finding them had been so easy. He'd been a fish on the line, and the shadows had pulled him ever forward.

Through winding passages, past long stretches of floods, down unlit holes and dangling ladders, until at last, he was here. To Cam, bloodied and kneeling before the assassin from the *Jana*. Before her brother, Garren.

It made sense now—why Cam had been hiding in that alley, who had attacked her by Pin's Keep, and why she'd continued to insist Vivia might not be behind the attack.

He would ask her about that later, get answers. Decide if he could forgive.

For now, though, Cam was in danger.

In a single bound, Merik dropped into the square. His winds coiled in for close combat. One man, turned. Merik snapped at his chest, felling him in a single swoop.

Two more men charged, cutlasses out.

Merik simply laughed at that—as if blades mattered to his winds. To his *rage*.

He flipped up both hands, funneling his power into a ball. With a flick of his wrists, every dust mote nearby flew at the men's faces. At their eyes.

They screamed.

Merik spun deftly back around, winds spraying outward like an extension of his body. Most men were running now, including the one who'd dragged Cam into the square. But Merik didn't let him go. In three long steps, he had caught up to the man and kicked him in the back of the knee. He hit the ground, a plume of dust rising that was quickly caught in Merik's winds.

Merik flipped the man onto his back. Unintelligible words babbled from his throat. He wasn't much older than Merik, simply bearded. Hungry too, if his hollow cheeks meant anything.

Merik straightened, lifting the man's cutlass with both hands. Ready—*hungry*—for the retribution that lived within this steel. He would sever the neck, the arteries, the spine—

"*STOP, ADMIRAL!*"

The words lanced through Merik's skull. He stilled, blade reared back. Winds crashing around him. The bearded man trembled, eyes screwed shut.

Merik turned and found Cam twenty paces away—a cleaver to her throat. Garren clutched her from behind.

Instantly, Merik's body went cold. Instantly, his winds stilled.

"Let her go," he tried to say, but his voice was a raw, intangible thing. Heat lightning when a full storm was required.

Garren understood. He smiled, his broken face stretching oddly. "Stay where you are, or the girl dies."

Merik dropped the cutlass and lifted his hands defensively. He needed to move with the stream, to move with the breeze. If Garren got spooked, Merik didn't doubt he would kill his own sister.

He'd certainly gotten close with the explosion on the *Jana*.

"Let her go," Merik ordered, his voice louder. "It's me you want dead."

"True." Garren's smile widened. "But you have proved to be a hard man to kill."

"I could say the same about you."

The man laughed at that, a piercing sound that set Merik's skin to crawling. "I know who you are, Prince Merik Nihar. But I wonder, do you know who *she* is?" The blade flicked. Blood blossomed.

Merik's heart lurched, but he stayed where he was. His fury was fast fading beneath the blood that dripped down Cam's neck. *Move with the stream, the breeze.*

"You were supposed to join the Nines, Cam." Garren's tone was silky as he examined her. "Take over after me and rebuild this city with the only vizer who cares about us. Instead, you ran off like a coward. And then, like a coward, you let me onto the prince's ship—"

"It's not like that!" Cam blurted.

"It's *exactly* like that." And with those final words, Garren snatched up her left hand and sliced off her pinkie.

Blood streaked out, a single dark line. She screamed. The finger hit the ground.

Merik was already there, ready to fling her aside before Garren could do more harm.

Garren laughed, stumbling back, before turning tail. He ran.

Good. Merik welcomed the chase. He took flight. Easy, easy—no rage now. Only cold, calculated death.

He landed two streets over, right before Garren, who had just rounded the corner. His face scarcely registered surprise before Merik's hands were around his neck. He lifted. Garren's feet dangled. Then he walked the man back, *back* until Garren hit a wall.

Fans of glowing mushroom flaked off. Still, the man

laughed. "You cannot kill me," he choked, clutching at Merik's fingers. "I'm . . . like you, Prince."

"No." Merik sucked in air, and winds coursed to him.

"I am, I am!" Garren grinned. "We're puppets now, you and I! We can come back from *anything*!"

"Are you sure about that?" came a new voice. One Merik knew, one he'd spent so many years hating. Yet now, as he allowed his head to turn, as he allowed his eyes to absorb someone other than Garren or Cam, he felt nothing but vicious relief.

For Vivia sprinted this way. Her eyes blazed, her face aflame with a familiar Nihar strength. Silver flashed. She lunged in close. Then, in a single move, Vivia decapitated Garren.

His head tipped, his head fell, and a half breath later, his body followed in a puff of ancient limestone dust.

"Come back from *that*," Vivia snarled, before lifting her gaze to Merik. Before a new expression settled over her features. One he'd never seen before. One that almost matched . . . regret.

"Merry," she said at last, a breathy, almost chuckling sound, "you look *awful*."

THIRTY

Safi had given up trying to still her tapping fingers, her jittering heels. Caden had given up telling her to stop.

After what had seemed like hours in the carriage, everyone was wound up. Even the Fareaster woman had taken to picking at the dirt beneath her fingernails, a furious movement that grew more animated, more impatient with each minute that passed.

Yet there was no accelerating the carriage. Once free of the crammed market, travelers to the arena filled every mud road through the marshes, every rickety bridge across the oxbows. Most people were hideously drunk—just as Admiral Kahina had described—and though Caden rarely peered beyond the curtain, there was no missing the sounds of revelry outside. Of petty brawls igniting, of slave wagers passing hands.

The landscape changed too. Firm earth shifted to uneven mud and shaky bridges. The ripe stink of a city softened into the sulfuric stink of a swamp. All the while the temperature within the carriage moved from bearable sunburned heat to unbearable choking humidity.

The only person who seemed unperturbed by it all was

Zander, who even tried to make conversation. "I've heard the Fareastern continent is even larger than the Witchlands. Which nation are you from?"

This earned him a withering glare from the slaver and an apologetic shrug from Caden.

When at last the carriage driver hammered on the roof and shouted, "Almost there!," no one was sorry to see the ride end.

The carriage lurched and jolted into an awkward descent. The outside din shrank to a stone-cuffed rumble, and any light that had slithered through the curtain's edge now vanished entirely. They had moved underground.

"The slavers' entrance," explained the Fareaster, sneering at the knife still held at her throat. "It is beneath the arena. Many armed men will be waiting there." She offered this less as a warning and more as a threat.

It prompted Caden to sit taller. "Zander," he barked, "I want you to exit first. Deal with any soldiers waiting—"

"Please," Vaness interrupted, authority dripping off her alongside the sweat. "Allow me." She didn't wait for a reply. The carriage was already clattering to a stop, and she was already reaching for the exit.

No one stopped her. By the time Safi was out of the carriage, all twelve arena guards had been shackled to the ground and gagged with iron.

The only people Vaness did not attack were the driver and the Fareaster, the former having dived for the glistening stones beneath the carriage and the latter still sitting on her bench, hissing profanities after them.

While the Hell-Bards gathered blades off the subdued

guards, Safi examined the cavernous arena entrance with its pitted ceilings and spluttering torches. Water seeped up between the mismatched flagstones. As if the arena were very slowly sinking.

It probably was.

Two archways caught Safi's attention. One seethed with shadows; the other seethed with sound. Every few breaths, roars and cheers rushed through. A living onslaught that set the stones to humming.

Whatever fight happened aboveground, it was a good one. And it meant the quiet tunnel was the one that led to the slave pens.

"Heretic," Caden murmured, appearing beside her. He offered her a crude short sword. Heavy but serviceable. "Any guess where the crew might be?"

"There." Safi pointed at the darker doorway.

A half-grin of approval from Caden, and after snagging a torch from its sconce beside the archway, he set off at a brisk jog into the bowels of the arena. Safi followed the commander, trying to reconcile her grip with the awkward blade, while Vaness hurried behind. The empress was weaponless, of course, though two new shackles rippled around her wrists like baby snakes. Lev and Zander trailed last, and though they glanced back to check for more guards, no one came.

Gods below, it felt good for Safi to move. Good to stretch her legs without Hell-Bards to goad her or Baedyeds to chase. Good to hold a sword again, even if it was meant for someone with hands twice the size of hers. None of that mattered.

Nor did it matter that every few steps, Safi's boots

344

splashed through puddles while water hit her head, icy and hard. She was *moving*.

Soon enough, all sounds from above had muted, replaced by murmuring, echoing conversations and the eternal slosh of a fortress half submerged. Here the entire floor was ankle-deep in thick, sulfuric water.

When the tunnels finally branched with a honeycomb of options, six guards appeared. Before surprise could register on their faces, Vaness had them locked against the damp walls. Narrow belts about their waists, iron gags across their mouths.

"Cartorrans?" Caden asked the nearest one, who dangled crookedly from a belt about three inches too high. His eyes shot to the central-most branch of passages—a look of such honest panic that it set Safi's magic to warming.

"This way," she called, already resuming the jog.

Lev cut in front. "Best let me lead. Just in case we encounter any witches."

Fair point.

Fire flared ahead, and conversations paused at the approaching splashes. Then they were there: a low dungeon exactly like something from a nightmarish fairy tale. On and on it spanned, lit by primitive torches. Stone cells with faces of all shades, ages, and sizes pressed against the crude bars. Many wore collars similar to the one the Hell-Bards had forced on Vaness.

"Cartorrans?" Caden shouted, thrusting his own torch high.

The response was instant. Almost every person in sight

345

thrust arms through the bars. "I'm Cartorran!" "No, I'm Cartorran!" "*Cartorra!*"

They were all very clearly not Cartorran, and though Safi hated the idea of leaving all these men and women enslaved to fight—to *die*—as sport for wagering pirates, she also wasn't naïve enough to think they could all be helped.

Escape. That was what mattered.

"*Here, sir!*" called Lev from farther down the line, and sure enough, by the time Safi caught up, Caden was speaking to a man in a Cartorran green uniform. It sounded like he was asking something about *the prince, where is the prince?*, but it was almost impossible to distinguish words with the slaves bellowing, splashing water, furious at being ignored.

Escape, escape. Her *own* escape. That was all that mattered.

Yet when Safi glanced at the Empress of Marstok, she saw something quite different glittering in Vaness's eyes.

"Majesty." Caden beckoned the Empress to the bars. "This is our crew. Free them, please, so we can find our ship and get out of this cursed land."

The empress did not move, and the slaves roared on. Water sprayed against her, against Safi. They were soaked, gowns hanging heavy. No longer mustard or forest green but simply saturated darkness.

"Your Majesty," Safi tried, approaching.

The empress speared her with a glare. "I do not trust them. They will take us both to Henrick."

"They won't," Safi argued. "They spoke the truth at the inn."

"Because there was a fire to spur them." Her eyes gleamed

like the crocodiles' outside. "I want another reassurance, Hell-Bard. Remove your chain, and let Safi read you again. If you refuse, then I free no one."

Caden's shoulders wilted, almost invisible were it not for the way his torch wavered.

"I'll do it, sir." Zander's hands reached for the noose at his own neck.

"No." The word lashed out simultaneously from Caden and Vaness.

"I'll do it," Caden finished, at the same moment that Vaness declared, "I want the commander's word."

Zander winced, but took the torch when Caden offered it. Then he and Lev stepped aside, with sadness in their eyes.

Sad, sad eyes. Safi didn't need her witchery to know that truth.

Caden slopped forward, stopping mere paces from Vaness and Safi. Then he leaned his blade against his leg and with an awkward fumble—as if he'd never done it before, as if he hadn't just done it an hour ago—he unfastened the noose.

Vaness moved. Up snapped her arms. Out snapped the shackles. They whipped around Caden's neck, while the blade at his leg coiled like a mangrove root. It towed him down. No one could move. No one could stop it. In half a breath, the Hell-Bard commander was bound to the ground.

Water rippled around him, and the slaves roared their approval.

Zander and Lev darted forward, but a palm from Vaness halted them both. "Stay where you are, or he dies." She glided to Caden, as if in a ballroom, and stared down. "We sail to Azmir, Commander."

347

"And ... if I ... refuse?" he huffed, a pained sound and with his face clenched. *Clenched.* Until Safi didn't think his eyes—or lips—could compress any more tightly.

"I will leave you like this. It will kill you eventually, will it not? I have heard tales of a Hell-Bard's doom. Like cleaving, but slow—and with your mind working the entire time. You have awareness, yet no control."

"Please," Lev begged. "Please don't do this to him."

Caden moaned. His fists balled at his sides, and though iron kept his wrists locked down, he hammered. And hammered.

This was only the beginning, though, for as Vaness knelt beside the Hell-Bard, waves shimmering outward, black began to crawl across Caden's face.

At first Safi thought she hallucinated it, what with all the shadows around them. Then when Caden's lips split with another groan, and black furled out from between his teeth, she knew it was all too real.

It was like the smoke from Admiral Kahina's pipe. Except ... this was magic. This was *wrong.* It set Safi's skin, her witchery to shuddering. Her gut rebelled too, for this was torture. Plain and simple. Whatever that noose did, without it, the Hell-Bard was in agony.

"Stop." Zander's voice drummed out, echoing down the cells, cells that had gone utterly silent. Every slave, every sailor, every man, every woman ogled the Hell-Bard commander.

Through it all, Vaness looked thoroughly unfazed. "We sail to Azmir, Commander. I want your word that as soon as we are on a ship, you will take me there."

348

Caden said something, but it was garbled. Lost to the splashing of his fists. To the writhing of his feet against the iron. Whatever he said, though, it sang with frantic truth.

Safi couldn't help it. She reached for Vaness. "*Please.*" No man should have to endure . . . whatever this was.

"Not until he agrees." Vaness leaned closer to Caden, and darkness wriggled over her like steam off a boiling pot. "Say that you will sail me to Azmir, Commander."

"*Yes,*" Caden gasped. Then again. "Yes, yes, yes, *yes,* yes, yes, YES YES YES YES."

It was too much. "He speaks the truth!" Safi shoved in, unconcerned when her elbows smacked against the empress. Unconcerned when Caden's dark magic rushed over her, at once cold as a midwinter kiss, at once hot as black sand on a boiling day. She dropped to his side, patting his hands for the chain.

He no longer held it, so she smacked at the water, spraying it all ways. Frenzied. *Desperate.*

Still Caden screamed, "YES YES YES YES."

The chain fell. Right onto his collarbone, and when Safi ripped her gaze up, she found Vaness holding an indifferent hand outstretched. Then the empress strode away, and the iron that had bound Caden chased after her like dogs at the heel.

Lev dived in to lift her commander while Safi clumsily groped the chain around Caden's neck. Once the two ends were near, magic whispered between them. They fused together, and instantly, the darkness sucked inward, moving in vague spirals back through the scars across Caden's face, his neck, his hands.

349

One of which, Safi now realized, was holding hers tight. White-knuckled and shaking. A grip to hold through hell-fire and back.

His eyes fluttered opened, the pupils swallowing everything, and he said, voice ragged and raw, "Thank you ... domna. Thank you."

THIRTY-ONE

seult had no idea what to do with the child.

When Aeduan had found Iseult, she had been standing on the Amonra's shore watching the mountain bat streak off to the south. Her stomach had bottomed out with surprise. With fear.

He was so quiet. So Threadless.

He was also bloodied. At Iseult's wide eyes, he said, "It isn't my blood." Then he beckoned for her to follow.

So she had, to a cluster of elderberry bushes tucked beneath a massive goshorn oak near the shore. Threads had pulsed within, a steady terrified gray. Iseult had ducked into the branches and found a girl huddled against the oak's silver roots, almost blending into the tree. A trick of the light, no doubt, yet it had taken Iseult three blinks and a scrub at her eyes to get a good look. To establish the girl's age, her frailty, her numb detachment.

The girl looked six years old, perhaps seven. She also looked lost and shattered. Her Threads hovered with endless shades of pale gray fear. No other colors. No other emotions.

Aeduan strode into the elderberries behind Iseult. He

pushed past her to crouch beside the girl. "Where do you come from, Little Sister?" He spoke crisp Nomatsi. "Did the Red Sails take your family?"

No response. The child was staring with big hazel eyes at Iseult.

A child. A *child*. Iseult had no *idea* what to do with a child.

Iseult dropped her rucksack to the knobby earth. They needed a proper shelter, and the girl needed clothes. Shoes. A fire wouldn't hurt either—assuming they could safely manage one with the armies approaching.

As Iseult inched toward Aeduan, the child's Threads flared brighter, hints of white panic within the gray. She backed deeper into the roots.

"I won't hurt you," Iseult said, schooling her face into what she hoped was an expression of calm.

The girl's Threads didn't change.

"Monk." Iseult wasn't sure why she used Aeduan's title. She supposed she didn't want to utter *Bloodwitch* in front of the girl.

Aeduan stood. The child tensed, and when he turned away, she grabbed for him. Her fingers crushed into his cloak.

His expression didn't change as he looked back. The stony stillness remained, yet he offered a gentle, "I'm not going anywhere, Little Owl." Her grip unfurled.

And sunset pink softly hummed through her Threads. A dazzling splash amid the gray. *The Threads that bind.*

"What is it?" Aeduan asked, drawing Iseult's attention back to the angles of his face. His pale blue eyes looked almost white in this frail light.

"Wh-why," Iseult began, only to instantly clap her lips

352

shut. She was tired. The mountain bat had unsettled her. "Why," she tried again, steadier now, "is this child here? What do you plan to do with her?"

"I don't know."

Iseult peered sideways at the girl, whose wide eyes were pinned on them. With mud mottled across her pale Nomatsi skin, she looked exactly as Aeduan had called her: like Moon Mother's littlest sister, Owl.

She needs a bath, Iseult thought.

"Did you find her with the Red Sails?" She looked back at Aeduan.

He nodded. "The same ones who hunted you."

"And . . . w-*where* are they now?"

"Gone." It was all the Bloodwitch said, but Iseult didn't need more. He had killed them, and that explained the blood.

Iseult knew she ought to be shocked. Horrified. Repulsed. Life was not meant to be claimed by anyone but the Moon Mother, yet . . . she felt only cool relief. Corlant's men couldn't hunt her anymore. "Can you smell the girl's family?" she pressed. "Or her tribe? Perhaps we can return her to them."

When Aeduan said nothing, Iseult slid her gaze back to him. He watched her, his face immobile. His chest immobile too, breath held. Whatever he thought, she couldn't guess.

A flash of heat raced up her spine. She snapped, "*What?* Can you or can you not track her family?"

The edge of Aeduan's mouth ticked down. "I can track them. There are traces of a tribe on her dress. But . . ." Aeduan's attention moved behind Iseult. His pupils pulsed. "Her family is north. Back the way we came."

Iseult's nose twitched. "If we don't continue on now,

though, we will not be able to pass. The Raider ships will land, their armies will block our way."

"They will block your way, yes."

It took Iseult three heartbeats to sort out what he meant. And once she did, ice dropped hard into her belly. A soft exhale escaped her lips.

This, then, was the end of their travels together. Their strange partnership would end, presumably forever.

"I cannot leave the child," Aeduan said, no inflection to his tone, no expression on his face. Yet somehow Iseult knew he spoke defensively.

"No," she agreed.

"She will be a burden to us if we continue on."

"Yes."

"The Truthwitch is southeast." He pointed toward the river. "Likely she is all the way at the end of the peninsula. Or perhaps even at sea beyond."

Iseult nodded. There was no argument here—nothing she could say . . . *would* say to try to keep Aeduan traveling with her. This was a divergence of paths, and that was it.

"If you stick to the river, it will be the most direct route. Though you must hurry if you intend to beat the Red Sails. I will carry Owl . . ." Now he was saying something about food. Something about sharing rations, and who should keep the Carawen cloak.

Iseult was no longer listening.

She looked at the girl again. Owl. The Moon Mother's littlest sister. More animal than human, she trailed silently wherever the Moon Mother went. In all the old tales, Owl's bravery came out only at night, and by day, she hid in the forest's darkest corners—just as this little creature did right now.

Why did he have to find her? Iseult wondered, heat splintering through her shoulder blades. For if Aeduan hadn't found this child, then Iseult wouldn't have to continue alone.

Safi was southeast; Safi was all that mattered. Safi was the rose in the sunshine, and Iseult was the shadow behind. Without her, Iseult was just a bumbling collection of thoughts that constantly led her astray.

Safi was the Cahr Awen. Iseult was merely the girl who wished she could be.

Iseult hated herself for that truth, but there it was. She wanted to go after Safi; she wanted Aeduan to lead the way; she wished this child would simply disappear.

Monster, she told herself. *You're a monster.*

It was at that moment that Iseult realized Aeduan had ceased speaking. He stared at her; she stared back. One breath. Two. On and on, while a breeze rustled through the hedge and insects buzzed.

Iseult knew what she had to do. She knew what Safi would do in this position. What Habim or Mathew or her mother or *anyone* with a backbone would do. So why was she finding it so hard to summon any words?

Iseult swallowed. Aeduan turned to go. There was nothing left to say, really, and in seconds, he had pulled Owl to her feet. "Would you rather walk, Little Owl, or be carried?"

The girl gave no spoken answer, yet Aeduan nodded as if he were the one who could see green determination flickering in Owl's Threads. A sign she wanted to walk on her own two feet.

Iseult turned then and dug herself back out of the elder-berry tangles. Something wrestled in her chest. Something she didn't recognize, at once fiery and frozen. If Safi were here, she would know what she felt.

Which was why Iseult had to keep going.

A patter behind her. Owl stepped free from the leaves. Then came Aeduan. Iseult looked at neither of them, her thoughts on the south. On the best route past the Red Sails.

A moment later, Aeduan silently—so silently—appeared directly beside Iseult. In his outstretched hand was the arrow-head.

When Iseult made no move to pluck it up, he gently grabbed her wrist and twisted upward. Then he dropped the iron into her waiting palm. It was warm against her skin, as were his fingers—fingers he now unfurled.

No words left his lips, and no words left Iseult's. She simply examined, almost numbly, the iron needle head as it glittered in the speckled sun.

Aeduan was back to Owl's side before Iseult could angle toward him, and they were already stepping out of sight, a sliver of movement amid the whispering green, before Iseult finally found her voice.

"Aeduan." She'd never said his name aloud. She was surprised by how easily it rolled off the tongue.

He looked back, his expression inscrutable as always. But laced with ... with *something*. Hope, she found herself think-ing, though she knew it was fanciful.

Aeduan was not the sort of man to ever hope.

"The talers," she went on, "are in Lejna. There's a coffee shop on the hill, and I discovered a lockbox full of coins in the cellar. I don't know how they got there. I simply found them, and I took them."

Aeduan's chest fell with a sigh. He wanted to ask more—Iseult could see it in the way his lips tightened. Readying for words.

But then he changed his mind and turned away.

So Iseult matched his movement, pivoting toward the river and setting off.

She did not look back.

Merik dropped to his knees beside Cam, all thoughts of Vivia or Garren or any of the Nines forgotten. Cam was curled in on herself, her left hand clutched to her belly. Blood streaming.

"We need to get you help," Merik said. He tried to lift her, but she resisted. Her head wagged.

"I'm sorry, sir," she whispered. "I didn't know what Garren was gonna do—"

"And I don't *care* about that, Cam. Stand up, damn it. We need to get you help."

Vivia's shadow stretched over them. "Pin's Keep," she said. "We can get a healer there, and it's that way." She motioned across the square.

"Then let's go." Ignoring Cam's arguments, Merik eased a hand behind the girl while Vivia moved to Cam's other side.

But Cam, stubborn as ever, shrugged them off. Her face was pale. Blood stained everything. "I can walk," she huffed. "It hurts like hell, but I know the fastest way. Come on." She stumbled over the corpses, leaving Merik and Vivia with no choice but to hurry after.

It was then, as Cam led them onto a side street, that Merik felt it—a cold draft from an unlit hearth. A frost to trickle against his ever-present rage.

He spun toward the sensation, and just as he knew he would find, just as he *felt* tugging in his belly, a wall of shadows met his eyes. It towered above the buildings. Blacked out the entire city, the entire cavern.

The wall moved this way.

"Run." The command fell from Merik's tongue, alive. Undulating like the creature he knew came toward them. Then louder, *"Run!"*

He grabbed for Cam, tugging her faster toward Pin's Keep—or whatever might lie ahead. But definitely *away* from the shadow man.

No one argued. Everyone ran.

Each step made Merik's chest clench. He was a fish on the line being reeled the wrong way. Block after block. Trying to keep panic at bay.

A distant voice began chanting.

It carried the words Merik had grown used to, the song that lived inside him now. These were the verses he'd forgotten, or perhaps never heard, and the song came from the city's heart. Far away, yet frizzing ever nearer.

"So on they swam deeper, till darkness took hold
and the only sound was click-click.
Daret feared it the sound of her claws,
but Filip assured him it wasn't."

Cam almost tripped. Merik caught her, keeping his arm sturdily at her back.

"What was that?" Vivia asked.

Merik didn't answer. He simply spurred them on, for the wall of darkness was catching up.

> *"Then fool brother Filip swam faster ahead,*
> *forgetting his brother was blind.*
> *For fool brother Filip had heard tales of gold*
> *that Queen Crab hoarded inside."*

The voice had reached a nearby street. The shadows grew thicker. Any moment now, they would roll over Merik and Vivia and Cam too, leaving all of them blind. Leaving all of them trapped.

> *"Queen Crab avoids fishes, she only hoards riches—*
> *at least so Filip believed.*
> *He also believed that money bought love,*
> *and that riches could make him a king."*

The road ended ahead, and a curl of air kissed Merik's face. A breeze. Cool, refreshing . . .

"Turn right," Merik barked, and Vivia and Cam obeyed.

> *"But this is the secret of Queen Crab's long reign:*
> *she knows what all fishes want.*
> *The lure of the shiny, the power of more,*
> *the hunger we all feel for love."*

Two more streets, two more turns, and more cold wind slithered over Merik. Yet as his lips parted to holler that they veer left, he realized—with a punch of dread in his belly— that he had taken them in a circle. That now, somehow, the wall of black waited directly ahead.

This was a trap. The baited line of Queen Crab, and he was indeed the fool brother. This wind he had been following belonged to the shadow man.

"*Stop.*" The word slipped from Merik's throat as he skittered to a clumsy halt, pulling Cam closer. "I've led us wrong."

Cam kept her calm even as she bled. "That way." She jerked her chin toward a new street. Thirty paces later, they hit the cavern's farthest wall, where a door waited.

Just in time, for the shadows were almost to them. Tendrils reached outward, like death across the sea floor. Heavy. Hungry. Unnatural.

Vivia shoved through the door first, with Merik and Cam behind. The stone passage looped up in sharp spirals before it abruptly reached a flurry of floods. Just like the Cisterns, the water funneled past at a speed no man could fight. Vivia lunged forward, as if to try.

"Wait!" Cam shouted. "The flood stops! Every sixty heartbeats, it stops for ten! You just gotta know how to count!"

"But we don't know how many heartbeats have already passed!" Vivia shouted. "In case you missed it, there's a *monster* hunting us!"

As if in reply, the shadow man's laugh oozed down the tunnel. "You need not fear me."

"I don't," Merik said, though he wasn't sure why he

360

answered. He wasn't sure why he even heard that voice atop the water's boom.

It was then that the floods broke off. A tail of choppy white flung past, leaving damp stones and a matching tunnel ten paces beyond.

Cam pulled free from Merik and ran. Vivia followed.

Merik did not.

Oh, he tried to follow, yet his feet felt bolted to the floor. It took monumental effort to manage one step. A second.

Then it was too late. The shadow man reached him.

Black crushed over Merik, just as it had in Linday's greenhouse, but tenfold stronger. A thousandfold stronger. This was not the soft snuff of a pinched wick or the gentle shrink of a Firewitched flame. This was sudden, and it was complete. One moment, Merik could see the tunnel ahead, could see Cam and Vivia wheeling into it.

The next moment, Merik was trapped in black. No up. No down. No sensing where he ended and the shadows began. *Eclipse.* That sensation of light where there was none, of pain with no source.

He fumbled forward, but there was no wall to guide him. Nothing at all to grab hold of. Only the words slinking up from behind.

"That song isn't Nubrevnan, you know." The voice was so close. A claw to scrape down Merik's spine. "The fool brothers are older than this city, their tale brought down through the mountains. Back when I had a different name. Back before I became the saint you call the Fury."

A wind trickled against Merik's face. He inhaled deep, letting air circle to him. Letting magic gather in. He could feel the tunnel now. Could feel the floods approaching to his right. All he had to do was run.

Or so he thought as he kicked into a jog. The shadow man laughed. "Oh, Threadbrother, you should not have used your magic near me."

With that statement, Merik went rigid. *Threadbrother.* It . . . couldn't be.

As if in reply, the darkness slithered away. Light resumed from the glowing fungus that had been masked by the shadow man's storm. It covered every inch of this tunnel— and it illuminated floods now hurtling this way.

They would hit Merik at any moment. He should move. He should fly.

He didn't. Instead, he turned his head and watched as, one by one, tentacles of darkness wound into the man striding this way. A tall man. Broad. With hair pale as ash, even as smoky shadows traced and danced across his skin. Even as they licked off his limbs and blackened snow circled around his head.

Kullen smiled. A heartbreaking, familiar smile. "Hello, old friend," he said. "Have you missed me?"

Merik had just enough time to think, *It can't be,* before the flood hit him.

THIRTY-TWO

I t wasn't supposed to be like this. It wasn't supposed to be the girl Cam screaming at Merik to run while Vivia watched numbly.

It wasn't supposed to be Merik, stolen away by shadows and flood.

But it *was* like this, and if ever there was a time to keep moving, it was now. "Get to the Keep," Vivia ordered the girl. "Get help, and keep soldiers *out* of the underground."

Then without another word, Vivia jumped into the flood.

The water swept over her. Stole her sight, her hearing, her touch. Friend. Mother. Self. All of it was a part of Vivia, and Vivia was a part of it all.

She felt Merik in the darkness, in the weight of these churning, booming underground waves. *Ahead.* Her brother was ahead. There was a fork in the tunnels; he was rocketing through. Spiraling right.

So Vivia launched herself, a creature of speed and power. She used her magic and her instincts to career faster than Merik. Faster than the bone-breaking current.

She was a shark riding the tidal wave. A sea fox on the hunt.

At a tunnel's fork, she shot right. Her lungs burned, but she knew that feeling. Welcomed it. The water was a mother to Vivia, a tyrant to anyone else.

She slammed into Merik, arms looping tight. If any air remained in his body, she had just punched it out.

But he was conscious—thank Noden—and his arms were around her now, and she was in charge. She could use the foam and the violence to propel them both.

Ahead, the tunnel would widen. She sensed a gap of air above the waves.

She cannoned them upward. They cleared the surface; Merik's rib cage sputtered against her arms.

Then she dove him back under before the tunnel shrank once more.

Vivia pushed them faster, grateful Merik didn't fight. That he instinctively elongated his body for maximum speed. It was the Windwitch in him, she supposed. He understood—he *became*—a creature of least resistance.

It was the one thing she'd always envied about him. So easy, he'd always had it so easy. Yet right now, *nothing* was easy.

Another fork. This time, Vivia charged left. A shelf waited ahead, and Vivia sensed it only because water sprayed across.

It would have to do.

She tightened her hold on Merik, and he tightened his hold on her—as if he knew that whatever came next, it wouldn't be nice.

Tide, she thought. *A tide to carry us.* She imagined the

skin-shredding force of a countercurrent. Beneath her and behind.

Then the water was there. It cut under her feet. It grabbed hold of her boots before launching them both upright. The full rage of the current battered them. Fought to flip them down.

Up! Vivia shrieked with her mind. With her witchery.

The tide finally complied.

Up they shot, toward a ceiling Vivia sensed was too close. Any slower, though, and she would lack the momentum to escape these rapids at all.

Head.

Body.

Feet.

Vivia and Merik cleared the water, their arms still anchored to each other. Then the water released them, and they toppled onto the limestone.

Vivia straggled upright. She knew where she was, for she could feel where dampness hit stone, where moisture gathered on walls. Where water had pushed its way into other tunnels, other stairwells—and which passages remained clear. Remained safe.

This was the cave-in, and here, through the spindrift, was a hole in the rubble she'd only just dug through.

She towed up Merik, feeling him strain to push his muscles. Once he was standing, leaning awkwardly on her shoulder, Vivia used the mist to guide her. There was so much she wanted to say as they shambled toward the surface. A thousand questions, a thousand apologies, and a thousand gruff older-sister criticisms. Yet like the water, fast building in the plateau, all these words Vivia yearned to say had nowhere to go. They simply pressed against her ribs, bowed against her mind.

So in the end, she said nothing at all.

Merik lived. She didn't know how, she didn't know why. But he lived, and for once in her life—for one single day—she felt as if she'd made the right choices. As if she could forge on, knowing she truly had no regrets.

Iseult was almost to the river when she came upon the first corpse.

This was not a forgotten skeleton of some ancient war but a new body. A young body.

She had just circled a fallen oak, its exposed roots home to bees that buzzed over everything, drowning all of Iseult's senses. Which was why she wasn't expecting to come face-to-face with the dead man.

He slumped against the other side of the oak, his brown skin not yet bloated. A recent death, for though flies buzzed over the gash across his neck, no maggots yet writhed in the wound.

Iseult looked to the sky. Buzzards and crows circled, suggesting more death ahead on the river's shore.

Iseult knelt beside the man. A boy, really, no older than she. His eyes were open, glass staring straight ahead, even as flies scuttled over. A golden serpent coiled across his belt, which Aeduan had described as the Baedyed standard. He looked nothing like the sailors Iseult and Aeduan had

366

watched from the cliffside, though. This boy bore no saber, only knives and a spyglass.

A scout. Iseult would need to move more carefully. Folding her hand in her sleeve, Iseult reached out to close the boy's eyes. Not because the Moon Mother demanded the dead be "sleeping" before entering her realm, nor because Trickster was known to inhabit the forgotten bodies of the forest.

No, Iseult wanted to close the dead boy's eyes simply because it was making her stomach spin to watch the flies crawling. With a sleeve-covered finger, she eased down the boy's left eyelid.

She moved to the right eye. Yet as the lid sank low, Threads tangled into her awareness. Hungry purple Threads, furious crimson Threads. They moved at the fringe of her magic, a frayed edge to warp around her. Focused blue Threads, hunting green.

Iseult scrabbled upright, and for the first time since finding the body, it occurred to her what it might mean. A dead scout amid an unstable alliance. Could this be an end to their fragile peace?

Doesn't matter, Iseult decided. For even if the Baedyeds and the Red Sails turned on each other, it wouldn't change Iseult's course. If anything, it meant she must travel more quickly.

She hurried away from the body, veering straight for the river. Away from the hunting Threads. Faster, faster she moved, and with much less care. She knew no one followed, and the time needed to hide her trail wasn't worth it.

More Threads pulsed into her senses, flashing from the

367

river. From the ships she knew sailed there, the ones she had to get past.

The foliage parted; the floodplain gave way to roots and spongy riverbank. Ships and soldiers and Threads. Three massive galleons, six smaller vessels—and more drifting beyond the next bend in the river, where others had already sailed ahead. A charge hung in the air, a shivering in the weave of the world.

Iseult knew that juddering, though she'd never seen it—never felt it—on such a massive scale.

The Threads that bind were about to break.

Without another thought, Iseult punched into a sprint. Her ankles rolled, her knees popped, but she *needed* to get past these ships, past these armies and these circling birds, before the world around her finally tore. Before the Threads connecting Baedyed to Red Sail finally snapped.

Iseult hadn't considered that she might find more corpses ahead. In fact, she had already forgotten all the buzzards and crows. Her world had pinpointed down to her feet, her route, her speed.

Stasis came so naturally when she had a plan. When she wasn't simply speeding for her life. Her plan, though, wasn't a good one—which she realized as soon as she tripped over another dead man. His arm, so brown amid the riverside grass, had looked like a root. She'd hopped ... and her heel had planted into ribs.

Iseult went sprawling. Her hands landed on a third corpse—on his leg—and her face zoomed in close to a fourth man's open eyes.

Flies kicked into her mouth. A crow squawked overhead.

Before Iseult could push upright, the Threads she'd sensed earlier—the vicious ones, the angry ones—scuttled into range. They were cantering for shore. They would reach her soon.

Iseult tried to stand, her fingers clawing into dead flesh. Still fresh enough to resist, but hard. Stiff.

Dead, dead, dead.

Once on her feet, she searched for cover . . . but there was nothing. No rocks large enough to duck beneath, no branches low enough to climb.

A frantic glance to the river showed a launch approaching, packed with men wearing violent Threads.

Nowhere to run. No time to plan. Yet for once, no panic battered in Iseult's throat. Nor a desperate wish that Safi were here to intuit a way free. Instead, Iseult's breaths stayed calm. Her focus keen. Her training at the ready.

With your right hand, give a man what he expects to see.

In a forest full of corpses, the solution was obvious. She dropped to the ground beside the nearest corpse, draped her body across his legs, and went limp.

Her eyes fluttered shut just as the Red Sails hit the river-bank.

THIRTY-THREE

As Aeduan stalked through the oaks of the Contested Lands, his pocket felt light without the arrowhead. He hadn't realized how accustomed he'd grown to its weight. To its iron presence.

But now it was gone, and that was that. No dwelling on it. Simply moving forward.

His muscles itched. His fingers flexed and fisted in time to his steps, and each time Owl tripped, he had to bite back frustration.

It was not Owl's fault that she was small and frail. It was not her fault that she demanded constant attention. Her stride was short, her body weak. She shrank, she huddled, she stared hard at anything that wasn't Aeduan's eyes.

For every one of Aeduan's steps, she needed three. For every rise in the earth that he crested easily, she had to crook, to scrabble, to examine thoroughly before each step.

There was nothing to be done for it. This was the path Aeduan had chosen, and it led north. Directly back the way he and the Threadwitch had come. He suspected, in fact, that the scents lingering on Owl's clothes might lead him to the same Nomatsi tribe who'd left the bear trap that shredded his leg. Like the Truthwitch's scent, though, the tribe's blood-smells were far. A week of travel; likely more at Owl's current pace.

And not in the direction of Aeduan's coins.

He was surprised by how much he *didn't* care about the talers. In fact, Aeduan found himself thinking more about the person who'd stolen his coins than the coins themselves. He wanted to know how the talers had ended up in Lejna. How the man—or woman—who smelled of clear lakes and frozen winters had gotten the money there in the first place. As soon as Owl was safe again, Aeduan had every intention of finding answers to his questions.

At that thought, more tension fretted through Aeduan's muscles. He wanted to run. To fight. He knew the feeling well by now—he'd encountered it often enough, whenever Monk Evrane had scolded or Guildmaster Yotiluzzi had schooled. It was a wall that hardened around Aeduan's heart and sent his heels slamming deeper, *harder* into the soil.

Until Owl whimpered, her hand crushed in his.

Aeduan ground to a stop. He'd been dragging her. Because he was a demon, and that was what demons did. His eyes snapped down to her wide, pitiful ones.

"I'm sorry," he told her, even though he didn't need to. She trusted him. Fool child. He couldn't believe his father wanted her. Why, why—after everything, *why?*

It was as Aeduan stared into her bloodshot eyes that a cannon boomed in the distance. South. Where the Thread-witch must now be.

Without thought, Aeduan drew in a long, deep breath.

371

His power stretched wide; his witchery latched on to the scent of his own silver taler, still dangling from her neck.

Yes, she was south. *Hurry*, he thought, for clearly violence was breaking loose.

It always did in the Contested Lands.

Aeduan let his magic subside, spool back in like a length of twine, when new blood-scents crashed against him.

Hundreds of them, rising from the forest, marched this way from the north, some on horseback. Some on foot.

Aeduan could only assume they were the same Baedyed ranks he'd passed yesterday—yet for some reason, they must have turned back. They now traveled south through the pillar-filled gorge.

Aeduan stopped. Right there in the forest with Owl at his side. The men on horseback would arrive soon . . . He sniffed, letting his magic swell and reach.

More people approached from behind, exactly as Aeduan and Iseult had seen from the ruins that morning. Soon, the two groups would converge.

Aeduan looked down at Owl, who surveyed him in silence. Always silent.

"We have to run now, Little Sister. I'm going to carry you. Will that be all right?" At her nod, he knelt. "Climb onto my back."

She obeyed.

Aeduan ran.

*

Safi had every intention of following the Hell-Bards and the Cartorran navy. After all, leaving the arena was undoubtedly the next logical step.

It would seem, however, that the gods had something else in mind. For as Safi raced after Vaness and the Hell-Bards, she caught sight of someone familiar.

Just a glimpse in the corner of her eye, and not instantly recognizable. She merely saw the man's square jaw, and the faintest recognition tickled at the base of her skull.

It wasn't until she reached the tunnel beyond that the words *'Matsi-lovin' smut* ran down Safi's spine.

Nubrevnans.

Not just Nubrevnans, but sailors from the *Jana*. From Merik's old crew.

Safi slung back on her heel midstride. In ten bounding steps and with water kicking high, she reached the man's cell.

Somehow, the slaves roared louder now. They clanged at the bars and sloshed water. *Free us, free us, free us.*

"You!" Safi yelled in Nubrevnan. She advanced on the square-jawed man, who made no move. Offered no reaction. "How did you get here?" When he didn't answer, she thrust close to the bars. "*How did you get here?*"

Still, the man held his tongue. His companions, however, did not. A bare-chested boy with braids scurried near. "We're part of the Foxes, lady. Out of Lovats."

It meant nothing to Safi. "You are not part of Prince Merik's crew?"

"No," said another sailor. An officer, Safi guessed, from his navy coat and the witch-collar strapped to his neck. "We work

373

for Princess Vivia. Our mission is to gather food and seeds and livestock—anything we can take back to our people."

"Nubrevna has turned to piracy?" called Vaness.

Safi flinched. She hadn't noticed the empress approaching. Hadn't seen her sidle close through the dim torchlight and water's splash.

"Hye," the officer told Vaness. "But we failed, for our ship was taken by the Baedyeds two days ago. And the crew—we were sold here to the arena."

"It's worse than that," the boy cut in, yelling over the building madness. "They took our ship and filled it with seafire. It's on its way back to Lovats *right now*, ready to kill everyone!"

Safi's jaw sagged, and even the Iron Empress swayed back a step.

"Help us," the officer begged, looking first to Safi, then to Vaness. "Please. Just free our Voicewitch. She can send a warning to the capital—that's all we ask."

"*Please.*" The boy's braids shook. "The pirates killed our prince, and now they'll kill our families." As he spoke, his words humming with truth, a new figure shoved through the ranks.

A woman with a collar. The Voicewitch.

Yet Safi hardly noticed. *The pirates killed our prince.* So explosive in all its simple utterance.

"Prince Merik," Safi repeated, "is dead?" When the boy didn't hear her, she slung in closer, shouting, "*Prince Merik is dead?*"

He reared back, before nodding. "The *Jana* exploded. Seafire."

Vaness turned to Safi. "Like my ship," Vaness said, though

no surprise crossed her face. As if she'd already known. *The message on the warship.* It must have told Vaness of Merik's death.

Safi didn't confront Vaness, though—not now. There was no point. Instead, she groped for her Threadstone.

Merik Nihar was dead.

I have a feeling I'll never see you again. Those had been Safi's last words to him. Thrice-damn her, though—she hadn't *meant* them. She'd just expressed what had been roiling in her gut after their lips had touched. It wasn't meant to come true. Merik Nihar could not *actually* be dead.

A click shivered through the air. The collar fell from the Voicewitch's neck, and instantly, the woman staggered back. Her eyes turned pink as she tapped into the Voicewitch Threads. Her lips began to move.

The slaves nearby rioted all the louder.

"Why," Safi shouted at the officer, "do the Baedyeds attack Lovats?" Yet either the man could not hear her, or he did not know, for he shrugged. A helplessness hung in his eyes.

"They attack to weaken us." The answer rumbled out from the square-jawed man. "The Baedyeds and Red Sails march over the Contested Lands as we speak, and Ragnor's raider armies gather in the Sirmayans. Once Lovats is flooded and dead, there will be nothing to stop them from claiming all of Nubrevna."

"How do you know this?" Vaness demanded.

"I heard the men who captured us."

"I heard it too." The boy clutched at the bars. "They'll kill everyone we love, destroy our home. Just like *that*." He shook the bars for emphasis.

And as he shook, the bars melted wide. Wide enough for him to step through.

He gasped, recoiling. Then all eyes shot to Vaness, even Safi's, but the Ironwitch gave no reaction beyond an imperious command. "Warn your people," she said. "And stop the Raider King." Then she turned to go.

"Wait!" Safi called. "You must free them all!"

Vaness pretended not to hear; the roars doubled.

"Please!" Safi lunged after her. "Both pirate factions are anchored for Baile's Slaughter, Empress! They won't set sail until tomorrow—we could leave this place in *shambles*."

Still, Vaness stalked on. She was almost to the archway. Almost gone.

"Think of your Adders!"

At that name, the empress finally stopped. Finally swiveled back, her face expressionless. Iron through and through. Up swept Vaness's left hand, as if she would ask Safi to dance. Then magic charged to life. It crashed over Safi, hot and alive, while a hundred locks groaned open at once. On doors, on shackles, on collars.

Between one breath and the next, the famed slave arena, where warriors and witches battled for coin, became a fight to simply stay alive.

Baile's Slaughter had begun.

THIRTY-FOUR

Hello, old friend. Hello, old friend. It was a rhythm to stumble by while Merik followed Vivia ever upward. Ragged breaths and the occasional burst of distant waves broke the silence, while wavering green fungus lit their way.

Hello, old friend.

Merik's feet dragged to a stop. Limestone gravel crunched beneath his boots. He snapped his head side to side, and water droplets splattered to the stone.

Vivia glanced back, strips of wet hair plastered across her forehead. "Are you hurt ... Merry?" It was the first words spoken since she'd hauled him from the flood.

He offered nothing in return. There was nothing to say.

Hello, old friend.

Merik had *seen* his Threadbrother cleave in Lejna. He had *seen* the corruption burn through Kullen, and he had watched as Kullen flew off to die alone. People didn't return from that. People didn't come back from the dead.

Except ... they did. They *had*. Garren Leeri, Serrit Linday—

Merik shook himself again. Harder this time. Almost

frantic—*legs!* He felt legs scuttling over him. He grabbed at his scalp, at his neck. Something crawled on him. Shadows to take control, darkness that lived inside—

Vivia smacked his shoulder.

He rocked back, fists rising.

"Spider," she blurted. "There was a spider on you." She pointed to the hairy thing, now trickling up the wall.

For several distant heartbeats, Merik watched the creature, his heart a battering ram in his throat. *Shadows. Darkness. Spiders.* None of it had been real. Of course it had not been real.

He forced himself to nod at his sister, a signal to keep moving. She hesitated, her lips opening as if she wanted to say more. There was nothing to say, though, so she cleared her throat and resumed jogging.

The tunnel came to an end. Vivia clambered up a rope ladder. Then light seared down, forcing Merik to squint at a square opening above. With the sun came fresh air, fresh wind, fresh *fuel* for the heat and the temper that had kept him fed for days.

Merik let it come. Let it ripple over him like thunder before a storm. Darkness might live inside him, but right *now*, he could rise above.

He ascended, winds gusting beneath him. No ladder needed, and rope streaming past. Until the gray light of day brushed over him. Until he was out of the tunnel and surrounded by hedges and ivy.

Leaves rattled, branches thrashed. Wind from his own cyclone as well as wind from a darker gale gathering overhead. Merik flew higher, clearing the plants before finally touching down beside a pond. It splashed with each gusting sweep of his magic.

His mother's garden. He hadn't been here in so long. It was overgrown and rippling with shadows, the weeping willow dunking its branches into the pond over and over again.

"Merry, you're hurt," Vivia said. She stood beside the marble bench, body squared to the gate but gaze lingering back. Wind hurtled through the cattails behind her, yet her waterlogged uniform barely moved.

Was this actually his sister before him? When Merik stared at her, he saw none of her swagger. None of her condescending strength or self-righteous Nihar temper.

Merik saw, in fact, his mother.

A lie, though. A trick. Just as what he'd seen below had not been Kullen.

"Your stomach," Vivia added. "And your leg."

Merik's eyes sank to a hole in his shirt, a hole in his breeches. Blackened, bloodied marks peeked through. He'd been hit by those arrows at the Cleaved Man; he remembered now. He pressed his fingers to the blood, but no pain followed. He felt only puckered skin below. It had already scabbed over.

"I'm fine," he said at last. His hands fell away. "But Cam. I need ..." Merik trailed off. He didn't know what he needed. He was cast adrift. Aimless. Sinking beneath the waves.

The holiest always have the farthest to fall.

For weeks, he'd been hunting for evidence that his sister had killed him. For weeks he had *wanted* that evidence, so he could prove once and for all that her approach to leadership was wrong—and Merik's approach was right.

That was the truth of it right there, wasn't it? He'd seen what he'd wanted to see, even though, in the deepest furrows of his mind, he'd known Vivia was not the enemy. He had simply needed someone to blame for his own failings.

The enemy was himself.

"Your friend," Vivia said, mooring him back in the present. "The girl? I sent her to Pin's Keep. We can go there, but I need to tell the Royal Forces what's happening underground—" She broke off, her forehead suddenly creasing. She twisted toward the gate, toward the city.

Then Merik heard it too. A wind-drum was pounding, its song almost lost to the black tempest overhead, where lightning crackled from a spinning heart.

A second drum joined in, then a third, until a hundred wind-drums hammered across Lovats. Louder than the winds, louder than the madness.

Attack at Northern Wharf, their cadence bellowed. *All forces needed. Attack at Northern Wharf.*

Merik didn't even think. He sucked in his magic, a wind to fly him fast and fly him far. He scooped it beneath his sister's feet, beneath his own.

Then together, the Nihars flew for the Northern Wharf. The gardens shrank back, revealing grounds that crawled with humanity. The streets of Lovats crawled too, like a tide carves through the sand leaving rivulets of water to chase behind.

Everyone ran in the same direction. Away from the Northern Wharf, away from the pluming smoke—black, choking, unnatural. It swept over the harbor, erasing all details. A cloud to burn through everything.

Yet the closer Merik and Vivia flew, the more Merik caught glimpses of what caused the smoke—of the black flames, spreading fast, with cores of pure, boiling white.

Seafire.

Merik had heard tales of entire fleets burned to ash atop frothy waves. Seafire ate through everything, and water only spread its reach. His own ship had succumbed to it—*he* had succumbed to it—and more ships burned now. Docks too, and buildings that hugged the wharf.

If the storm swirling above finally broke, then nothing could stop this fire from claiming the city.

Merik's eyes streamed as he strained to see where, amid the smoke and wildness, the Royal Forces charged. He fell lower, Vivia tumbling behind him. Then lower still until he caught sight of a blockade forming at the end of Hawk's Way. Stone and sand piled higher, higher, blocking the river. Blocking the streets.

It held back the seafire.

Before Merik could reach the blockade, a familiar whisper trailed down the back of his neck. A leash being pulled. A reel being tightened.

His flight slowed. He flung his gaze back. Toward the storm's eye. Toward a slithering darkness that tentacled down into the city.

The shadow man.

"*What is it?*" Vivia screamed over Merik's winds. Her uniform flapped—dry now—and her hair fanned in all directions. She wobbled and grasped at air.

"It's the shadow man," Merik answered. He didn't shout, but he didn't need to. Vivia had already seen, had already understood.

She didn't argue when Merik swooped them lower—faster, faster, smoke rushing over their faces—only to release her near the blockade.

Nor did she argue when Merik didn't land beside her. When instead he spun away, riding an updraft of thick, flaming air back toward the rooftops.

Rain began to fall.

Vivia hit the ground. Shock pummeled through her heels, ankles, knees. She almost fell, but soldiers were there to catch her, to help her to rise. Then they pointed her to the nearest man in charge.

Vizer Sotar.

Stix's father towered above all others, bellowing commands at Windwitch officers lined beside the blockade. "*We must keep the stones dry! Keep the smoke back!*"

Spotting Vivia, he charged over. Lines of smoke-clogged rain ran down his face.

"Update me," Vivia ordered, as soldiers and civilians scurried past, carting stones and bricks for the blockade.

They carted bodies too. Some still living and screaming, but most charred beyond recognition.

"Our Voicewitches received word from Saldonica," Sotar shouted, "that a ship was on its way with Baedyeds and seafire. We instantly halted all river traffic, but we were too late." He pointed to where the river fed into the Northern Wharf.

"The ship was already here, and when we tried to board for a search, a hose appeared. Seafire started spraying."

"What ship?" Vivia demanded, having to pitch her voice louder. Having to cover her nose and mouth against the smoke. "How did it get past the Sentries?"

"It's one of our ships, Highness! A two-masted warship—one that you had authorized yourself."

Vivia recoiled. "I authorized it? I didn't . . ." *Oh*. But she had. A Fox ship with two masts. A Fox ship that had gone missing off the cost of Saldonica.

"It's sailing onto the water-bridge now!" Sotar continued. "We fear it heads for the dam, but we haven't been able to stop it! Every Windwitch we've sent out there has not returned."

Vivia nodded mutely. The rain, the smoke, the heat and the noise—it all settled into a dull background buzz.

No regrets, she tried to tell herself. *Keep moving*. There had to be a solution here. A way to stop the ship before it reached the dam. And yet . . .

For half a smoky heartbeat, the world around her smudged into a vague cityscape suffocating with jagged black flames. She doubled over. The cobblestones of Hawk's Way wavered.

She *did* have regrets. Thousands of them, and the weight was too heavy for her to keep moving. She was a ship that could not sail, for its anchor—its *thousands* of anchors—locked it to the sea floor.

"Highness!" Sotar was beside her, saying something. Trying to lift her. She didn't hear, she didn't care.

Ever since her mother's death, Vivia had tried to be something she was not. She had worn mask after mask, hoping one of them would eventually take root. Hoping *one* of them would force out the emptiness that lived inside her.

Instead, the regrets had built and gathered and swelled. Feeding the emptiness until it could not be denied.

And now ... *Now* look at what Vivia had done. This conflagration, this death—it was her doing. She had started the Foxes. She had stolen the weapons that had allowed her fleet to grow too bold.

And she, Vivia Nihar, had left her brother to die. She couldn't outrun that truth any longer. Just as she could not outrun these flames.

"Get a healer for her highness!" Sotar shouted. He tried again to lift her, but Vivia resisted. Anchored. Stuck.

Until she heard him say, "We already lost Prince Merik! We cannot lose the princess as well—get her to safety."

Prince Merik. The name slipped through Vivia's awareness, settled over her heart and stilled her muscles. For they had not lost Prince Merik, and Vivia had *not* lost her brother.

The one with true Nihar blood boiling in his veins was still alive and fighting, for Merik could no more sit still than she could. That remained true, and at least, in that one characteristic, Vivia *was* like her father. She *was* like Merik.

And there it was—*that* was who she was. Split right down the middle, she bore her father's strength, her father's drive. She carried her mother's compassion, her mother's love for Nubrevna.

As that certainty settled over Vivia's heart, she knew exactly what she had to do. It was time to be the person she should have been all along.

She straightened, breaking free from Sotar's grasp, and in

a burst of speed, Vivia charged for the blockade. There was a gap in the stones on the left. She could pass through. She could reach the wharf. She could *reach* the ship before its seafire and rage spread any further.

Sotar hollered for her to stop. "The fire will kill you!"

Of course it would. Vivia knew that death awaited her on the water-bridge. Those black, unnatural flames would hit her skin and burn, unsated, until they hit the bone.

But Vivia also knew that she could not leave thousands of people—*her* people—to die. If the dam broke, the seafire would only spread. First the city would burn. Then the city would drown.

Vivia dove headfirst into the wharf. Through smoke, through flame, until she was too far below for the seafire's bite to reach her.

Then she swam as fast as her magic would carry her onto the northern water-bridge.

THIRTY-FIVE

seult's heart had never pounded harder.

Surely the men around her could hear it. Surely they *saw* it fluttering through her body, one booming beat after the next.

Twelve men stood around her. Nine from the shore, three from the trees. One had his boot planted mere paces away, and a sound like steel on a whetstone shivered into Iseult's ears. He was sharpening his knife.

She had splayed her hair and lifted her collar as best she could to cover her pale skin. It didn't keep away the flies. They crawled on her ears and hands. Even down the back of her neck and into her cloak.

She didn't move. She just breathed as shallowly as she could through parted lips.

The men were silent, waiting. Then the final man joined them. Even with her eyes closed, Iseult sensed his Threads of violent gray and of flaming red. *Firewitch*. He was the man in charge, for the instant he arrived, the others' Threads turned mossy green with deference.

The Firewitch tromped through the slaughter. "They have the child."

"The Baedyeds?" asked the man with his boot nearby. He leaned deeper into his stance; bones crunched.

"Who else is there?" Heat curled out as the Firewitch spoke, as if he sent fire coiling along each word. His Threads certainly flashed with the orange tendrils of fire magic at play.

"I thought," spoke a third man, his accent thick, "that Ragnor had told only *us* about the child."

"And Ragnor clearly lied." The Firewitch was closer now. Iseult sensed his Threads, heard his breaths as he nosed around the corpses, like a dog on the hunt.

Her heart banged harder. She was definitely shaking. *Please don't come here. Please don't come here.*

"Maybe," said the first speaker, "the Baedyeds don't know what they've found. Maybe they took her by accident."

"And killed seven of ours to get her?"

Owl, Iseult realized—and fast on its heels came another thought: *Aeduan killed seven men.*

The Firewitch snooped closer. He'd found something he liked. His Threads flared with interest and desire.

Then fire whooshed out. Heat seared against the side of Iseult's face.

The man with the boot rocked back, hissing curses.

The Firewitch simply laughed, and a smell like burned hair slithered into Iseult's nose. He was burning the corpses.

"Stop," said the man with the boot, his Threads paling into beige revulsion. "The Baedyeds will see the smoke."

"Does that matter?" the Firewitch snapped. Though he did clap his hands, and the fire did wink out. Only the smell and a *hiss-pop!* left behind. "We could win their ships. And their horses. All of Saldonica, even, if we attack now. All at once, while the Baedyeds are unprepared."

At those words, every set of Threads in the area bruised into hungry shades of violet. They wanted what the Baedyeds had.

"But what of Ragnor?" asked a new voice. "What of the child?"

"We reclaim the child, and we sell her. If her magic is so valuable that Ragnor wants it, surely someone else will want it too."

Another shiver of agreement ran through their Threads. Yet although the men spoke on, Iseult stopped hearing. She *couldn't* listen, for the Firewitch was now stepping toward her.

The whole world shriveled down to his boots closing in on her left. One pace, two.

Then he was there. He stepped on her arm, and her mind erupted with white. Her lungs strained. She couldn't inhale, couldn't move, couldn't think. The urge to open her eyes scored through her muscles.

The Firewitch knelt—more a *sense* than anything else, for Iseult couldn't see him. Couldn't watch as his knee dug into her elbow, shoving the joint in a way it was never meant to be shoved.

She heard each of his breaths. Harsh exhales that smelled like smoke and dead things. Closer. He was leaning in closer, his fingers grabbing onto her salamander cloak—

A horn ripped through the air. Deep, rumbling, and shimmering with blood lust.

As one, the Threads around Iseult flashed with turquoise

surprise. Then came tan confusion. So quick, it was almost lost before crimson fury took hold.

Then a cannon sounded—once. Twice.

The Firewitch released Iseult's cloak, pushing to his feet. Snarling and with flames licking out to gust over Iseult. Still she moved not a muscle.

Not until he'd stepped away, not until he'd joined with the others and they had roared their rage to the sky.

The instant the men were gone—the *instant* Iseult knew their Threads were far enough away not to see her—she clawed herself upright.

The salamander cloak was untouched, but her breeches were scorched below the knee. A bright, shrieking patch of blister already peeked through. But she was alive.

Moon Mother bless her, she was *alive*.

For several guttering breaths, Iseult hesitated. Half standing, half crouched, and with a blackened corpse still smoking nearby.

She had to run. Now. Before a full battle erupted. Which way, though—that was the question, and though Iseult knew what she wanted to choose, what she *needed* to choose, her wants and her needs no longer aligned.

Iseult fumbled for her Threadstone. It had left a mark below her collarbone, as had the silver taler strung beside it. Iseult squeezed them both, fingers white knuckled. Her Threadwitch logic told her to travel one way. To speed, to race, to *outrun* what was coming. Her heart begged to go that way too—the Threads that bind tugged her south.

It was only half her heart, though. The other half . . . it

longed to go north. The foolish way. The one where survival seemed impossible.

More cannons thundered in the distance. Smoke plumed across the sky. The battle had begun, and it would soon reach where Aeduan and Owl ought to be. If Iseult would just turn south, she could leave it all behind.

It was then, as she stood there in agonized indecision, that magic roared over her. A hurricane of power and fiery Threads. It laced over the sky, heat to set the forest aflame.

In that moment, Iseult knew what she had to do. Logic didn't matter, nor Threadwitch practicality, nor even the opposing halves of her heart.

What mattered was doing the right thing.

So Iseult made her choice, and she ran.

Aeduan carried Owl on his back. She bounced and jostled, her fear a palpable thing.

But like her namesake, Owl was a fighter. She held tight and didn't once resist the onward sprint. Aeduan's blood, alive with magic, drove him to speeds no man could match. No man could stop.

Or so he hoped. Aeduan had never had to dash like this while protecting another person.

A horn split the air with a single, long bellow. *A-ooooo!*

Then fire erupted in the distance, an inferno ignited by magic.

Firewitch. Aeduan didn't know if it was the one from yesterday—and it didn't matter. A vast conflagration of heat and flame rolled this way. He had to outrun it.

Then the horses were there, breaking through the forest with Baedyeds on their backs. Color flashed on their saddles—streaming and bright against the gray haze that now drifted between the trees.

Aeduan swung Owl around and yanked her to the ground. An arrow punched into his back, he stumbled forward, crouching over Owl.

No arrows hit her, though, and that, Aeduan thought, was at least one good thing.

He pulled Owl closer to him, protecting her while he cataloged pain and damage. *Broken rib. Pierced left lung. Pierced heart.*

The impaled heart would be a problem—*that* would slow him. For without blood to pump easily through his veins, Aeduan couldn't tap into his full power. He would be slow, he would be weak.

And now a second arrow hit. Directly into his neck. Blood spurted.

Always. There was always blood where Aeduan went.

The fire was closing in now. Smoke sawed into his throat, into his tear ducts. His eyes streamed, and the oaks, the riders, the soldiers now charging from beyond—they all seemed to snake and blur.

Run, my child, run.

The river. If Aeduan could just get Owl to the Amonra, then they might escape this growing firestorm.

He rose, snapping the arrow's shaft from his neck as he did so. Voices and blood-scents crashed around him. Deer and squirrels and moles fled.

Without a word, Aeduan hefted Owl onto his shoulder

391

and resumed his run. A stag ran too, and Aeduan forced himself to keep pace with it. To follow its route through the trees.

Not once did Aeduan check on Owl. He'd have to crane his neck to look at her, and there simply was no time. Not when every step had to be perfectly placed to keep them out of the fire. Not when every inch of his attention had to be given to holding her tight.

At last, he, Owl, and the stag outran the roar of distant flames. In its place, steel clashed. Blood-scents crawled up Aeduan's nose. War had come to the Contested Lands once more.

Aeduan didn't slow. If anything, he pumped his legs faster. Owl shook against him, but his grip—and hers—held fast.

Ahead, the trees ended. The river opened up, but it was covered in ships aflame and cannons firing.

The stag reached the end of the forest.

Arrows slammed into him. The creature reared, and blood bloomed.

Aeduan barely had enough time to stop himself. To wrench around before more arrows loosed, whizzing past. Two crunched into his left arm—but he twisted, releasing Owl to the ground.

Nothing hit her. She was safe, she was safe.

Aeduan was not, though. Too many wounds; too much blood rushing out of him; too much smoke in his lungs. Worse, he was at the river, and he saw no way through.

Run, my child, run.

Aeduan yanked Owl back into the trees. Too hard, though—he pulled her too hard. She stumbled, she fell.

Her eyes, panicked and streaming, lifted to meet Aeduan's. So much terror there, so much confusion and trust.

The earth trembled, moving almost in time to Owl's panting breaths. So sudden, so strange—the tremor turned Aeduan's legs to dust. He fell, tumbling out of the trees and onto the shore.

Arrows pummeled him, one after the other.

He turned toward Owl, hoping to tell her to *run!* To *hide!* Just as his mother had told him so many years ago. But he was too slow. A Baedyed rider was snatching her up. Then the rider reeled his horse about and galloped back into the smoky trees.

Aeduan dragged himself after. The earth still shook, a thousand aftershocks that rattled each arrow deeper into his flesh. He couldn't remove them or his body would begin healing with full force—and if he healed, he would pass out.

His breath hiccupped. Blood sprayed from his mouth. His vision quivered, black swarming at the edges.

He sniffed, almost frantic, for Owl's blood. Or for the man who'd nabbed her, but Aeduan was simply too weak, and there was no magic to be spared.

He listed and swayed through the trees. Creatures still ran and birds streaked, all while flames licked in closer. Yet Aeduan scarcely felt the coming heat. Owl had been carried this way, so this way he would go.

Until a figure appeared before him.

At first, Aeduan thought it an apparition. That exhaustion and smoke inhalation played tricks on his eyes, creating dark shadows to stride through the burning trees.

Then the figure walked from the fire. His hands flung up

like a maestro's, and wherever his wrist twirled, new fires erupted. Trees, hedges, and even birds—they all ignited in a burst of fiery death.

Aeduan knew he should circle away, but there was nowhere to go. The forest burned; he was trapped.

The Firewitch turned to ignite a birch, and his eyes—glowing like embers—caught on Aeduan.

The man smiled, a flash of white in a world of flames, and Aeduan recognized him. It was the one from before. The Firewitch who'd tried to kill him.

As that awareness cinched into place, a fresh surge of energy roared through Aeduan's muscles. Smoke laced and fire singed, it was enough power to send him racing forward. If he could kill this man, maybe the fire would end. In three magic-sped steps, Aeduan reached the Firewitch. He rasped his sword free.

The Firewitch opened his mouth, and fire spewed out.

Aeduan barely managed to lurch left before the onslaught funneled past. So loud, it ate all other sounds. So hot, it boiled away all senses.

Aeduan swung. His blade hit only fire—and pyres were now igniting beneath his feet. Sparks and smoke to blind. *Run, my child, run.*

He heaved left again. More fire. He tumbled right. Endless flames. He spun around to move backward, but now he found only stone. *The pillars in the gorge.* No escape.

Aeduan turned to face the Firewitch, still wearing that cursed smile. Gloating and gleeful.

So this is how I will die. Aeduan had never thought it would be flames. A beheading, perhaps. Old age, more likely.

But not fire—not since he'd escaped that death all those years ago.

The world shivered and smeared before him. Still, his training took over. With his free hand, he checked that his baldric was still in place. The knives ready for the grabbing.

Then he readied his stance, for though blood might burn, Aeduan's soul would not.

The Firewitch lifted his hands for a final blaze. Even with the smoke, Aeduan smelled the attack gathering on the man's blood. Aeduan's muscles tensed, waiting for the perfect moment to charge. He'd have to go directly into the flames if he wanted to reach the man's neck.

The attack never came, though. As Aeduan stood there, bracing and ready, shadows crept over the fire. At first, he'd thought clouds—a rainstorm—except the longer he stared, the more he realized the shadows came from the Firewitch.

Lines ran over the man's body, rivulets of darkness. He started convulsing, screaming. He clutched at his blackening, bubbling arms. He scratched, he clawed.

Cleaving, Aeduan realized, and as that thought flickered through his mind, the Firewitch stilled. His eyes turned pure black. His fires snuffed out one by one around him.

A figure in white coalesced behind the Firewitch. She walked stiffly, her hands extended and her eyes rolled back in her head. The salamander cloak's fire-flap covered half her face. Ash coated her brow.

Aeduan didn't know how the Threadwitch was here. He didn't know why either. He only knew he couldn't look away.

The Threadwitch walked, each step evenly spaced, to the Firewitch. He was a monster fully cleaved now, yet when he wriggled and snarled at Iseult, she showed no fear. No reaction at all.

Instead, she lowered the fire-flap on the salamander cloak, then with her mouth stretched wide . . . she snapped her teeth at the air.

The Firewitch collapsed. Dead.

THIRTY-SIX

Vivia launched herself to the water's surface halfway down the water-bridge. Here, the seafire had stopped. Here, no ships sailed, and she rode atop a tide of her own making.

Even through the wildness of her waters, Vivia recognized her Fox warship ahead.

Heat erupted in her chest at the thought of Baedyed pirates onboard. A blistering thing that pressed against her veins, her skin, her lungs.

The Nihar rage.

Finally, it came to her. *Finally,* she could tap into the wild anger of her father's line, she could embrace the berserking strength that consumed all fear.

Vivia shot up from the water, enough violence scorching through her to carry her high. Sailors saw Vivia. They pointed, their mouths bursting wide as other sailors scrambled to defend.

But they were too slow and Vivia too enraged. She rocketed onto the ship's main deck. Midair, she punched her fists, *punched* her waves. Men crashed back. Into each other, into the river, and one man, directly onto a saber he'd tried—too late—to unsheathe.

Then Vivia hit the deck, wood splintering under her knees as she crunched down. A sling of her left hand, and a tide whipped up to yank more men overboard. A slice of her right, and shards of water cut through flesh. Tore open necks.

Blood, hot and glorious, splattered across Vivia's skin.

She barely noticed, her attention already locking on the hose at the stern. She'd never seen seafire before this day, but she could recognize its source. A massive leather tube, the width of an oak, pumped resin from belowdecks. Its spout was a modified cannon that could be spun around and aimed.

A sword swung at Vivia's head. She ducked. Too slow. Steel clipped her left shoulder, taking skin and cloth and blood. Heat—distant and meaningless—gathered up her arm. But Vivia was at the hose, and there was nothing these sailors could do. With her left arm, spurting, she yanked it around and aimed for the main deck. Then she hauled at the spout's crank—

"Stop! Stop!" A figure hobbled toward her, hands flailing and robes flipping.

Serrit Linday.

Vivia stopped, shock staying her hand. *Here* was her culprit tucked somewhere in Nubrevna, *here* was where the jumbled mess from her spies would ultimately lead. Linday was the one working with the Baedyeds, the one working with the Nines—and *he* had tried to kill Merik.

Vivia didn't know how, she didn't know why, but she couldn't deny what stood before her. Everything really did lead back to Serrit Linday.

"Stay where you are," Vivia ordered.

Linday halted. His robe was torn, his face smeared with black. Ash, Vivia assumed, except that the darkness seemed to move. To circle and twine.

"If you release that seafire," Linday called, "you will ignite a thousand firepots belowdecks. I will die, and you will die too."

Vivia couldn't resist. She laughed. A hollow, rusty sound. "Why are you here, Serrit? Betraying us to the Purists wasn't enough for you?"

His face constricted. The darkness pulsed against his skin. For several moments, his throat wobbled like he might gag.

Through it all, the ship still coasted onward toward the dam. The misty valley below, still so green and alive, slid by.

Then finally Linday squeaked, "I did not want to betray Nubrevna. Ragnor promised me your throne." His voice snapped off. He doubled over. Hacking.

Black tar flowed from his mouth. The shadows on his skin swirled faster. Bubbled faintly, like a Cleaved.

Vivia stepped away from the hose and stalked three steps toward her least favorite vizer. The sailors collectively lunged as if to attack, but Linday growled through bursts of black tar, "Stand down."

"What's happening to you?" Vivia asked. "Are you cleaving?"

Three more coughs, then Linday's head lolled up, eyes shining. When he spoke again, his voice was honeyed. Accented. "The dead cannot cleave, Princess. Not truly, for the dead . . . their Threads are already torn asunder. I simply scoop them up before they shrivel away."

"Who does? Who *are* you?" The question was so soft it

was almost lost to the breeze of the bridges, to the distant boom of storm and seafire behind.

But Linday—or whoever it was that controlled him—had no trouble hearing. "I'm the one you should be afraid of, Princess, for once the dam breaks and the city is dead, I will be the one who marches in and claims everything. Including that Well your family had hidden all these ages ago."

At those words, the world seemed to stretch into a strange, sluggish thing. A hundred thoughts colliding at once. A hundred little details to stand out.

The dam loomed with its massive crack, so strangely quiet. So strangely calm. Gulls circled, and a hawk caught air currents drifting beside the bridge. The breeze caressed Vivia's skin, and the sailors watched the sky as if waiting for something.

Or for someone.

In a cumbersome move, with the scene blending like fresh paint beneath the rain, Vivia looked behind her. At Lovats, where black plumed in contained columns. Already weaker than when Vivia had set off.

The storm was leaving too. No more rain, no more lightning. Just black, spinning clouds rising away from the walls, like poison sucked from a wound.

Lovats would survive this day, but only if Vivia could keep the dam from breaking. *Only* if she could keep this boat from traveling any farther. And though she didn't know if the water-bridges' magic would hold, she felt the consequences from a flooded valley were better than those from a flooded city.

She swiveled her head left. Staring at the patchwork farms

so far below. The same view her mother had seen before she'd left this life forever.

It was, Vivia decided, not a bad view to end on.

With that thought, time lurched forward. The world resumed, and Vivia vaulted for the seafire spout. She gripped the iron crank and pulled the handle into place. A shiny resin hacked from the end. Then a full stream burst forth, spraying across the planks, the mast, the sails.

Fire erupted. Black and white and spreading too fast to escape.

The remaining sailors ran. Not Linday. He simply stood there, letting it spew over him, even as his body ignited like a torch. Even as he burned and burned and burned.

Vivia turned to the bulwark and jumped. She dunked beneath the waves and swam with her magic to propel her back toward Lovats.

Too slow, though—she was too slow.

The ship exploded. A burst of energy slammed over her, catapulting her to the surface. Then came the sound, but she was already flung up. Flung out.

As her body left the water-bridge and the valley appeared below her, dappled by shadows and flame, Vivia could do nothing but smile. For though she might now be falling to her death, at least the water-bridge had held.

And at least the dam had held too.

Safi wanted to break something. She wanted to break, to shred, to pummel, and to slay.

Then perhaps the world would make sense again.

For Merik Nihar could not be dead. That truth boomed in time to her heart. In time to her loping steps forward.

Slaves charged past her on all sides, their limbs long unused. Witcheries ready to let loose. Screaming, racing, hungry. Bursts of fire to her right; lashes of wind to her left; stones rattling underfoot. A maelstrom of color and violence, of hunger and freedom so true, true, *true*. The slaves thundered into the tunnels, every cavern identical. There was no telling which way traffic traveled versus which way traffic fled.

Fingers clutched Safi's elbow. She wrenched her sword high . . . but it was only Lev, her eyes huge and scars stretched long. "Where is the empress?"

Safi didn't know, so she didn't answer.

"We need to go," Lev continued, squeezing Safi tighter. "The slaves are freeing other slaves, and this place'll be overrun with guards at any moment."

Good. Safi smiled. She would hack this place to the ground, starting with the Baedyeds who'd killed Merik.

Lights blared to life. Alarm-stones nestled in the walls flashed, summoning guards.

Safi's smile widened.

"*Lev!*" Caden shoved through the crowd, Cartorran sailors dispersed behind him. "We can't get through the way we came in. Zander's gone to find another exit . . . Where's the empress?"

This was directed at Safi, but she only grinned all the more. Zander, whose head towered above the fray, waved at them to follow.

Safi set off immediately, glad to be moving. To be fighting.

She body-slammed her way forward, elbows out and teeth bared.

All the while, the alarm-stones dazzled on.

The madness spat Safi out before Zander, who waited beside a passage that was eerily quiet, eerily empty. Some slaves sprinted into it, but most moved very distinctly *away*. "It's the way to the arena!" Zander's bass roar was almost lost to the chaos. "But I think there's a cutoff that'll take us outside!"

"Lead the way!" Caden ordered before turning to the Cartorran crew, counting them as they pelted past.

Safi stalked after Zander, following his shadowy bulk upward. The puddles thinned out. A strange vibration took hold of the floor.

At first Safi thought it simply a result of all the noise, all the slaves fighting their way free. Yet the closer they got to the fork ahead, the more a shuddering quaked through her legs. She felt it all the way in her lungs with each panting inhale.

Even the torches sputtered in their sconces.

"What's that?" one of the sailors asked.

"It's coming from the arena," said another.

"Which is why we won't go *into* the arena." Lev pushed ahead and reached the forked pathway first. Then with a holler for everyone—"Hold up a moment"—she launched left into the darker tunnel.

The moments slid past, and everyone gathered at the fork. Safi's pulse beat with the same rhythm as the vibrations through the stones—faster, faster—until she was certain the blackened hallway Lev had chosen was wrong, wrong, *wrong*.

She rounded on Caden. "Call her back. Something's down there."

"What—" Caden began.

Wrong, wrong. Safi shot past him, cupping her hands. "Lev! Come back!"

"Just a moment!" came the distant reply. "I see something—" Her words broke off, swallowed by an ear-splitting shriek.

Then orange light blazed at the end of the tunnel, and Lev's voice came clattering down the stones: "*FLAME HAWK! THEY HAVE A RUTTING FLAME HAWK! RUN!*"

"Oh, shit," Caden said. Or maybe that was the crew. Or maybe Safi herself had said it. She was certainly thinking it as she turned tail and ran as if demons of the Void were after her.

Flame hawks. Demons. Close enough.

Noise built behind her. A growing roar like a waterfall approaching fast. Except not. *Definitely* not, for waterfalls did not make the ground wobble or turn darkness into day.

Next came the heat. She felt it searing against her, clawing and nipping at her shoulders, long before the fiery glow caught up.

And when the glow *did* catch up—holy hell-gates, Safi had never run so fast in her life. She passed sailors, she passed slaves, she passed Caden and Zander, and oh, there was the empress, just stepping through a sunny doorway.

"*RUN!*" Safi screamed. She reached Vaness and clapped her hand on the empress's arm. With all her strength, she shoved. Out the doorway, out of the flame hawk's path.

404

Yet what Safi shoved herself and Vaness into wasn't much better than the flame hawk. They had reached the arena.

All across the gravel-floored basin, Baile's Slaughter rampaged. Lightning sliced out, singeing Safi's cheek before it crashed against a stalagmite now punching up from the earth. A Stormwitch battling an Earthwitch. *Excellent.*

Safi vaulted left, scarcely avoiding a flurry of ice shards that were quickly sizzled up by a wall of flame. All lines had faded between friend and foe, slave and slaver, Red Sail and Bae-dyed. Everyone fought. Every single thrice-damned person alive in this arena grappled body to body, blade to blade, or magic to magic.

Oh, and there was the matter of the flame hawk. It had reached the arena's surface and now careened from the tunnel in a streak of white heat.

Thank the gods Safi's muscles were smarter than her brain, for at first sight of the beast—a streak of fire as long as a galleon with wings twice as wide—she would've happily stood there, awestruck.

Her legs, however, wanted to *move.* She dove for a stalagmite, but it crumbled the instant she got close. So she scrabbled on—cover, cover. She needed cover. For the hawk was circling now and screeching its rage to a keen, blue sky.

Then it folded its wings close and dove. Directly for Safi.

She tried to bolt, to duck, to wheel sharply aside, yet even as she evaded, she knew—in that base, survivalist part of her brain—that this wasn't a creature one could escape by simply *twisting fast.*

Her hearing was swallowed by noise, her sight a raging inferno. There would be no escape. Not this time.

A body rammed into her from behind. She hit the ground, chin cracking hard on the gravel. "*Close your eyes!*" Caden shouted.

Safi closed her eyes. The flame hawk hit.

The old life ended.

When she was a child, Habim had told her that the Marstoks believed flame hawks to be spirits of life. Of birth. To meet a flame hawk—and to survive—was to be given a second chance. A new beginning. A clean break.

Safi believed it, for in that space between one heartbeat and the next, while the beast roared over her with light and heat and sound, Safi's entire being focused into a flash of thought. A memory, sharpened like the finest of blades.

Everything you love, her uncle had said, *gets taken away, Safiya . . . and slaughtered. But you will learn soon enough. In all too vivid detail, you will learn.* Then he'd told her: *If you wanted to, you could bend and shape the world. You have the training for it—I've seen to that. Unfortunately, you seem to lack the initiative.*

Well, Safi was calling horse shit on that. She didn't lack initiative—she *was* initiative. Through and through.

Initiate, complete.

Safi was ready to bend the world. Ready to *break* it.

And with that thought, a new life began.

The flame hawk shrieked past. Caden clambered off Safi's back. Her hair was incinerated to half its length. And her gown had enormous holes along the edges.

Caden offered a hand. As before, his scars oozed with darkness that whispered of *wrong*. His pupils had spread to the limits of his irises.

"Next time," he panted, the words mingling with shadows, "you see a flame hawk, how about *not* standing in its way." He turned as if to stagger away.

But Safi's fingers whipped out. She grabbed his noose and yanked him close. "What," she hissed, "are you?" Even as she asked the question, the shadows were already receding. His irises were melting back into brown, and no more smoke-like darkness curled off his tongue.

"If we get out of this alive," he said, looking once more like the Chiseled Cheater she'd known, "then remind me to tell you. But for now, Domna, we keep moving."

THIRTY-SEVEN

Merik knew this storm. He'd survived it in Lejna, flying against the same charged winds in search of an eye. In search of the source.

Today, when Merik found the storm's heart, the same man flew. Today, though, Kullen was not collapsed and dying but rather hovered, stiff as if he stood upon mountain peak.

Once, in boyhood, a fire had swept through a house on the Nihar lands. The people who'd lived within had escaped; their dog had not. The shiny, charred shape of its corpse amid the wreckage had been forever etched into Merik's mind after that.

Now here he was, facing it again. Remains. A corpse. Horrifying, yet unmistakable, even as his mind whispered, *Stop seeing what you want to see.*

Kullen spotted Merik. Lightning flashed, illuminating a toothy smile. His lips stretched in a way that was simultaneously familiar and thoroughly inhuman. Black winds spiraled endlessly behind him, carrying debris, autumn leaves, and sage.

"No words of welcome, Threadbrother?"

"You aren't my Threadbrother." Merik was shocked by how evenly his voice came out. "I saw my Threadbrother die."

"You saw me *cleave*." Kullen spread his arms, almost languidly, and lightning laced from his fingertips. "Cleaving need not be the end, though."

"What are you?"

"You know the answer to that. I am vengeance. I am justice. I am the Fury."

At those words, ice, anger—they sank claws deep into Merik's chest. Yet distantly, Merik knew they were not his own.

"I asked you to kill me," Kullen continued. He swept in closer. Closer still until there was no missing how shadows lived inside his flesh. Inside his eyes, glowing with each crack of lightning below. "Remember that, Merik? In Lejna, I asked for the wind-clap. Thank Noden, you refused, for otherwise, neither of us would be here today. You would be dead, I would be dead, and we'd both we waltzing with the Hag-fishes."

Merik tried to answer. Tried to utter some response, but no words would come. Nothing beyond, *You would be dead, I would be dead.*

Kullen laughed. "*Yet only in death, could they understand life. And only in life, will they change the world.*" He tapped his head, that unnatural grin spreading all the wider. A smile that didn't reach his dead, dead eyes. "The Fury's memories were always here, Merik. I just had to die to unlock them.

"Now I will make you a king!" Cold radiated off Kullen. Power begging to be used. "Together, we can claim this city! Claim this whole nation!"

"No." Merik's head shook. Tears flew from his cheeks. Vanished into the storm. "I don't want that, Kull! I don't *want* to be king—"

"Oh, but you do." Before Merik could blink or resist, Kullen had clutched him by the neck. He drew the air directly from Merik's lungs. "If you do not join me, Threadbrother, then I will deem you enemy. And remember, *I am sharp as any edge.*"

"Please, Kull." Merik hammered at Kullen's arms. "This isn't you!"

"This *is* me, Merik. My true self finally set free." Kullen's fingers gripped tighter, searing into Merik's skin.

"Stop this storm," he rasped. "Leave, Kullen, *leave.*"

"No." Kullen chuckled, a throaty sound that set thunder to rumbling. They were high, so high. "I made this city, and so I will destroy it too."

"I won't let you," Merik wheezed. His lungs were aflame. He blazed from the inside out.

Kullen's grip dug in. Black ice to pierce Merik's skin. Snow fell around them. "Do you think you can stop me, Mer? I am bound to the Loom, and you are bound to me. If you send my soul past the final shelf, then yours will follow. Threadbrothers to the end."

With that statement, he released Merik. Breath roared in while winds kicked under Merik. Keeping him aloft. Kullen's winds, he knew, yet he felt his own power writhing in there too. As if they both controlled the magic, as if this witchery—this *rage*—was a river stretched between them. A well they both pulled from.

And in that moment, Merik understood.

He *was* a dead man. Just like Garren. Just like Linday. And, worst of all, just like Kullen soaring before him. The saint of all things broken, more grotesque than even the Hagfishes. Kullen was the Fury, through and through.

"I see you understand," Kullen said, and though the words were lost to the tempest, Merik felt them rattling in his soul. "The explosion on the *Jana* killed you, but we are bound as Threadbrothers. The same weaving magic that keeps me alive has stretched into you. If one of us dies, though, the other one goes too. And so, what choice do you have but to join me?"

Light flared behind Kullen. So bright it sent Merik's eyes snapping shut. His hands rising. Then came a boom to shatter the earth. By the time Merik had his eyes open again, it was to find Kullen staring below.

Through the clouds and chaos, Merik saw it too: the ship with seafire had exploded.

Kullen's attention whipped back to Merik, his eyes pure black. No lightning now. Only ice and wind and rage. "Your sister might think she has won, but I will simply break the dam on my own. This city will be returned to its rightful ruler one way or another."

Merik wasn't listening anymore. Through watery eyes and storm, he saw figures plunging into the valley, specks of color amid a world of smoke and dark flame.

One person tried to pull water toward her. Tried to tow herself back to the water-bridge. *Vivia.* She fell to her death, leaving Merik with only two choices.

Save the city.

Or save his sister.

The answer, he knew, was obvious. One for the sake of

411

many—he had lived his entire life by that creed, sacrificing himself, giving up Safi, and ultimately losing Kullen for what he'd thought would be the greater good.

It hadn't worked, though.

It *never* worked. Merik had always been left empty-handed, with a darkness digging ever deeper. Soon, there would be nothing left inside him, nothing left to give.

Merik saw that now. What did he know of this city? What did he know of the vizers or the navy? He'd tried—Noden *knew* he'd tried to be what his people needed, but the payoff had only ever been ashes and dust.

Vivia, though . . . the sister Merik had never understood and forgotten how to love, the Nihar who could lead this nation to safety, to prosperity, who could—who *would*—stare down the empires as easily as she stared down a tide . . .

Vivia was meant to be queen. She'd been born to it; she'd been honed for it.

"Come," Kullen commanded, summoning Merik's attention. Winds and frost pulsed across the Threads that bound them. "It is time to remind men that I am always watching."

The need to obey crystallized in Merik's bones. The need to use Kullen's cyclone, to succumb to the endless power. To break and scream and shred and ruin.

But Merik fought it. This time, he dug deep inside himself. Until he found the temper. The kindling of Nihar rage. *That* was his magic—weak and tiny but wholly his own. It would have to be enough.

Otherwise, Merik would never catch his sister before the hungry Hagfishes.

So with that thought, Merik turned away from Kullen, using only his own magic, only his own will.

Many for the sake of one.

The escape from Baile's Slaughter was a blur of steel and blood and magic. Safi's steel. Others' blood. Vaness's magic.

Near the main exit out of the arena, they rejoined with Zander and Lev, who still had most of the Cartorran crew trailing behind them.

"Piss-pies," Safi swore once they were outside—for somehow, the bedlam around the arena was even worse than what had warred within.

"Piss-pies," Caden agreed. The single road toward the wharf overflowed with people, fleeing and fighting. Two bridges had collapsed from too much weight while three more were engulfed in flames.

The final kick in the kidneys, though, were the waters circling the arena. They foamed with blood and movement. With crocodiles writhing and rolling and snapping up any person, living or dead.

"There is absolutely no way," Safi hollered, "we can reach the harbor."

Caden tossed her a smirk of absolute smugness. "This is nothing," he said. Then he shouted, "Hell-Bards! In formation! Everyone else, get behind! *You*"—he pointed at the empress—"We need three shields. Big ones."

Vaness matched his smirk, and with the same control that marked all her movements, all her magic, she swooped up her arms. Three iron shields—*big* ones—gathered and formed

413

from any iron nearby. Safi's own sword wriggled from her hands before reshaping into a curved chest-high shield for Caden.

"Move behind!" Caden shouted.

Safi moved behind.

"Move out!"

Immediately, the Hell-Bards triangulated themselves. Zander at the fore, Caden and Lev just behind. Then they shot forward in a full-speed charge.

Followed by a pause.

Followed by a charge.

Safi had never seen anything like it. They worked in perfect concert. *Charge. Pause. Charge. Pause.* While a brave few assaulted their formation from the sides or rear, the sailors were well trained.

In this pattern, the Cartorrans crossed the marsh. Time lost all meaning. It went from seconds and breaths to bursts and lulls. To blades arcing up and jaws snarling near. *Charge. Pause. Charge. Pause.* On and on beneath a perfect, cloudless sky.

Until at last, they reached the harbor.

Until at last, they reached a ship.

They weren't the only ones to reach the Cartorran cutter at the end of the dock. Sailors already crawled across its deck while a woman with gray hair trumpeted orders from the stern.

She saw them approach before her crew did. She smiled—a false thing that scuttled over Safi's magic—and then trilled, "You're too late to reclaim your ship, lovelies!"

One by one, her men swiveled about to see who'd arrived.

414

And one by one, they drew knives, cutlasses, and Firewitched pistols.

Vaness's arms rose, and Safi saw exactly where this was headed. More fighting, more bloodshed, more wasted life.

Then she thought of initiative. Of bending and breaking, and she found herself shoving in front of the empress. In front of the Hell-Bards. "*Wait!*"

Kahina waited, eyebrows slinging high.

"We don't have to do this," Safi said. Merik might be dead—and countless others too—but that didn't mean anyone else had to join him today.

"Walk away." Kahina strode to the bulwark. Her own sword clanked against her hip. "I have no quarrel with you, but I claimed this ship. Now I keep it."

"Play me for it." The words tumbled out. Stupid—*so* stupid. But also something they would never see coming.

Caden and Vaness pivoted toward Safi, faces aghast.

Admiral Kahina, however, looked delighted. A feline smile spread over her face, and she leaned a hand onto the bulwark.

"Not taro," she drawled. "But a duel. Me." She splayed her fingers to her chest. "Versus you. No weapons. Just brains and brawn. *Then*, whoever comes out alive keeps the ship."

"No." Caden reached for Safi. "No."

But he was too late. Safi was already agreeing, already nodding and marching for the gangway onto the ship.

Initiate, complete.

THIRTY-EIGHT

Aeduan couldn't tear his eyes away from the Threadwitch. Smoke whispered up around her. Without the Firewitch to sustain the flames, only charred earth remained—and Aeduan could finally get his bearings.

He and Iseult were at the southernmost edge of the pillars, where the river smoothed out into ancient battlefields.

Aeduan sagged against a pillar and watched Iseult's approach. She had cleaved that man. As easily as Aeduan stilled a person's blood, she had cut the bonds that connected the Firewitch to life. He'd seen that magic before. Dark magic. Void magic like his own. But never—never in a thousand years of living—would he have guessed that the Threadwitch . . .

Was not a Threadwitch at all.

As he waited, the morning's rhyme flickered through his mind. *Dead grass is awakened by fire, dead earth is awakened by rain.* That moment in the ruins felt like lifetimes ago. But it wasn't. Iseult was still the same woman who'd sparred with him. Who'd raced him.

Who'd come back for him.

Rain began to fall, dowsing the Firewitched flames. Cannons continued to blast, and pistol shots popped. Voices charged in through the drizzle, a sign the battle had reached the gorge.

Iseult reached Aeduan. Ash ran down her cheeks, black rivers of rain, and for half a breath, she looked as corrupted as the man she'd just killed.

Then the illusion broke. Her fingers landed on Aeduan's shoulder, and without a word, she angled him around. Not gently, but efficiently. She gripped the arrow lodged in his lungs and heart.

Aeduan knew what Iseult intended to do, and he knew that he should stop her. Now. Before he owed her any more life-debts.

He didn't. Instead, he let her brace a foot against the pillar. He let her wrest the iron from his heart.

Pain washed over him, heavy as the smoke-choked rain. He sank forward against the stone. His chest gulped and heaved. Blood oozed.

"They have Owl," Iseult said.

Aeduan nodded, his forehead scraping against the rock.

"She's not merely a child," Iseult forged on. "The Baedyeds and the Red Sails both want her. Whatever she is, she's special."

Again, he nodded. He'd guessed as much, though he'd yet to think through what it might mean.

"They're coming for her, Aeduan." Iseult's voice was harder now. Louder than the dribbling rain.

Aeduan opened his eyes. Black droplets cut lines through the ancient striations of the pillar.

Two more arrows popped free from his flesh. One from his thigh, one from his shoulder. Instantly, his vision sharpened.

Another two arrows burrowed free, and Aeduan's spine straightened to its full height. Three more arrows, and his magic expanded as well.

"People," he said, turning back to Iseult. "Hundreds are coming this way."

She showed no surprise. In fact, she was the one to nod now. "It's the Red Sails from the river. They want Owl back, which is why we must find her first."

It was then—at that moment—that it hit Aeduan square in the chest. Iseult was here. Not hunting after the Truthwitch but here, standing tall in a land of smoking embers. Before he could speak, before he could ask her how she knew of the Red Sails, an inhuman shriek filled the air. Louder than the receding rain, louder than the cannons' roar.

It was the mountain bat, returned and plunging right for them.

Aeduan barely yanked Iseult sideways before its talons crashed into the stones.

Merik could not reach Vivia.

Kullen's cyclone fought him on all sides, even as Merik tried to send winds to grab Vivia. Even as he tried to send himself breaking free.

It was as if Kullen sensed what Merik would do next. It was if he *sensed* the tiny, pitiful heart of Merik's true power.

He and Kullen were bound. Their souls, their magics,

418

which meant . . . No magic. Merik could not use his Wind-witchery here.

It left his chest aching and his body limp, but Merik did it. He released the wind. He released the magic. He released the fury.

Then Merik fell, a nosedive straight down the storm's heart. A free fall toward the water-bridge. He felt Kullen's scream blast in his skull. The magic lanced through Merik's belly, through his limbs. *Use me, use me, use me.*

Merik did not use it. He hurtled on, no self, only black seafire zooming in fast.

Then he was passing the water-bridge. Heat consumed him. Shadows raged. But below—below, green valley awaited.

Through the smoky, wind-raised tears, Merik saw his sister. With her hands and legs outstretched, water writhed to her in vast webs. Over and over they shattered as she plummeted through. Not strong enough to save her from the valley's floor, but enough to slow her descent. Enough for Merik to catch up.

He squeezed his arms to his sides, pointed his toes.

Water sprayed his face; droplets lost from Vivia's control.

Faster, *faster*. No magic to push him, only the power of Noden. The power of the fall. *Move like the wind, move like the stream.*

Merik reached her. Water crashed into him, a thousand cuts that sliced him apart. His arms tore around her. He held tight.

They spun. Around, around, no sight. No sound. Only water and wind and the feel of death rushing in fast.

But now—now Merik could fly. *Now* he could use the power that bound him to Kullen.

An eruption of wind. It snapped beneath their bodies, flipped them hard into a new spiral. More, more. Merik summoned *more* in a roar of heat that Kullen could not contain. Enough air to stop them. Enough wind to send the grass flattening outward. A vast circle above which Merik and Vivia slowed. Finally stopped.

They landed on their feet, legs crumpling beneath them. Merik's hands sank into wet grass and soil. Such a bright, living smell after all the smoke and storm.

"Merry," Vivia tried to say. Her shoulder was bleeding.

"Your arm," Merik replied. He stood, shaky. Had there always been so much grass? Already it sprang back to its full height, as if Merik's winds had never come.

"I'm fine." Vivia stood beside him. "I can't feel it. Merry, I need to tell you—"

A loud crack echoed through the valley. As if a mountain had fallen. As if the earth itself had split in two.

The dam was breaking.

Safi versus Kahina.

They fought on the cutter's deck while the crews watched from the dock. No weapons, no shoes, and no one else on board. Just the two women and gulls circling overhead.

The rest of the world fell away. No more distant roar from the arena. Nor even the nearer creak of the ship's planks. The world fell away because Safi *made* it fall away, just as Habim had taught her almost a decade ago. Her gaze hung chest level at Kahina, the better to see all of Kahina's body. All of her twitches and twists. Then Safi planted her soles on the rough wood—the better to feel how the ship might pitch and yaw.

Kahina was shorter than Safi, but Safi wasn't fool enough to think this was to her advantage. She could already tell Kahina was an experienced, comfortable fighter. It was in the way she bounced foot to foot, arms up and fists loose.

It was also in her ears: lumpy and swollen from decades of being pummeled—and from getting back up again.

What made Kahina especially formidable, though, was her freshness. She hadn't spent her morning on the run from flames or Baedyeds or an arena gone mad. In fact, Safi's greatest challenge would be in staying alert. Focused—

A fist swooped in. Safi swore. Kahina was already on the attack. Another swing, then another. Safi could scarcely block in time. She had no choice but to skip back.

Too soon, she ran out of space. The bulwark loomed, which meant Safi *had* to move offensively or be caught in a corner. She kicked—just a feint to send Kahina's hands dropping. It worked, and Safi's fists connected in a double punch.

One set of knuckles hit Kahina's nose. The other slammed into her chest—not for pain, but for power. For the distance it gained when Kahina stumbled back.

But the admiral was smiling, all her stained teeth bared, and though her eyes watered, Safi hadn't broken her nose.

Kahina sniffed. "You know, girl, I do not know your name." She stomped her left foot, catching Safi's eyes, before darting in fast. A flat hand sliced against Safi's throat. Next came a hooking punch to Safi's nose—and Kahina *did* manage to break it. A final kick sent Safi windmilling back.

Blood spouted from Safi's nostrils. Her eyes gushed tears. At least, though, the pain was a distant thing. She was used to getting hit; it didn't slow her.

Though she *was* on the retreat again. Kahina was speaking again too. An intentional distraction.

"How delightful for me"—jab, cross, kick to the ribs— "that you like a wager as much as I do, girl."

More blood. More pain. *Don't listen, don't listen.*

"Do you know what I like more than a wager, though?" Kahina ducked beneath Safi's punch. Then hopped back before Safi's foot could connect with her knee.

Safi kept charging. Snap kick, fingernails across the face, back fist. The harder she pushed, the less Kahina seemed able to block. Until soon, Safi was landing blow after blow, and she was close enough for a knee to the gut. An elbow to the chin—

Kahina flipped her.

One moment, Safi's view was of wood and sailcloth and sky. Then the whole world turned to only sky.

Safi's head cracked. Stars swept over her vision. Then pain erupted in her ribs. Kahina was kicking her. Once, twice.

Safi curled in, grabbing for a leg, a foot—anything. What she got was a fistful of Kahina's pants. It was enough. She yanked down the pirate.

Or so she attempted. Instead, though, Kahina used the momentum to tow Safi upright—directly into a waiting fist.

Safi's already broken nose crunched. Black rushed over her eyes. She swayed back, and once more, her skull slammed to the deck. Not that she felt it.

Blink. She was falling. *Blink.* She was down. *Blink.* Kahina

422

was straddling her. *Blink, blink.* Kahina's forearm braced against Safi's windpipe. Except Kahina paused here—no force in her pinning hold. Just a gentle lean while her other hand braced beside Safi's head.

"You didn't answer me, girl. So I repeat: Do you know what I like more than a wager?" Kahina's jade ring flashed sunbeams into Safi's eyes.

"What?" Safi barely got out that word. Blood, blood. It fringed everything she saw. Every breath too.

"I like a good bargain."

Safi had no response for that. There was no point in using her wits against Kahina—not when she'd already lost. If Kahina wanted to distract her with words, so be it.

Except that as Kahina uttered, "Tell me your name," it occurred to Safi that maybe this wasn't a distraction technique but rather a *stalling* one. *More important than the words spoken,* Mathew always taught, *are those unsaid.*

"You . . . want to lose." Safi captured Kahina's gaze. They were both using these moments to catch their breath. "Why?"

Kahina's eyes thinned. No—they crinkled. She was grinning. "Because I do not need this ship. However, a favor from the future *Empress* of Cartorra. Why, imagine what I could do with that, Safiya fon Hasstrel."

Dread, bleak and booming, filled Safi's lungs. Of course Kahina would have learned who she was. The information wasn't exactly secret, and at least Kahina didn't seem to realize Safi was a Truthwitch. *That* still remained private.

"Here is my bargain, girl." Ever so slightly, Kahina bore down her weight—and ever so slightly, darkness woozed in. "I will let you win this fight, and my crew and I will depart.

423

In return, though, you will owe me. Anything I want, I will one day collect from you." Kahina's words were laden with truth. "Do we have a deal?"

Safi writhed. Safi fishtailed. Safi strained. But there was no breath here to sustain her, and grappling had never been a skill she'd bothered learning. The sky, Kahina's face, the ship—it all wavered in and out. Leaving Safi with no choice. She *had* to agree.

Though she still choked, "Two . . . conditions." It was inaudible—*no air!*—but Kahina understood and eased up enough for Safi to squeak out: "I will kill no one for you, and I . . . will not give my own life."

Kahina's smile spread. "Then we have a deal." As she spoke those words, a hiss of magic brushed over Safi's skin. A glow flashed in the corners of her eyes.

Kahina's jade ring, humming with magic inside.

"Now flip me, girl, and start punching until I beg for—"

Safi flipped her, a bucking of her hips that actually worked this time. Distantly, she was aware of cheers from the dock. The Hell-Bards. The Cartorran crew.

False, false, false. Kahina's back hit the deck, and Safi piled on. *False, false.* More cheers, more blood—and more wrongness to scrape against her magic. Lies of her own making. Lies to set them free.

"Stop," Kahina groaned. "*Stop.*" Her eyes were sinking back in her skull. "Enough, girl, *enough!*"

Safi stopped. Then dragged herself off the stronger, smaller, wiser woman. "We claim," Safi panted, loud enough for the crews to hear, "this ship. Take your men and go." *False, false, false.*

424

Kahina only sighed, sinking back against the deck in mock defeat. Her face was pulp. But lies—all of it lies. "I will go. The ship is yours once more."

And that was the end of it. The duel was done, the deal was final.

Safi did not watch the admiral leave, though. Nor did she observe the Cartorran crew marching on board, nor the Hell-Bards and Vaness arguing on the dock. Safi simply hauled her broken body to the stern and looked out at the murky bay. Behind her, a growing war thundered across Saldonica.

Yet while Safi's eyes stayed locked on the soft lull of Saldonican waves—blood drip-dripping from her nose, her cheeks, her mouth—her thoughts were stuck elsewhere.

For resting on Safi's palm was her Threadstone. It flickered and shone, a sign that Iseult was in danger yet again. A sign that Safi could do absolutely *nothing* to help her except stand here and pray to whatever gods might be listening.

THIRTY-NINE

A mountain bat. *The* mountain bat from earlier. Iseult didn't know why she was so surprised to see one. After all, they were creatures of carnage, and a battle raged here.

Time seemed frozen as she held her ground beside Aeduan, taking in the monster. A shudder moved down the beast, rippling through its dark fur. Rain sloughed off.

Then it lunged for Iseult's head, teeth bared and jaws wide.

Her instincts took over. She twirled sideways, ripping her cutlass free. *Strong.* She felt stronger than she'd ever felt before. And she couldn't help but wonder—a smattering of thought between breaths—if it was because . . .

Because of the Firewitch.

Her speed was still nothing compared to Aeduan's. His sword was already there, slicing roughly. He connected with the mountain bat's fur, and mossy brown tufts fell with the rain.

Its silver Threads shone brighter. Iseult didn't think she could cleave those Threads—and the fact that she wanted to, *desperately*, sent sickened heat punching up her throat.

But now was not the time for guilt. Nor revulsion. Nor

426

regret. Iseult had to use this new strength to get herself and Aeduan *away*.

As if on command, Aeduan charged low, but the bat was rolling down in a blur of shrieking forest shades. Aeduan careened directly toward its fangs.

Iseult charged, a war cry building in her throat. "*Me!*" she screamed. "*Come for me!*"

A half second—*maybe* Aeduan gained that much from Iseult's distraction, but it was enough. He shot for the nearest pillar, and in three steps, ascended.

Then he dove out, ready to impale the beast from behind. Positioned as the mountain bat was, with its wings outstretched for leverage, the creature couldn't possibly twist around in time.

Aeduan's sword slung up, ready to drive all strength and magic into his blow . . .

Iseult saw it, then: the silver Threads shimmered with a new color. One that made no sense—one that Iseult hadn't known possible. Yet there it was, sunset pink braiding and twining within the silver.

The Threads that bind.

Aeduan's blade met flesh and fur. The tip of a pointed ear—a chunk of meat as large as Iseult's head—splattered to the rain-soaked earth.

The mountain bat roared, its breath rushing over Iseult and knocking her back. Then it heaved its enormous serpentine form around, wings crashing outward. Each step set the earth to shaking.

Four more haggard steps, and it took flight.

Sunset Threads flared more brightly, wisping off toward

the waterfall. Toward a faint, distant smattering of terrified, broken Threads. *Familiar* Threads.

Owl. The mountain bat was bound to Owl.

Aeduan staggered to Iseult, blade and body coated in bat blood. His cheeks were scarlet, his eyes swirling red.

"The . . . Falls," Iseult panted. "Owl is at the Falls. And the bat . . . is bound to her."

A blink of confusion. Two shuddering breaths. Then understanding braced through him. "That must be why the pirates want her. A child who can control . . . a mountain bat." He wiped his face on his shoulder, then offered Iseult his hand.

She clasped it tight, her fingers lacing between his. Together they ran.

The world blurred into striated stone and smoky rain. All Iseult saw was the scree underfoot and the pillars ahead. Her white cloak flapped around her, and Aeduan's grip never loosened.

Just as the mountain's bat screams never subsided. Its diving attacks resumed. Silver Threads galvanized by pink, they spun in closer. Closer. But now Iseult knew they were aimless. It attacked without reason because Owl was trapped without reason.

At least, through it all, Iseult could see where the mountain bat would dive next.

"*Left!*" Iseult bellowed, and as one, she and Aeduan lurched around a column of stone thin as a tree.

Silver Threads. Screams of the damned. The mountain bat crashed down.

The pillar crashed down too.

Aeduan was zooming into the lead. Yet this time, as his fingers dug tight into Iseult's forearm, Iseult realized the mountain bat was hanging back. Rather than darting high for another hard dive, it was hovering above.

Owl. They must be near her.

"The river!" Iseult shouted, and instantly, Aeduan's course changed. They dove out from behind the pillars, and the Amonra greeted them. Its white chop had turned red; corpses floated downstream.

Here, a battle waged. Arrows fell; fire-pots erupted; blades endlessly clanged. It was chaos, and neither side cared whom they killed. Violent, lusting Threads saturated Iseult's vision. Blood saturated the soil.

Habim had told Iseult once, *War is senseless.* She'd always thought he'd meant it figuratively. Now she knew he'd meant it *exactly* as he'd said. War *was* senseless, overwhelming her sight, her touch, her hearing. Even her witchery. Every *piece* of Iseult was crushed. Crumbled. Shattered to shreds.

Ahead, at the base of the falls, Owl waited. Her panicked, jittering Threads shone through the fog off the river.

A *snap!* shook through the air. Instantly, the sky turned black as arrows pelted down, a great swarm from the cliff.

Aeduan cut right, yanking Iseult behind the stones. Just in time, for the arrows hit their marks. Soldiers and steeds, Red Sails and Baedyeds—all fell like wheat to the scythe.

No stopping, though. Only running onward through the weak rain. Men charged with blades, but swords were so easy for Iseult to evade with Aeduan at her side. Together, they arced, they lunged, they ducked, they rolled. A fluid combination of steps built on blood and Threads.

They were almost to the waterfall now. They were almost to Owl.

The mist cleared, whipped away on the mountain bat's wings. It scooped in close, talons outstretched and mouth wide.

The fog swept back completely, and there was Owl. Ten men guarded her. The rest were carcasses smashed on the rocks or already lost downstream—for that was the mountain bat's method. Even now, its claws were hooking over a thrashing Baedyed. Then, the bat launched into the air, snapping the man once to the side, before dropping him into the river.

Another screeching nosedive from the mountain bat sent the mist scattering, and in that brief flash of time, Iseult glimpsed all she needed: nine soldiers now—soon to be eight—blocked Owl, who cowered against the rocks, a bag over her head.

A Red Sail pounced from the right; Aeduan froze the man's body with a chop of his wrist. But he didn't kill the man, just left the soldier still as a statue and already behind.

Fog rolled over them. The mountain bat swooped low, and it was time to make a final move.

"*Get Owl!*" Iseult roared at Aeduan, and in that moment, she ripped her arm free from his grasp.

She turned to face the remaining soldiers. They had troubles enough with the mountain bat, so they hadn't yet noticed her in their midst.

With a hard grunt, Iseult launched herself at the closest soldier, whose gaze was pinned on the sky. On the mountain bat careening closer.

She swirled behind, her left foot hooking back. Out went his knee; down he fell. The stones were so slick here, and the Amonra thundered close—a foe Iseult knew no one could face.

Which was why she kicked with all her power into the soldier's neck.

He toppled into the river. Another victim of the Amonra. Seven more men remained, though, and now the earth was shaking.

No, not the earth—the stones. The river-smoothed gravel of the shore. It undulated and rippled, like waves upon a sea. All of it guided by almost invisible Threads of dark green.

Iseult's eyes traced the Threads through the mist . . . to Owl. They were *her* Threads. This was *her* magic.

There was no time to consider what that meant—or to try to stop it. Another man had seen Iseult. His saber lashed out.

Iseult dropped low. The air whistled overhead. Too close—the blade had been too close, and the man was too close. Iseult needed space.

Or silver Threads would work too. Iseult fell to the gravel, and the mountain bat did her work for her, taking out three men at once.

Four men left.

At that moment, Aeduan yanked the sack off Owl's head. And her Threads lanced out, explosive in a way Iseult had never seen before.

The earth rumbled. The mountain bat screamed, Threads of Earthwitch power laced over everything.

Iseult's legs buckled beneath her. She fell to the slick rocks, blade lost and hands grabbing. The Amonra rushed in close.

Iseult tumbled for it. Then the water's bite crashed over her, stealing all air from her lungs, all thought from her mind.

For three long, echoing heartbeats, the frosty, bloodstained waters churned around her. She was trapped in place. Towed underwater.

Then the earth boomed beneath her. It crunched and rocked, lifting her like a mother carries a child. All the way out of the water. All the way back to shore. Then the stones dropped Iseult into Aeduan's arms.

He eased her to her feet, shouting something. *Run*, Iseult guessed. *Hurry*, she assumed, but she wasn't actually listening. Her attention was trapped by the shriveling-in Threads of an Earthwitch who had done all she needed to do.

Iseult strained to see Owl, clambering roughly up the cliffside—all while the mountain bat hovered and flapped. It was a guardian that let no soldiers approach. That beat down arrows the instant they were near.

It made no sense. A child who could move the earth. A child who could control a mountain bat. Yet there was no denying what Iseult saw.

They caught up to Owl in moments, and without a word, Aeduan hefted her onto his back. She hugged his neck tight, her Threads burning bright with that same warm sunset.

Then together, the three of them continued up the rainy cliffside while a creature of legend, a creature of battlefields, cleared the path ahead.

Merik and Vivia stood on the water-bridge. Merik on one side and Vivia on the other.

Whitecapped water hurtled toward them. Tall as the dam. Tall as the city. The flood would hit them in seconds. Winds, warm and weak but wholly his own, gathered to Merik. Vivia too, summoned her tides.

They looked at each other. Two Nihars. Two magics. A brother and a sister who'd never known each other, never even tried.

The flood arrived.

Out flung their arms. Wind, tides, power. A wall of magic to meet white foam. Merik slid back, his planted feet dragging across the slick stones even as his winds roared ahead. He screamed, a sound that tore from his throat. Sent his jaw slinging low, and more winds, more power coursed out of him.

More, more. An untouched well, deep inside him. Bound not to Kullen but to his own Nihar blood. To his sister battling the flood beside him.

No rage, no hate, no love, no past. Just now. Just this water, slowing, sweeping, splashing.

Stopping.

Merik lifted one leg. He stepped forward, pushing himself, pushing the wind, pushing the flood.

A second step became a third. One foot after the other, over a green valley and under a sky now flickering with blue.

Across the bridge, Vivia walked as well. Their steps matched. One. Two. Fight. Push. Three. Four. Keep moving.

And inch by furious inch, the flood withdrew. Fight. Push. Keep moving.

Then ice thundered across the water-bridge, crunching

over the river. Up the flood—and briefly distracting Merik. Briefly letting the flood stutter forward and gain a few inches.

Stix, Merik realized. She raced toward them, running atop the ice she'd made. Then she fell into step beside Vivia, mimicking the Nihar pose and joining the fight.

The flood stumbled back.

Fight. Push. Keep moving.

More people arrived, more witches. Wind and Tide. Stone and Plant. Civilian and soldier, everyone pulsing forward on that same Nihar beat.

Back, back, they gained ground, they gained speed, and soon everyone was walking upright. Then jogging.

Then stopping entirely, for they were back at the broken dam. The water was slippering inside its old home, while ice and roots and stone slowly ascended. One level after another, a wall made by hundreds of witches. Hundreds of Nubrevnans.

Until there was nothing left for Merik to do. He turned, and again he met Vivia's eyes. She nodded once, and something almost like a smile settled on her lips.

Merik nodded back, already easing up his ripped, sodden hood. Already swiveling away to return to Lovats. His sister had control of this battle, of these witches, of this new dam growing before their very eyes.

She didn't need any clumsy attempts to help. Especially not from a dead man.

So it was that Merik stepped off the water-bridge and flew for Pin's Keep.

*

Aeduan had been walking for hours, with Owl on his back and the Threadwitch five paces behind—and with the mountain bat always crisscrossing the sky.

They were out of the Contested Lands, but only barely. And though Aeduan had veered north of where he and Iseult had originally traveled, he didn't dare slow.

Nor did he dare put down Owl. His shoulders had long since moved past pain and into mind-numbing agony, but the girl slept peacefully. If she awoke, if he put her down ... Too slow, she would be too slow.

Only once the sun began fading and the pines of western Nubrevna left long shadows to darken their path did Aeduan finally allow them to stop.

They'd come upon a pond, crisp and clear and jagged through the trees. A forgotten wall, half submerged, jutted out into the pond's farthest edge.

"We're alone," the Threadwitch croaked, her voice ruined by smoke. "We should stop."

It was the first thing anyone had said in hours, and for half a moment, her words were gibberish to Aeduan's ears.

Then he realized she spoke in Dalmotti instead of Nomatsi. He assumed so Owl would not understand.

"I've sensed no one near since long before the sun began to set." She pointed vaguely at the horizon. "And ... I'm thirsty." That was it. The end of her reasoning.

Aeduan's lips parted to argue, but now Owl was shifting in his arms. She yawned.

So, muscles screaming, he eased her to the ground. Then she was on her feet, stretching as if she were nothing but a normal child waking from a normal nap.

Four whooshing riptides of air swept over the water, flapping at Aeduan's coat as he peeled it off his sore shoulders. Then the mountain bat was there, settling atop the sunken wall, where its long tail could slither around the ruined corners. The tufted tip sank beneath the water.

Owl showed no interest in the enormous beast—who now cleaned itself like a cat, starting with its bloodied right ear. Instead, Owl was thoroughly absorbed in making her way over the boulders that lined the pond's edge. When she reached the water, she tentatively mimicked Iseult, spooning out mouthfuls of water with her hands.

"Little Sister," Iseult said while the girl drank. "What's your true name?"

Owl ignored her, and Iseult flung a helpless glance at Aeduan.

He shrugged. After all, Owl wouldn't be the first child to lose her words to war.

Still the Threadwitch pressed, and a strain pulled over the words. "Can you speak, Little Sister? C-can you tell us the name of your tribe? Anything?"

Owl merely continued lapping at the pond, acting as if Iseult wasn't even there.

With a hard sigh, Iseult finally abandoned her attempts. She pushed upright and hopped over the stones. Even silhouetted against the dusk, there was no missing how filthy she was. The tips of her black hair were shriveled from flame.

This was not the Threadwitch who had cornered Aeduan beside a bear trap. Nor the Threadwitch who'd sparred with him that very morning. This was a woman changed.

Aeduan knew because he'd been there before himself.

Soon she would learn—just as he had—that there was no outrunning the demons of one's own creation.

Forever after today, she would flex and furl her fingers, precisely as she did right now. She would roll her wrists and crack her neck. She would stretch her jaw and wonder who might next die at her hands. Who might not get away.

And forever after tonight, she would be hungry to outrun the nightmares. She would race and she would fight and she would kill again, just to make sure the ghosts were real.

They were.

Aeduan wondered if perhaps he should feel remorse. After all, she had cleaved to save him. He felt no heat in his chest, though, no sickness in his belly. She would have found her true nature one way or another.

"Your friend is moving again," he said as Iseult took up sentry beside him. Her hands dripped water to the stones. "My guess is by sea. You would not have reached her in time had you continued on."

Iseult gave no reaction. But she did stare hard into Aeduan's eyes, which he knew must be spinning with red. It took all his power—what little was left—to reach for the Truth-witch's scent.

"Owl's family is probably dead," she said at last, gaze still pinned on Aeduan.

"Probably," he agreed.

"Where will you take her, then? I doubt many families will welcome a mountain bat to their ranks." She spoke with no inflection, as always, yet there was no missing the twinkle of humor beneath her words.

So Aeduan answered in kind. "Nor will they welcome a Bloodwitch."

Her lips ticked up. Then instantly flattened. "Nor a Weaverwitch, I suppose." The word fell like a hammer between them.

Aeduan didn't contradict her. She was what she was, and fighting one's nature only brought pain. Sometimes death too.

Which was why he found himself saying, "No one is ever turned away from the Carawen Monastery."

"Not even mountain bats?" Again came that flickering hint of a smile.

"Not so long as they serve the Cahr Awen."

Iseult stiffened, and Aeduan wondered if he'd spoken too soon. It was hard enough staring into the Void, but what did one do if the Void looked back?

It was certainly looking back now. That sway to her stance. That fevered flick of her tongue along her lips. If she was indeed a Weaverwitch, then she was bound to the Void. And if she was indeed a Voidwitch, then *she* could be the Cahr Awen. She saw that now.

Aeduan saw that now too.

"The Carawen Monastery." The words fell from her mouth like a prayer. Then she blinked and said, "I thought you were no longer a monk."

"Which is why"—he stretched his shoulders—"I won't stay. I'll leave Owl, I'll leave the bat, and I'll leave you. Then I'll go to Lejna for my coins." *And perhaps hunt for Prince Leopold too.*

Iseult nodded, as if this plan suited her. For some reason,

the movement bothered him. Her easy acceptance made his lungs stretch tight.

Whatever that feeling was, though, it passed in an instant, and now Owl was splashing deeper into the shadowy pond. The mountain bat, meanwhile, slapped its tail against the wall with what looked to be displeasure. Though it might have been amusement. Impossible to guess which.

Iseult marched away from Aeduan, calling for Owl to be careful.

Which left Aeduan, as always, on the edge of a scene, watching while the world unfolded without him beneath a darkening sky.

FORTY

I've been here before, Safi thought as she surveyed the lines of white trailing the Cartorran ship. The marshy shoreline of Saldonica had long since faded, and now a sunset smeared fire across the waves. Across the blurry, salt-sprayed view through the window.

She *had* been here before. On a ship bound for Azmir while someone tended her wounds.

Pain came in bright bursts, a shuddering onslaught each time Caden's needle pierced the skin above Safi's eyebrow. Were her chair not stiff backed and sturdily armed, she would have fallen off ages ago, for as gentle as Safi knew the Hell-Bard tried to be, it still hurt when he stitched the cut left by Kahina's fist.

For an hour, Safi had been in the captain's cabin. First, Lev had come to rebreak and then set her nose. Despite her best attempts not to, Safi had *howled* and more blood had gushed. Even after all the pain and resulting tears, Lev had still been forced to leave with an apologetic, "Not sure it'll ever look the same again, Domna."

Safi had simply shrugged. Without any bewitched healer

supplies on board—Kahina had claimed them all—Safi knew she'd wear scars and a crooked nose for the rest of her life. It didn't bother her much. Not when there was so much *actually* worth worrying over.

Like her Threadstone.

It had stopped blinking. Iseult was safe again, but for how long?

"I misjudged you," Caden said, scattering Safi's thoughts. They were his first words beyond, *Tip up your head* or *Close the eye*. "In Veñaza City, I thought you reckless. Naïve and selfish too."

Safi couldn't help it: she glared up at him. "*Thanks?*"

The needle pricked hotter. Caden stiffened atop his stool. Then sighed. "Stay *still*, Domna."

With a sniff, Safi attempted to relax her face. He resumed: "Your bravery earlier, on the ship—fighting the Admiral. It was *still* reckless, but it was also clever. And not selfish at all. Plus, what you did back in Saldonica, at the inn . . . I misjudged you."

"And I," Safi muttered, careful to keep her face perfectly still, "do not accept this attempt at an apology."

Caden grunted once, almost a laugh, before leaning in close to tie off the hemp embedded above Safi's eye. Seconds slid past, pain thudded through her skull, and Safi had nothing to stare at but the gold chain dangling from Caden's neck.

The Hell-Bard's noose.

He sank back. "Good enough. Give me your right wrist."

Safi complied, and he held it toward the window, toward the light streaming in across the sea. His fingers dug uncomfortably into bruises swelling on her forearm.

441

"Hell-Bard," she said.

"Hmm?" He set her arm, palm up, over his knee. Then he reached for his needle and a fresh length of hemp.

"Did you tell the emperor what I am? What my magic is?"

"I did not." The answer came without hesitation as he threaded the needle, the copper winking in the sunset. "But I did confirm for the emperor what he'd already heard from other sources."

"Ah." Safi exhaled roughly, and her muscles weakened. She slouched back, watching as Caden cleaned the long cut with a water-soaked linen. Fresh blood welled, and fresh pain with it.

Safi forced herself to keep speaking. "How can you tell what my magic is? What is it that Hell-Bards do? You told me if we survived that you would explain."

"I was hoping you would forget that." His eyes flicked up. "Can't trick a Truthwitch, I suppose."

"Answer the question."

"Let's just say . . ." He chewed his lip for a moment. "Let's just say that we Hell-Bards were once heretics too. Just like you." Here he paused to set aside the bloodied linen and grasp the needle once more. "Our magics were taken away from us, Domna, as punishment. Now we serve the man who took them from us. To remove the noose is to die."

Safi gasped. Her eyes winced shut as pain barked from the needle's stab—and a memory formed. Of Uncle Eron removing his chain, his noose—though only for a few breaths at a time. Long enough for Safi to read his truths.

Then Eron had always slipped it back on.

She opened her eyes to find the top of Caden's head so

near. He had freckles on his forehead. She hadn't noticed them until now.

"When the noose is on, you're protected against magic. How?"

"I can't tell you all my secrets, Domna. Otherwise, you'll run off and then the emperor will hang us all—and with a real noose this time." He laughed, but it was edged with sadness.

Before Safi could demand more answers, hinges sang.

The Empress of Marstok swept in, her stained mustard gown swishing. Like everyone else, she wore what she'd fled Saldonica in. Admiral Kahina had left nothing on board beyond barrels of fresh water and furniture.

Vaness positioned herself between Safi and the window. Her face was serene—*falsely* serene. For though there was no sign of the blood sickness from earlier and though the cutter was indeed sailing them all straight for Marstok, the truth was that the empress never relaxed her guard. Ever.

"How much longer here, Hell-Bard?" Vaness asked.

"A few more minutes."

"Then I will have this conversation with you present."

"Good enough." Caden moved no more quickly, no more slowly than before. Just his usual cautious concentration, and the usual steady swipes of pain.

"We will reach Marstoki shores in the morning, Safi. As an expression of my gratitude for all you have done since we left Nubrevna, I wish to give you a choice.

"You may either remain in the care of the Hell-Bards and return to your homeland, or you may go with me to Azmir. Once you have helped me purge my court, you will be free to leave. And I . . ." She paused here, and for a fraction of a breath, the cool mask faltered. Earnest hope shone through. "I will gift you with enough funds to travel wherever you wish. To start a new life somewhere."

The statement—the offer—settled through the cabin like a sheet billows atop a mattress before it finally sinks down. Before it finally *connects*.

"A . . . choice," Safi repeated, and there was no missing how Caden's careful movements *did* slow now.

With her left hand, Safi gripped her Threadstone. Her bruised, cracked knuckles brushed against the steel chain Vaness had first looped there seventeen days ago.

So much had happened in that time. With Vaness. With the Hell-Bards. Neither were her enemies any longer.

True, true. Safi's throat pinched tight at that thought, and chills raced down her torn flesh. If she went to Cartorra, she would lose her freedom, and then Iseult might never find her again, never *see* her again. Safi would be trapped as the emperor's bride, trapped as the emperor's Truthwitch, and trapped in a cold castle she could never escape.

But in Marstok . . . In Azmir . . . Safi stood a chance. Once she was done weeding out corruption in the court, she could leave. Better yet, she could leave with money to sustain her, and she and Iseult could finally—*finally*—start their lives somewhere new.

What of the Hell Bards, though? To return to Cartorra without Safi was a death sentence—Caden had just revealed as much. And Safi hadn't saved their wretched skins just so Henrick could kill them off.

She had already lost Merik Nihar. She would not lose more people if she could help it.

"I will go with you to Azmir," Safi said, trying to pump authority into her words, "and the Hell-Bards will go with me. As my personal guards."

The words echoed in the small cabin. Vaness looked puzzled, while Caden stopped stitching. He regarded Safi with wide eyes, something almost like a frown playing on his lips.

The silence dragged on for several heartbeats. Until at last, Vaness sniffed. "I accept your terms, Safi. And . . ." She bowed her head, her face relaxing into real, honest serenity. "Thank you for staying by my side."

The Empress of Marstok strode out exactly as she had come in. It wasn't until the door had clicked shut and the ship had swayed—left, right—four times that Caden finally spoke.

For some reason, heat flamed up Safi's cheeks as he did so.

"Why do you want us with you?" His voice was so low. "You know that ultimately we must take you back to Cartorra."

"I know." Safi bounced her left shoulder and tried to look casual as her grip finally fell from her Threadstone. "But you know the old saying, *Though we are safe with our friends near . . .*"

"I see." He snorted. The needle lifted. Copper flashed. *"Though we are safe with our friends near, we are safest with our enemies nearer."*

"No." Safi tensed, waiting for the needle's bite to come. "Just the friends part, Hell-Bard. Not enemies. Not anymore." She smiled, if strained, and he smiled back.

Then he stabbed her with the needle. Once. Twice. The final beats of pain before her wound was patched up.

Iseult waited until the sun had set and the stars had risen before she made her move.

They'd found a clearing, uphill and beside a creek that burbled down to the pond. It was wildly indefensible to Iseult's eyes, and Aeduan's—for he'd said as much when Owl had led them up here. The trees groaned too loudly, and the water trickling past wouldn't deter a flea.

Yet here the girl had sat, cross-legged and stubborn. Then *here* the mountain bat had lumbered, before heaving its massive body down behind Owl. Its silver Threads had dimmed then, as if sleepiness muted its ferocity, and soon it was snoring.

It *ought* to be incredible, Iseult thought—exactly the sort of tale she'd want to tell Safi once they were together again. Except that the bat stank, and flies buzzed across its thick fur. It ruined some of the wonderment.

Not that Owl seemed to notice the stench or care, for as soon as the beast had curled into a ball on the rocky shore, Owl had hunkered beside it and fallen asleep.

Leaving Iseult to finally, finally claim a moment of peace to herself.

"Where are you going?" Aeduan asked as she skirted past him, heading back toward the pond.

"Not far." She motioned vaguely ahead. "I need . . . a drink from the pond. I'll be back soon."

He frowned, and though he didn't argue, it was also clear

he didn't approve—and heat flushed in Iseult's cheeks. They had come far in this odd partnership to now be holding each other accountable.

Iseult reached the pond, breathing heavier than she ought. But at least there was no one to disturb her. No one to hear her creep to the pond's edge and crouch above the water.

Her reflection stretched across the surface. It wobbled ever so slightly at the edges, as if it didn't know who it was.

Sever, sever, twist and sever.

Iseult looked away, fingers rising to her Threadstone.

She looped off the leather thong and peered at the ruby. It rested atop the silver taler, in her palm.

"Safi," she whispered. Her other hand clamped over the stone. "Safi," she repeated, straining. Stretching. Feeling for Threads.

Safi was out there, and this stone was bound to her. If Esme could do this dream-walking, and if . . .

Well, if Iseult was truly like Esme, then she could perhaps dream-walk too.

But nothing came. Nothing, nothing, thrice-damned *nothing.* "Weasels piss on you," Iseult whispered, and heat plucked at her eyes. She sniffed, and held the stone tighter. "Where the *rut* are you, Safi?"

Swearing doesn't suit you, Iz. You are simply too poised to pull it off.

"Safi?" Iseult fell to her haunches. A rock pierced her thigh. "Is that you?"

Who else would it be? It's my dream.

It was working. Iseult couldn't believe it, but it was *working.*

"This isn't a dream, Saf. I'm really here. I'm really talking to you."

Of course it's a dream. I think I would know, since I'm the one sleeping.

"Saf, it's Thread . . ." Iseult hesitated, cold spiderwebbing through her chest. For this wasn't Thread magic, was it? This was Esme's magic, and Esme was not a Threadwitch.

Whatever it was—whatever this witchery could do—it couldn't be all bad if Iseult could talk to Safi.

She swallowed. "It's magic," was all she said at last. "And trust me, this is real."

A pause stretched between them. Then giddy pink Threads filled Iseult's mind—and warmth too. A beam of Safi's sunshine to chase away the cold.

Goddess, Iseult had missed that feeling.

And *goddess*, she had missed her Threadsister.

Well, weasels piss on me is right! Safi's dream-voice took on a breathy, elated quality. *We're actually talking right now, Iz! Can you thrice-damned believe it?*

Iseult couldn't help it. She laughed.

Safi laughed too, and sunset colors shimmered over their bond. The Threads of friendship.

Before Iseult could revel in that perfect shade, a figure caught her eye. A shape moving amid the pines.

No Threads. Her heart jolted. It was Aeduan—of course it was Aeduan, yet why did he have to come this way now?

Iseult spoke faster. "Where are you, Safi? Are you safe?"

I'm on a ship to Azmir, and yes. I'm safe. We should arrive at the capital tomorrow. Where are you?

"I'm c-coming for you." Iseult's tongue was turning fat. She

448

had so much to say. This couldn't be over already. But now Aeduan was almost to the submerged wall. He would be close enough to hear Iseult soon. "I-I won't be in Azmir for a while, Saf, but I'll get there as soon as I can. I have to go now."

Wait! Stay! Please, Iz!

"I . . . *can't*," she gritted out.

Just tell me, are you safe? And don't lie, Iz. I'll know.

Iseult couldn't help it. Her stammer slid away, and she smiled. "I'm safe, Safi. We'll talk again soon. I promise." Then she lifted her hand from the ruby.

In two breaths, Safi's Threads had drifted away. Iseult's heart was left cold as she slipped the leather back around her neck.

Then Aeduan stepped onto the shore. He stayed silent as he crossed the rocks, and to Iseult's surprise, she found her frustration already leaching away.

For, of course, she could simply dream-walk again. Her time with Safi wasn't over. It was only just beginning.

Aeduan stopped nearby and inspected his reflection like Iseult had done. No sitting, of course, for Iseult doubted he ever sat. Or relaxed. Or did anything that normal humans did.

Then again, Iseult supposed, she wasn't precisely normal either. *Weaverwitch*—

No. She would not think of that.

Iseult plunked her hands into the water. Its icy grip banished her thoughts. Deeper she dug, until her elbows were under. Her biceps—

"Fireflies."

"What?" Iseult splashed upright. Chill bumps raced down her arms.

"There." Aeduan waved across the pond. "Fireflies. They're good luck in Marstok, I've heard. And children make wishes on them." There was something light to Aeduan's voice, as if he . . .

"Are you making a joke?" Iseult pushed to her feet. Water droplets splattered across the stone.

"No."

Iseult didn't believe him. Nose twitching with a smile, she slid her own gaze to the lights twinkling among the pines. The air, the sky, the water—it was so much like their encounter two nights ago.

Yet also nothing like it at all. Iseult and the Bloodwitch had been enemies then, bound only by coins. Tonight, they were allies bound by . . . Well, Iseult didn't know precisely. Owl, certainly, and perhaps the mountain bat too.

Iseult sucked in air, marveling at how her lungs could feel so full against her ribs. Then she closed her eyes. She wanted to make a wish, but there were too many choices. She wished for Safi at her side. She wished for Habim and Mathew too. And, though she couldn't *quite* understand why, she wished for her mother.

More than anything, Iseult wished for answers. About her magic. About the Cahr Awen.

I wish I could learn what I am.

Her eyelids fluttered open. Aeduan was still observing the fireflies. "Did you make a wish?" she asked, and to her surprise, he nodded. A curt bounce of his head. "What did you wish for?"

450

He flexed his hands. Then shrugged. "If it comes true, then maybe one day I will tell you." He pivoted and set off across the shore, slowing only once at the trees, to call back, "Be careful when you return, for the bat has stretched its tail across your rock."

Iseult watched him until he was nothing more than another streak of darkness within the pines.

She realized she was smiling then—though over Aeduan, over the wish, or over Safi, she couldn't quite say.

After easing onto the rocks, Iseult removed her boots and dipped her toes into the pond. The cold braced her. Grounded her, so when she clutched at the Threadstone and whispered to Safi once more, the connection was almost instant.

The night slid past. Perfect in all its dimensions, while Iseult and Safi giggled and listened and shared every tale that they'd been saving for the past two weeks.

All the while, the pine trees swayed, the pond rippled, and the fireflies danced.

FORTY-ONE

The Battle Room. Yet again, Vivia faced its oak doors—but this time, the footmen hopped too.

This time, Vivia wheeled her father before her.

First came the scent of rosemary mingling with sage. Then came the sea of iris-blue robes, with more than thirty faces swimming above. The vizers and their families turned as one at the opening doors. Their murmurs quieted, and a wave rippled out as they collectively rose and bowed.

Vivia's dress boots clicked, her own robe swishing in a living counterbeat to the squeak of the wheels on her father's rolling chair.

"Highness, Majesty," Vizer Eltar's eldest daughter murmured as Vivia approached. She curtsied, and Vivia couldn't help but smile in return. This was the first time in her memory that other women had joined her in the Battle Room.

After today, after the memorial, Vivia intended to make it the first time of many.

Upon reaching the head of the table, she knelt to lock her father's chair in place.

It was meant to be a day of grief, yet no one at the table wore sadness on his or her brow. How could they lament, truly, when the city had survived such seafire and storm? When, despite all odds against them, they had come out stronger for the fight?

The people of Lovats now knew of the under-city, and already engineers and witches combed through the streets to ensure it was habitable. Already, the first shipment of supplies from Hasstrel farms in Cartorra had arrived, and already a new treaty with the Empire of Marstok was being drafted— for now that Vaness apparently *lived*, she had a very different set of negotiations in mind.

It was especially hard for Vivia to be anything but buoyant today. She knew something these people did not. While the city believed the Fury had helped her on the water-bridge, she knew it had been Merik.

Merik lived.

He had said he would leave the city though. That he and his two friends—the girl Cam and another who'd just arrived named Ryber—would head north into the Sirmayans.

"Ryber says we can find answers to my . . . *condition*." He'd waved at his face, steeped in the shadow of his hood. "And there is little good I can do here. You have everything well handled."

Vivia hadn't agreed with that sentiment, but she also hadn't argued. Merik had found her in the main hall of Pin's Keep, where a hundred other voices competed for space in her brain. Where she hadn't the time or space to offer him a suitable response.

Besides, if Merik truly wanted to leave, she felt she had no claims to stop that. So she'd nodded and said, "Please update me when you can, Merry. The royal Voicewitches work all hours."

"I'll try," had been his only answer. Then he'd ducked deeper into his hood—a new hood, for Vivia had insisted he be well clothed before departing—and sauntered out of Pin's Keep forever.

He wouldn't try to contact her. Vivia had known that at Pin's Keep, and she knew it now as she tugged at the itchy wool collar on her robe.

Vivia rose and cleared her throat. The vizerial families all thought her father would speak, now that he was well enough to return. They certainly all stared at him expectantly. Yet Serafin had urged Vivia to "be the queen they need and soon a true crown will follow."

She cleared her throat again. All eyes snapped to her. Finally, no resistance.

"Though we've gathered to remember my brother," she said, using the same forceful boom she'd heard her father use a thousand times, "there are many more we must also honor. Hundreds of Nubrevnans died in the attack three days ago. Soldiers, families, and . . . one of our own. A member of this very council."

A shifting of postures across the room. A sinking of everyone's gazes to the floor. No one knew the truth of Serrit Linday; Vivia had no plans to tell them.

At least not before she knew who exactly had controlled him—and how.

"So," she went on, pitching her voice louder, "for each leaf you toss from the water-bridge today, I ask that you

454

remember the people who fought for us. Who died for us. And I ask that you also think ahead to the people who continue this fight, and who may still die.

"This war has only just begun. All too soon, our recent victory will be a memory, but let us never forget those who passed Noden's final shelf to win it for us. And let us never forget..." She wet her lips. Stood taller. "Let us never forget my brother, the prince of Nubrevna, and the admiral of the navy, Merik Nihar. *For though we cannot always see the blessing in the loss...*"

"*... strength is the gift of our Lady Baile.*" The room shook from all voices rising as one. "*And she will never abandon us.*"

There were disadvantages to being a dead man.

Merik Nihar, prince of Nubrevna and former admiral to the Nubrevnan navy, wished he'd considered *living* a long time ago.

Then maybe, right now, he wouldn't be filled with so much regret. Maybe, right now, he would have more memories of Kullen and Safi—and even Vivia—that were worth hanging on to. As many memories, perhaps, as the leaves that drifted off the water-bridges.

Merik, Cam, and Ryber had ascended the hillside near the dam. The plan was to travel north, following the river into the Sirmayans, but on their way, the funeral had begun.

The girls wanted to watch, and as morbid as it was, Merik had wanted to watch too.

The leaves tumbled at different speeds, orange and vibrant, green and alive. Some rode air currents, popping higher, while others hit slipstreams and coasted down. Some were aflame with smoke tails that chased behind. Others simply shone, unlit yet still brilliant in the sunset.

"It's beautiful," Cam said beside Merik, her left hand held across her heart. The healers had told her to stand that way, and for once she was doing what she'd been told.

No, no, not "she," he reminded himself, for Cam was a boy. Though Merik had been shamefully slow to put it all together, he understood now – and he had weeks of travel ahead to correct his mind and grow accustomed to calling Cam "he".

"It is beautiful," Ryber agreed from Cam's other side. She swatted a braid that dangled before her eyes. Unlike Cam, she had kept her ship-boy braids, and though tied back, one kept popping free.

"I've seen enough," was Merik's eventual reply, and he turned away. He'd had enough of the macabre for one day.

He adjusted his hood, tucking it as low as it would go. Too many people lingered nearby. Farmers who'd climbed up from the valley and soldiers off-duty from the dam's watchtowers. With his scars healing, his hair growing back, and his true face now peeking through the dark, lacy shadows, Merik couldn't risk being seen.

He needed the world to think him dead. Not merely so he could hunt for Kullen in peace, but also because the world didn't need him in it. *Vivia* didn't need him in it either, and Merik knew her life would be easier without him around.

One for the sake of many.

It was while Ryber and Cam were joining Merik on the shore of the Timetz, where the hoof-carved trail they sought cut into the trees, that Cam began humming a familiar tune.

Instantly, Merik's hackles rose. He walked faster. Trees soared up around him, birch and maple and pine. "Not that song, please."

"Why?" Ryber asked. She lengthened her stride to join Merik as well. Her boots rolled in the grooves of the path. "That rhyme has a happy ending."

Then, before Merik could stop her, she sang.

> "Blind brother Daret, with senses so keen,
> smelled danger lurking ahead.
> So he called to the Queen, I am bigger than he!
> Release him and eat me instead!

> "Her maw then swept open, and Filip raced out,
> to where Daret waited nearby.
> Then fin-in-fin the two brothers fled,
> leaving Queen Crab far behind.

> "Said fool brother Filip to blind brother Daret,
> once they were free of the cave,
> I was wrong to leave you and hurry ahead.
> My brother, my friend, you are brave!

> "So forgive me, dear Daret, for now I can see
> that I was the one who was blind.
> I do not need riches nor gold nor a crown,
> as long as I've you by my side.

"See? A happy ending." She grinned, and two gold-backed cards slipped from her sleeve. She flipped them Merik's way, revealing the Nine of Hounds and the Fool. They fluttered on the breeze, not entirely natural.

Merik halted. His sack dropped to the ground with a *whoomf*. Then he doubled over to plant his hands on his knees.

His heart pounded against his lungs. The mud and scree blurred, streaks of red and gray that wavered in time to his quickening pulse, his quickening winds.

> *So forgive me, dear Daret, for now I can see*
> *that I was the one who was blind.*

Merik was the fool brother. He had been all along—it was so clear now. He'd wanted something that wasn't real, something he could never have, and he'd wanted it for all the wrong reasons.

Seeing what he'd wanted to see.

His story, though, just like the two brothers', had a happy ending. He was still here, wasn't he? And Kullen was still out there too—and maybe, just maybe, both he and Kullen could still be saved.

Ryber had told Merik she knew how to heal him. How to stop this strange, half-cleaving that had taken hold. She'd said the answer waited in the Sirmayans, and since Merik had nothing to lose—and everything to gain—by trusting her, he'd packed up his supplies and set out.

Cam, of course, had refused to be left behind.

At the memory of Cam's stubborn jaw and pursed lips, Merik's shoulders unwound. His breath loosened.

He straightened, listening to the dusk around him. Crickets, owls, nightjars—they drifted into his ears. The sounds that he and Kullen had grown up with. The sounds they would listen to again one day soon.

"Sir?" Cam murmured, approaching. Her . . . no *his* dark eyes shone with worry—so familiar and yet so unknown. He'd forgiven Cam for hiding the truth of Garren and the Nines.

But this is the secret of Queen Crab's long reign:
she knows what all fishes want.
The lure of the shiny, the power of more,
the hunger we all feel for love.

Merik had forgiven Ryber too, for leaving him in the Nihar Cove. For keeping her secrets, and even for claiming Kullen's heart, Kullen's time, Kullen's love.

After all, both Cam and Ryber had come back for Merik when no one else had.

Well, no one but Vivia.

He smiled at them then. He couldn't help it.

"Come," he said, slinging his bag onto his back. For the first time in weeks, he felt alive. "We've a long way to go, and the sun will be gone soon."

Then Merik Nihar set off, content with no riches, no gold, and no crown, as long as he had friends by his side.

ACKNOWLEDGMENTS

They say it takes a village, and never was it more true than with *this* book. I simply could not have written it without the support of so many incredible people.

First and foremost, I must thank my editor, Whitney Ross. This book is as much hers as it is mine, and she went above and beyond. Thank you, Whitney. *Fighting!*

Dear, dear Sébastien, thank you for your patience, for your love, and for your unflappable good nature. *Je t'aime.*

Joanna Volpe and the rest of the New Leaf gang: I could not function without you. Thank you for all you do, day in and day out.

For my incredible team at Tor: you're the hidden stage-hands working tirelessly behind the scenes to turn my drivel into something real. Thank you, thank you. There would be no *Windwitch* without you.

To my wifey, Rachel Hansen: I never could have reached The End without your help. Thank you. (P.S. The hand flex is for you. P.P.S. Make haste!)

I must also thank, from the bottom of my heart, some amazing writer/reader friends. When I called, you *immediately* answered: Amity Thompson, Erica O'Rourke, Mindee Arnett, Melissa Lee, Leo Hildebrand, Akshaya Ramanujam (Aks Murderer!), Madeleine Colis, Savannah Foley, Kat Brauer, Elise Kova, Biljana Likic, Meredith McCardle, Leigh Bardugo, Meagan Spooner, Amie Kaufman, Elena Yip, and Jennifer Kelly. (Like I said, this book took a village.)

Oh yeah, and to Erin Bowman and Alexandra Bracken—I have only one word for you: #cattleprod.

For my friends at Fabiano's, especially Sensei Jon Ruiter and Sensei Brant Graham, thank you for letting me beat you up in the name of a good fight scene.

For my dear, *dear* #Witchlanders, you are my patronus. Real talk here: you are my guardians against the darkness. You're the reason I keep writing every day, the reason I didn't give up even when this book almost killed me, the reason I want to tell this story at all. Thank you from the bottom of my heart.

For Mom and Dad, you're my heroes and always have been. I aspire every day to be more like you.

And finally, to David and Jenn: Sorry I wasn't always the best big sis. Like Vivia, it took getting comfortable with myself before I could get comfortable with you. I hope you know though, that I will do anything for you—yes, *even* plummet to my death in a valley filled with seafire. Though let's avoid that if we can.

AGAIN, THANK YOU SO MUCH TO THE WINDWITCH STREET TEAM . . .

AETHER CLAN

Melissa Lee
Jillian Coffey
Angel King
Asteria Gonzalez
Jen Stasi
Karina Romano
Lizzie Shillington
Julia Espejo
Mishma Nixon
Cassie Frye
Diana Connors

AIR CLAN

Kelly Tse
Brian Gould
Roxanne Stouffs
Theresa Snyder
Casey Marie Sennett
Cristian Gallego Dominguez
Katie Steele
Jordan Bishop
Jessica Lindon
Meg McGorry
Becca Fowler
Duane Grech

EARTH CLAN

Kelly Peterson
Meredith Coffman
Samantha Smith
Hannah Mae Astorga
Adriana Marachlian
Adriyanna Zimmermann
Tiffany Jyang
Hannah Martian
Melanie Richel
Fallon Vaughn
Isabel Coyne

VOID CLAN

Danielle Fineza
Michaela Gustafsson
Nori Horvitz
C.J. Listro
Elena M-ski
Laura Ashforth
Karen Bultiauw
Olivia Walther
Lauren Johnstone
Thissi Logan
Ava Mortier

FIRE CLAN

Jana Lenart
Aneli Aguillon
Faith Young
Megan Miklusicak
Sondra Boyes
Emily Louie
Nancy López
Rachel Cartwright
Daphne Tonge

WATER CLAN

Louisse Ang
Charlene Cruz
Alyssa Susanna
Shanna Hughes
Kim Lüneburg
Olivia Whetstone
Carine Verbeke
Madeleine Kennedy
Katrina Tinnon
Stephanie Kaye
Alejandra García
Cat Moll
Shanna Hughes